Children of the Cross

A Novel

Lawrence Van Hoof

Published by Lawrence Van Hoof
ISBN 978-0-9879208-8-1

For my Parents

Prologue

The day started warm and clear when the Walters family left Ottawa, heading to a cottage they had rented near Algonquin Park. Mom and Dad sat in the front, Dad behind the wheel, while Nathan played his Nintendo. Cora eyed the pastures that dotted the low rolling hills, in between scruffy woods and the occasional marsh. For the last three years, she had wanted to take riding lessons, but Dad said they were too expensive and too much driving. She had to settle for looking at horses from the wrong side of the fence.

As well as horses, Cora hoped to spot a deer before they got to the cottage. Last summer she had seen two of them, a doe and fawn, along with three raccoons, and a fox that had zigzagged through one of the wide ditches near Barry's Bay like it was confused or drunk. Nathan had called the fox Uncle Charlie—since their Dad's friend always stank of beer—but Dad had not laughed and stopped the car long enough to box Nathan on the ears. Mom had said the poor thing had rabies and made them close the windows.

~

Around eleven-thirty, Dad drove through the town of Renfrew and grumbled about the price of gas. Cora settled back in her seat and toyed with the straps of her white sandals, and Nathan glanced up from his Nintendo.

"Don't be such a dumbie," he said. "You're not gonna see a deer. We're not going in the park."

"Don't call your sister that," Mom said. "You're in enough trouble already."

"It wasn't me. I never touched that stupid tent."

"Watch your mouth," Dad said.

Nathan made a face, which Dad didn't see luckily, and went back to playing the Nintendo.

Ten minutes later, while they drove through a stretch of farm-land peppered with scrub, Nathan started playing faster, battling some sort of boss. Cora shoved his left arm.

"Hey!" he said and elbowed her. She shoved back. He elbowed her harder, and she slapped his arm. Then he punched her in the arm, and she cried out.

"Stop it! Both of you," Mom said.

Dad hit the brakes, stopping the car in the middle of the road. Cora and Nathan froze.

"She started it," Nathan said. "It wasn't me."

Dad reached over the seating and slapped Nathan across the head. "I don't give a goddamn who started it."

"Why don't we just drive?" Mom said. "I'm sure they'll be quiet now."

Dad ignored her. "I don't want to hear another goddamn word out of you," he said to Nathan. "You're lucky you're coming along at all."

Silence filled the car, and Cora glanced at Nathan. He was too busy blinking back tears to notice. Dad must have hit him harder than usual.

"Can we go?" Mom said. "There's always people driving too fast on these roads."

"Then shut them up," he said and put the car in gear.

For next few miles, Cora shifted back to her window and watched fields and woods whizz by. Nathan stared at Mom's seat, trying to look tough.

Cora slipped a hand over to touch his arm. He shook her off and glared at her.

They drove into a town where cars had pulled over and people roamed yard sales lining both sides of the road. Mom wanted to stop. Just for a minute. She didn't really need anything but what if the cottage didn't have a good frying pan? They were always handy anyway. Or maybe a new lamp for Nathan's bedroom. The old one had chunks missing.

Dad gave her a look that said, "Over my dead body."

Once the yard sales disappeared behind them, Cora turned her attention to the woods ahead, trying to picture the deer she had seen last year. She hated when her parents fought. It always made her feel bad. Sometimes it even made her a little sick.

Cora rubbed her stomach saw a dead raccoon on the side of the road and a flattened piece of gray fur that might have been a squirrel. Gross. Then she heard a hiss and a pop from the speakers in the back of the car and glanced between the headrests. Had Mom turned the radio on?

Nothing else came out of the speakers, though, and Mom stared down at her hands, still upset, while an empty logging truck sped toward them down a long shallow hill.

"What the hell," Dad said.

For a moment, Cora thought he meant the truck since it would scare away all the deer. They weren't stupid. But then she spotted the gold fire surging out of the woods a hundred yards behind the truck and forgot everything else.

Nathan craned his neck to look too and dropped his video game. The logging truck jerked. Its tires screamed and smoked. A gold face appeared in the fire and roared past the truck, trailing a tail that shimmered like scales. Dad yelled and wrenched on the steering wheel. Everything slammed sideways—stomachs, lungs, kidneys, hearts, legs, brains. The car screeched. Mom screamed. Nathan screamed. The gold fire smashed into them and exploded. Cora's body snapped tight. Her skin blazed. Then the tail end of the logging truck crashed down, and she knew no more.

~

Cora woke up feeling terrible. Her head throbbed. Her chest ached. Everything looked fuzzy and far away, and a chainsaw roared nearby.

She sucked in a breath, her lungs like wet sand. Two people shouted and appeared in front of her; both wore dirty armor with bright yellow stripes that reminded her of Dad's uniform. A third man, with bionic arms, chewed on the car where Mom had been, her seat twisted like wet licorice.

Cora let her eyes drift shut. Had Mom gone to the washroom? When had they stopped?

The shouts of the men drifted closer, and Cora struggled to open her eyes. The men pulled a deer out of Dad's seat. Someone

3

had shot up the deer real bad, but she couldn't focus on it and didn't really want to. Her whole body felt tight. Her stomach wanted to burst open and make a mess. She didn't want to make a mess. She just wanted to find Mom and go to the washroom.

The men in dirty armor returned and attacked the twisted seat in front of Cora. She remembered Nathan. Where was he? She could feel him beside her, but her neck didn't want to work, and he wouldn't look at her.

Maybe he was still mad at her.

Cora tried turning her head again and opened her mouth to say his name but managed only a weak gurgle.

The men shouted and backed out of the car. A loud crunch tore off the roof. Sunlight blinded Cora. The men surged into the car, and she wriggled her fingers, trying to touch Nathan. Pain shot up her arm. Her vision went dark.

One of the men in dirty armor shouted and attacked the seat in front of her. She gasped and stretched her hand a little more. Another jolt of pain surged up her arm. Her fingers brushed a thumb. The burning of the sunlight intensified. The men shouted and ripped out the seat, and she grasped the thumb—yes, Nathan's thumb—but the men didn't care and grabbed her and pulled and pulled until the darkness swept in and claimed her once more.

Chapter 1

It was a few minutes past midnight when Cora walked into her apartment, her head throbbing like a second heartbeat. More than anything, she wanted to sleep. Her bed felt so close—the sheets and pillowcases she had laundered that morning. But she had to get rid of the lawyer's smell first, or she would wake up with him; and she never wanted to make that mistake again.

Next to the breakfast counter, she dropped her handbag on a stool and eased out of her high-heeled sandals. She brushed her blonde hair from her face, rubbed her forehead, and picked a bottle of water out of the fridge. The aspirin she had taken at the hotel hadn't done much good. One more wouldn't hurt. She just hoped she would get some decent sleep. No crazy dreams. No calls from Nathan.

In the master bathroom, Cora flicked on the wrong switch, and the big bulbs over the mirror blazed to life. She winced and pulled out the aspirins from the medicine cabinet. God, that was stupid.

Two pills later, she slipped out of her black evening dress and draped it on the rattan hamper. In the hamper, she tucked her lacy, black bra and matching panties, not looking at the latter too closely. She hated seeing the stains and the wet patches. Something always oozed out afterwards.

She shivered, sipped her water, and spritzed vanilla air freshener over the hamper. Her cellphone chimed from the kitchen. Probably Katrina? She always checked on Cora, especially after difficult customers.

On the toilet, Cora heard her cellphone chime again. She flushed the toilet and scrubbed her hands. She hoped it wasn't her brother. Tomorrow she could handle him. Now she was too tired. Her head hurt too much.

She washed her hands again and pulled on a plush white bathrobe. In the kitchen, she fished her cellphone from her handbag and checked the list of calls. Yes, the last two had been from Nathan.

She sighed and pressed one to check her voicemail. The first message hissed for a second before cutting out.

During the second message, her brother said, "Geez, would you fuck off. I just want a pizza."

Cora pressed a hand to her forehead and deleted the message. At least it wasn't the police. Nathan just sounded a little confused.

She wiped the screen of her phone on the bathrobe and pressed two. Her brother's number was busy, so she went back to the bathroom and turned on the shower.

Over the next twenty minutes, she scrubbed every inch of her body, focusing in particular on her groin and inner thighs and breasts. The lawyer had oozed sweat like a pine tree. She also washed and rinsed her hair and washed her mouth with a bar of peppermint soap she kept solely for that purpose.

Once finished, Cora grabbed a towel from the rattan storage tower and dried herself off. She spent another ten minutes brushing her teeth and gargling and plugged in the blow dryer, trying not to think about the roar in her ears and the pain spiking behind her eyes. The aspirins hadn't helped at all.

Back in her bedroom, she slipped on a pair of white cotton panties flecked with pale blue flowers and a white cotton nightie. Her cellphone chimed from the bathroom. Cora rubbed her forehead and wondered if she should turn the volume off. Nathan would probably spend half the night trying to order a pizza.

She yawned and sat on her comforter. Even if she ordered the pizza for him, she would get the ingredients wrong. The pizza was always wrong, even when Nathan ordered it himself. He always changed his mind while waiting for the pizza to arrive, and the pizza in his head was what he expected the deliveryman to bring.

After another yawn, Cora shuffled into the bathroom and pulled out her cellphone. As frustrating as Nathan was sometimes, she couldn't blame him. Having schizophrenia wasn't his fault. It was stupid to even think about. He did what he did, and all she could do was hope for the best. That was her life. She had to live with it.

The phone showed one voice message and one text message, the latter from Katrina.

Call me tmrw re lucky no7.

Cora deleted the text message and closed her eyes. The last thing she wanted to think about was her client tomorrow. James—lucky number seven—was nice enough but old enough to be her grandfather.

The voice message was from Nathan. "Fuck, it's a goddamn pizza. Stop screwing it up."

She shook her head and called his number. After three rings it switched over to his voicemail, and she hung up and washed her hands. She wasn't sure why she had even bothered adding the service to his phone. He never checked his messages anyway. She only ended up listening to them herself and worrying all the same.

~

With dawn crawling around the edges of her venetian blinds, Cora jarred awake from another dream: trapped in a hotel, the rooms and beds and halls crawling with shadows, all of it filled with the grunts and groans of men. One of the men wore an expensive suit, his penis hanging out like a dog's tongue. The next one wore a lab coat and bent her over to thrust thermometers and pens and spoons and other long objects inside her. A pale man wanted to spank her with a pizza while a little nun from the Red Cross, her hair yanked back in a severe bun, chased after Cora with a giant needle. Nathan was hiding somewhere too, but he couldn't get away. They had him tied down in a straitjacket.

Cora tugged on the drawer of her nightstand. She pushed aside the aspirins and lip balms and fumbled with the sleeping pills she had gotten from her doctor. Even though they rarely helped, she had to take something.

Pink pills skittered on the nightstand. More fell on the carpet. She glanced down, bleary-eyed, and shook another pill out of the bottle. Not too many. She had to be careful. She had promised. The rest she would pick up in the morning.

~

It was late, almost eleven, when Cora rubbed her head—what felt like a stuffed cabbage—and fished her wine-colored slippers from under the bed. She had to get up. She had to go to Nathan's. Being consistent was important. Keeping promises. Like every other day she would get through it.

Still blinking the sleep out of her eyes, she shuffled into the bathroom and stopped abruptly. The lawyer's stink lingered in the air: his sweat, his cologne, his cigarettes. How was that possible?

Cora rubbed her nose and flicked on the fan. From under the sink, she grabbed a big plastic bag and wiggled in the black dress from last night. The undergarments she stuffed in a smaller bag. She dropped both bundles in the bathtub, scrubbed her hands, and lit the beeswax candles sitting on blue saucers beside the tub.

Even though leaving the candles alone made her uneasy, the residue of too many stories from her father about burned-down homes and destroyed families, she shut the door to the master bathroom and hurried to the spare bathroom.

A few minutes later, back in her bedroom, she opened the sliding windows and checked her cellphone for messages. Nothing new. She hoped that meant Nathan had ordered his pizza. Otherwise he might have stayed up the whole night, fretting about conspiracies between the phone companies and the doctors and the superintendent.

Cora glanced at her alarm clock and called her brother. The line switched over automatically to his voicemail. Was he up yet? Some days he stayed in bed until she got there. Other days he woke up with the sun and disappeared in one of the parks near his building. There was no rhyme or reason. For him, time didn't matter. He had nowhere to go. He had nothing to do.

It was sad, sometimes exasperating, but he didn't have any interest in the programs meant to help patients integrate back into the community. He didn't see the point. Nor did he trust them. He had had too many bad experiences already.

Cora headed back to the spare bathroom and turned on the shower. She pulled out a new razor and toothbrush from the extras she kept in the storage bin under the sink and hurried through her morning ritual—soaping, shaving, plucking, shampooing, conditioning, rinsing, moisturizing, brushing, flossing. Her nails she would worry about later. They looked fine. Good for another day or two.

Even so, it was already past noon when Cora, wearing a fresh bathrobe, circled around the beige couch in the living room and opened the door to the balcony. She picked up the pink watering can and filled it in the kitchen and soaked the basket of pink geraniums hanging on the balcony and watered the small plants that lined the window ledge inside the apartment. The whole week had been hot, more like August than June, and the sky was clear, reaching over Lake Ontario like a giant blue magnifying glass.

After returning the watering can to the balcony, she called Nathan again. His voicemail answered. She said she'd be there soon, on the off chance he actually listened to his messages, and changed into a yellow tank top and a pair of slim-fitting blue jeans. She also pulled out a red T-shirt with a tiny hole in the back from her dresser, which was painted white and had a big rectangular mirror, and tucked the T-shirt into an old H&M bag. She kept a few spare things at Nathan's apartment for when she cleaned, but most of them needed to be washed.

Her cellphone chimed. For a second, she thought it might be her brother, but the screen flashed *Kat C.*

Cora slid the H&M bag on the dresser and answered the phone.

"I wanted to see how you were doing," Katrina said. "I know you weren't too thrilled about last night."

"Well, maybe it wasn't that bad," Cora said. "Except for his sweating. I think I was just tired."

"You must have done something right. He already called to book you for his next trip into the city, but I wanted to check with you first."

"Oh?"

"Can you talk? Or are you at your brother's?"

"No, but I have to go soon," Cora said. "I should be there already."

"Don't worry about it, then. There's no rush. Just think about it, and we'll talk later." Katrina turned away from the phone for a second and spoke to someone in Chinese. Probably one of her cats, in the midst of causing mischief. "I also wanted to update you about James. He changed the restaurant to Sassafraz, which is about a block from his hotel. But I have a feeling he'll change his mind again. He's like a little puppy, peeing all over the place."

"I know, he gets excited."

"I'll call around five to confirm the details," Katrina said. "Right now the plan is for Straw to pick you up at seven so you can be in the restaurant by seven-thirty. I don't want to take any chances with traffic."

"That should be fine."

"I've also got a package from Paul for tomorrow. I'll courier it over after I get something to eat. Should be at your place by four."

"So you looked it over already? For labels or anything?"

Katrina made a clucking noise with her tongue. "I'm a professional, sweetie. Discretion is everything."

"Sorry, I know. I just worry too much."

"That makes two of us," Katrina said. "Us mother hens. Cluck, cluck."

Cora laughed a little and sat on the white wicker chair in the corner beside the dresser.

"Anyway, I have to go," Katrina said. "Call me if you need anything."

"I will."

"I know I can rely on you. You're the one person around here who really knows what that means."

"Don't worry. I'll be back in time. I promise."

Chapter 2

Around quarter after one, the cab dropped Cora off in front of Nathan's apartment building. It was a brownish-yellow three-story with bricks crumbling in dozens of places, cloudy windows, and black paint peeling off the wood trim. To the right stood a garden center surrounded by green plastic fencing. To the left, on the other side of a dead-end street, rose a second apartment building, which had a sign on a striped pole that reminded her of an old motel.

She rummaged through her purse for her keys and walked up the steps of Nathan's building. Since the foyer smelled vaguely of urine, the second time that month, and his mailbox was empty, Cora hurried up the front stairs. She didn't want to bump into the superintendent either. Sometimes it felt like he stalked the halls, waiting for her to show up.

When she reached the third floor, she noticed her brother's door was ajar and darted forward to knock. Normally he was quite careful about locking up. The neighbors seemed okay, but you never knew for certain. Temptation changed people.

"Nathan? It's me. Are you home?"

After waiting a few seconds, Cora called his name again and nudged the door open. What she saw made her want to pull it shut again. Shirts, pants, socks, and underwear covered the green faux leather sofa. Spoons, forks, knives, and dishes were scattered on the rusty brown carpet, forming an arc around the door. All the windows stood wide open: the one to the left of the couch had already been missing a screen, but the screen to the right had a new hole the size of her head.

"Nathan?"

She stepped through the minefield of dishes and utensils and glanced in his bedroom. His sheets were tangled on the bed; his pillows lay on the floor. In the kitchen, she checked the stove was off. There were no taps running. Nothing looked broken. She walked back to the living room, rubbing her hands together, and noticed the gash on the top of the cherry-finish end table that Nathan had picked out at a garage sale the year before. When she had tried to point out a better coffee table, one without a gash, he had gotten upset so she promised herself to never say another word about it. Instead she had settled for hiding the worst of the damage with the phone.

But where was it? She didn't see the phone anywhere.

The wall jack was empty too. There was no phone cord visible in the living room or the kitchen.

Cora turned to stare at the hole in the window screen. No, he didn't. He couldn't have.

She leaned against the couch and pressed a hand to her forehead.

When she felt steady again, she checked the bedroom and bathroom. Thankfully everything else looked normal.

After washing her hands, she took an aspirin and glanced at her phone. She wondered if she should look for Nathan. Sometimes he didn't mind. Sometimes he did. She had a feeling he was close by.

She maneuvered through the utensils and dishes and fished her keys from her purse but needed both hands to tug the apartment door shut. Was that why he had left it ajar in the first place? The superintendent really needed to fix the stupid thing.

She took the back stairs down to the laneway behind the apartment building. One of Nathan's more unfortunate habits was hiding out behind the garbage, perhaps because no one else wanted to be there.

With a hand to her nose, Cora hurried around the wooden fence surrounding the garbage bins, both of which reeked of rot and soiled diapers. No Nathan, thank goodness. She unlocked the rear door and darted back inside.

On the basement level, she passed the laundry room, thinking of the clothes strewn on his couch. He rarely did his own wash, but it wasn't impossible. Maybe he had gotten confused.

She poked her head inside the room. A dark-skinned woman wearing a black hijab pulled clothes out of one of the washing machines while a pair of small girls with curly black hair played a game of patty cake. The woman avoided looking at Cora, but the girls stared at her like she had two heads.

Cora managed a smile and headed to the front door. Once outside she turned right, crossed the dead-end street, and walked past several apartment buildings, the last of which had white paint peeling from the walls. She glanced down a lane leading to the tennis courts behind the Alexander Muir Memorial Gardens. Beyond the tennis courts, the lane turned into a path that meandered through a series of ravines and eventually merged with the Don Valley, but she was positive he was a lot closer. She couldn't explain the feeling—she'd probably sound crazy if she tried—but she could practically hear him shifting around, trying to get comfortable.

She continued north on the sidewalk, beside the green hedge of the Memorial Gardens, until she reached a black wrought iron gate that opened onto a brick path bordered by evergreens and shrubs. The path led to the heart of the gardens, but that still didn't feel right, so Cora walked a dozen more feet and peered at the skinny park on the other side of Yonge Street.

About halfway in the park, amid the shadows of the maple trees, she spotted someone sitting on a bench, hunched over, wearing a black T-shirt.

Yes, Nathan.

She glanced left and right and darted across four lanes of Yonge Street, most of the traffic stopped for red lights. When she reached the other sidewalk, she paused to adjust the strap of her left sandal, and a car honked at her from the small gas station next to the entrance of the park.

She ignored the honker and walked between a pair of flower beds, onto an asphalt path. She could see Nathan's hands twitching on his legs while his right foot tapped like he was listening to fast music. He probably didn't even realize he was doing it. The bench had a fresh coat of green paint, covering up the graffiti from the winter and the spring. Behind the bench there was a row of scraggly shrubs and a concrete retaining wall, half of it repainted, the other half still splattered with graffiti.

"Nathan?" she said, stopping a few yards from the bench.

Her brother blinked and shook his head, his sandy brown hair scruffy and long enough to hang in his eyes. He needed to get it cut. He also needed to shave the bristly, brown growth off his face and throw out his T-shirt, which had a large hole in the right side.

Nathan flashed her a smile, almost feverish in its intensity. She sat beside him.

"It's really nice out today," she said. "Especially here in the shade."

"This is better," he said. "The new spot. Much better. That bastard was too close."

"Why? What happened?"

"He's always trying to rip me off, it's never enough, that cockroach motherfucker, god up his ass and down his pie hole."

"Do you mean the superintendent? Did something happen?"

"The pig says I broke it, I saw him do it," Nathan said. "But he just wants to blame the man, the one below, and blow it out his ass, like a good fucking leprechaun."

Cora closed her eyes and took a deep breath.

Nathan continued. "I was just looking for something, something important, I know it was, but I don't remember."

"I know, it's always the important stuff." Cora touched Nathan's arm, but he pulled away and clamped his trembling hands between his knees. "Do you want me to call the doctor?" she asked. "Maybe there was something wrong with your last needle?"

"Bastards," he said. "Fat bastards."

"I know it's hard sometimes. But the doctor's doing his best for you."

"Yeah, they love doing it, sticking it to you. Stick, stick, stick. Always laughing, laughing their asses off."

Cora touched Nathan's arm again. He hummed under his breath and shook his head. She felt the twitches shooting up his arms, the electricity he couldn't control. Sometimes she wondered if it was actually something in his brain or just a side effect of his medication.

"It's all right, Nathan. It'll be okay."

"Yeah, bye," he said.

"No, I'm not leaving," she said. "We're just sitting in the park, having a talk. It's a beautiful day. Quiet. Relaxing."

Nathan laughed, harsh and loud. "Like a dog."

"It's nice here," Cora said. "Not too hot. Just right."

"He won't like it." Nathan pointed to the half of the concrete wall spattered with graffiti. "He's really fucking loud, all that shit music. Enough to drive you nuts. I can't get him to shut up."

"It's all right," Cora said. "It's just temporary. He'll be gone soon."

Nathan slapped a leg and swore. Cora waited. After a few more curses, he settled down and she rested a hand on his arm again. Normally he hated people touching him. He said it made him itch all over, like he had something growing under his skin, trying to push out. With her, though, it seemed to help. It reminded her of the first month after the car accident, when he lay in the hospital and the doctors thought he would never wake up again. She used to sit beside him, holding his hand, watching the respirator move his lungs. Aunt Clara didn't think it was a good idea: Cora was too young, she needed to go outside and play. But that only reminded her their parents were dead and Nathan was the only one left. She had to be there to help him. She had to help him come back.

And for four years he did come back. He even managed to stay out of trouble throughout most of grade nine. The following year, he started getting suspended for fights and such and drove Uncle Abner crazy. It wasn't until Aunt Clara developed cancer that Nathan settled down again. Yes, he still skipped class, but he spent a lot of that time in the hospital with her. The chemotherapy alone almost killed her, all for one more year of suffering.

At the west end of the park, a dog barked—a golden Labrador running after a ball—and Nathan jumped a little. The owner, a man wearing dark jeans and a red shirt, stood on the path, smoking a cigarette, looking in Cora's direction.

Nathan muttered a curse. "I wish he'd shut up. I can't sleep anymore. He's always so fucking loud."

"We'll find something to help," Cora said. "We just have to keep trying. Have faith."

He shrugged. "*C'est la vie, n'est-ce pas?*"

Cora frowned.

"Don't look at me like that," he said. "I'm not a retard."

"Sorry. It's just . . . you always hated learning French," Cora said. "It used to make Dad really mad."

"I don't remember," Nathan said. "I don't want to."

"I know. I jus—"

He jumped to his feet. "Christ, would you shut up. You always want to talk about that stupid shit."

"Please sit down, Nathan. I won't talk about it anymore. I promise."

"I don't want to remember any of it. It's all crap now. It just makes it hurt more."

"I know, I'm sorry," she said. "I shouldn't have brought it up. It's just hard sometimes. I still miss them."

Nathan hovered in front of the bench, shaking his head like a big shaggy dog.

Cora touched his arm. "Why don't we just sit and enjoy the weather? We don't have to talk."

Still shaking his head, he sat down. Cora fanned her face with her other hand. There was no breeze in the park, and Nathan really needed a fresh shirt and a shower. She already had enough bad smells in her life.

Nathan coughed and jerked his arm away from her. She glanced down and noticed his right foot had stopped twitching. His hands, too, which was strange. He shouldn't change moods that quickly.

A few seconds later, her cellphone chimed and Nathan jerked away from her. "What the fuck is that?"

"Nothing." She pulled out her phone and sent the call to her voicemail. "Nothing important."

"Sounds like a bunch of fucking church bells."

"I think they're relaxing."

"You never had any taste."

Cora let the comment pass, remembering some of the thrashy metal he had listened to in high school, and switched her phone to silent mode.

"You're bells are fucking again," Nathan said.

She glanced down. Her cellphone started to flash, telling her she had a new message. She frowned and slid the phone back in her purse.

"I was going to make supper," she said. "Would you rather have potatoes or rice?"

"I just wanna take a piss." Nathan pointed the scraggly shrubs behind the bench. "Water the lawn."

"Someone else will take care of that. It's supposed to rain this weekend anyway."

"That's no fun."

Cora studied him for a few seconds. Was he making a joke?

"You seem a lot calmer," she said.

"Thanks," he said and stood up.

"Wait, you're kidding, right?"

"Yeah, yeah. Don't nag."

"Sorry. I didn't mean to. It's just, you know."

"Bing! Another shit deal for the Walters clan. Claim your prize."

Cora stood up. She still wasn't certain if Nathan was joking or diving back into the dark twists of his brain. It made her nervous when he had swings like that. She had no idea what to expect.

"When you coming back?" he asked. "I'll surprise you with something, if that fucker doesn't steal it. Tomorrow, maybe."

"I don't have to go. I can stay for a while."

"I'm good," he said. "A happy clam. Totally baked."

"Are you sure?"

"What do you want me to say? No?"

"Of course not," she said. "I just thought we could eat something. It doesn't have to be at home. We can go to Tim Hortons, if you want, get a soup and sandwich."

Nathan shook his head. "Too much noise. I'm gonna hang out by the river, go fishing."

Cora rubbed her forehead, the ache intensifying behind her eyes. What else could she do? She didn't want to sound like she was arguing. He would only get defensive.

"Okay, I'll be at your apartment," she said. "For a couple of hours anyway. I'll make potatoes and roast and maybe beans. I don't think there's any pork chops left."

"I got it," he said.

Without looking back, Nathan sprinted to the hill at the west end of the park.

"Be careful," she called after him.

He waved a hand and chugged up the green slope, ignoring the stairways on either side, built with old railway ties. When he reached the top, he cut across Duplex Avenue without seeming to check for traffic, and Cora clutched her purse. Then he disappeared—no honks, no screeches—and she swallowed, her throat like a frozen garden hose. Someday he was going to get hurt if he kept doing things like that. He just didn't think. And there wasn't much she could do about it either, not without sending him back to an institution.

Cora took a deep breath and walked back to Yonge Street. She never wanted to go through that again: seeing him trapped with patients whose nightmares never stopped. She still remembered the man with red and purple blotches scarring his face and arms after he had tried to set himself on fire; and the beautiful, old woman who swore all the time and yelled about cunts and cocks and pussies and wanting to get it up the ass. Nathan only needed the right medication . . . a safe place to live. Then he was almost normal. Sometimes it seemed short-lived; some weeks were better than others. But at least he had a chance. He had a hope for a better tomorrow.

Everyone needed that.

Chapter 3

Teresa stood in the unlit interior of the boarded-up nightclub where she kept Father and breathed in the stink of death. After six centuries, it no longer bothered her. If anything, the blend of urine and feces and corrupt human flesh had become almost comforting. While the rest of the world spun around her, changing every minute, every day, death remained the one true constant. No mortal escaped it. She alone would stay outside of time. The rest simply deluded themselves, selling their souls for empty promises.

She brushed a hand over her silver crucifix and inhaled more of the foul air. At first glance, people often mistook her for a gawky fifteen-year-old, her face plain and too long for her short thin body, her arms like spindles. The effect was heightened by her hair, which was black and hung loose down to her hips. She also wore her staple dress: made of midnight blue velvet, the hem grazing the floor, black lace encircling her neck and wrists.

Beside her, Mobius stirred and cleared his throat. Teresa glared at him, and he bowed his head.

"My apologies, mistress," he said. "Do you wish the lights on?"

Her scowl deepened. How long had she stood there daydreaming? Five minutes? Ten?

"Yes, it's time," she said. "I need to see what he's doing."

"I could have one of the others deal with this, mistress."

"Now!" she said.

Mobius bowed and flicked a switch on his right. Nothing happened. He flicked the switch up and down several times, but the interior of the building remained dark. His cantaloupe-shaped head turned to one of the side rooms, his skin peppered with sweat.

"I'll check the fuse box, mistress."

"Hurry up," Teresa said. "I have better things to do than suffer your incompetence."

Mobius bowed his head and disappeared into the room on their right. A few seconds later, a hiss slithered out of Father's room, echoed by the screams of people who had died long ago. Teresa blocked them out by thinking about the music she would listen to later and felt the shadows shift around her, rippling her dress.

Overhead a pair of florescent lights snapped on. Teresa stepped into Father's room and passed a hand over her eyes. Although she no longer needed such lights to see Father, she preferred using them. They made him seem more human. They helped keep him in one place.

Shadowy faces spurted out of the black floor and screamed, spewing anger and hatred: the Cardinal, her mother, her childhood friends, the boy she had wanted to marry. Teresa shook her head and stepped through them. The faces were only an illusion—Father's way of trying to break into her mind.

A mix of florescent lights and spotlights flickered on in the nearest corners, revealing two of the four cages, each of which held one prisoner. Four still seemed enough to keep Father in check, but she wondered if she would have to increase their number soon. In the last month, the prisoners had died too quickly for the shipments from the Orient to keep up with the turnover, and the war between the drug cartels continued to disrupt the shipments from Mexico.

In the far left corner, still shrouded in darkness, a prisoner twitched and released a faint croak. Teresa crossed herself and touched her crucifix. At least one of the girls was still alive. A good sign.

More lights snapped on. She kissed the crucifix. In the center of the room, a former dance floor, stood a concrete slab covered with a white tarp, holding up a long glass box, inside of which lay an old man on a bed of purple velvet. He was naked and hairless, his arms and legs little more than bones hanging in sacks of flesh, his nose a flap of leathery flesh surrounded by a mass of wrinkles that swallowed the rest of his face. Sometimes his mouth hung open, a dark hole that promised eternal suffering and damnation; but today his mouth was closed while shadows swirled over the glass and the white tarp, mocking her, their whispers of death and destruction rising and falling like waves on a rocky shore.

Teresa kissed her crucifix again and stepped on the old dance floor. A split second later, a blast of putrid air and hatred knocked her back a step. The prisoner in the far left corner screamed. A spotlight exploded. Teresa dropped into a crouch, and blackness rolled over her. Pain sliced into her arms, shoulders, and her chest. She clenched her teeth to stop from screaming, and one of her molars cracked. The blackness pushed at her eyes.

"You have no place in me," she said. "Your tricks won't work."

The pain cut into her belly and her thighs, and a voice like molasses filled the room, hisses and rasps promising suffering without end.

"I'm free of you. Your pain only makes me stronger."

The pressure on her eyes intensified. Teresa rubbed her arms, aggravating the sensation of knives cutting into her flesh.

"Go back to sleep," she said. "Go back to your prayers."

The phantasmal knives jabbed her a few more times, the pain dwindling with each failure.

"You still have time," she said. "We haven't found him yet."

A guttural rumble shook the floor. Teresa slapped her arms and eased her eyes open. They burned, but the darkness around her remained absolute. She prodded her left eye. It still felt intact. Father must have damaged the retina. She prodded her ears too and heard the crinkling of her flesh, though the rest of the room remained silent. He had sucked the life out of everything, even the microscopic life harbored in the bowels and on the skin of the prisoners.

In one of the adjoining rooms, a door creaked open, and a pair of feet shuffled across the floor.

"Are you well, mistress?" Mobius asked, his voice sounding frayed.

"Of course," she said.

"Your command?"

"Tell them to bring more prisoners. We need to keep him distracted, for as long as possible."

"The warehouse is getting low," Mobius said. "The next shipment won't arrive until Sunday."

"Then grab locals. It won't matter soon."

"Yes, his rising is near."

Teresa grimaced. She hated when he made everything about Father sound prophetic.

"Just get out," she said. "Have them send whatever's left."

"Yes, mistress."

Mobius shuffled to the entrance, and white splotches formed at the edge of Teresa's vision. She waited a few more seconds, caressing her crucifix, until the room snapped back into focus. She then circled the room and checked the prisoners.

All four of them were dead. The third must have been dead the whole day, considering the stink rising from her ripening flesh.

Teresa grimaced and rubbed her nose. She turned to face Father. Though he looked like nothing more than a broken puppet, the shadows around him were jagged and alive in a way she had not seen since the Second World War. It was foolish to forget he had already survived two millennia.

"Don't worry," she said. "The net is closing fast. We'll have your fish soon."

Just not the way you want it.

In the glass box, Father's left hand twitched, and a thud hit the floor in front of Teresa. She hopped back a step and tripped on the hem of her velvet dress, tearing it.

She muttered a curse and freed her skirt from the strap of her sandals. He shouldn't have been able to do that.

"Mistress?"

Teresa pivoted and glared at Mobius, who stood in the opening leading to the main entrance.

"What do you wish?" he asked.

"Call everyone," she said. "Tell them to redouble their efforts. We must find the Light. He must be close."

"As you wish, mistress."

"Nothing else matters. There's no more time."

~

Teresa squinted as she walked out of the former nightclub and raised a hand to shield her face. The sunlight felt like paper scraping her eyeballs. A moment later, she remembered she was not alone and dropped her hand to her crucifix. Security teams occupied the surrounding buildings; Mobius watched her every move from her SUV, the tinted windows masking nothing; and a man with a tangled beard shuffled on the sidewalk, his blue shirt splattered with filth and pictures of pineapples, his pants even filthier—one of the legion of beggars that plagued the city. Unfortunately Father had lost interest in them a long time ago and killed them too quickly to make them useful.

Nonetheless, Teresa considered stuffing the beggar in a cage as he veered toward her, holding out a dirty red baseball hat. Doors banged open from multiple directions: two on the SUV, one in the house across the street, two in the old paint factory next to the nightclub. Men wearing black uniforms and flak jackets scrambled onto the street, several of them clutching pistols.

Teresa waved one hand and dismissed them. In a matter of seconds, the security men scurried back to their hiding holes while Mobius hovered in front of the SUV, ready to throttle the beggar.

The beggar glanced around, his face twisting with fear. Teresa lifted a finger, and Mobius hurried to her side. In the daylight, his scalp looked like a crocus bulb with the skin peeled off.

"Could you spare some change?" the beggar asked. "For some food?"

"Give him a dollar," Teresa said. "One dollar."

Mobius stared at her. She glared back, and he bowed his head and ducked inside the SUV to get change from the driver. Then Mobius ran back to her side and dropped a loonie into the beggar's hat.

"Now go away," she said to the beggar, "while you still have legs."

He bobbed his head, mimicking Mobius, and scurried to the corner of King Street.

Teresa frowned at Mobius. "Do you think I need protecting?"

"No, mistress."

"How long do you think it would take to kill all these apes you've hired?"

"Not long, mistress."

"Then get back in the car and do something useful. The sun's annoying me."

Mobius bowed his head and scurried into the SUV. Teresa turned to look at the nightclub. On the outside, it could have been any of a hundred industrial leftovers in downtown Toronto, waiting for its chance to be torn down and replaced with a loft for young professionals and divorced yuppies; but Father's presence permeated every brick and board and hung over the roof like a mushroom cloud. Even the air stank of him, something more complex than rotting flesh and feces, more like dead pigs mixed with brimstone and overripe cheese.

From within the building came a vague rumble, and the ground quivered.

Teresa spat on the sidewalk. "May you die horribly, old goat. I'm tired of you."

Then she kissed her crucifix, hitched up her skirt, and slid into the back of the SUV.

~

About ten minutes later, the SUV turned onto the Gardiner Expressway, heading east past a line of condominiums that blocked Teresa's view of Lake Ontario. Mobius typed on his Blackberry and muttered to himself in a Tuscan dialect from the nineteenth century, pausing every few seconds to scratch his cheeks, and flecks of pale skin fell like dandruff on the jacket and pant legs of his gray suit.

"What about the prisoners?" Teresa asked.

"Yes, mistress. They're being prepared."

"Call Alex. He'll handle the exchange."

Mobius opened his mouth to disagree but stopped short of actually speaking the words. Teresa ignored his impudence, distracted by a sharp pain behind her eyes. Images flashed through her head: a fishing boat; storm clouds; olive trees; men weeping; a temple on fire.

Teresa looked out her window and focused on the last of the condominiums, the windows stretching up forty or fifty stories. She pushed everything else away. The memories did not belong to her. She did not want them.

"My boys can do it," Mobius said. "Alex is too soft."

Teresa grimaced and turned her dark eyes back to him. "What did you say?"

"Nothing, mistress," he said, bowing his head. "Only making a humble suggestion."

"Do you think those idiots of yours could last five seconds if he surged again?"

"He won't. Not so soon."

"We can't assume that anymore," Teresa said. "He's starting to wake up. I'm just surprised none of your apes have died yet. The whole block is going to feel it soon."

"Perhaps we should move him to a safer location."

Teresa leaned forward and flicked a finger against Mobius's nose. He flinched but didn't pull away.

"I'm going to pretend you didn't say that," she said.

"Yes, mistress."

"And turn on some music. I don't want to hear him anymore." Teresa rubbed her forehead. "I can feel him scratching already."

~

Alex sat in his car, waiting at a red light. The University of Toronto spread out on his left, kids with backpacks chugging across the intersection and along the sidewalks. When he had gone to school, more than seventy years ago, he never had a backpack. His family had scrounged for one, and his older brother had been the smart one. Sometimes Alex had gotten to carry the backpack through the fields and woods during their long walk to and from school, but he didn't get his own until he joined the army, and those packs weighed a hell of a lot more than a few books.

Not that his school had had many books either. Maybe in the big cities like Montreal and Toronto but not the piss-poor backwaters of Manitoba. That was part of the reason he had run off to Europe and joined the ranks against Hitler. He had wanted to get out of that shithole and be a hero. He had wanted to be like the other boys and chase the girls—to kiss them and fuck them. The army would fix all that. It would make him a real man, one his father would be proud of.

Now his father was long dead; his three brothers, too. His two sisters lived somewhere out west, probably senile. Alex, on the other hand, didn't look a day over twenty. The only real change was his clothes. In the old days, he never had money for fancy suits. Those were reserved for bankers and railroad tycoons. His one suit, for church, had been a faded hand-me-down from a cousin in the city.

The car behind Alex honked, startling him. He swore and reamed on his horn. Other cars echoed him. Then he noticed the green light in front of him and stomped on the accelerator.

At the next intersection, he slammed on the brakes for another red light and swore again—though what did it matter? He wasn't in a rush. He was only driving around in circles anyway, searching for the Light. The problem was he didn't know what the hell the Light looked like. It was supposed to be hiding in some guy—real useful in a city with millions of people. The only other information Teresa had given everyone was that they would feel his presence.

Yes, they would feel the Light. Even more useful.

Alex leaned sideways and pulled a beer out of the case wedged in front of the passenger seat. He drained the bottle and shoved it back in the case. In the car on his left, a man with a Pinocchio nose and a ring of a gray hair stared in disbelief, probably wishing he had his own beer.

Alex saluted and opened another bottle. He would have to buy another case soon, maybe Heineken this time. Drinking them faster didn't help much but at least tilting back the bottle still reminded of the sensation of getting drunk—the numbness, the ignorance.

The traffic started moving again. He guzzled the rest of his beer and drove three more blocks, past the Ontario Legislative Building, and turned right at Bay Street, a hub of condominiums and office towers. The liquor store across from the mall was probably his best option, even if parking was a pain in the ass.

Alex shoved the empty bottle in the case and braked for a red light at Elm Street. His cellphone buzzed. He muttered a curse and tugged it out of his jacket.

"Yeah?" he said.

On the other end, Teresa spoke, sounding annoyed. "Where are you?"

"Sorry, mistress. Didn't mean any disrespect. Didn't know it was you."

"Shut up and answer the question," Teresa said. "Or did you sneak off to one of your bars again?"

Alex grimaced. She was spooky sometimes. He couldn't have a private thought anymore.

"Bay Street," he said. "Heading south. Then I'll loop back west."

"Anything to report?"

"Nothing particular."

"What about last night? At the hotel?"

"Peter was the only one who felt something," Alex said. "The rest of us got there too late."

"I already know that, idiot. Otherwise we would have the Light, and this conversation would be irrelevant."

On the phone, a man muttered in the background—that cockroach Mobius. Alex also heard classical music, a concerto with piano. He didn't care for that stuff but knowing what kept Teresa happy had saved his skin a few times.

"You'll be handling the prisoners," she said. "Be there in an hour."

"What about Leroy? I thought—"

"Are you questioning me?"

"No, mistress. As you command."

"That's right. You forget that—all too often."

"No, never," Alex said.

"Oh? You're too smart? Or are you just an exceptional liar?"

"No, mistress," he said. "I was reborn through you and only through you."

Silence followed. Alex drove to next set of red lights, turned right, and pulled into a parking lot across from the Greyhound bus terminal. He left the car running and eased another beer into his lap.

"Be ready," Teresa said. "He'll know you're there."

Alex bit back a curse. "Of course, mistress. I'm always ready to serve."

"We'll see," she said and hung up.

Chapter 4

A few minutes after Cora walked into Nathan's apartment, the superintendent, Maurice, called her cellphone. Though she didn't want to talk to him, she put down her bottle of aspirins and answered the call. Maybe he would actually fix something for once. With Nathan out, it would make things a lot easier. She had already waited weeks for Maurice to look at the window stuck half-open in the bedroom and the faucet dripping in the bathroom. He had completely ignored her complaints about the paint peeling off the ceiling in the shower, which had started months ago, when Nathan moved in.

After an abrupt hello, Maurice said, "Yes, I come for problem. Twenty minutes."

"Uh, okay," Cora said, glancing at the mess in the living room. "That's fine."

He paused, perhaps trying to think of something else to say, then simply said goodbye. Cora hung up and started picking up the utensils and plates on the floor and piled them beside the kitchen sink. She still didn't see Nathan's phone anywhere, something she would have to ask him about later.

Or maybe she should just get him another one? She had a spare landline at home she would never use anyway.

She turned on the hot water to fill one of the sinks and sorted Nathan's laundry into three piles on the couch: a few pieces of light-colored clothing she could wash with his sheets; the towels; his jeans, socks, underwear, and dark T-shirts. As always, she felt tempted to throw out the shirts with tears and holes in them, but Nathan ignored the new ones she had given him and got upset if any of the old ones went missing. One was a Nirvana shirt with a drowning baby he had bought in grade eleven when he was in love with Lucy Miller. Another shirt used to say Limp Bizkit, but most of the letters had flaked off, and there was a reddish stain on the bottom that wouldn't come out. She used to think the stain was sauce from spicy chicken wings or spaghetti, but it was probably paint. The rip in the Metallica shirt had happened the second time the police threw him in jail, before they realized the pills in his back pocket were actually a medical necessity.

Cora sighed and dropped the Metallica shirt on the pile of darks. For once she wished the washing machine would do her a favor and eat all his old shirts. He wanted to forget everything else from their past. Why couldn't he at least wear something decent?

She circled the couch, checking for stray socks, and eyed the torn window screen. If the superintendent noticed, he would probably get upset and leave without fixing anything. He was always looking for an excuse—seeing her was the only thing he cared about, sneaking a touch if he could.

Cora pushed thoughts of his hairy hands aside and retrieved her sewing kit from its hiding spot in the coat closet. She made a few loops with a needle and thread to lift the torn flap of the screen back in place and shut the window halfway to hide her work.

In Nathan's bedroom, she checked for more stray clothes and found one of his black sneakers, crusted with dirt, sticking out from under the bed. She kneeled down and found the other shoe, also dirty, and a *Playboy* with the smooth, glossy look of a new magazine. Probably the July edition. She hoped Nathan had actually paid for it. She didn't want any more trouble with the local shopkeepers.

Cora eased the sneakers out from under the bed and left the magazine alone. Over the years, she had found enough of them, mostly *Playboy* and *Maxim* and *Penthouse*, which Nathan kept stashed in his dresser. She didn't care, as long as he didn't bring home anything with underage girls. That had happened once, a few weeks ago, something from Japan or China he had left on the coffee table. She had no idea where he had gotten the magazine nor had she mentioned it, but made it disappear and hoped he wouldn't notice.

In the bathroom, Cora pulled on a pair of yellow rubber gloves, scrubbed the dirt off the shoes, and put them on the edge of the bathtub to dry. She moved to the kitchen, switched to a green pair of rubber gloves, washed and dried the stacks of forks and knives and spoons and plates, and put everything away.

While tucking the green gloves back under the sink, she heard a knock on the apartment door. She rinsed her hands and dried them on a hand towel. Through the peephole, she saw the superintendent plucking at his thick swollen nose, his face screwed up with impatience.

Cora took a deep breath and unlocked the door. It was stuck, though, and she had to use both hands to yank it open.

Maurice gave her a sour smile. "You have problem with door?"

"Yes, I guess you can see that."

"Hm, yes. Always problems," he said and scratched his unshaven chin. Black hair sprouted out of his gray shirt like weeds, and he had enough body odor to knock over a bus. "Many people complain. Your brother make always noise when people sleep."

"I'm sure they're exaggerating. He just has bad dreams sometimes. Everybody does."

Maurice grimaced and snorted. His gaze drifted down to her breasts.

"I'm not sure what's wrong with the door," Cora said. "It was sticky before, but now it's a lot worse."

The superintendent ran a thumb over the latch of the door and peered at the strike plate. After a grunt, he pushed the door open until the knob touched the wall of the bathroom and scowled at the hinges. The top one hung a little loose, and the heads of the screws stuck out like tiny gophers.

Maurice muttered to himself, sounding annoyed. "Have to put new in. Hinge maybe, too."

"How long will that take?"

"You pay," he said. "This your brother do."

"How could he?" Cora said. "It's probably just old. Like everything else in this building."

"Okay, smart girl. You wait," Maurice said. "Lock man come Monday. He fix for you."

"What about tonight? How is Nathan supposed to close the door?"

"Maybe he quiet, then. Less problem."

Cora crossed her arms. Maurice turned to leave.

"Wait, okay," she said. "Can you fix it? Today?"

"Many people need help. They little trouble."

"Please," she said and touched his hairy arm. "It won't take long."

Maurice wet his lips, staring at her.

"I would really appreciate it," she said and squeezed his arm.

He took a shaky breath. "Maybe have time. Will see."

"Before four-thirty? I have to leave."

He grimaced and licked his lips again and glanced at the stairway.

"Please?" she said.

Maurice nodded slowly and turned to leave. Cora waited until he reached the stairs, then shoved the door shut and darted to the bathroom to wash her hands.

~

At the corner by the gas station, Nathan used the bottom of his T-shirt to wipe the sweat from his forehead while the traffic on Yonge Street stopped for a red light. Too many shadows in the ravine kept scaring away the fish. Later would be better.

He gave the cars on his left the finger, in case they got any ideas, and ran across the intersection. At the billboard advertising the local parks and ravines, he ducked into the Alexander Muir Memorial Gardens and ran between the spruces and cedars and pines and various shrubs until he reached the courtyard, which had a rectangle of bricks at its center, surrounded by grass, walkways, beds of flowers, and more shrubs. At the far end, a stone wall overlooked a grass lawn, a scattering of small flower beds, and the tennis courts. Two boys huddled against to the wall and made explosion noises while lobbing pebbles on the lawn but stopped when they noticed him.

Nathan walked towards them. "Bashing the yuppies? You need bigger rocks."

The boys glanced at each other. They were about nine years old, dressed in jeans and T-shirts and shiny sneakers. Between the boys lay a small pile of stones, two cans of Coke, and a green backpack.

"Fuck off," said the chubbier of the pair.

The smaller boy, who wore glasses, stared at Nathan like he was a bug.

"Yeah, look who's talking," Nathan said. "Four eyes."

The chubby boy grabbed the backpack and elbowed his friend. Together they sprinted between two of the flower beds on the north side of the courtyard and ducked into a path bordered by rosebushes. The smaller boy paused to give Nathan the finger before disappearing behind the thicker branches of some evergreens.

"Okay," Nathan said. "More for me."

He sat down beside the pile of pebbles and pushed it closer to the wall. Something jabbed his left palm. He jerked his hand back and swore. A piece of glass, brown like a beer bottle, stuck out his palm.

Those little shits.

Nathan huddled against the wall and flicked the glass out of his palm. Blood bubbled to the surface. He shook his head and closed his eyes. Everything was okay, as long as he didn't look. Looking only made it bleed faster.

"Here, take this," a woman said.

Nathan straightened up, bumping his head on the cap of the stone wall, and swore.

The woman stood on the grass only a few feet away, tall and thin, in her thirties, with pale blonde hair down to her shoulders. Her tank top and sandals were pink, and she held out a pink handkerchief with her left hand. Her Capri pants were lime green and cut low, revealing the knobs of her hip bones and a belly as pale as milk.

"No, you're not real," he said.

The woman coughed and waved the handkerchief impatiently. Her face looked powdery, like she had sneezed in a bag of flour, and her lips were as glossy as candy.

"You're a dream," he said. "You're not supposed to be here."

"Take it," she said. "Or you get blood on your shirt. Do you want to explain to your sister?"

"Fuck no, she'd freak." Nathan glanced at the blob of red dribbling down his palm and winced.

"Hurry. The sun burns more each day."

"Okay, fuck you," Nathan said and grabbed the handkerchief. "Bitch."

With a snort of disgust, she turned and strode toward the other end of the courtyard. He lurched to his feet and wrapped the handkerchief, which smelled of baby powder, around his hand. Her pants fit so tight they revealed the triangle of her thong while her cheeks pulsed up and down in a rhythm both beautiful and painful.

Nathan clenched his bleeding hand and backed up to one of the stairways leading down to the grass lawn. The woman darted up the limestone steps leading to Yonge Street and turned right on one of the brick paths, disappearing behind a cluster of spruce trees. He hesitated. What if she tried to sneak up on him again? Or was it his turn? How was it supposed to work again? Take her from behind?

He sprinted across the courtyard and turned into the same brick path, but she had already reached the edge of the Memorial Gardens and darted across St. Edmund Drive. He ran after her, and a car jammed on its brakes and honked at him. He gave the driver the finger and continued running, into a park shaped like a lopsided bowl. She flew up the slope on the opposite end of the lopsided bowl and disappeared between the parked cars.

Nathan charged up the slope, crossed another side street, into a second park, and passed a playground and the Locke library, a rough-hewn stone building that reminded him of a bunker. Ahead of him, the cars heading west revved their engines. He ran across the intersection, giving them the finger.

For a second, he thought the dream woman had disappeared in the subway station, but then he spotted a flash of pink at the next corner and chased her through an apartment complex, an alley, and a series of streets before she finally ducked into a Shoppers Drug Mart.

Nathan hunched over outside the store, gasping for breath. What the hell was he doing? This wasn't a fucking marathon. He didn't even know her name. That was important, or she wouldn't fuck him. Those were the rules. After, it didn't matter.

Still breathing hard, Nathan grabbed some flyers from the entrance and used them to hide his face while glancing down the aisles of the store. People gave him strange looks and hurried away from him. He told them to fuck off, but not too loud. She might hear him and run again.

In the aisle with the freezers and bread, a security guard wearing a black uniform stared at the shelves, too busy daydreaming. Nathan ducked behind a display of granola bars on sale, then hurried to the opposite end of the store—the makeup section—and glanced at the handkerchief wrapped around his right hand. Yeah, that made sense. She wanted to look pretty. Girls were obsessed with that. They spent more time on it than God. Except God was bullshit. Everybody knew that.

Nathan sniffed his armpits. Okay, no shit smell. That was important.

He stuffed the flyers in a shelf with jars of face cream and waved the handkerchief in front of his eyes. The blonde woman popped out of the shadows in front a section of compacts and lipsticks, her glare as pointy as icicles.

Nathan gave her the finger. She spun on her heels and clicked down to a different section of lipsticks, pretending he didn't exist.

"Yeah, fuck you," he said. He didn't need her either. Her green ass could go to hell.

With the handkerchief clutched in his right hand, Nathan stalked to the other end of the store and rummaged through the bags of potato chips. Salt and vinegar. Classic. Lightly salted. Sour cream. Dill pickle. Ketchup. Doritos. Tostitos. Fritos . . .

The security guard appeared at the end of the aisle, talking to a tiny Filipino girl in a blue and gray uniform. Nathan grabbed two bags of chips and sprinted back to the aisle with the makeup, but Blondie had disappeared. He swore. The guard strode out of the junk food aisle. Nathan hurried to the back of the store. She was probably hiding from the guard too. She couldn't have disappeared. She was real. He still had her handkerchief.

He backed up against a display of shampoo and waved the handkerchief in front of his face. At first, nothing happened. Then a woman with bulging breasts walked out of aisle three and stopped in front of the pharmacy counter. He dropped one of the bags of chips on the floor. She was probably twice his age but wore a pink blouse, a black mini-jacket, and a tight black skirt that showed off a trim waist and smooth legs—ten times better than an anorexic in green pants.

The woman ran a finger over the bottles of pain relievers, her black bra showing through her thin blouse like a neon sign at a strip club. Nathan shook his head. She probably had huge nipples too, like in the pornos, and sweaty skin and a shaved vagina, the kind that tasted like banana or strawberry or blueberry. He had never licked one before but tried all the flavors in the store—a lot better than the fish and cheese in high school.

Unless she was too good to be true? He had to watch out for that. Doctor's orders. Stop. Take a reality check.

The woman picked out two packages of Tylenols and strode back into aisle three, her breasts bouncing like basketballs. Nathan wished he could squeeze them. That would be a good reality check.

He shifted his erection, squashed as it was against the crotch of his jeans, and noticed an Indian man in a white robe staring from behind the counter.

"Hey, fuck you, you queer," Nathan yelled.

He whipped his second bag of chips at the pharmacist, but it bounced off the counter and flopped on the floor. The pharmacist ducked behind a metal rack. Nathan grabbed a bottle of mouth-wash from the display behind him as the security guard stumbled out of aisle five, yelling in broken English.

Nathan dropped the mouthwash and bolted past deodorants and razors. People jumped back against the shelves, including a cute girl with pale breasts popping out of her blue paisley dress.

He charged through the checkout counters and out the exit. God was such a fucking joker. He practically hit you over the head with them—tits falling out everywhere—then kicked you in the nuts.

No wonder people didn't believe in him anymore.

~

While waiting for the superintendent to return, Cora ate lunch: half a bagel with low-fat cream cheese, the last of the baby carrots, and a small yogurt. Nathan didn't like the raspberry much anyway.

Afterwards, she changed into a spare pair of jeans, which she kept in the cabinet beside the front door, and the red T-shirt she had brought from home and washed her plates and utensils, scrubbed the counter, sink, stovetop, and microwave, and pulled out the stepladder from the coat closet to clean the top of the fridge. She thought about doing a load or two of laundry, but if the superintendent came back while she was in the basement, he wouldn't wait for her.

After sliding the stepladder back in the closet, she checked her cellphone and saw she had missed a text message from Melissa:

Vote no 2 grubie dicks.

Cora pressed four on her speed-dial, but the call switched over automatically to Melissa's voicemail.

"Hey, just got your message," Cora said. "Hope he wasn't that bad. I'm fine until seven, so call me if you want."

She tucked the phone back in her purse and turned on the TV to check the weather forecast. No rain expected for the next twelve hours. None tomorrow. Probably showers on Sunday. That meant she was safe wearing the black evening dress with the spaghetti straps and the new shoes she had bought at Holt Renfrew. James liked red, but she had already worn the red dress for him last time.

Cora switched to a channel playing top 40 and went into the bathroom. She pulled out the bucket and yellow rubber gloves from the vanity and cleaned the mirror and scrubbed the toilet, the sink, and the floor tiles. Once finished, she stowed everything back under the sink and washed her hands and checked her cellphone again.

No, nothing from Katrina yet.

In the kitchen, Cora poured herself a glass of water and sat on the stool tucked beside the window overlooking the garden center next door, mostly a view of the green plastic roof. She thought about making a cup of tea but already felt hot from the cleaning. What was taking Maurice so long? Was he even coming back?

She sipped her water. The apartment door banged open and smacked the plastic disc meant to protect the bathroom wall. Cora started, sloshing water on her shirt and jeans. For a moment, she thought the superintendent was barging in like a madman, but then she saw Nathan and exhaled in relief.

"How was the ravine?" she asked.

"They're fucking everywhere," he said, breathing heavily, and slammed the door shut. "Always trying to beat you down, keep you in the mud."

"Are you hungry? There's still some soup in the fridge. Or I can make you a sandwich?"

"Yeah, soup," he said. "That's the stuff. Makes your hair grow."

Cora slid her glass on the counter and noticed a pink cloth wrapped around her brother's right hand. She frowned and paused by the fridge.

"What's that around your hand?" she asked.

Nathan shook his head.

"Is your hand okay?" she asked.

"Jesus, would you fuck off," he said and pushed past her. After grabbing a cup from the cupboards, he pushed her away again and grabbed the orange juice from the fridge. "It's fucking stinks in here."

"It's probably the vinegar. I did some cleaning."

"Bullshit," Nathan said and grabbed a banana from the fruit bowl by the toaster. "I know that smell."

Cora nodded and waited until he had finished the glass of juice and the banana. "Can I look at your hand, please? Just quick. Then I'll warm up the soup."

Still grumbling, Nathan let her unwrap the handkerchief from his right hand, revealing a cut at the base of his palm.

"I'll clean that and put a bandage on it. Just to be safe," Cora said and turned get the first aid kit from the bathroom.

"Hey! Give that back." Nathan yanked the handkerchief out of her hand.

"Sorry, I—"

Nathan swore and stormed into his bedroom and slammed the door. Cora closed her eyes and took a slow breath. Then she stepped into the bathroom and dug the bottle of rubbing alcohol out from behind the toilet paper and rummaged through the first aid kit and cut off a strip from the roll of bandages.

She knocked on the bedroom door. "Nathan? Can I come in? I

just want to clean your hand."

She waited. He didn't answer.

"Please? I just want to put a bandage on it."

"Go to hell."

"It'll only take a second. I promise."

Behind her, someone knocked on the apartment door.

"Tell that shit to fuck off," Nathan said.

Cora closed her eyes, took a deep breath, and walked to the peephole. Yes, it was the superintendent.

After setting the rubbing alcohol and bandage on the cabinet on her left, she tugged the door open, and Maurice gave her a sour smile. He had a tool belt slung over one shoulder, a screw gun in one hand, and a Ziploc bag in the other, holding a couple of hinges and a variety of screws.

"Don't let that fucker in here," Nathan yelled from the bedroom.

"Sorry," Cora said. "He stubbed his toe."

"Always problems," Maurice said. "Always yelling."

Though tempted to argue, she put on her best smile and tapped the door. "I really appreciate you coming back so quickly."

"Yes, you hold. Will be faster."

He gestured for her to open the door all the way, which she did, and he used the screw gun to remove the top hinge. Cora felt redundant holding the knob, but he wanted her to help, and she wanted the job done. A small sacrifice. Especially when compared to the rest of her life.

"No good," Maurice said, interrupting her thoughts. "No good."

He pulled a hammer and a block of wood out of his tool belt and kneeled in the hallway. Cora turned her head to avoid looking at the tangles of dark hair bursting out the back of his pants. He banged on the hinge a few times, muttered, and shook his head. From the Ziploc bag, he pulled out a new hinge and held it up against the holes in the door.

"Have you ever wanted to go anywhere?" Cora asked. "You know, travel?"

"Too much money," Maurice said.

"But if you could?"

"Why? Everywhere fighting. No good."

He finished screwing in the new hinge and waved Cora away from the door. After swinging it back and forth a couple of times, he picked up his tool belt and tugged at his pants.

"Your brother lucky," he said. "I have extra. But next time will cost."

"Yes, thank you," Cora said. "I really appreciate it."

She was tempted to ask him about the bathroom sink too, but Nathan shouted another curse, and the superintendent's face furrowed up like an old dog. Cora thanked him again and touched his hairy arm. The faucet could wait. It wasn't dripping that bad.

After a grunt and a lingering look at her breasts, Maurice started down the stairway. Cora locked the door, washed her hands, and knocked on Nathan's bedroom.

"Get out of here, you fuck," he said.

"It's me," she said. "Just me."

"I told you to get rid of that fuck. He's always stealing my shit."

"He didn't come inside. He just fixed the door. It wasn't closing properly."

The bedroom door jerked open. "Yeah? What about my shoes?"

"They're in the bathroom," Cora said. "I cleaned them and put them on the tub to dry."

"Fuck you," he said and slammed the door in her face.

She stood there for a few seconds. It felt like much longer. Then her eyes began to film over, and she wondered where she had left her purse. She needed a tissue.

When she felt calm again, Cora washed her hands and made him a peanut butter sandwich, using two slices of white bread, and cut off the crusts and took the pot of chicken noodle soup out of the fridge and ladled fours scoops into a Tupperware container. She slid the container and the sandwich beside the microwave and wrote Nathan a note: *Microwave on high four minutes with the lid loose. See you tomorrow. Call me if you need anything.*

While wiping the counter, though, she remembered Nathan's phone was missing and glanced at the scarred end table in the living room. He couldn't call her, even if you wanted to.

Cora washed her hands and wrote her brother a new note, this time omitting the sentence about calling her. She would bring her spare phone tomorrow. Or maybe his old one would show up again. She didn't have much hope of that, but with Nathan anything was possible.

Chapter 5

Two blocks shy of Father's building, Alex's throat tightened up, and his head began to throb. The pubs he drove past called out to him, telling him to turn around, don't be an idiot, but he simply saluted them with his last Heineken and guzzled its pale contents.

At the corner with the old paint factory, he turned right and passed the front of the boarded-up nightclub, and turned right again, into an alley. He drove to the loading dock at the back end of the nightclub and parked beside a brown dumpster, behind which stood a couple of broken chairs.

He stepped out of the car and waved a hand for the security cameras before any of the guards decided to bother him. They were all morons. Mobius's finest.

Alex wriggled out of his gray jacket and draped it over the head rest of his seat and opened the case of Steam Whistle sitting on the passenger seat. Three beers later, he told himself to slow down, or he wouldn't have any left when he finished with the prisoners. Swapping them was bad enough, but shadows already slid across the walls of the alley and the grime on the asphalt, making faces at him, mocking him. Most were from the war, the friends who had gotten shot and blown apart: Jimmy, who lost four of his fingers to the rats; Patterson, who stepped on a mine and got his foot blown into his crotch; Big John and Al and Henry, all hit by Germans; Lewis, the first to die because of Father; Wilson, the second; Patrick, the third.

Fuck, so many of them had died badly.

Alex rolled the beer bottle between his hands and shook his head. Back then, in that mud pit called Holland, he used to think the war was the worst hell possible. But he didn't really know hell until a scrawny girl and her bald stooge killed six of his men and marched Alex and the remnants of his unit off to dig out a corpse from the rubble of a manor bombed by Germans—or maybe the English. Nobody knew for certain. Nobody cared.

With the rain pouring down, Alex could only watch while the rest of his men died, two of them killing each other, seeing things that weren't real, shadows spurting out of the ground, hissing and growling, the voice in their heads promising death, destruction, suffering.

A horn blared behind Alex. He twisted right, sloshing beer on the passenger seat. A white van pulled up behind him, honked again, and backed up to the bay door of the nightclub. The side of the van said SKYEARTH PRODUCTIONS, a front company created by the accountants in Teresa's security force.

The driver of the white van honked a third time. Alex swore and climbed out of his car.

"Open the damn door yourself," he shouted.

At first nothing happened. Alex tossed his beer bottle in the dumpster and yelled at the van again.

Without any particular hurry, Fernandez stepped out of the passenger side of the van and sneered at Alex.

"Stop fucking around," Alex said. "You have work to do."

Fernandez shrugged and swaggered to the small gray door beside the loading dock. He was short and tanned and wore a black sleeveless shirt showing off the tattoos on his shoulders and arms: skulls, barbs, imps, and tiger claws. His dark hair was slicked back like a duck in an oil spill, and his beard looked like someone had used a thumb to make an inkblot on his chin.

The driver, Schwartz, straightened out the van and backed up again till it covered the bay door. Fernandez tapped in the security code to unlock the gray door and disappeared inside the building, releasing the stink of shit and rancid meat into the alley. A few seconds later, the bay door slid open. Alex rubbed his nose and grabbed another beer from his car.

Schwartz stumbled out of the van. "Fuck, that reeks."

"Just get your fat ass inside," Alex said.

Schwartz stared at the beer for a couple of seconds before rolling his shoulders and grabbing a can of pop from the front of the van. He was pale and freckled and had short red hair, most of it covered by a black baseball cap with the new logo for the Blue Jays. He also wore a green jersey with a picture of a basketball above the words "BIG BALLS".

Alex drained the beer and tossed the bottle in the dumpster. The bang made Schwartz jump, but Alex didn't find it particularly funny and walked to the gray door.

In the loading area, the stench of death was even stronger and seemed to pulse from the walls, as if Father beat it out with his shriveled heart. Fernandez pretended not to notice and leaned against the back doors of the van, smoking a cigarette.

"Get those doors open," Alex said. "You can smoke later."

"Awh, scared of little cigarette?"

"Yeah, that's why I'm still alive," Alex said. "Which you won't be if you're shoving that in your face when he wakes up."

Fernandez took a drag and shrugged. Alex glanced at Schwartz, who wiped sweat off his face with a bandana and looked like he had swallowed a rotten egg.

"I don't care who does it," Alex said. "Just get it done."

Schwartz continued to wipe his face. Fernandez sucked on his cigarette and blew smoke at them.

"That means now," Alex said, glaring at Schwartz.

"Yeah, yeah," he said and shoved his bandanna in his jeans.

"Oh, pussy, pussy," Fernandez said. "Here, pussy, pussy."

Still muttering to himself, Schwartz pushed Fernandez aside and opened the back of the van. Inside, three women and a child sat on a pair of long wooden boxes, black sacks pulled over their heads, their hands and feet secured with zip ties.

"What the hell is that?" Alex asked, pointing at the child.

"He come with the girls," Fernandez said.

"That's not what you're supposed to bring," Alex said. "Father's not interested in little boys."

"You take him, then," Fernandez said. "You like it. Special gift."

Alex sprang forward and shoved Fernandez into one of the van's doors. Fernandez bounced off the door and punched Alex in the face. He stumbled backwards, punches hitting him in the stomach and the face, but they didn't hurt much, and he rammed a shoulder into Fernandez's chest, knocking him off his feet. Arms grabbed Alex from behind. He spun in a half-circle and flung Schwartz against the van.

The snap of a switchblade jerked Alex's attention back to Fernandez.

"How far do you think you're going to get with that?" Alex said.

"Far," Fernandez said. "Plenty far."

"Yeah? Then what? You're going to call the mistress and tell her what a stupid shit you are?" Alex turned his back on Fernandez and said to Schwartz, "Get them out of the van before we stink up the whole block."

Schwartz muttered under his breath and climbed into the van. The prisoners trembled and whimpered and tried to pull away from him. He grabbed the nearest woman, wearing a thin, flower print dress, and hauled her out of the van. After dropping her on the floor beside Alex, Schwartz climbed back into the van and grabbed the legs of a woman wearing blue jeans and a green T-shirt.

Alex shook his head and opened the door of a storage room. Still holding the switchblade, Fernandez lit another cigarette and toed the woman on the floor. Schwartz dropped the other two women next to the first and started to pull out the boy, but the boy grabbed hold of one of the wooden boxes and struggled to kick his feet. Schwartz swore and latched on the zip tie around the boy's ankles and yanked him out of the van. The boy whacked the concrete floor, and a cry of pain pierced the bag covering his head.

Fernandez grabbed the boy by the shirt and hauled him to his feet. Again the boy cried out.

"You shit your pants? Heh? Little shitter?" Fernandez pressed his knife against the boy's throat. "I throw you in the river, make you food for fish."

Alex grimaced at the bile in his mouth and rubbed his nose. From deeper in the building came the rumble and hiss of a voice, promising death, destruction, eternal suffering.

Next to the van, Schwartz slapped his head. Alex focused on the nearest prisoner, a woman with dried blood around her neck, probably because of the cord from the bag covering her head.

"Lock them in the storage room," he said. "I need to get the old ones out first."

"Alone?" Fernandez said. "No run off?"

"Get those goddamn boxes out of the van and get the hell out of here," Alex said. "I don't have time for your bullshit."

"Awh, big pussy now. Pussy everywhere."

"Would you shut up and help," Schwartz said and dragged the woman wearing the blue jeans into the storage room.

Fernandez shrugged and flicked the ashes from his cigarette on the woman wearing the flower dress. Schwartz muttered a curse and dragged the rest of the women into the storage room. The boy struggled against his zip ties and kicked his feet, scraping Fernandez's shoes.

He swore and kicked the boy in the kidneys. The boy yowled. Alex sprang forward and flung Fernandez at the van. His switchblade banged off the bumper.

With surprising grace, Fernandez dropped into a crouch and grabbed his switchblade off the concrete floor. He flicked the blade back and forth, daring Alex to come closer.

"Go ahead," he said. "I'll shove you in a cage and see how long you last."

"I am right for choosing," Fernandez said. "Not like you."

Schwartz, who looked pale enough to shit cream cheese, threw the boy in the storage room and scrambled to get between Alex and Fernandez.

"The mistress wants it done, that's all that matters," Schwartz said. "Through her we're reborn."

Fernandez made a sour face but glanced in the van.

"I'll unhook the boxes," Schwartz said. "You just need to get the end."

"No, I do it," Fernandez said. "You watch shitface."

The blade of his knife snapped back into the hilt as he shoved Schwartz aside. Once in the van, Fernandez released the straps holding the front of the boxes and heaved the right one at Schwartz. Even though he managed to grab the handle on the end of the box, he stumbled and dropped it. The box hit the concrete floor with a loud crack.

Alex swore and shoved Schwartz out of the way and hoisted the box out of the van. Despite the awkwardness of the box's girth, he swung the whole thing around and eased it on the floor.

"You could have done that sooner," Schwartz said.

"I'm not your fucking mother," Alex said. "Just hurry up with the other one. Father's waiting."

Schwartz and Fernandez exchanged scowls but unloaded the second box and slid it on top of the first one. Without another word, Fernandez grabbed his cigarettes from the bumper and stomped out of the building.

"Come back in an hour," Alex said. "Load the boxes. Take them straight to the crematorium. No fucking around."

"Yeah, yeah," Schwartz said.

He slammed the van doors shut and yanked down the bay door.

In the alley, Fernandez yelled, "Fuck you, asshole."

Schwartz swore, scampered outside, and started the van. From deeper in the building spilled other noises—the screeches of the dead, the hisses, the promises of destruction—and Alex wished he had brought some beer inside.

The van rumbled and spit gravel. Alex muttered a curse and hoisted the top box, which felt empty, on the floor. Inside the second box, he found five black body bags and a can of pine air freshener—someone's stupid idea of a joke. Probably Schwartz. Fernandez wasn't that bright.

Alex eased the body bags on the floor and walked out to his car. After grabbing the two bottles of Stella from the back seat, he rubbed his nose, hoping to dislodge the stink stuck in his nostrils, but rubbing only pushed the foulness deeper.

He guzzled one of the beers and tossed the bottle in the dumpster. From the trunk, he pulled out the smaller of two canvas bags. He didn't have time to lollygag, especially with Mobius's goons watching from the surrounding buildings.

Back inside the loading bay, Alex dug out a black rubber slicker, a pair of rubber boots, and leather gloves from the canvas bag. He drained the second beer and swapped his black leather shoes for the boots, first taking a flashlight out of the right boot. After pulling on the slicker and the gloves, he slung the body bags over a shoulder, picked up the flashlight, and walked to the door leading to Father.

No more time to think, only time to do. Like a good little soldier.

Alex shoved the door open, keeping the beam of the flashlight on the floor in front of him, and stepped into the next room. It stank, of course, but not as bad as he had expected. More like an old cesspool than a hellhole.

He stepped past a paint shaker covered by a dirty gray tarp and slid three body bags on the floor. The other two bags he carried to the left, heading to the cage beside the deejay booth. He avoided shining his flashlight anywhere near Father. Seeing him only made things worse, made the air heavier, the noises louder, the shadows stronger. How the prisoners survived more than a few hours mystified Alex.

Inside the first cage, the prisoner lay crumpled against the door, her hands secured behind her back with a zip tie, a gray gag in her mouth. Alex unlatched the door and eased her to the floor, careful not to bounce her head on the floor, and used a knife from his overcoat to cut the zip tie and the gag. She was tiny, little more than a skeleton in a soiled gray dress, one of those girls from Vietnam or Thailand or China who had already been small before Father sucked her dry.

From the direction of Father's glass box came a tap, almost too soft to hear. Alex shook his head and slid the girl's feet into the bottom of the body bag. As quietly as possible, he lifted the rest of her and wiggled her inside the bag, keeping her face away from him. He hated when they stared at him with their dead fish eyes.

He eased the zipper shut and carried her to the loading bay and lowered her into one of the boxes. He resisted the urge to grab another beer from his car. First he had to empty the cages, or it would only get worse—listening to all the screams, seeing the dead faces. He just had to do his job, get out. Pretend the world was his friend.

At each of the remaining three cages, he eased the girls on the floor before cutting their zip ties and gags and sliding the girls into their body bags. Each time, he thought he heard a tap from the center of the room, but the noise was so faint he hoped he had imagined it.

While carrying the last girl to the loading bay, Alex stumbled on a loose flap of floor and dropped his flashlight. It rolled down a step and fell on the old dance floor, and Father's shriveled body jumped out of the darkness, hitting Alex like a punch in the face. He fell to his knees. Noises exploded in his head: sheep, Nazis, rain, howitzers, dogs, fire, tanks, screams, storms, drowning, dying, breathing, rifles, boots, mud, mud, mud.

Alex clenched his hands and dug his nails into his palms. The noises slowed. Cold air ruffled his coat. Then they struck him full force again, crashing like waves in a storm, and he slapped his ears and shook his head until the noises tumbled out and crawled back to whatever hellhole they had escaped from.

With his eyes squeezed shut, he groped around for his flashlight. His fingers felt like popsicles. His throat burned, filling his lungs with poison. No matter how many years went by, he always had to fight the same tricks—that bastard and his fucking tricks.

Alex coughed and shoved the flashlight into his overcoat and pounded on his chest. Still coughing, he grabbed the end of the body bag with the girl and dragged her into the loading bay.

He kicked the door shut, sank to his knees, and spit out wads of phlegm. The burning sensation in his throat subsided. A shadow pulled away from the body bag and melted into the floor. Alex spat and staggered to his feet and heaved the body into the nearest box.

After another bout of coughing, Alex stumbled into the alley and grabbed the case of Steam Whistle from his car. He didn't care who was watching anymore. They could all go to hell.

Back in the loading bay, he guzzled three of the bottles in between coughs. While drinking the fourth, the coughing stopped. Part of him wanted to wait a little longer, but the rest of him told him to finish and get out.

He gulped half of his fifth beer, stuck the bottle back in the case, and opened the storage room. The prisoners huddled against the walls, trembling and moaning. Father was already toying with them, poking their minds like a hot stick in a snow bank.

"Pray it's quick," he said.

The woman wearing the flower dress buckled at his touch and flopped on the floor. He muttered a curse and scooped her up and hoisted her over a shoulder. She was too weak to do more than murmur to whatever God she believed in.

At the door to Father's room, Alex paused, tempted to pray too, but he had never been very good at that charade. He had always felt phony, especially with a minister who thought it was fun to jiggle your trousers.

Alex eased the door open, keeping his gaze down, and stepped across the threshold. He pulled out his flashlight. He didn't want to turn it back on, but he needed to see something. He just had to be more careful.

When he reached the deejay booth, he turned right. Even though the floor was relatively smooth, he tripped twice—Father playing his mind games—but Alex kept a firm grip on the flashlight and the prisoner. Not that she cared. She had passed out. If she was lucky, she would never wake up again. It was less painful that way. Less suffering.

Alex wedged the flashlight between the bars of the cage in the far corner, pointing the beam of light at the back wall, and eased her inside. She flopped against the bars like a bag of onions. Not a whisper. Not a hope.

Back in the loading bay, Alex swigged the rest of his open beer and pulled the boy out of the storage room. He had soaked the front of his shorts with piss and kicked at Alex like a newborn lamb. Alex closed his eyes and tried not to think about the wrongness of it all. In the war, he had pissed himself too, when he thought he was going to die, mortars falling around him, his buddies getting blown into hash, bullets ripping through their heads and bellies. But at least he had had a chance then.

He wiped at the sweat on his brow and boosted the boy on a shoulder. The boy mewled and wriggled until they reached the door to Father's room, then slumped and fell silent. Alex hoped the boy had passed out. It would be easier for both of them.

Once across the threshold, Alex turned left and passed the paint shaker. The boy fluttered his legs, trying to kick, but he had no energy left. The air was too heavy for him. The air was too dead.

Alex stuck the flashlight between the bars of the cage beside the deejay booth and maneuvered the boy inside the cage. He made one last croaking sound through his hood, and Alex latched the door shut and marched out of the room. Only two more. Then he could try his damnedest to get drunk.

In the storage room, he found the last two women curled on the floor. He carried them, one at a time, into Father's room and eased them into their cages. Neither of them struggled. Neither of them made a noise. He wanted to tell them to fight—they would never get another chance—but his footsteps already felt too loud. Something in the room had changed, swallowing the shadows and their whispers. That was always bad.

Alex shut the door of the last cage, and his flashlight highlighted the black bag covering the head of the last prisoner, transforming her into a nightmarish doll. He grimaced and tugged the flashlight from between the bars.

A cold draft prickled the skin on his neck and face. He eased to his feet. Where the hell had that come from?

His flashlight flickered. The darkness in the middle of the room jerked and rumbled. Not just the usual games Father liked to play, but something big and angry.

Alex sprinted toward the door for the loading bay. The flashlight clattered on the floor. A surge of darkness slammed into him. He tumbled and hit a railing. Cars whipped through his head. Buildings. Streets. High-rises. Trucks. Trees. Walls and windows ripped apart. Debris smashed into him, all of it screaming, rushing inside him.

Alex screamed and convulsed as he hit the floor. He continued to scream and convulse until his voice gave out and his limbs went numb.

Then there was only Father, rumbling and hissing within his glass cage. Promising death. Destruction. Eternal suffering.

Chapter 6

From the back of a cab, Cora watched the corner of Eglinton and Yonge flash by, people streaming in and out of the mall, the restaurants, the banks, the coffee shops. She did not want to think about Nathan. She did not want to think about the door slamming in her face. It wasn't his fault. Sometimes he just didn't realize what he was doing.

She brushed her hair from her eyes and glanced at her fingernails, idly checking them for chips and scratches. When he first became ill, five years ago, the outbursts used to bother her a lot more, often keeping her awake at night, perhaps because he still had the power to surprise her then, and she still had hopes for a recovery, as if schizophrenia was only a broken bone or a bloody gash. She hadn't truly grasped the severity of his disease. She hadn't grasped how it would twist up her life and turn it into a farce.

The cabby honked at a black car drifting into his lane. Another block of shops and offices and condos zipped by. She fished her cellphone out of her purse and called Nathan's psychiatrist, but the number switched over automatically to an answering service. No surprise. It was almost five. The doctor was probably on a golf course.

Cora left a short message requesting an appointment to discuss Nathan's medication. Hopefully they would get back to her on Monday. The cabby honked at the black car as it squeezed in front of them. She opened her window a little to let in some air and called Melissa, who picked up after the first ring.

"Hey, I was just going to call you," she said.

"Sorry about canceling cancelling yesterday," Cora said. "My brother's been all over the map this week."

"Are you there now?"

"No, I'm on my way home. I have to get ready for tonight."

"Yeah, I'm heading home too," Melissa said. "I don't have the next boy wonder till nine."

"Is he new?"

"No, it's Vince. Kind of a pain in the ass. He's totally obsessed with getting the real thing, whatever that means." Melissa snorted. "I don't think he'd know the real thing if it bit his nuts off."

"So you don't have to be a virgin again?"

"God, no, I hate that."

"It's not that bad."

"Well, you're probably good at it," Melissa said. "You look so wholesome."

Cora murmured, "Oh?" She didn't feel very wholesome.

"Honestly, I don't know how you do it. That shit with your brother would drive me crazy. It's like being a nurse but worse."

"I wouldn't say that. I mean, it's hard sometimes, but—"

"Please," Melissa said. "I've heard enough about him to write a book."

"He's okay most of the time," Cora said. "I just wish he had more good days, days where he's really himself."

"Geez, you're such a selfish bitch."

Cora surprised herself by laughing, though the laugh sounded startled, like a rabbit darting across a highway.

"Anyway, gotta go," Melissa said. "I'm almost at my garage."

"What about lunch? Maybe Monday or Tuesday?"

"I'll call you tomorrow," Melissa said. "I need to check a couple of things first."

"Okay, talk to you then."

Cora hung up and settled back in her seat, her gaze drifting to the trees on the other side of the Yonge Street, and wondered if Melissa would be willing to grab lunch near Eglinton again. It made going to Nathan's afterwards a lot easier.

The cabby, an Indian man with a bulbous nose, scratched his mustache and glanced over his shoulder. "You, pretty lady, should not look sad."

"What?" she said, surprised.

"It is a crime. Very wrong."

"Please watch the road. That would make me plenty happy."

The cabby shook his head and waved a hand over the steering wheel. "Life is a sweet song, like a bird. Feed it good things, and it flies."

Cora peered past him at the high-rises ahead. How much farther did she have to go? Ten minutes? Fifteen?

"I have never seen a game of baseball," he said. "I have been meaning many times. And you are next door."

"I don't like baseball," Cora said.

The cabby nodded and passed a truck with a giant maple leaf on the trailer. "Cricket is much better. The sport of a man."

Cora mumbled, "Oh," and held down the two on her cellphone, activating the speed dial. She hoped it would stop him from talking.

Nathan's voicemail clicked on, and she hung up and said, "I just wanted to know if you were going to the mall later. There's a pair of shoes I want to get."

After a pause, giving the imaginary person a chance to reply, Cora continued the conversation while the cabby turned onto Church Street and passed through the construction zone on Bloor. A few blocks later, she pretended to hang up again and took her time reading her old text messages, deleting them one by one, until the cab stopped in front of her apartment building.

She avoided the cabby's gaze while paying her fare and didn't wait for change. On the sidewalk, she hurried past the potted cedars and the flower urns and the tourists who seemed to be everywhere, enjoying a hot afternoon at the Harbourfront.

Once inside her building, she avoided the trio standing by the empty concierge's desk—the two men eyeing her—grateful she had an elevator to herself. No matter where she went, men were all the same. Black, white, brown—it didn't matter. They only wanted one thing. They never had enough.

~

After what felt like only a few seconds, Cora woke up to the chime of her cellphone and pushed herself out of the cushions of her sofa. God, what time was it? She shouldn't have fallen asleep. She had to get ready.

Her cellphone started to chime again. Cora wished she could

ignore the call but knew she didn't have that luxury.

Yes, it was Katrina.

"Hi, sorry," Cora said, answering the phone.

"I was talking to Rex," Katrina said, "the surgeon from Montreal. He wanted to see you next week, but I told him you didn't have time."

"He was here a couple of weeks ago? For a conference?"

"Yeah, him. Apparently he couldn't wait to see you again." Katrina paused. "That makes two today. Plus a couple of calls from newbies."

"I guess I should be flattered," Cora said.

Katrina snorted. "You don't have to sound so excited."

"I didn't mean it like that. Rex was nice."

"I suggested an alternative, but it had to be you. He was crystal clear about that."

"When is he coming?"

"Friday, when you're with Fred C."

Cora leaned back in the sofa and wiggled her toes. Which one was he again? The developer?

"I don't know what your secret is," Katrina said. "But it sure works."

"I just try to be what they want, I guess."

Katrina laughed. "Don't tell Ang that. She'll throttle you."

Cora said nothing, though she was inclined to agree. Ang was one of the older girls, who also handled some of the bookings, and weighed every second of her life in terms of money.

"Anyway, I have to go," Katrina said. "Straw will be at your place quarter to seven. Dress for the restaurant. But I'll call Ling again to confirm."

"I wouldn't mind somewhere quieter," Cora said. "If that's what he's thinking."

"I'll keep that in mind," Katrina said and hung up.

Cora set the phone beside her and sank into the cushions of the sofa and yawned. She wished she could doze off again. She felt like she could sleep forever, without ever having to dream.

From outside came the rumble of a plane, and Cora opened her eyes again. She glanced out over the balcony. A white plane appeared for a second or two on its descent to the runway on the island.

Yes, enough stalling.

She pushed herself out of the sofa and fetched a bottle of water from the fridge. In the master bathroom, the stink of male sweat and cologne lingered like week-old pizza, and she realized she had forgotten to take the dress from last night to the dry cleaners. She grimaced and picked the bundles with her clothes out of the bathtub and stuck them on the balcony. They would have to wait until tomorrow. Then she washed her hands and pulled out a pair of yellow rubber gloves from under the sink and scrubbed the bathtub with soap scum remover.

Somewhat mollified, Cora lit the beeswax candles in front of the tub and showered in the smaller bathroom. After drying herself off, she pulled on a fresh bathrobe and walked into the spare bedroom, where she kept all her work clothes. She opened the mahogany wardrobe sitting against the far wall and stroked the sleeve of a scarlet cocktail dress, the fabric soft and slippery. For the next few hours, she needed to forget her everyday life. She had to be the girl who was always fun and sexy and full of smiles and moaned and wriggled at the right times and salved the man's ego if he went limp. Or worse, if he couldn't come at all. That always got them upset.

Cora pulled out the black cocktail dress with the spaghetti straps and posed for the mirror standing beside the wardrobe. Her cellphone rang from the living room. She stuck the dress back in the wardrobe and hurried to answer the call.

"Ling decided on an in night," Katrina said. "So Straw will take you straight to the hotel."

"Still three hours?" Cora asked.

"Yes, he's already paid the extra. You just have to knock on his door. Room 3013. I'll text it to you as well."

"Okay, that's fine."

"And call me after," Katrina said. "I want to know if he manages to stay awake for more than five minutes."

~

The clock said three to seven. Cora sat at her vanity, adding the last touches to her eyeshadow, when her cellphone buzzed with a message from Straw.

Waiting.

She sent back, *5*, and used the toilet. She could finish her makeup in the car.

While washing her hands, she looked herself over and wondered if she should have put on proper earrings. Ling wanted her to look more refined, more cultured, even if they were only staying in the hotel. Melissa said no. Stay away from jewelry. She didn't even like to wear stud earrings when she was working. Katrina was more philosophical. If he bought it for you, absolutely.

Cora's cellphone chimed with another message from Straw: *Waiting 2.*

Cora hustled into the spare bedroom and opened her jewelry box. The minutes ticked by. Finally she settled on a pair of faux diamond teardrop earrings and put them on.

On the elevator, she received a third message: *Waiting 3.*

She hurried out of her building and spotted Straw's black sedan parked in front of the grocery store next door. Across the street, a cluster of Chinese tourists took pictures of the Amsterdam Bridge. Meant solely for pedestrians, the bridge arced over a small slip holding about a dozen boats, white cables stretching up from the span to resemble sails.

Cora tapped on the passenger window of the sedan. Straw turned to frown at her, one arm draped over the steering wheel. He had a thick face with a black stripe for a mustache and an avocado-shaped beard.

The back door clicked, and she ducked inside the sedan.

"You get lost again?" Straw said.

"Sorry, emergency."

"You know Kat's gonna bust it if you're late. She hates looking bad."

"It'll be fine," Cora said. "It's not that far."

"Yeah, whatever." He tapped the steering wheel with his fingers and checked the mirrors. "I don't need Kat chewing me out for driving so fucking slow."

"Sorry, it really was an emergency."

"Yeah, and my ass is blue."

Cora opened her handbag and pulled out a pink purse, hoping it would end the conversation. He could be such a jerk sometimes. She couldn't understand why Melissa mooned about him.

"What was so important anyway?" Straw asked. "You got a new boyfriend?"

"That's the last thing I need."

"Sounds like a piece of work."

"What does that mean?"

Straw shrugged. "I hope he's richer than God."

"Can we just go? Or I really will be late."

"Whatever," he said but accelerated past the cars parked in front the neighboring restaurants.

At the first intersection, he turned up the radio. The thump of rock music filled the car, something dark and grungy Nathan would have loved as a teenager. Cora fished out a mirror and dark gray eye pencil from the pink purse. She brought the mirror close to her face, looking at the freckles on either side of her nose, and rubbed the left side with a finger. Sometimes she wished she could say a few magic words and make them disappear . . . like certain men who continued to glance at her in the rear-view mirror.

By the time they reached University Avenue, about ten minutes later, she was already sick of the music and asked Straw to switch it to something else. He shrugged and flipped to a station playing top 40 and drove past a cluster of hospitals, including Mount Sinai, where Nathan's psychiatrist had his office.

"Did I tell you my cousin opened a restaurant in Liberty village?" Straw asked. "Mostly fusion. Best food you've ever had."

Cora glanced at him, startled. He sped through a yellow light, and the street curved around the Ontario Legislative Building, its pink sandstone muted from years of smog.

"You should tell Melissa," she said. "She loves everything fusion."

"I'm telling you."

She murmured in reply, slipped her mascara back in her purse, and picked out a pale rose lipstick. Straw stopped for a red light across from the Royal Ontario Museum, the evening sun gleaming off the glass of the new Crystal expansion.

"When's the last time you laughed?" he asked.

"What?"

"You look burnt out, like a fucking crackhead. You need to relax, have some fun."

"It's nothing," Cora said. "I just had a long day."

"Bullshit. I know the look."

Cora slid her lipstick back into her bag and focused on the people passing by on the sidewalk: the students wearing shorts and carrying backpacks, a plump woman wearing black spandex pants that made her look like a hideous balloon, a pale thin woman with three small children in tow.

Straw snorted. The traffic light turned green. Two blocks later, he stopped in front of one of the smaller entrances for the Four Seasons hotel, tucked between the lounges and restaurant.

"You better hope he isn't picky about you being late," he said.

"It's only a couple of minutes."

"Yeah, that's fucking helpful."

"All right, fine. Don't come back. I'll take a cab."

"Yeah, right. Kat would chew my ass." He scowled at Cora. "I don't why she makes such a big deal about driving you around like fucking Miss Daisy. But she wants me to do it, so that's what I'm going to do."

"I wish she didn't."

"Just call me when you're done."

Cora slid out of the car, careful of her dress, and slammed the door. She didn't have time to argue with him.

Once inside the hotel, she paused beside an escalator to smooth her dress and moved her handbag to her other shoulder. She took a deep breath, walked past a pair of lounges, her heels like a barrage of pistols, and pressed the up button for the elevators. She already felt the eyes of the men behind her and the concierges, perhaps wondering, speculating.

To distract herself, Cora pulled out her cellphone and set it to vibrate mode and scrolled through her contact list until the elevator arrived. Luckily it was empty, and she checked her makeup in the mirrored walls and smiled. No lipstick on her teeth. She also double-checked her phone to make certain it was silent. She wished all her clients were as considerate. Sometimes they ignored their phones, sometimes they didn't, but it was her problem if they had a hard time becoming erect again.

On the thirtieth floor, Cora knocked on the door of Ling's suite. She waited, smoothing over her dress, and tried to relax.

After a second knock, the door jerked open and Ling murmured an apology and waved her inside. He was a thick man in his mid-sixties with dyed black hair, whose youthful affliction with acne had left parts of his cheeks bumpier than granola, and wore a blue-black suit perfect for a business meeting.

"I think I make mistake with time," Ling said, looking both excited and relieved.

"No, it's me. I got delayed. There's construction everywhere."

Ling laughed. "You see Beijing. More cranes than people."

Cora kissed him on the cheek and took his right hand and led him into the central room of the suite. The carpet and walls were the color of cream, and the curtains were dark beige with burgundy stripes. Ling pointed to a plush burgundy sofa, next to which stood a cart with a silver bucket holding a bottle of champagne and a silver platter with a variety of crackers, cheeses, pâtés, and caviar. On the dark chocolate coffee table sat two smaller platters: the first had a circle of pinkie-sized shrimp and baby carrots around a cluster of small Chinese oranges; the second was filled with an assortment of colorful Asian sweets Cora disliked, especially the bean curd coated in sugar.

"You hungry? I not know what you like."

"Yes, a little bit. Thank you." She gave Ling's arm a squeeze. "It's very sweet of you to think of me."

Ling smiled and poured two glasses of champagne and plunked beside her on the sofa. She nibbled a carrot and sipped her champagne and asked him where he had come from, he was always flying somewhere. He said he had gone to Montreal for meetings, after a fishing trip in northern Ontario with some American businessmen, where he thought the bugs would eat him alive. Tomorrow he would fly back to Vancouver for more meetings with his business partners from China.

"You must visit," he said. "I do everything. Hotel. Car. You want nothing. Everything done."

"I wish I could," Cora said. "It would be wonderful."

"Nothing better. You come. See."

She stroked Ling's face and smiled at him. The last time she had tried to go away for a few days, Nathan had moved into his bedroom closet and built a cocoon with blankets he must have found on the streets, judging by their stains and stench. Even worse, he had poured cola around the door of the apartment before laying down his gauntlet of utensils, and she had to hire a cleaner to bring in a machine and do his best to remove the stains. The superintendent kept calling too, with a list of complaints from the neighbors, and freaked when he finally saw the discoloration in the carpet.

Ling squeezed Cora's leg and tugged her closer. She leaned against him and whispered, "You're such a bad boy."

He tried to pull up her skirt, but it was too long and slippery, and she shifted his hand up to her breasts. He squeezed hard, hard enough to hurt, and she murmured in his ear. Ling replied in Chinese and rubbed against her, his penis poking through his pants like a butcher's thumb.

Worried he might damage her dress, she put down her glass and slipped away from him. He tried to pull her in again, but she stepped around the side of the sofa and told him to wait. He could watch while she took off her dress. She had wanted to take her time, give herself more time to relax, but he already looked anxious enough to burst.

To keep his hands busy, she told him to take off his jacket, and he threw it on the sofa and fumbled with the buttons of his shirt. He also knocked a pair of Chinese pastries off the coffee table, onto the carpet, but he didn't notice and stepped on them.

Cora slipped her earrings into her stilettos, wiggled out of her dress, and draped it over a burgundy wingback chair before circling back to him.

"Ride them cowboys," he said and slapped her buttocks.

She pushed him playfully and fingered his belt. "Maybe you should take this off first? It might be in the way."

Ling nodded and scrabbled at his belt. From her handbag, she pulled out a green purse and took out a condom and a small bottle of lubricant and a packet of wipes. Then the room wobbled sideways for a moment, and she stumbled against the sofa. Gold light flickered across the floor. Something far away screamed.

She twisted sideways, her gaze darting around the room. Ling groaned and threw the belt aside and struggled with his pants. Cora glanced at the opening to the bedroom. Maybe he had the other TV on? A movie?

Ling stumbled, his pants caught around his knees, and she reached out to steady him.

"Be careful," she said.

Ling pulled her closer, squeezing her buttocks, and pressed his face into her breasts. She stroked his dyed hair and realized she had dropped the condom and lubricant on the floor.

"Maybe you should take your shoes off first," she said. "Then we can get the rest of these things off."

"Yes," Ling said, blushing. "Shoes."

She steadied him while he sat down on the sofa. He fumbled with his laces, and she kneeled, picked up the condom, and flapped it like a flag.

"Would you like a present?" she said.

"I give extra."

"I know, but then we have to stop."

"You hard girl."

"Not as hard as you," she said and tugged on the band of his white boxers. He reached for her head, but she leaned away from him. "Oh, you're naughty."

"No!" he said. "Give more. Give extra."

"Say, 'Yes.' I'll give you a present."

"Oh . . ."

"Yes," she repeated and opened the condom. "All you have to do is say, 'Yes,' otherwise we have to stop. I don't want to, but—"

"Yes! No stop!"

"Good. I'm glad." She pointed to his pants, and he wiggled his feet out and pushed his shoes away. "Now we can have fun. Lots and lots of fun.

Chapter 7

Alex's head snarled like a broken muffler. Darkness surrounded him. A minute or two passed before he realized something was pressing against his left shin, burning the skin. He tried to shift the leg, but it was numb all the way up to his hip. The rest of his body was groggy too, but he managed to wriggle his arms to one side and pushed himself into a sitting position.

Pain lanced through his lower back and left leg. He swore and squinted into the darkness. What the hell was going on? He remembered that idiot Fernandez; the boy; dropping the flashlight. Father was there too, his mind whirling like the blades of a helicopter, waiting to lop off heads and serve them for breakfast.

The pressure against Alex's left leg increased, and the burning intensified. He tugged on his left thigh. Something resembling a melon bounced against his shin.

He froze. How could she have gotten out of her cage? She was supposed to be tied up.

With both hands, he yanked on his left leg, daggers of pain shooting up his back. Her head clunked on the floor. Sensation rushed up his leg like steam from a kettle, and he clenched his teeth to stop from yelling.

She let out a sharp, sucking noise. Alex rolled onto his knees and lurched to his feet.

She sucked in another breath and gurgled. Alex stumbled and grabbed at a railing. She jerked an arm towards him, desperate to pull him back in. A pig-like gasp escaped her throat. Her body convulsed. He slapped his legs and told them to move. The woman gurgled again, like she was choking on vomit, and her arms and legs thudded on the floor. She was trying to crawl.

Alex stumbled up a pair of steps and yanked on the door for the loading bay. The light from overhead jabbed his eyes. He tripped and fell.

A meaty hand clapped him on the back of the head. "Hey, dip-shit."

Alex rolled onto his side, grabbed the arm above him, and heaved. Cloth ripped. A man yelled and hit a stack of black wooden chairs.

The man sprang back to his feet and kicked the chairs, smashing several legs. The chairs fell over.

"What the fucking are you doing?" he yelled. "You ripped my suit. It's fucking ruined."

Alex squeezed his head between his hands and grimaced. Next to the chairs, a stocky man with pasty skin and a bald head, shook off the charcoal gray jacket of his Armani suit and jammed his fist through the gaping hole in the left shoulder.

"Hey! I'm talking to you," Leroy said. "See? This comes out of your comp."

"You're lucky I didn't rip your head off," Alex said.

"Yeah, fuck you. You're such a goddamn pussy."

Alex sank down on one of the boxes in the middle of the room and coughed up a wad of phlegm.

"You look like shit," Leroy said.

"Yeah, you're beautiful too."

"You must have had a good time with the old man." Leroy pointed to Father's room. "How long you been in there?"

"I don't know. What time is it?"

Leroy shrugged.

Alex scowled. "How long have you been here?"

"Don't know. You busted my watch."

"Go fuck yourself."

"Maybe later," Leroy said. "Right now I'm gonna piss on your grave."

"You're such a fucking clown," Alex said.

Leroy's face clenched up like an angry dog, as if clown was the biggest insult in the world.

"We'll see who's the clown after Mobius hears about you fucking around in here."

"Yeah, run to mommy," Alex said.

Leroy growled and pulled on his torn jacket. "Don't be pulling this shit now. It's getting too close. I can feel it. It's like fucking Christmas."

A gob of phlegm caught in Alex's throat, and he hacked until he managed to spit the damn thing out.

"I have to go," he said, "get out of here."

"Keep dreaming," Leroy said. "There ain't no out."

"I don't mean that. The prisoners are dead, the ones I just put in there. You have to get new ones."

Leroy swore. "Don't pass your shit on me."

"Just get it done," Alex said. A sharp pain cut into his left side. He spat more phlegm and cupped his head between his hands. "I'm not going back in. Not yet."

Leroy glared at Alex, looking angry enough to put a fist through his face.

"If you want to call Teresa, go ahead." Alex eased to his feet. "Just be quick about it. Don't give him time to poke around. He tried to change one of the girls. But she was dead already."

Leroy swore and pulled out his cellphone. Instead of calling Teresa, though, he called the warehouse in Mississauga and ordered another load of prisoners. No, he didn't care where they came from. Just bring them. Now!

Alex threw his gloves on the floor and limped to the exit, keeping one hand against the wall.

"You owe me," Leroy said.

"I'll buy you a doormat."

"Just get the fuck out of here. You're only making it worse."

Alex slipped out of his overcoat and dropped it beside the exit. "You can keep that. Consider it a down payment."

Leroy scowled and stepped toward Alex.

"Yeah, see. You think you're funny too," Alex said and opened the door to the alley. He flinched. It felt like sun wanted to cut out his eyes.

Compared to Father, though, that didn't seem so bad, and Alex stumbled outside and yanked the door shut behind him.

A few minutes later, sitting in his car, he cracked open one of his last beers and rested his head on the steering wheel. He resisted the urge to fall asleep. First he needed to get some distance, at least a few blocks, so Father would shift his attention to someone closer. He loved to twist and grope, turning brains into chicken soup.

Alex rubbed his face and started the car. Beer spilled between his feet. He swore and guzzled the rest of the bottle before putting the car in reverse. The alley seemed to stretch on and on, the shadows thick and crawling with the faces of the dead. His ears roared. Guns blasted from every direction. Shells exploded. But none of them were real. None of them! The war was a long time ago. All those boys were dead—Lewis, Jones, Wilson, a thousand others, all of them screaming, full of hatred and pain and misery.

Alex jerked on the steering wheel, avoiding the face of his mother, and the car scraped the corner of the building as he spurted out of the alley.

On the street, a silver minivan honked and swerved. He yanked the steering wheel the other way and jammed on the brakes. The minivan sped away, still blaring its horn. He sucked in a couple of breaths and eased the car alongside a No Parking sign. The screams continued to come in waves, slapping at his brain.

From the old paint factory stepped a pair of guards wearing black flak jackets. Both were armed with pistols. Alex swore and slapped his head. At least a dozen eyes were watching him, reporting everything to Mobius, that goddamn cockroach.

One of the guards tapped on the passenger window. Alex stepped on the gas, his legs trembling, and jolted to the corner. The guards yelled after him. Alex was tempted to yell back, but what was the point? If they wanted to go to hell, they only had to cross the street.

Chapter 8

To Cora's dismay, Ling surprised her with more erections than seemed humanly possible for a sixty-seven-year-old man. It felt like fighting a Hydra. He seemed just as surprised and barely gave her time to wash before calling out to her, demanding her attention. Normally he just fell asleep. Then, before she left, she would wake him up with a blow job, and he would look at her like she was a miracle worker.

Today, though, Cora carried the champagne into the bedroom, hoping the alcohol turned off his penis. She had had trouble with erectile medication before, but nothing this extreme. She wanted to tell him enough, but he had paid the extra, and his excitement teetered on the edge of mania. Playing along seemed safer.

Finally, around quarter after ten, he collapsed on top of her, gasping for breath, and she nudged him in the ribs to shift his weight to one side and slid out from under him, careful to keep the condom from slipping off his shriveling penis. She yanked tissues from the box she had put on the nightstand and used them to toss the condom in the wastebasket beside the bed. Ling groaned and murmured in Chinese. She hoped he wasn't having a heart attack.

After his breathing calmed down, she ducked into the master bathroom with her handbag, scrubbed her hands, and hopped in the shower, goo leaking down her right thigh. A few minutes later, while drying herself off, Cora peeked into the bedroom. Ling still lay on the bed, flopped out like a rag doll. God, what if he really did have a heart attack? It had almost happened last month with a fat lawyer from Ottawa. He ended up taking one of his heart pills and seemed fine after and kept apologizing for scaring her.

Ling snorted and wriggled onto his right side. Cora ducked back into the bathroom and scrubbed her hands again. While sitting on the edge of the tub, she used a clean towel to wipe off her handbag and her cellphone. She had two messages: a text from Melissa, a voicemail from Straw.

Melissa's message said, *Fast as fast can be.*

Cora sent back, *I wish.*

Straw said he was at the parking garage next door. When she was ready, he would meet her in the underpass of the hotel, by the revolving door at the back.

On the bed, Ling began to snore. Cora slipped out of the bathroom and used a tissue to pick up a stray condom wrapper and an unused wipe and added them to the garbage. In the sitting room, she found another condom wrapper in the tray of carrots and shrimp on the coffee table. She picked up the wrapper and used two tissues to dab at a blob of lubricant on the carpet.

After one more circle of the sofa, Cora tied shut the garbage bag from the bedroom and scrunched the bag in the garbage container in the sitting room. She walked back to the bathroom, washed her hands, and sent Straw a text message.

Leaving 5.

In the sitting room, Cora clipped on her bra and slipped into her panties and dress. A snort came from the bedroom. She leaned against the armchair, waiting for Ling to quiet down. Normally she would have woken him up to say goodbye, but she didn't want to take any chances. Enough was enough.

A minute or two ticked by. She picked out the earrings from her stilettos and slid them into a pocket of her handbag. Ling snorted again and returned to snoring.

Cora sighed, carried the stilettos to the door, and brushed a hand over her hair. At least the night was over. Now all she had to do was go home.

~

On the elevator, Cora studied her reflection in the mirrored walls and smoothed back her hair. Her face looked flushed, like she had consumed too much champagne, even though she had only taken a few sips to coax Ling into finishing his glasses. She also had a red spot on her collarbone, where he had gotten too excited and used his teeth.

She shifted the straps of her dress, trying to obscure the bite, but only ended up looking lopsided. She had some face powder in her handbag, but by the time she fished out the compact, the elevator slowed and binged for the ground floor.

Her stomach growled and tightened. She dropped the compact back in her pink purse, zipped up her handbag, and wished she had avoided eating the carrots. They had been mixed with shrimp, and seafood sometimes bothered her. She wasn't allergic exactly, but she had suffered cramps too many times to ignore the connection.

The doors of the elevator slid open. Her stomach clenched even harder, and she stepped into the lobby. In front of her stood a tall man with thin blond hair, wearing a gray blazer, who stared at her with bulging eyes.

"Sorry," she said and tried to step around him, brushing against his right arm. He yelped and jumped back, dropping his Blackberry. Her stomach kicked. She stumbled and clutched her belly.

The man swore and hunched over to retrieve his Blackberry. She hurried to the revolving doors in front of her, her stomach still churning. God, no!

Once outside, in the underpass that served as the main entrance for the hotel, she glanced at the black limousine and the dark green sedan parked there, but neither of them belonged to Straw. On her left, the doorman and bellboy turned to stare at her.

She darted between the cars and passed windows displaying wooden cabinets and brass lamps and vanities that gleamed like treasure and then the entrance for parking underneath the hotel. A man wearing a black suit called after her, but she stumbled out of the underpass and turned left. Above her hung bright red canopies. Her throat burned. She ducked her head behind the green fronds sprouting from a large concrete pot filled with mixed flowers, next to a window displaying exchange rates, the diodes for the numbers glowing like hundreds of little red eyes. Her stomach continued to clench and roll. People strolling on the sidewalk gawked at her, but she didn't dare move.

One woman in her thirties, wearing a light blue dress, stepped closer, like she wanted to help, but a tanned blonde wearing a black cocktail dress pulled her friend along. Cora closed her eyes and straightened up a little, keeping her left hand pressed to her stomach. She needed to calm down. Breathe. Everything was okay. She had only eaten a two or three carrots. She would be fine.

After several minutes, the churning of her stomach slowed, turning into a medley of gurgles and rumbles. People continued to walk by and gawk at her. She stepped to the next concrete planter, paused for half a minute, and then moved slowly to a cobbled walkway between a shop selling luggage and a shop selling bedding.

In the walkway, she paused again to steady herself and glanced at a bright pink suitcase in the neighboring window. The reflection in the glass showed an Asian woman wearing a purple blouse behind Cora, and she turned, startled.

No one was there. There was only a window showing off a cream-colored quilt decorated with wildflowers.

Her cellphone chimed, and she jumped. Her stomach rumbled. She hunched over, trying to ease the discomfort, and fumbled with the pockets of her handbag. God, what was wrong with her?

The text message from Straw said, *Waiting rear door.*

She wiggled the phone back into her handbag and crept past the window displaying the pink luggage. All she had to do was find the car. Then she could go home. Lie down. Take a long shower.

The walkway opened into a courtyard where people sat on the patio of a brasserie, jazz music drifting from inside. She shifted her handbag to her right shoulder, keeping the bag between her and them, and strode to the walkway on the other side of the courtyard. Once there, she rested between a pair of display cases, her stomach grumbling, until a couple in their late forties walked past, the man staring, the woman shaking her head.

Cora walked past the rest of the display cases, most of them advertising shops in the neighborhood, and stopped beside a large planter with flowers and small palm leaves. Nearby she saw a pair of black cars parked on the Yorkville Avenue, but they didn't look right. One was definitely the wrong shape.

On her left, past a Starbucks with several people sitting out front, she spotted trunk of another black sedan parked in the north entrance for the underpass of the hotel.

She took a deep breath and hurried to the sedan and grabbed the handle of the back door. It was locked.

Cora rapped on the driver's window. Straw, holding a cup of

coffee, frowned at her.

She rapped on the window again. The back door clicked. She grabbed at the handle and ducked into the sedan.

"What the hell is going on?" Straw asked.

"Nothing. Can we go?"

"Yeah, try again."

"Please? I just want to go home."

Straw shoved his coffee on the dashboard and shook his head.

"It's nothing," Cora said. "I just ate something bad. Some seafood."

"Hey, don't be puking in my car."

"I won't. It's just a stomachache."

"Yeah, whatever. I'm not a fucking retard."

"I'll be fine. I promise."

Straw scowled and took a swig of his coffee. "I don't care. You're still fucking cleaning it up."

"Fine, whatever. I just need to go home."

~

About fifteen minutes later, Straw stopped in front of Cora's condominium and turned up his rock music. She shimmied out of the car, careful of her dress and her sore thighs.

On the sidewalk, in the breeze from the lake, she felt a lot better. Her stomach had calmed down. She didn't even have a headache—a rare reprieve.

She walked between the potted cedars and the concrete basins planted with purple and red flowers in front of her building and rushed through the first glass door. Madison, the concierge, buzzed her through the second door. He was a squat man in his late fifties with a long drooping mustache that reminded her of Colonel Mustard from the board game Clue.

"Thanks," she said and hurried past him.

"Oh, Ms. Walters? There's a package for you."

Cora paused. Even though she just wanted to go upstairs, Katrina had said something about a gift for tomorrow night.

Madison grinned and stepped into the small room behind his desk. Cora sighed and rested her handbag on the black granite counter while he squinted at the shelves.

"Here we go," he said and pulled out a white box with a pair of red stripes and black Japanese calligraphy across the top. "A right pretty box."

She nodded and brushed hair from her eyes.

"Everything okay, Ms. Walters?"

"Yes, thank you," she said and glanced at the names on the delivery stickers on the side of the box. A big loopy K followed by a lot of scribbles. "Is there anything else?"

"No, just this." Madison passed Cora the clipboard with the log of deliveries, and she signed it. "Can I get the elevator for you?"

"No, I'm fine," Cora said. "It's not that big. But thank you."

"Sure. Always glad to help."

~

In her apartment, Cora slid the package and her handbag on the kitchen counter. She needed to sit down. Her stomach felt squirrelly again, and her skin itched, especially on her thighs. Most of all, she needed to pee and flicked on the shower light for the bathroom.

A few minutes later, while washing her hands, she heard the chime of her cellphone from the kitchen. Katrina. She always wanted to know everything and wasn't very patient.

Cora draped her dress and bra on the laundry basket. After another thorough wash of her hands, she pulled on a white bathrobe and headed to the kitchen to check her cellphone.

Yes, Katrina had called.

Cora picked out a bottle of water from the fridge, took a sip, and called back.

"How are you feeling?" Katrina asked. "Straw said you didn't look so good."

"No, I'm okay," Cora said. "I just ate something bad."

"Like what?"

"The shrimp, I think. Sometimes it makes me queasy."

"Ling didn't try anything?"

"No, not really."

"What does that mean?"

"Nothing," Cora said. "He just had a lot of Viagra."

"Oh, one of those. I always—" Katrina paused. "Hold on a

sec."

A dull hissing noise replaced her voice, and Cora sat down on a breakfast stool and sipped her water. It made her stomach grumble, though, and she pushed the bottle on the counter. Maybe she should try a cup of tea instead.

Katrina returned to say, "I'll call you back," and hung up.

Ten minutes later, during the middle of Cora's shower, her cellphone chimed again. She waited, hoping it was only her imagination. The phone continued to chime and switched to her voicemail. Less than a minute later, her phone chimed again.

Cora turned off the water and fished the phone out of her bathrobe.

"Sorry," Katrina said. "Everything's beeping at me."

"That's okay. I know you're busy."

"I wanted to make sure you're all right. I know Ling tries to go the old-fashioned way, as if a bit of latex is going to kill him."

"No, that was fine," Cora said. "I can handle that. He just wouldn't turn off."

"You're too nice. Don't let him get away with anything." Katrina paused to shoo one of her cats off of her computer. "You're in charge. Don't ever forget that."

"He was fine last time," Cora said and shivered. "More like normal."

"Maybe he's eating rhino balls," Katrina said. "My grandmother used to make a killing on that stuff, back in Shanghai. Tiger livers, elephant tusks . . ."

"I can do without them."

"So you're all right?"

"Just tired."

"Okay, get some sleep, then. I'll call you back tomorrow," Katrina said. "Which reminds me. Did you get the package from Paul?"

"I haven't looked at it yet."

"You'll like it. He has great taste." Katrina sounded amused. "It's probably even the right size."

Cora murmured in agreement.

"But let me know, just in case," Katrina said. "Try it on in the morning."

"I will."

"Good. I have to go. Sweet dreams."

Chapter 9

Alex rubbed his face and muttered a curse. He wished he had remembered to close the blinds. He might have actually managed to sleep a few more hours. Now the morning sun cut into him while the TV rambled on about a garbage strike.

He grimaced and dug between the cushions for the remote. Where the hell was it? He fumbled behind his head, and the lamp sitting on the end table wobbled and crashed on the floor.

Alex swore and pushed himself upright. Empty beer bottles covered the coffee table beside him, and the remote lay on the floor beside the couch. He scooped up the remote and turned off the TV. The cable box said 6:57, three hours until the beer stores opened. Another good reason to sleep in.

From his bedroom, which overlooked the alley behind the apartment building, came the rumble of a garbage truck. He limped into the kitchen and pulled a Heineken from the fridge. His pants hung on a chair, his jacket on another. Dozens of empty beer bottles covered the cheap wooden table and the Arborite counter. He guzzled the Heineken, banged his left leg against a cupboard door, and grabbed another Heineken from the fridge.

Back in the living room, lying on the floor, his cellphone rang. He wondered how many calls he had missed. Mobius was probably frothing at the mouth, trying to convince Teresa to punish the unworthy—namely Alex. Those security clowns couldn't keep their mouths shut about anything.

He took a swig from his second beer and picked up the phone. The caller was Sebastian, the youngest of the reborn. Teresa was the oldest, Alex the third, Leroy the fifth—nine in total. None by choice.

Alex answered the phone. "Yeah, you want beer, we got beer."

"Where have you been?" Sebastian said. "I've been trying to call all night."

"Yeah? Why?"

"I don't know what to do. I screwed up so bad."

"Welcome to immortality. Ain't it grand."

"She was right in front of me. But I didn't know what to do, I didn't think. I just let her get away. She's going to kill me."

"What the hell are you talking about? Where are you?"

"Wait, can you come here? Maybe you can find her. You would know better."

"Where the hell you are?" Alex said.

"In Yorkville," Sebastian said. "In a coffee shop. They just opened. I kept walking around, hoping I'd see her again. The whole night."

"All right, I'll be there in half an hour," he said. "I just have to pull on some pants."

~

In the east end of Toronto, on the bluffs overlooking Lake Ontario, stood the smallest of Teresa's mansions. Compared to her estates in Madrid and Rome and Prague, the building was a pumpkin but sufficient for the short time she needed it. Sometimes she wondered if living downtown would have been wiser, close to where her men patrolled for the Light, but she had to keep her mind clear of Father. She had to be ready. Her men might be stupid, but the Light couldn't hide forever.

Teresa picked up her red wine from the whitewashed table filling the breakfast room and opened one of the French doors to the back terrace. The scent of roses drifted inside, along with the faint slosh of water from the base of the bluff. She only needed the men long enough to capture the Light and discover his secrets. Beyond that, she didn't care. She would only get one chance to destroy Father.

From the hallway came the paddle of slippers and the swish of robes. A timid knock followed. Then a soft cough.

"Come in, *pater*," Teresa said. "You must be hungry."

The Monsignor stepped into the breakfast room and bobbed his head.

"I hope the dogs didn't disturb you last night," Teresa said, switching to Spanish. "They must have found some rabbits in the trees."

"No, I didn't hear anything," the Monsignor said. "I've always been that way, never hear anything. Like a stone."

"That happens a lot, I've noticed. All cut from the same cloth."

The Monsignor smiled weakly and sat at the table. He was a bland-looking man with eggshell skin, wispy hair, and a bulbous nose and wore a purple *pechera* around his neck and a robe made of black velvet. Before him, the table was set for twelve and had three candles at the center, between which sat a pair of crystal bowls overflowing with fruit and a small clock adorned with gold leaf. On the wall connecting to the dining room hung an ornate mirror similarly gilded. Opposite the mirror hung two large paintings of people shopping for paintings, mirrors, vanities, and other decorative items, one of which had belonged to Louis XV. The second was a forgery by a Frenchman, circa 1950, which the Louvre had bought for twelve million dollars.

After crossing himself, the Monsignor clasped his hands together and closed his eyes to offer a prayer. Teresa grimaced and sipped her wine. She hated when he hid behind his false piety. He was actually thinking about what he would shovel into his mouth, like all the other priests. Their faith was only a veneer for their short and shallow lives.

The Monsignor finished his prayer and fidgeted in his chair. "When would you like Mass to begin?"

"You already know," Teresa said.

"Yes, excuse me," the Monsignor said, keeping his gaze on the table. "I only want to be certain."

"There are better things to worry about," Teresa said.

"Yes, many things."

Teresa frowned and rang a small, silver bell sitting on the table. A tiny, lopsided woman wearing a black cotton dress scurried in from the kitchen. Teresa told the servant to bring the Monsignor's breakfast. She bowed and brought in a series of trays: dark bitter coffee, milk, and orange juice; sausages, bacon, and slices of ham; crepes with maple syrup, scoops of French vanilla ice cream on the side, fruit danishes, cinnamon buns, and bowls filled with sliced bananas, strawberries, and blueberries.

The Monsignor eyed the dishes, distress twitching his face.

"The servants told me you prefer a continental breakfast," Teresa said. "But this suits your temperament better."

"You are too generous."

"Yes," Teresa said and glanced at the terrace. She sensed Mobius approaching from the west, coming up the stairway from the rose garden. A few seconds later, he stepped around the statue of a marble lion missing its right ear and bowed to her.

She waved a hand, and he stepped inside.

"Forgive me, mistress, for interrupting your time with the cloth," Mobius said.

"Yes?"

"Sebastian and Alex are meeting," he said.

"And?"

"It's about Him."

Teresa flicked a hand to dismiss the Monsignor.

"Yes," he said, looking relieved. "Thank you for the invitation to breakfast. It was generous." He bowed his head, hurried to his feet, and fled into the central hall.

Mobius eyed the backside of the priest with disdain.

"What do you want?" she said. "Have you secured more prisoners?"

"We monitored a call between Alex and Sebastian. They're hiding something important from you."

"Obviously."

"Alex was with Father for several hours yesterday, but he said nothing about it. He explains nothing."

"I'm not interested in petty accusations."

"I have the conversation for you, mistress." Mobius pulled an MP3 player from his jacket. "Their deceit is clear."

Though annoyed, Teresa listened to the recording of Alex and Sebastian. She frowned. Sebastian had done something stupid, that much was obvious. But that could mean anything from spilling coffee on someone's dress to killing a woman on the street. He was the most incompetent reborn she had ever suffered, with sobbing fits and manic episodes well into his second year. That was why she had tried to kill him—multiple times. But Father kept bringing

Sebastian back to life, just to spite her.

Mobius bowed his head. "Mistress, they are meeting right now to discuss their plans."

Teresa hissed, and her wine glass cracked, slopping red liquid on the white tablecloth. "I already know that, idiot."

"We can't trust them."

"I don't trust any of you."

"Yes, mistress. Very wise."

Teresa glared at him. He bowed his head again.

"I'll deal with Alex myself," she said. "So don't come back until you have something useful to tell me. You've already ruined breakfast."

"My humblest apologies," Mobius said. "I live only to serve."

"Then find the Light," she shouted. "And stop wasting my time with your childish stupidity."

~

Alex walked into the Starbucks at the base of a high-rise overlooking the concrete sidewalks of Bay Street and spotted Sebastian sitting near the washrooms. He was tall and lanky and had thinning blond hair he combed to cover the bald spot on his crown. He wore black slacks and a dark gray blazer, contrasting sharply with his pale skin.

"Thank God," Sebastian said, his gaze jerking up from the coffee clutched between his hands. "I wasn't sure, you took so long. I thought you'd changed your mind—"

"Christ, would you relax." Alex sat down across from Sebastian. "And stop blathering like a damn woman."

"I didn't mean to screw up. I really tried."

"That means start at the beginning. I can't help if I don't know what the hell's going on."

"Sorry, I know, it just happened so fast. I wasn't sure. It didn't start very strong."

Alex straightened up. "You felt a presence?"

"I didn't know where it was coming from, so I wanted to be sure. I didn't want to make a mistake."

"Teresa doesn't like mistakes."

"That's why I waited. I just waited." Sebastian wrung a hand through his hair and looked ready to cry. "Then I felt this awful burning in my throat, and it got hard to swallow. I couldn't breathe, like she was strangling me."

"She?"

"Yeah, she ran into me, off the elevator. Right in front of me. And I didn't do anything. I just stood there."

"Are you saying what I think?" Alex asked. "You're sure?"

"I know it was her. It hurt so bad."

"Teresa always talked about a he."

"That's what I was thinking the whole night. What if I was wrong? If it was someone else, and I missed him?" Sebastian shook his head. "But I know it wasn't. She was right there, right in front of me."

"Where was this? Another hotel?"

"Yeah, the one at the end of Cumberland. The Four Seasons. Just after ten-thirty. I looked at my watch." Sebastian winced and rubbed a hand over his thin hair. "That's the only smart thing I did."

"Too late to worry about that." Alex leaned back and scratched his chin. "As long as we move on it before Mobius finds out."

"What do you mean?"

Alex shrugged and pulled out his cellphone.

"Wait!" Sebastian said. "What are you doing?"

"Good question." Alex scrolled through his list of contacts and paused when he reached the number for Sydney, the head of Teresa's security force.

"That might work," Alex said. "You got a good look at this girl? You'd remember her?"

"That's when it happened," Sebastian said, "as soon as I saw her. It was like getting punched."

Alex pressed call, and Sydney answered on the first ring. "What can I do for you, sir?"

"When are you getting the surveillance tapes for the hotel from Thursday night?" Alex asked. "The ones from the Royal York."

"The copies should arrive in the next couple of hours."

"Consider it a priority. I need to see them."

"Sorry, sir?"

"You damn well heard me."

"I'd have to clear it with Mobius. No disrespect, sir."

"I don't care what you do," Alex said. "But I told Teresa we've got pictures to show her, so you'd better have something for her. By tonight."

There was a long pause. "Yes, sir. I'll send someone over, as soon as we get them."

"You also need to get the surveillance tapes for the Four Seasons, the one in Yorkville, at the end of Cumberland. For last night."

"Uh, yes, sir."

Alex hung up and eyed Sebastian, who stared back, his face stuck somewhere between perplexed and terrified.

"You should get some sleep," Alex said. "I'll call you when they bring the surveillance—if those jackasses don't fuck it up."

Sebastian nodded, but his hands crumpled the top of his coffee cup. Fortunately it was mostly empty.

"You could just call the mistress," he said. "Tell her everything. It'd be a lot easier."

"Yeah. But I've never been very good at doing it the easy way. Too stupid."

Sebastian shook his head. "I never thought it would be this bad."

"Don't start with that. You can't go back your wife. You doesn't exist anymore." Alex grabbed one of Sebastian's hands and squeezed hard. "You belong to Teresa now. She's your redemption. You need to keep saying that until she believes you."

"I know. I jus—I—"

"What? You want to keep punishing yourself? Drive yourself crazy?"

Sebastian licked his lips and buried his face in his hands.

Shit, Alex thought. He turned to look at the sign listing all the drinks. Why couldn't they at least have one kind of beer? Something with alcohol? Anything?

"Be right back," he said.

Sebastian snuffled and looked up. "What?"

"Nothing. I just need a drink."

Alex ordered a coffee, black, and tossed a twenty on the counter. The Chinese girl serving him gave him a big smile so genuine it made him turn away. He didn't want to think about the prisoners anymore. With the bags over their heads, he didn't have to see their faces. He didn't have to know how old they were or where they came from.

He gulped half the coffee and walked back to the table. The two men sat without speaking for several minutes.

Once Sebastian finally finished crying, he lowered his hands and wiped them on his slacks.

"Has anyone ever gotten away?" he asked.

Alex grimaced. "That's a dangerous question."

"I mean from Father."

"It doesn't matter. You can't separate the two."

"I know, but—"

"Christ, would you listen? I mean, really listen."

"I'm sorry, I can't help it."

"Too bad. You have to anyway," Alex said. "None of those crazy plans you've got running through your head are going to work—just disappearing one night and never coming back." Sebastian looked startled. "Father has something inside you, and you can't get it out. It's always there, always waiting. You think you can run, but . . ." Alex guzzled the rest of his coffee and crushed the cup. "It starts itching at first, like you've got lice in your belly. You get real thirsty too, except nothing you drink makes it go away."

Sebastian shook his head.

"There's buzzing in your ears too," Alex said. "And dizziness. Gets worse the longer you're away. Your dreams start coming alive, the shadows coming out of everywhere."

"They're bad enough already."

"That's the point. You start seeing them all the time, even when you're awake. You start living with them, until you're ready to beat your head on the wall, just to make it stop." Alex tapped his skull. "That's what happened to Leroy. Teresa sent him to Hong Kong, and the snakeheads there found him unconscious, next to a big hole in the wall. Peter tried to jump off a building, around the same time, but Father wouldn't let him go. You should have heard him screaming. Took him days for his bones to pull back together. The worst fucking torture you can imagine."

Sebastian shuddered.

"Yeah, you've probably thought about jumping too," Alex said. "But Father can hold onto you, leave you dying over and over until he gets tired of you. You just have to—"

Behind Alex, the door jangled. He glanced over his shoulder, and a skinny blonde woman wearing black tights and a pink tank top walked up to the counter. Something in the air felt different too, a prickliness he should have noticed already if he hadn't been so busy flapping his jaw.

"What's wrong?" Sebastian asked.

"Nothing," Alex said and stood up.

On Bay Street, an Asian woman wearing a purple blouse peered through one of the windows of the store but darted left, out of view, as soon as he turned towards her. He swore, grabbed Sebastian by the elbow, and steered him to the door. Mobius would never use a woman to follow them, but the clowns running the security force were probably more open-minded.

Once outside, Alex scanned the lengths of Bay Street and Cumberland Street. He didn't see the Asian in the purple blouse anywhere, which was a nice trick considering the regular stores were still closed and not many people were out yet.

Sebastian looked around and fidgeted with his blazer. "What's going on? Did you—"

Alex's cellphone rang, making them both jump. He pulled it out of his jacket and swore. He hadn't expected Teresa to call that quickly.

"Yes, mistress?" he said, answering the phone.

Though already pale, Sebastian's face turned even whiter.

"Where you are?" Teresa asked.

"Yorkville," Alex said. "On Bay Street."

"I know that. The question is why."

"I had to talk with Sebastian before coming to see you."

"Why?" she asked.

"That's what I want to talk to you about," Alex said, "as soon as

it's convenient for you. I know you'll want to hear this in person."
He waited a few seconds, but she remained silent. "I already told
Sydney to get the surveillance tapes ready, but I'm sure you'll want
to know all the details. I can come right now."

A long pause followed. Sebastian kept glancing around the
streets, ready to bolt, and Alex closed his eyes to stay focused. It
was like lining up the sights on a rifle. He just had to take a deep
breath, relax the eyes, and let the target come to him.

Finally, Teresa said, "You have twenty minutes."

Then the phone clicked and went silent, and Alex shoved it in
his jacket. Sebastian opened his mouth to say something, but no
words came out.

"It'll be fine," Alex said. "I'll take care of it."

~

With an audible crack, Teresa struck Alex across the head, and
he tumbled on the marble floor of her solarium. Pain scissored his
brain. An animal screamed. Darkness rolled in. The world shattered.

After what might have been an eternity, jagged pieces of sunlight broke over him, and the pain roared to life once more. Alex
groaned and tried to fall back into the darkness, the silence, the
emptiness, until the bob and weave of violins and violas and cellos
and the thunder of kettle drums yanked him back to the sunroom.
He sucked in a breath. Agony surged through his temple.

"You look like a worm," Teresa said. "A big, dead worm."

He sucked in another breath. Flashes of lightning cut across his
brain. A moan trickled out of his mouth. Time escaped and returned.

Finally, the pain and lightning eased enough for Alex to take
another breath. The bottom half of his face was sticky. His eyelids
twitched.

"The Light is a he," Teresa said. "The firstborn always said so."

Scattered thoughts flicked through Alex's head. He. Mistress.
Light.

"You were smart not to bring Sebastian," Teresa said. "I would
have ripped his head off and smashed it into jelly."

Without thinking, Alex shifted his head toward her voice. Pain knifed through his skull. Far away, her voice continued, but the screams within his body gobbled up the words.

When he could breathe again, he licked his lips and tasted blood. It had hardened on his right cheek, becoming crud-like. He probably had a crack in his skull, over the left ear. She had hit him hard enough.

He saw Teresa's toes first, sticking out from beneath the hem of her midnight blue dress. She sat in a white wicker chair with red cushions, her left hand rubbing her crucifix, classical music drifting in from one of the neighboring rooms. Alex waited. There was nothing else he could do. He didn't trust his voice yet.

Ten or fifteen minutes passed, and the music built into a final crescendo and stopped abruptly.

"Oh, yes. You," Teresa said. "I interrupted, when you had something so incredibly important to tell me."

Alex licked his bloody lips. "I b—believe him. Sebastian."

Something burst near Alex's head. He jerked a little, and a wave of agony blotted out his vision. He barely noticed the hot wax spattered on his face.

"The firstborn never doubted," Teresa said. "He knew the Light would return, even if it took centuries." Behind Alex, another pair of candles burst and rained hot wax on him. "Time doesn't matter to them, the light and the dark. They're all the same."

"W—what if . . . d—didn't know?"

For a moment, the entire room seemed to quiver. Windows creaked. A leaf fell from one of the trees hanging over Alex.

"Why do you think that?" Teresa said, her voice soft and dangerous. "You're not even strong enough to get up, and you think to question the centuries."

"Must mean s—something. All this time. Waiting."

Teresa scowled and stepped through a gap in the plants to the west wall of the solarium. While she glared across the lawn to the trees that hid the neighboring mansion, Alex let his eyes drift shut. He wished he could sleep, fall back into the darkness. No dreams.

Instead he forced himself to open his eyes and wriggled his left hand across the floor to loosen some of the wax hardening on his face. He had to stay conscious, just a little longer. To finish this.

The music from the next room returned, another orchestral piece with a piano, and Alex shifted his gaze to Teresa.

"What about Sebastian?" she asked. "Why does he think it was this girl?"

Alex coughed and winced. "She touched him."

"What!"

"He was t—trying to serve. But she surprised him."

"You didn't say that the first time. You just said he saw her and felt a presence."

"Mistress. No offense. But you hit me. I couldn't finish."

She stepped towards him, knocking over a potted plant. Alex sucked in a breath and waited. What choice did he have? She was close enough to kick him, and black and purple splotches clouded his vision.

"Sometimes I wonder if you are incredibly stupid," she said, "or too clever for your own good."

He was tempted to say, "Both," but kept it to himself.

One of the panels along the west wall exploded, hurtling shards of glass across the lawn. Teresa turned away from him. A second glass panel exploded. A few seconds later, a third panel, this one along the south wall, burst outwards, and a dog howled in pain. One of the Rottweilers must have come too close to the house. Usually they were smarter than that.

The next explosion sounded deeper and denser, more like stone than glass, and the howling ended with an abrupt yip. Silence followed. Even the music from the next room had stopped.

Alex took a slow breath, fighting back a cough. Needles of pain skittered beneath the crack in his skull. Then a chunk of glass fell from one of the broken windows and shattered on the marble tile of the solarium.

"Is there anything else you forgot to tell me?" Teresa demanded.

"Called Sydney. Made a plan."

"Meaning what?"

"S—surveillance. He can look. Sebastian. Knows her face."

"Did you tell Mobius?"

"Sydney will. You know . . . how they work."

Teresa's scowl deepened. "When you get up, tell one of the men to drive you back downtown. You'll deal with Sebastian. One way or the other."

"Yes, mistress."

The slap of her feet left the marble tile of the solarium and disappeared on the Persian rugs of the hall. Alex waited until he was certain she was gone—a loosening in the air, a brightening of the sunlight—then closed his eyes and prayed for a long sleep.

Chapter 10

While Cora stood in front of the mirror in the master bathroom, tweaking her eyebrows, her cellphone chimed with a text message from Katrina.

Dress?

Cora sighed, traced a finger over her eyebrows, and put the tweezers back in the rattan storage tower. After washing her hands, she walked into the kitchen and used a bread knife to slit the stickers on Paul's package, some of which Katrina must have added to keep out the concierges.

Inside the box, Cora found a note on top of a champagne silk dress patterned with Japanese-style flowers, purple and red petals on long black stems: *Red lace thong. Bring the brassiere.*

She ripped the note into small pieces and added it to her green bin. The dress she eased out of the tissue paper for a better look. Did she have the right shoes? Maybe the stilettos from last night? Or the slingbacks she had bought at Holt Renfrew? They were about the same shade of red and a little demure. Paul seemed to like it when she played shy. With Alastair, it didn't matter. He was just the penis, always in a rush to take off her clothes, while Paul watched from the shadows.

In the spare bedroom, she pulled the slingbacks from the closet and compared them to the flowers on the dress. Yes, the reds were almost a perfect match.

She frowned and put the shoes beside the mahogany wardrobe and hung the dress inside. Paul was spooky like that. He always seemed to know everything, always watching and waiting. But he was exceptionally generous, as Katrina liked to point out, so it was worth putting up with a few eccentricities.

Back in the kitchen, Cora flattened the box, wiggled it under the sink beside the green bin, and washed her hands. While drying them on a tea towel, she remembered she needed to dig out Uncle

Abner's old phone too. Nathan's was probably still missing.

She returned to the spare bedroom and pulled out the folding footstool from the closet. On the shelf over the shoe rack, she rummaged through the boxes of cleaning rags, shoe polishes, sprays for leather and suede, and candles, and tugged out the landline phone Uncle Abner had given her when she moved to Ottawa to find Nathan. She wasn't sure why she had kept it. She didn't even know if it worked, and the plastic had turned the dirty yellow of smokers' teeth.

"There's nothing you can do," Uncle Abner had said when she first told him about her plans to find Nathan. "He's not your brother anymore."

"How can you say that?" she had replied. "Nathan's just sick. He needs help."

"You've been spending too much time in that loony bin. Those damn people are crazier than tarnation. That's why they're locked up. If the government wasn't such cheap bastards, they would have left Nathan there too. He'd be better off. You, too."

"But he's probably living on the street somewhere. We have to find him."

Uncle Abner shook his head and scratched his beard and told her she had college to think of. She had a future. She couldn't throw it away. Life was made of hard choices. That was just the way it was.

At that point, Cora had bolted upstairs to her bedroom, on the verge of tears. Uncle Abner came up later and knocked on the door, but she refused to change her mind. Eventually he went back downstairs and drove to town to pick up supplies from the co-op and the hardware store for repairs to the horse barn. She didn't pack much—mostly clothes, a few books, a set of sheets, a pillow, some cookware sitting unused in the camper, and the comforter Aunt Clara had made in the months before she died of stomach cancer.

When Uncle Abner came back from town, he threatened to shoot anyone who helped Cora move. He didn't have the heart to go through with his threats, though—not after Aunt Clara had suffered so much—and ended up moving Cora himself.

Two weeks later, the neighbors found him sprawled on the concrete floor of the horse barn, next to Thunder's stall. A massive coronary, they said. Never had a chance, the poor bugger. Cora had already managed to find a part-time job at a bar in the Byward Market and found Nathan locked up at a nearby police station for disturbing the peace.

"Yeah, the Walters, all fucked up," he said, after hearing the news about their uncle. "Shit out of luck. Strike three. The house is falling down."

Nathan didn't go back for the funeral, though. He refused to even talk about it, and Cora spent half the service worrying he would disappear again. But he simply ended up sleeping on the streets for a few days near the Parliament Buildings, getting into arguments with the homeless who had lived there for years.

~

Around quarter after twelve, Cora knocked on Nathan's door. He didn't answer. She unlocked the door and found most of his laundry lying on the floor around the couch. She closed her eyes, took a deep breath, and put the groceries and the phone from Uncle Abner on the kitchen counter.

The bedroom door was closed, and she knocked on it. "Nathan? Are you home?"

He muttered something that sounded like, "Wait," or, "What?"

"Have you had lunch yet? I could make some pancakes."

"Are they any good?"

"I haven't made them yet. I just got here. And I bought apples, so I can put them in, if you want. There's bananas and raisins too."

Her brother remained quiet.

"Nathan?"

"Yeah?"

"Can I come in?" Cora asked.

"I don't know, can I? May I? I always hated that shit."

She eased the door open, and it jammed on a blue towel lying on the floor, reminding her of when they were kids and played firemen, rescuing her dolls from certain doom. Nathan had always wanted to wear their father's helmet, but she refused to play unless she got to put it on once in awhile. They had to be careful not to drop it, though, or dad would go ballistic.

"So pancakes are good?" she asked.

"If you don't burn them," he said from the other side of the chest of drawers.

"Were they too dark last time?" she asked. "I'll be more careful."

Nathan muttered something.

"I'll make some of each kind," she said. "Then you can pick whatever you want, and we can try out the maple syrup I picked up last week. It's supposed to be organic, the best you've ever had."

"Fuck, would you come in," he said.

Cora slipped her right hand through the crack and teased the towel away from the door. Even with the window stuck half-open, the room was hot, and the sheets on the bed were still smooth, which probably meant he had not slept on it last night. Nathan sat with his back against the door of the closet, staring at the window. In his hands, he clutched the pink handkerchief from the day before, the dark splotch with his dried blood visible.

"How did you sleep last night?" she asked.

"I don't know. It was dark."

"I'll wash your sheets today. Then they'll be nice and fresh."

"Why? Do I stink?"

"No, I didn't mean that," Cora said, even though he did need a shower.

"Yeah, fuck you too," he said.

"I just meant it would be nice to have fresh sheets. It's just too bad we can't hang them outside to dry. That's one thing I miss about having a laundry line."

"Yeah, they fucking steal everything, even the phone, that fucking pig."

"It's okay, I brought a new one," Cora said and sat down in front of the chest of drawers. "Or, well, an old one. You can have it. I don't need it anymore."

"You took it?" he said, scrambling to his feet. "You're always taking my shit. Leave it the fuck alone."

"No, I brought you another phone," Cora said. "I saw yours was missing so I brought one, a spare one I had. I don't know where yours went."

He didn't listen, though, and stalked out of the bedroom. The bathroom door slammed shut.

Cora rubbed her forehead and leaned against the chest of drawers. At least he was still in the apartment. He would probably calm down by the time she made pancakes.

She stood up, adjusted her jeans, and walked into the kitchen. After washing her hands, she pulled on an apron with a picture of a cow on the front and searched through the cupboards for the white flour and the baking powder and the vanilla extract. Nathan was always rearranging things. She also wanted to make some chamomile tea but couldn't find the box on any of the lower shelves.

She opened the closet by the bathroom to get the footstool and found the laundry basket wedged between the coats, three of them Nathan's and two of her spares. She wiggled the basket out, careful not to break it, and straightened the coats. In the bathroom, the shower started. She glanced at the laundry scattered on the floor and decided she might as well take a load downstairs. Sometimes Nathan took forever in the shower. What he was doing she didn't want to think about.

While pulling the sheets off Nathan's bed, Cora heard the bathroom door open. A black T-shirt, pants, socks, and underwear flew into the living room. She shook her head and added them to the pile of darks.

In the basement, two of the four washing machines whirred and thumped like a pair of bad opera singers. She shoved the sheets in the washing machine that had WC scratched on the lid and the darks in the older machine wedged in the corner and dug through her purse for change. Shoot, she only had enough for one load. When did she use up all her quarters?

Cora started the washing machine with the sheets and headed back up to Nathan's apartment and wondered how much change was hiding under the couch.

She found her brother standing in the kitchen in a pair of black boxers, poking through fridge, looking so skinny and pale it made her pause. It was like he had an old man's body, wasting away to nothing.

He grabbed a pop from the fridge and snapped open the tab. "See, I'm starving. Like those kids on Jeopardy." He ran a finger over his ribs and the pink scars from the car accident, almost nine years old. "Mirror, mirror on the wall, who's the thinnest of them all?"

"I'll start the pancakes in a minute," Cora said. "I just need to get the other load of laundry going."

"I can't wait till summer."

"Do you have any change?" she asked.

"No worries. That's a good color on you."

"I mean loonies or quarters. For the laundry."

Nathan frowned and walked into his bedroom. Cora poured herself a glass of water and glanced down at the light blue tank top she was wearing. If Nathan liked the color, did that actually mean it was a good color? Or a bad color?

In the bedroom, Nathan called out, "Here quarter, quarter, quarter, quarter. Here quarter, quarter, quarter."

Cora slid her glass on the counter, washed her hands, and lined up an apple and an egg and filled a small measuring cup with Sultana raisins. Just to be safe, she put the egg in a coffee mug, and Nathan came back into the kitchen with a mix of quarters and nickels.

"We'll trade," she said and took a twenty out of her purse. "In case you want to go to Tim's later and get a coffee."

He stuffed the twenty in his underwear, and Cora averted her gaze and added the change to her purse. She wasn't going to say anything. After all, what made living with Nathan impossible also made it possible for her to help him with the things he didn't consider important—like the apartment, the rent, the food. He was too busy juggling his own thoughts to notice his checks from the government didn't match his expenses.

"There should be a clean pair of jeans in the chest of drawers," she said. "I just need to start the other washing machine, and we can have lunch."

"Where are we going?"

"I'm going to make pancakes. With raisins or apples, whatever you want. Or I can mix in bananas."

"As long as you don't burn them."

"Yes, I'll be careful."

"Good. May the force be with you."

Nathan strode to the bathroom but didn't bother shutting the door, and the stream of urine hitting the water in the toilet echoed through the apartment.

"I'll be back in a couple minutes," she called and hurried out of the apartment. Hopefully he would have some pants on by the time she came back.

~

While in the laundry room, Cora heard a door slam down, and a man started yelling in a language she didn't know, quickly joined by a shrill woman. Probably the Indian couple by the stairway. They always seemed to be fighting.

A door opened, and the yelling spilled into the hallway. Cora moved into the corner and toyed with her cellphone. The superintendent never bothered them, though. He just picked on Nathan.

A few minutes later, the yelling stopped, and a door slammed. Cora peeked into the hallway on the main floor. Thankfully she didn't see anyone and darted up the back stairs.

The door to Nathan's apartment stood ajar, and she hurried closer. Had she left it open?

No, she couldn't have.

Inside the apartment, everything was quiet. Her brother wasn't in the kitchen or the bathroom. She called his name and tapped on the bedroom door, but it hung open enough for her to know he probably wasn't in there either. To be certain, she checked the bedroom closet and looked around for his black sneakers. How could he have left? She hadn't been in the basement that long.

Was he coming back?

She leaned against the kitchen counter and pressed a hand to her face. He was like a little kid sometimes. When he got an idea, it became his whole world, and nothing else mattered. At least, until he got the next great idea.

~

With no particular need to rush the pancakes anymore, Cora

washed her hands, took an aspirin, and wiggled the footstool out of the coat closet. She searched the top shelves of the kitchen cupboards for her chamomile tea and found it hiding in a box of granola bars, perhaps meant as a joke.

She turned on the tea kettle, mixed the batter for the pancakes, and peeled a Granny Smith apple. While throwing the peel in the garbage, she heard a knock on the door and glanced around the fridge. Had Nathan forgotten his keys?

Cora rinsed her hands, grabbed the tea towel from the stove, and peered through the peephole. Two police officers stood in the hallway.

Oh god. What had he done now?

She opened the door, recognizing both of the officers. Back in April, Nathan had walked out of a store without paying for the magazines in his coat. Officer Kaczynski was the older of the two, with a stout belly and the furrowed face of a potato farmer. She had forgotten the name of the other officer, who reminded her of Justin Timberlake, except shaved and tanned.

"Ah, Ms. Walters, good to see you're here," Officer Kaczynski said. "Makes things easier."

"Why? What happened?"

"Is your brother here?"

"No," she said and stepped back to let the officers in the apartment. "Please, come in."

For a second, Officer Kaczynski looked like he was going to decline, but his partner nudged him, and Kaczynski nodded his thanks. "We won't take much of your time."

They lined up beside the couch, reminding Cora of boys wearing tuxedos for the first time. She smiled, glad she had cleaned up the laundry.

"Would you like some coffee?" she asked. "I was just going to make some."

"No thanks," Officer Kaczynski said. "But we do need to talk to your brother. When will he be back?"

"I'm not sure," she said. "Can you tell me what happened? Maybe I can help?"

"We had a complaint yesterday from one of the local merchants," Kaczynski said.

Cora nodded and crossed her arms, a shiver building in her spine.

"The drugstore," the second officer said. His name tag said A. Roberts. "The one across from the Dominion supermarket."

"Did he take something? He forgets, sometimes, that he has to pay. He doesn't do it on purpose."

"You know it's not that simple," Officer Kaczynski said.

"Why? What happened?" she asked. "I can go talk to them. I'm sure they'll understand."

Kaczynski scowled, as if that was beside the point. Officer Roberts, though, outlined the incident: Nathan yelling and throwing several items at the pharmacist and knocking over a display.

"No one was hurt," Roberts said. "Some minimal damage to property."

"I'm sorry," she said. "It's been a difficult week. But I'm going to talk to his doctor. I think his medication needs to be adjusted."

"When did you say your brother would be back?" Officer Kaczynski asked, still looking annoyed.

"I have no idea. He could be gone all day, especially if the weather stays nice."

"Then we won't take any more of your time," Officer Kaczynski said. "But we will come back to talk to him."

"Of course," Cora said. "I'll be here tomorrow too, if that helps. In the afternoon, after church."

Officer Kaczynski nodded and marched out of the apartment, but Roberts paused and opened his mouth, like he wanted to add something.

Instead he cleared his throat and fidgeted with his belt and nodded to her.

"Thank you," Cora said, touching his right arm.

By the stairway, Kaczynski coughed and shot his partner a dark look. Officer Roberts began to flush and nodded again and wished her a good afternoon before the two men tromped down the stairs.

~

Nathan hopped over the guard rail along Duplex Avenue and gave the finger to a car honking at him. Those fuckers needed to slow down. What if he had been a turtle? They weren't no fucking ninjas.

He scooped up pebbles from the curb and headed down a steep path of hardened dirt into the Chatsworth ravine, pushing the odd branch out of the way. At the bottom of the path, a small stream poured into a big maw sealed off with metal bars, heading where the sun don't shine, and he started tossing his pebbles into the maw, one at a time, watching them arc through the air and disappear.

"Kowabunga, dude," he said and stepped on the concrete rim of the maw and tossed in the last of his pebbles. What would it eat when the stream dried up? Kids? Dogs? Lots of little ones, he hoped. They were always trying to bite him in the ankles, the little fuckers.

Nathan hopped down from the concrete rim and circled it to the south side of the stream. The north side was too soggy. Ahead the dirt path broadened, and he followed it to a small pool of dark brown water surrounded by crud-covered rocks. He dug a few pebbles out of the dirt and tossed them one at a time into the pool, but no fish chased after them. No minnows. They were too smart.

He looked around for a stick to spear them, like the Indians, but all the branches were chunky and rotten. Good for dogs and campfires. All he needed was some marshmallows. A couple of patties. Steak. Potato salad. Corn on the cob.

His stomach rumbled, and he glanced at his watch, but someone had stolen it. He swore and turned in a circle. The ravine stared back at him.

Nope. Nobody.

At least nobody he could see. Sometimes they hid in the shadows, waiting for him to close his eyes.

Nathan ducked down and sprinted to where the path split in two. The shadows whispered and pretended not to follow him. He darted along the right branch of the path and followed it onto a footbridge that crossed the stream, the metal rails painted with graffiti and the sides made of chain-link fencing.

In the middle of the bridge, he stopped and pulled out the pink handkerchief stained with his blood and waved it in front of his face. On the opposite side of the ravine, next to a pocket of poplar trees, a blonde woman wearing a red top and white pants appeared.

"This is my ravine," he yelled. "Go find your own."

She ignored him. He charged across the footbridge and up the dirt path leading to the poplars, but she still managed to disappear.

He swore and waved the handkerchief in front of his face again. A few seconds later, he spotted her at the top of the slope, on the other side of a chain-link fence, standing in front of a wooden shed and a house built of rusty red bricks, pierced by large windows with white trim.

"I see you," he yelled. "You can't fool me."

She waited but said nothing.

He waved the handkerchief over his head. "Do you want it back? Don't be such a bitch."

She shook her head and walked behind a thick maple tree. Nathan ran through a patch of wild flowers and clambered over the chain-link fence. Where had she gone? She couldn't have climbed the tree. He glanced up at the branches, the lowest of which was at least fifteen feet off the ground, and frowned at the smaller trees in the yard and the trees on the other side of the fence. A black squirrel clung to the trunk of one of them, staring back at him.

"What are you looking at?" he yelled and grabbed a small yellow ball from the ground. The squirrel raced up the trunk and disappeared into the foliage.

Nathan swore and opened the door of the shed. It was smaller than he had expected, more like a fancy outhouse with a window on the side for perverts. The interior was jammed with empty flowerpots, shovels, rakes, and other garden tools that looked like attachments for amputees, and a bag of dirt with its top gashed open. No other way out.

He circled the shed and looked around at the trees again. Maybe she really was a squirrel, jumping from tree to tree. Like Tarzan but blonde.

At the front of the house, a car honked and revved its engine. Nathan dropped the yellow ball and sprinted up the brick walk on the east side of the house. Too late, though. The car had already reached the end of the block: a blue Ford or a GM. Turning right.

A moment later, Nathan realized someone was staring at him and glanced over his shoulder. About twenty feet away, a woman stood in front of a flower bed, holding a trowel in one hand and wearing a giant straw hat. She looked ready to pee herself or fall and go boom.

From a neighboring yard, a man yelled, "Hey!"

Nathan sprinted after the blue car, turning right at the same corner, and then ran down into the park where the dogs liked to shit. Next to the wall spattered with graffiti, he scrambled over a chain-link fence and cut through several yards, dodging patio chairs, basketball nets, and a yappy white terrier with brown spots. Three blocks later, he cut through a lane and an alley and the parking lot of a funeral home and dropped behind a green dumpster heaped with splintered lumber, floor tiles, and ratty shingles, gasping for breath.

What the hell was he doing? Why was he running? That stupid hag could fuck herself. The squirrels, too.

He pulled out the pink handkerchief and balled it up and threw it away, but the handkerchief opened up and fell on the pavement by his feet. He swore and kicked at it, which didn't work any better, so he shifted to the other end of the dumpster. She was out there, watching. He could feel her. She was moving closer.

"Go fuck yourself," he yelled. "You're not getting me. None of you are."

For several seconds, nothing happened. He heard the chirping of birds, the rumble of a car on the far side of the funeral home, and the barking of a dog.

"Fuck you," he yelled. "Fuck the police. Fuck you all."

"If you keep yelling, they're going to come get you and lock you up," a woman said. "They'll tie you up and hack you open and yank out those useless brains of yours."

Nathan froze against the dumpster. She was the devil, straight from the mountain. Black hair, black eyes. Flaming tongue.

"Is that what you want?" she asked. "I can call them right now. They would love to get you. You would save your sister a lot of trouble."

"Fuck you!"

"I would rather do it myself, but I'm not allowed to have fun. He's always been picky that way. Too much Buddhism. He should have stayed with Christianity. At least they're allowed to hurt people."

"I don't believe in you," Nathan said. "You're not real. You're all a bunch of bullshit."

"I don't care what you believe," the devil said. "Just stop pestering Tania. It's hard enough for her already, keeping you contained. You have no control."

"I can't hear you," Nathan said and covered his ears. "Go away. Fuck you."

"We're growing tired of you," she said. "Your time will run out. The others will find you."

Then the heels of her shoes clipped on the pavement—three, four, five times—and vanished.

~

With the sheets still warm from the dryer, Cora made Nathan's bed and folded the underwear and socks and put them in the chest of drawers. She finished ironing the last of Nathan's T-shirts, which sported a tattered picture of the rock band Kiss, and hung them up. She turned off the TV, halfway through the movie *The Pursuit of Happyness*, and wiggled the ironing board back in the coat closet.

After washing her hands, she put plastic wrap over the plate of pancakes and slid them in the fridge. At least they were good cold. She could leave instructions for the microwave too, in case he wanted to warm them up. Thirty seconds for each pancake would probably be enough.

Next to the fridge, her cellphone chimed. She fished it out of her purse and glanced at the ID. Yes, it was Katrina. The usual checkup.

"One of Paul's little helpers called," Katrina said. "She wanted to make sure you got the dress. He wanted something that suited your skin and the candlelight."

"Paul talks about light a lot," Cora said. "I think he used to paint."

"Yeah, I believe that. Painters are all crazy. Otherwise they wouldn't paint. Maybe it's the fumes."

"He's okay. I almost forget he's there sometimes." Cora paused. "I mean, not really, but sort of."

"He probably likes it that way. Makes it feel more authentic, more exciting for him."

"I guess so," Cora said.

"Hold on, I have another call. Be right back."

"Okay," Cora said and unplugged the water kettle and wiped off the kitchen counter.

Katrina came back on the line. "God, what a moron. He wanted to pay by check."

"Somebody new?"

"Yeah, that too," Katrina said. "Anyway, I know Paul's done a lot for you, but don't let him push anything on you. Those kind of guys always have a surprise, sooner or later. They always want to push things a little further."

"I know."

"I feel like a harpy, saying it a million times, but I'm just looking out for you. Don't let him get away with any crap. You're in charge."

"I'll be careful."

"Good, I know you will," Katrina said. "Call me if you need anything."

Chapter 11

Alex lay in the back of his car, his head cushioned on his jacket, while a skinny Quebecer with a cigarette stuck behind his right ear drove to a parking garage near the Four Seasons Hotel in Yorkville. Conversation with the driver was nonexistent. He simply drove, parked, and glanced back once to check if Alex was still alive. Then the bastard pulled out his cellphone to call Mobius and walked off.

"Yeah, fuck you too," Alex said and closed his eyes.

At least once or twice, he fell into a churning, heaving darkness that gnawed at him like a rabid squirrel. The rest of the time, he listened to the chirp of people and the rumble of cars on Cumberland Street and tried to remember if he had any beer left in the trunk. He hoped so.

Half an hour later, Alex eased upright, scooped up his keys from the front seat, and opened a door, careful not to whack the black BMW parked next to him. It probably had an alarm like an air raid siren.

Once on his feet, he peered over the railing to the street below and cursed. Why did that bastard have to park on the third floor? Now he had to go down all those stairs.

Still swearing, Alex opened the trunk of his car and found three beers under his duffel bag. He drained the first two while sitting on the bumper, rolled the empty bottles under the BMW, and dug a pair of sunglasses out of his glove compartment to cover his eyes, which looked like giant prunes.

He opened up the last beer, walked to the nearest stairwell, and pulled out his cellphone. The screen was cracked, but it still winked on.

Alex sat at the top of the stairs and called Sebastian.

His nasal voice came on the line. "Are you okay? What happened?"

"Yeah, the doctor says I'll live," Alex said. "Lucky me."

"Why? What did she do?"

He took a long swallow of his beer. "Have you heard anything from Sydney or Mobius?"

"No, nothing."

"Good, I'll take care of that. Are you at your apartment?"

"Yeah, but I couldn't sleep. I kept thinking about my wife and the baby. I couldn't stop myself. It just keeps running through my head, over and over."

"You might as well meet me in the plaza east of the hotel. We're just waiting for the surveillance anyway."

"I can be there in ten minutes."

"Make it twenty," Alex said and hung up before Sebastian could ask any more questions.

Alex finished his beer, shoved the empty bottle against the wall on his left, and limped down another flight of stairs and sat down to call Sydney.

The head of security answered with a polite hello. "We've got everything ready," he said. "We can have a van to you in half an hour."

"Make it twenty minutes," Alex said. "The plaza on Cumberland Street."

"Yes, sir. It'll be one of the plumber refits."

"Good," Alex said and hung up.

At the south end of the parking garage, he found Cumberland Street jammed with cars, including a red Ferrari and two classics from the fifties or sixties, driven by men with nothing better to do on a Saturday. Alex grimaced and raised a hand to shield his face from the sun. He wished he had a hat. It felt like the sun wanted to fry his face off.

He turned left and passed a patio full of people nibbling food and sipping drinks, their glasses full of froth and bright liquids. He backed up and walked through the doorway at the back of the patio and sat on a stool in front of a black bar with brass rails and ordered two Heinekens.

"You all right?" asked the girl behind the bar.

"No, just got in a fight with a Frenchman." Alex tilted up his sunglasses. "He's pretty good with a bat."

The girl stared at him, too shocked to say anything. She had blonde wavy hair that belonged in a shampoo commercial and big hoop earrings checkered black and white.

"Actually, I tripped and fell on my face," Alex said. "Stupidest thing I've ever done."

The girl laughed a little and leaned down to open a refrigerator. "Sorry. I didn't mean to—"

"No, laugh all you want. I deserve it."

She smiled, set a pair of green bottles in front of him, and reached into a black cabinet for a drinking glass.

"Don't worry about that," Alex said. "These beauties won't last long."

He drained the first beer and glanced at his watch. Sebastian would show up early, probably fretting like a damn monkey. The girl behind the bar asked Alex where he was from. He had an accent.

"I spent a lot of time overseas," he said.

"Have you been to France? I've always wanted to go. Italy too." Alex nodded. The girl beamed. She planned to go at the end of the summer, if everything worked out. She still had to get the time off. Her friend, too.

Alex finished his second beer. He ordered a third. For him, France had been a shithole, nothing but bombed-out buildings and hungry people. Why Teresa had wanted to stay there so long, he had no idea, especially after the war ended. Then came four years in Rome, three in Madrid, five in a little shit town near Bonn, two in London, and each time they had to move Father without drawing too much attention. Fortunately they had access to trucks again, sometimes trains, as long as nobody asked too many questions. In '44, carting him from Nijmegen to Paris had taken almost five weeks since horses hated going near his shriveled body, dogs ran off, and birds fell silent. Sometimes they even dropped out of the sky.

The bartender started to talk again. Alex chugged the rest of his beer and slapped two twenties on the bar. He crossed Cumberland Street, cutting between a Porsche and a Mazda, and walked past an entrance to the Bay subway station and a mammoth-sized rock that had a bunch of kids crawling over it, perhaps meant to represent the Canadian Shield. On the other side of the giant rock, people sat on shiny silver chairs around shiny silver tables, and Alex grabbed a newspaper from one of them and held the paper over his head. The man sitting at the table glanced up, startled, but didn't say anything.

Alex walked around the south end of a waterfall and a procession of metal archways connected by wooden benches and ducked into the shade of some trees where more shiny silver chairs were padlocked to shiny silver tables. Alex plopped into one of the chairs and tossed his newspaper on the table. Next to him, three teenage girls stopped their chattering—two with each other, one on her cellphone. An Indian couple sitting at one of the other tables glanced at him and then stared at each other. The woman reached for her purse.

"You gals got any beer?" he asked the teenagers.

The girl on her cell phone scowled at him. The other two simply looked surprised. The Indian couple stood up to leave.

"I'll pay you double," he said. "Triple if it's good."

The girls hurried out of the shade, toward the waterfall, and the Indian couple headed to the boutiques on the other side of Cumberland Street. Alex shrugged and spotted Sebastian coming from the east, glancing around like a frightened dog. Alex whistled and raised a hand. Sebastian darted through a rock garden, passing an old man with a scruffy beard and dirty trousers. The old man began to swear and yell, and Sebastian fumbled with his wallet and threw some coins on the ground.

When he reached the trees, Alex said, "That was brilliant. Really touching."

"I shouldn't have let you go. It was my fault," Sebastian said.

"Oh well. Too late."

"I never meant for this to happen. I never wanted any of it."

"Who does?"

"But I can't stop. I can't. Every time I see kids, strollers, even those stupid little stuffed pandas."

Alex slapped the table. "Yeah, your family's gone. Kaput. And the sooner you accept it, the better. The only one thing you need to remember is they're safer without you."

"I would never do anything to them," Sebastian said, looking alarmed. "Never."

"Yeah, well, maybe," Alex said, "But you've got a piece of Father inside you. It's a part of you, feeding you. Do you want that near your kid?"

Sebastian sucked in a shaky breath and shook his head.

"And what about Teresa? Or Mobius?"

Sebastian's head jerked up.

"I'm not saying they would." Alex said. "Teresa doesn't care where you're from, as long as it doesn't get in the way of what she wants."

"You're sure? I'd do anything to protect them. Anything."

"Then why give her ideas?"

Sebastian shook his head and clapped his hands over his face. Alex leaned back and watched a sparrow hopping near the edge of the trees, chasing a piece of beige fluff. For several minutes, neither of them spoke, the crying starting all over again, until a white van crept into view, painted with a plumber's logo that looked like a wrench clubbing a snake.

"That's us," Alex said and strode to the sidewalk. He raised a hand and gestured to the side street at the east end of the plaza. The man sitting in the passenger seat of the van saluted.

With Sebastian in tow, Alex cut through the rock garden and a cluster of evergreens surrounded by concrete rings and waited next to a No Parking sign. Because of the steady trickle of pedestrians cutting across Cumberland Street, a minute or two passed before the van moved a hundred feet, and Sebastian danced from foot to foot like he had a bladder infection.

Finally the van stopped beside Alex, and the man in the passenger seat hopped out. He had short blond hair, slim rectangular glasses, and a dumpy androgynous body wrapped in a white-collar shirt, brown slacks, and black sneakers.

"Praise to the mistress," he said, echoed by the driver, a dark Hispanic man with a jagged, purple scar on the right side of his neck.

"Yeah, praise be," Alex said. "Do you have everything?"

"Yes, sir, whenever you're ready."

"Then we'd better get started. She's bloody hell waiting."

"Yes, sir."

Alex yanked the side door open and told Sebastian and the androgynous man to get in the back. Heavy gray blankets covered the floor, and workbenches and storage racks filled the sides of the van, loaded with thick canvas bags, a garden hose, a large tool chest, and a diesel generator.

Alex climbed into the passenger seat. "Find us a spot to park," he told the driver. "The quieter the better."

"Yes, sir."

Ten minutes later, the driver pulled into a parking lot sandwiched between a dirty white apartment building and a residential neighborhood lined with small maples. Alex told the driver to take a walk for a couple of hours and moved into the back of the van, beside Sebastian. The androgynous man had already pulled out three black carrying cases with laptops and linked them together. Each screen showed a different part of the main lobby in the Fairmont Royal York—one pointing to the bar, another focused on the main doors, and the third angled towards some of the elevators.

"What time do you want them to start at?" the androgynous technician asked. "I can run them simultaneously."

"Let's try eleven," Alex said. "We'll go back further if we have to."

"Is that when you got to the hotel?" Sebastian asked.

"No, closer to twelve," Alex said. "But Peter had already been there half an hour."

"I heard he had his car towed."

"Yeah, lucky for him. Otherwise the boss would have been more upset."

Sebastian dropped his gaze, and the androgynous man coughed and fiddled with the cables.

Alex continued. "He'd been driving down Front Street when he felt that kick in the gut, kind of like you did, and pulled over to find the source. But the feeling was gone by the time he got inside the hotel."

"I was so stupid," Sebastian said.

"Yeah, well, done is done." Alex gestured to the technician, and he started the surveillance footage. "At least we have something to work with."

Or so Alex hoped. Otherwise they were both up shit creek.

~

After watching the laptops for close to an hour, Alex leaned back against the driver's seat and wished he had told the driver to bring a case of beer. He already had enough to worry about without Sebastian twitching and dripping sweat, which made the technician fidget and sweat, until they both had giant stains on their backs and under their armpits.

Alex yawned. Father loved it, though. He loved people pissing their pants and sweating buckets and bleeding their lives away, especially if the bleeding was slow and unpredictable. Mobius used to experiment with the prisoners, gauging Father's reaction, but Teresa didn't care anymore. She only wanted to find the Light. For sixty years, she had talked about it. Yet Alex still didn't understand how the Light was supposed to manifest. Was it like them? Reborn? Forever young? Or hiding in the body of an old man? Alex suspected Teresa didn't know the answer either but liked to pretend otherwise.

"Wait! That's her," Sebastian said.

Alex opened his eyes and saw Sebastian pointing at the screen showing a cluster of elevators. The androgynous technician paused the surveillance footage. Alex leaned in to get a better look at the four people walking in various directions, three of them women.

"Which one?" he asked.

Sebastian pointed to a woman with blonde hair, wearing a black dress, but the man closer to the camera hid half of her face.

"Are you sure? That's a lousy shot."

"I wouldn't forget," Sebastian said. "Not in a million years."

The technician backed up the footage thirty seconds and played it at a slower speed. Unfortunately the man was in the way for most of the shot, and then she turned and walked out of view.

Alex frowned and glanced at the other laptops and watched

them for another ten minutes, but she failed to reappear.

"I should have footage for the elevator she came from. It'll just take a minute," the technician said.

"Do it," Alex said.

They waited while the man changed footage on one of the laptops and set the time frame to 11:40pm. The screen was a composite of shots from four elevators, two of which were empty. After about thirty seconds, a blonde girl in the same black dress stepped on one of the empty elevators and checked her face in one of the mirrored sides.

"Yes! That's her," Sebastian said.

Alex leaned closer to the screen. She wasn't what he had expected. She was young, for one thing, pretty, and he had the strangest feeling he should know her from somewhere—maybe because of all the bars he had frequented over the decades, all those waitresses schlepping drinks.

"I can do some work on the image," the technician said. "Enhance the resolution. Increase the size."

Alex nodded.

While they waited, Sebastian's excitement faded, turning back to fear. "What do we do now?"

"We'll keep looking at the surveillance," Alex said. "Make sure we have the best pictures for Teresa."

"And then?"

Alex frowned. He wished Sebastian would stop asking so many damn questions. There wasn't a damn thing they could do about it anyway.

The technician glanced up from his work, sweat from his chin dripping on the keyboard. He didn't look happy either.

"We'll do what we have to," Alex said.

Sebastian chewed his lips, staring at the image of the girl. Maybe he was thinking of his wife. She was a pretty blonde woman too, his pictures of her carefully preserved in his wallet.

Alex put a hand on Sebastian's neck. "That's the way it is now. You're either with us, or you're against us."

Sebastian nodded.

"Don't kid yourself," Alex said. "That's exactly how Teresa sees it. Her will is God's will."

"I know."

"Praise be," said the technician.

"Exactly," Alex said and leaned back against the driver's seat. "And don't ever forget it."

Chapter 12

Straw said only five words to Cora during the drive to Paul's building. "Call me when you're done." The rest of the time Straw kept the music loud and obnoxious, and she slid out the back, careful of her skirt, wondering why men were such jerks. They practically turned into three-year-olds when they didn't get what they wanted.

She paused on the sidewalk to smooth her silk dress before climbing the steps of Paul's building. Prior to its renovation into lofts, it had been a haven for artists and drug dealers, a storage facility for one of the local breweries, and a warehouse for textiles, along with a few other more transient roles over the course of its hundred years. Paul had also told her bits of history about the surrounding buildings, which was often interesting, but she wished he had left out the part about the ghosts and the furniture store that sold coffins.

Cora pressed the buzzer for Paul's apartment. Straw honked at a cab and sped westwards, even though he was supposed to wait until she went inside. On the sidewalk, a pair of skinny guys wearing baggy pants and shirts and carrying skateboards slowed down to gawk at her. She resisted the urge to press the buzzer again and glanced at her cellphone.

The intercom crackled. The door buzzed. Cora hurried into the foyer and passed a dark-skinned Indian security guard, her heels clacking on a granite floor variegated with shades of salt and pepper. Behind a trio of brown leather couches hung a large landscape painting that reminded her of Algonquin Park—a lake, pine trees, rocks—though she found the overall effect garish, too many oranges and reds.

On the elevator, she turned off the volume of her phone and pulled out her compact. She had kept her makeup simple: nude beige lipstick, bronze eyeshadow, a bit of darker eyeliner. Paul would tell her if he wanted more. Alastair, the penis, didn't care.

At the end of the hallway on the third floor, a light bulb flickered like a giant firefly. Cora patted her hair, fiddled with her dress, and took a deep breath. Her stomach squiggled. She slid her compact back in her purse, brushed a hand over her belly, and walked to Paul's door.

She stopped short of knocking. The door was already open a crack. Had Alastair come early? Usually Paul wanted to look at her first and talk about his old books and trinkets. Each time, she did her best to sound enthused about philosophy, religion, and history that smelled of dead moths, dust, and shriveled librarians, just like she did her best to sound enthused about being treated like another trinket. By now she was used to it. A lot of her clients did the same thing, in one way or another.

She listened for a few seconds, heard nothing, and knocked. After waiting a minute or so, she knocked again. This time she thought she heard a "Yes" and poked her head in the apartment, the central room of which combined a huge kitchen, dining area, and living room and had three wooden columns supporting its twenty-five foot ceiling. The tables, cabinets, cupboards, and trim for the walls and counters were dark European oak. The couch, loveseats, and reclining chairs were Italian leather, dark burgundy in color, and faced a huge fireplace. Five large windows faced the main street, each covered with thick burgundy curtains. Several dozen paintings, a mix of contemporary and classical, hung on the walls, interspersed with three large crosses: one made of dark oak from Germany, one of cedar from Jerusalem, one of iron from Russia. On her right, a staircase with a black iron railing spiraled up to a walkway, leading to the master bedroom and bathroom. There were also two doors under the walkway for the study and the guest room.

From the direction of the study, Cora heard Paul's voice: a sharp word or two in a language she didn't know. Then he appeared in the doorway of the study and waved a hand. As always, he wore black slacks, a black buttoned shirt, and a black hat with a wide brim. If he had had hair, he would have looked like a cross between a Christian rock artist and an orthodox Jew.

Cora stepped into the apartment and closed the door. "I wasn't sure," she said. "It was so quiet."

"Yes, a strange night," Paul said.

She started to circle the kitchen counter, across thick rugs and hardwood flooring, but he raised a hand to stop her.

"Please sit," he said and pointed to the couches. "Or did you want a tea? I'm sure you remember where everything is."

"Yes, thank you," Cora said, pressing a hand to her stomach. "I will. In a minute. Unless you want something? I can make it for you."

Paul strode to one of the couches and studied her—dress or body, it was hard to tell. For him, there didn't seem to be much difference.

"How do you find the dress?" he asked.

"You have incredible taste," she said and lifted her skirts to flash Paul her panties. "I hope this is what you wanted. I brought something else along, just in case."

"It is the one in my mind." Paul pointed to one of the leather loveseats. "Alastair will be late. You should be comfortable."

Cora stretched out on the nearest loveseat, and Paul glanced over his shoulder in the direction of the study. She shrugged inwardly. She would never figure him out, that much was obvious. Nor did she want to, if she were honest with herself. He was too different, too strange. In the six months she had known him, he had never once touched her. The first penis had been Hank, an otherwise charming man who had treated her breasts like bean-bags. Next came Williams, a thin man with a scratchy beard and a crooked erection. Number three had loved showing off the scar on his right arm from a skiing accident in the Alps. Now the penis was Alastair, in his late thirties, the youngest so far, always impatient, always pulling at her clothes.

Still standing behind the couch, Paul shook his head and said something Cora did not understand.

"What was that?" she asked. "German?"

"Mmm? No," he said. "*Fiat lux*. Let there be light."

"Oh," Cora said and glanced up at the wedge-shaped lights overhead, their frosted glass surfaces filling the room with a glow reminiscent of moonlight. "They're very pretty, the way the glass looks."

"Yes, I keep forgetting them. The residue of the mind. You see so many things, but you see nothing."

"Sounds philosophical."

"Yes, seeing is different than understanding. Too many forget that." He glanced at the study again. "But understanding is the only way to freedom."

Cora nodded and rubbed her legs together in a way she hoped looked suggestive. The apartment was colder than usual, and goosebumps prickled her arms.

Paul murmured a few more words but peered at the study, so she decided to remain silent. Her gaze drifted to the three white candles burning on the coffee table. Amidst them stood several small Indian statues, a miniature shrine in the Japanese style, Tibetan prayer beads, and a porcelain bowl filled with water. Paul had explained how they all fit together into one way of being, like the universes themselves. Fortunately nodding had sufficed as a reply.

Voices drifted from the direction of the study, and Cora sat up, surprised. Wasn't Alastair supposed to be late? Who else was there?

She started to stand, but Paul raised a hand. She hesitated before settling back against a throw cushion.

A pair of women strode out of the study. The smaller of the two was a thin Asian woman with straight ebony hair that fell to her shoulder blades. She wore a purple blouse and silk black pants and pulled along a second woman with dyed blonde hair, who wore cream-colored Capri pants and a red blouse that made her look like an ironing board.

Cora sat up again. What was going on? There wasn't supposed to be anyone else except Alastair. That was the arrangement. Definitely no women. Some of her clients had wanted threesomes, but she said no. She couldn't see herself doing that.

"You should have waited," Paul said.

For a second, Cora thought he was talking to her, but the Asian woman shook her head.

"I'm going to take her back," she said. "That's what you wanted."

"Not like this," Paul said.

"I would have jumped out the window, but you don't have one in there."

"Sorry," the blonde woman said. "I did not want to be difficult. But the pain was too much."

"It won't be much longer," Paul said.

The Asian woman glared at Cora. She picked up her handbag, and her stomach clenched. No! Not now!

Paul frowned and glanced at her. She stiffened, and her stomach rolled again.

"Get out," he said.

Cora stared at him, her thoughts darting a dozen different directions. Her stomach rumbled. The Asian woman grabbed the blonde woman, and they sprinted out of the apartment.

"Be gentle with yourself," Paul said. "The discomfort will pass. You should be used to it by now."

Cora shook her head and clutched her abdomen. Dark spots danced in front of her eyes.

"Hurry, then," Paul said. "The bathroom."

Cora clapped a hand over her mouth and stumbled to a small door tucked beside the coat closet. Once in the bathroom, she fumbled for the light switch, the burning in her throat, and dropped her head over the sink. Her stomach lurched. Her mouth burned. The bathroom counter spun in front of her—the beige tiles, the mirror, the foam green towels. She retched again and clamped her hands on the counter. Her legs wobbled. Her stomach kicked a third time, and her throat clenched. This time, only a bit of liquid dribbled out, and she stumbled, bumping her head against the mirror. Her legs buckled. She sank against the counter, onto her knees, and her stomach kicked a few more times.

After a minute or two, Cora fumbled with the faucet, all too aware now of the smell, the chunks, and the liquid. Though her stomach continued to churn, she eased to her feet, careful not to look too closely at the sink. She splashed water around the basin until the worst of her vomit had swirled down the drain, then rinsed her face and mouth.

Her legs began to shake again, and she sank to her knees. While resting her head on her right arm, she tugged at the smaller of the hand towels but gave up and closed her eyes.

Once her nausea settled into a dull gurgle, she returned to her feet and washed her face and rinsed her mouth several times. Thankfully she found multiple sets of fresh towels in the vanity and bundled her first towel in the corner furthest from the door. After that, she sat on the lid of the toilet, covered her mouth with a hand towel, and rested for a few minutes. She also remembered Paul. He was still waiting for her. Sooner or later he would knock. She couldn't stay in the bathroom forever.

With one hand resting on her stomach, Cora stood up and studied her reflection. Thank God she had pinned up her hair—or it could have been a lot worse. How could she have been so stupid?

She washed her hands and searched the vanity for mouthwash or disinfectant. No, only a bottle of liquid soap and more toilet paper. No gloves. No sponges.

Cora closed her eyes. What choice did she have? She had to make do. Improvise.

She took a deep breath, then cleaned the sink using the liquid soap and wads of toilet paper and dropped the wads in the toilet. She didn't dare use the soap to rinse her mouth. The thought alone made her stomach twist. She should have put one of those little bottles of mouthwash from the hotels in her handbag. Instead she had to settle for gargling with water and managed to find a peppermint breath mint in one of the pockets of her handbag.

After flushing the toilet, Cora washed her hands and leaned against the bathroom door. She didn't hear anything through the burnished oak and eased it open.

A voice drifted from the kitchen. She froze.

"It is always what you want," the Asian woman said. "It has to be your way. We are too stupid, too blind."

"It won't be much longer," Paul said.

"You keep saying that. But Tania can't keep running around like this, especially when that fool hurts himself. You could easily tell Teresa where to find them."

"You always want to fight the inevitable," Paul said. "But it will happen in its own time."

"Really? How? You've forgotten what it means to live, to take action. Nothing happens by itself."

"That is the mentality of flesh. Of desire."

"If you won't do something, I will."

"It will only make the situation more difficult," Paul said.

"For who? You?"

The click of heels came closer, and Cora tugged the bathroom door shut and locked it. God, what now? Why couldn't they just leave? Go upstairs? Just long enough for her to get out?

She sat on the toilet and pressed a hand to her forehead. Her stomach gurgled.

After a minute or two, she dug her phone out of her handbag, tempted to call Katrina. What would she say? She was probably going to freak, screwing up a big client like that.

Cora hugged herself and pushed her phone back in her handbag. The minutes crawled by. Not a sound came through the oak door.

She washed her hands and listened at the door. Still nothing. She unlocked it and eased it open. The room beyond remained silent.

With her handbag clutched in front of her, Cora slipped out of the bathroom. The door to the hallway hung wide open, the light on the right wall flickering like a firefly. For a moment, she thought of darting out, but—

From somewhere behind her, Paul spoke. "How are you feeling?"

Cora jumped and twisted around. Her stomach lurched.

"Sorry," he said, stepping out of the shadows beside the fireplace. "I forget sometimes."

"No, it's my fault. I'm sorry," Cora said. "I didn't mean to—I wouldn't have—"

"I understand. It was my poor judgment."

"I'm so sorry. I never meant to be like this." Cora leaned against a low shelving unit filled with knickknacks from the Orient. "I must have eaten something bad, some shrimp. I try to be careful."

"Yes, your body didn't agree with something."

"I'll make it up to you, I promise. You've always been so generous."

"Perhaps. If time allows."

Cora opened her mouth to apologize again, but something in his face made her stop and made her stomach tighten.

"I wish it could be like when we first met," he said. "There was still time then."

"I'm so sorry," she said.

"There is no need to fret. We will settle this in the future. You have enough worries in your life."

Cora stared at him. What did he mean? Did he want to reschedule?

Her stomach began to hurt, though, and she pressed a hand to her belly.

Paul walked to the far corner of the living room, next to a large antique grandfather clock.

"It is better you go," he said. "It is hard enough already."

At first, Cora thought he meant his penis, but the feeling was all wrong. He wanted her to leave.

"Yes, go," Paul said. "You will need rest. Tomorrow comes quickly enough. A day for other worries."

Still uncertain, Cora glanced around the apartment. "Thank you for understanding. I—I really wanted tonight to be special. After everything you've done. This beautiful dress."

"You can close the door behind you," he said.

"Sorry," she said. "I'm so sorry."

He nodded and waved her out. She walked to the apartment door, trying not to look like she was rushing.

In the doorway, she stopped to say goodbye, but that seemed wrong too, somehow. Everything felt wrong.

As quietly as she could, she eased the door shut and hurried to the elevators. Once outside, she leaned against a tree and waved for a cab. For once, no one honked. No one bothered her.

During the ride home, she stared at her cellphone, expecting a call from Katrina any moment. She had a knack for finding out things quickly. But the only message came from Melissa, complaining about an asshole from Texas who thought deep throat meant sticking his dick through her tonsils. She wanted to go shopping too, on Monday, to find something for her niece's birthday. They could make it a lunch date.

Cora saved the message and massaged her temples. Her whole forehead throbbed, but the thought of swallowing an aspirin made her stomach squirm.

When she got home, she headed straight for the shower and spent forty minutes washing, scrubbing, rinsing, brushing, flossing until her skin hurt and her gums ached. After pulling on her night-gown, she sent Straw and Katrina the same text: *Finished early. Cab. Will call later.*

Over the next half hour, her phone chimed several times with a mix of text messages and calls from Katrina and Straw. Cora turned down the volume and buried her head in her pillows. What could she say? How could she make it all go away?

Finally, after the fourth call from Katrina, Cora answered the phone. She had to. She couldn't avoid it forever.

"You had me worried," Katrina said, sounding furious. "First you send a strange message, and you don't return my calls. I was about ready to call the police."

"Sorry, I wasn't feeling well," Cora said. "My stomach was really bothering me."

"You sound fine to me."

"I know, I'm sorry. It must have been the shrimp from last night, when I was with James. I can't handle it. I'll have to be more careful. I think I might be allergic."

"That's all?" Katrina asked. "What happened with Paul?"

Cora tried to think. "It was . . . different."

"What does that mean?"

"It's easy to misunderstand him. He's not like anyone else."

"That's still pretty vague," Katrina said. "What did he want you to do?"

"He talked and watched," Cora said. "Like he always does."

"Oh, I see. How did you find that?"

"Okay."

A pause followed. Cora picked at the folds in her bedspread.

She would work things out with Paul. He was reasonable. The evening had just been a lot of bad luck.

"So everything's good?" Katrina asked. "Alastair was satisfied too?"

"I think so," Cora said cautiously.

"You'd better be sure. I don't know what their financial arrangement is."

"Oh? I didn't think of that."

"It wouldn't be the first time," Katrina said, "especially if somebody has a reputation to protect. Never assume anything."

"You're right," Cora said. "And I'm really sorry about not calling sooner. My stomach still feels a little weird but a lot better than an hour ago. I'm sure I'll be fine tomorrow."

"All right, I have to go anyway," Katrina said. "But we'll talk about this again. You need to call me, I don't care if it's for five seconds. Especially when there's a problem—with him or anybody else."

"I know, I will. I promise."

Chapter 13

Teresa sat on the front left pew of her chapel, waiting for the Monsignor to begin the Eucharist. Above her, dark oak beams cut across the rounded ceiling, dividing it into a dozen sections, each of which portrayed a story from the Old Testament—the fall of Adam and Eve, the drowning of sinners in the great flood, Moses holding the Ten Commandments, David cutting off Goliath's head, Solomon threatening to cut a baby in half. Behind the altar, ten scenes from the Passion of Christ formed a large arc over a pair of large French doors, both of which glowed with images of the Virgin Mary holding the Christ child. More images of Mary adorned the side walls of the chapel, between the red drapes and the fat white candles, while in the back the red drapes enveloped a pair of confessional booths the servants used every day to seek penance for their sins, after which the Monsignor chose one of the women to serve as the communicant for the midnight Mass.

Today it was Maria—one of three in the mansion—who knelt before the altar, crossing herself, sweat soaking the back of her dress. As the chosen one, she was also responsible for keeping the prisoner inside the altar alive for the next twenty-four hours, a task she had failed twice earlier in the month. Perhaps she would be the next one in the altar, if she failed again.

Teresa nodded and caressed her crucifix. She could feel the prisoner's fear seeping into her chest, nurturing the darkness that kept her young. Siphoning the man's energy was much harder. Despite decades of practice and hundreds of prisoners, she could still only take a fraction of what she needed. The rest came from Father. He shoved it into her and expected her to thank him. He expected her to be grateful.

A whimper came from the altar, escaping through the air vents. The Monsignor squeezed his eyes shut and murmured a prayer.

Maria echoed him and crossed herself.

"Hurry up," Teresa said. "Enough stalling."

At the back of the chapel, a door between the confessional booths slipped open, and the Monsignor's head jerked up like a chicken. Teresa felt Mobius step into the sanctuary. She raised a hand to silence him and nodded at the Monsignor to continue. He coughed and adjusted the sash of his robe and announced the body of Christ while Mobius slunk down the center aisle and slid into the pew behind Teresa.

Maria said, "Amen," and opened her mouth to receive the bread from the Monsignor. After a brief silence, the Monsignor said, "The blood of Christ," and offered Maria the chalice. She said, "Amen," again, her hands trembling, and sipped the transformed wine.

Teresa glanced over her shoulder. Mobius passed her a photograph.

"This is the last one," he said. "From the doors at the side of the hotel."

Teresa eyed the picture of the girl with the blonde hair and black dress. It was similar to the previous two pictures, perhaps a little clearer, and she had her head turned to the left, rather than the right. She also looked more tired, something about the eyes.

"I've sent copies to everyone," Mobius said, "as you wished. The soldiers too."

"They must call immediately, did you make that clear? Or those idiots will replace this one." Teresa flicked a finger toward the altar, and the man inside whimpered.

"Yes, mistress."

On the rug in front of the altar, the Monsignor stood frozen, his gaze locked on the rich red weave between his feet. Maria kept her head bowed, her hands covering her eyes.

Teresa kissed her crucifix and slipped it back inside the bosom of her dress. "You'll patrol Sebastian's area. He can move southwards to overlap with Peter and Dmitri. Those idiots don't know what they're doing either."

Though Mobius's face clenched up, he bowed his head.

"You've served me a long time," she said. "That means nothing.

There's only what you do for me today and what you do tomorrow."

"My only concern is your wishes," he said. "May they not be led astray by the greed of one."

Teresa scowled, and two of the candles on the altar exploded. The Monsignor flinched and stumbled over his own feet.

"These hotels must be important," she said. "It's the third time this month. A clear pattern."

"With respect, mistress, the firstborn never spoke of a girl," Mobius said. "Not once."

More candles exploded. Teresa turned to face the front of the chapel.

"Yes, mistress," Mobius said and hurried from the sanctuary.

The Monsignor straightened up, his hands clasped before him, and began to stammer one of the Lord's prayers. Teresa returned her attention to the man dying in the altar, pushing aside the thoughts whizzing through her head—the girl, the Light—and felt the ripples of Father's anger coming from miles away.

Yes, he was always listening. Always trying to find a way in. But she would find the Light and destroy him before she ever let that happen again.

Chapter 14

The sermon had already started when Cora slipped into the sanctuary of the church. She wished she could have slept longer, but she had needed another long shower to rid herself of last night before putting on her Sunday best—a pale blue dress, white sandals, white purse, the silver necklace and silver bracelet that had belonged to her mother. Like most weeks, half the pews were empty, many of the parishioners old enough to remember the Second World War. Cora had heard rumors the congregation would have to merge with another in a newer building, but most of the parishioners didn't want to move. She didn't either. Finding a church where she felt reasonably comfortable had taken months.

Behind her, one of the oak doors creaked open. She stepped closer to a wooden pillar supporting the balcony above her and brushed a hand over the skirt of her dress. Two women in their seventies trundled into the sanctuary: the first, Mrs. Joyce Williams, wore a stiff, green dress and had pantyhose clumping around her ankles; the second wore a shorter dress the color of porridge and had dyed her hair a gruesome reddish-brown.

At the podium, Reverend McLachlan waved a hand to welcome them in. The two elderly women shuffled up the center aisle, turning heads right and left, and settled in a pew close to the front. A few people glanced at Cora too.

She stifled a yawn, crept over to the far right, and slipped into the back pew. In the middle sat an old woman wearing a tidy brown dress and a small necklace of pearls. The man in front of them stank of diesel and french fries. Cora leaned back in her pew, wrinkling her nose. Why did men think they never had to shower?

The old woman frowned at Cora. She put her purse beside her, pretending not to notice. The old woman turned back to the front, shaking her head, and Cora pulled out the book of prayers. Sometimes it felt like she could never do anything right. Someone was always mad at her for something.

At the front of the church, the Reverend slapped the podium, and she looked up, startled. He started talking about how he had stayed with a couple in Montreal whose son served overseas in Afghanistan. Together they had watched the news about the deaths of three more Canadian soldiers. Not their son but tragic nonetheless.

"We want to remember those soldiers and hold them in our prayers, along with all the dedicated soldiers who serve there. Every day they make sacrifices to protect the freedoms we are so lucky to have here. They struggle every day to give others the chance for those same freedoms."

The old woman in the brown dress frowned at Cora again. She flipped through the pages of the prayer book. Had she used too much perfume? She knew some people were sensitive. That was why she had only used a bit.

"It's important for us to pray every day," the Reverend said, "and allow our prayers to reach out to those truly in need."

He began to read a passage from the Bible, and the old woman returned to squinting at her prayer book. Cora brushed a hand over her skirt. Nothing was wrong. She simply hadn't slept well. Too many bad dreams. Too much unpleasantness. That was all.

~

Cora's cellphone chimed while the Reverend's voice boomed through the church, "The Lord will show all who seek him the light of truth."

She scrambled to open the clip of her purse, answered the phone, and hung up.

"He is compassion and love. He will take away the shroud of misunderstanding and reveal the true path."

Cora glanced up. It seemed like everyone had turned to stare at her. Some shook their heads. Some whispered.

Behind her, a man said, "Amen."

She jerked forward and glanced over her shoulder. No one was there. Her stomach twitched. Then her phone chimed again, and she fumbled with the buttons, sending the call to her voicemail.

Eyes turned toward her again. Didn't she have any decency? What was wrong with kids these days? They had no respect for anything.

Her hands trembled as she switched off her phone and closed her purse. The old woman in a brown dress shook her head and returned to the pages of her prayer book. Cora took a shaky breath and glanced into the back of the nave.

Nothing but shadows shifted along the wall. Big ones. Little ones. The rest was only her imagination.

~

Nathan huddled beside the TV and peeked out the window the broken screen. On the other side of Yonge Street, at the intersection, Blondie in the white pants shielded her face from the sun, giving him the death glare. Cars slowed down. She walked across the street and turned into the walkway for his building. He swore and tightened the bedsheet wrapped around his body. That was how she knew everything. She snuck in when he wasn't looking and stole it. She was the fucking thief, the angel of stealing.

He ducked down, scrambled to the kitchen, and freed his right hand from the bedsheet to open the drawer beside the stove. The utensils were armed and ready to go.

"Shhh," he told the drawer and slid it shut and paced in front of the stove—one, two, three, one, two, three, one, two, three—and pulled a mug out the cupboard. She was too close. She heard everything.

He used the mug to add water to the coffee machine and flicked it on. "You got a job to do, donkey man. Hup hup!"

With the tap still running, he grabbed the carton of orange juice from the fridge and dumped the contents in the sink. They always poisoned the orange stuff first so you couldn't taste it. Medication they called it. Good for you, good to the last drop.

Nathan shoved the empty carton back in the fridge and gave the finger to the floor. Blondie was down there with that fat fuck and his cabbage soup, making them run like dogs. But he would stop them this time. He knew what they were up to.

He eased open the drawer beside the stove, pulled out the forks, and spread them in front of the apartment door, making certain they were prong up. Like penises.

Which was totally gay.

Nathan darted into his bedroom and yanked a pair of Playboys from the bottom drawer of his chest. He rubbed them against his crotch but didn't have time and threw the magazines on the chest. The rest would have to wait. He had to get the spoons and knives and dishes and bowls ready, or she would break in and steal everything.

~

As soon as the Reverend finished the service, Cora ducked into the stairway in the corner and hurried to the basement. She sped through the room where the children used to gather for Bible studies and locked herself in the washroom on the far side of the kitchenette. She hoped no one followed her. They had the other washrooms, the bigger ones, by the main set of stairs.

Cora balanced her purse on the dispenser for the paper towels, washed her hands, and spread a layer of toilet paper on the toilet seat. It was easy to imagine everybody talking about her over tea and biscuits like a geriatric version of high school. No one had ever let her forget how Nathan had snapped during English class, smashed a window, and tried to jump out, screaming about the shadows. Even the guys who used to stare at her like she was a blow up doll turned on her.

"Watch your back, or she'll freak on you."

"Carrie, Carrie, she's so scary."

They thought they were so hilarious. She could still picture them standing by their lockers, snorting and laughing—

Someone tapped on the door of the bathroom. Cora froze, one hand on the roll of toilet paper. She waited. If she stayed quiet, maybe they would go away.

The knock came again, quickly followed by a third.

"Just a minute," she said.

In her haste, she scattered the toilet paper from the seat and hurried to pick up the pieces. The knock returned. She flushed the toilet, washed her hands, and wondered what was wrong with the person on the other side of the door. Were they deaf?

Cora looked herself over in the mirror, ruffled the hair over her left ear, and straightened her dress before opening the washroom door. Mrs. Williams stood a few steps away, scratching her belly and muttering to herself.

"Sorry," Cora said.

"Everything all right, dear?" Mrs. Williams asked. "You look awfully pale."

"No, I'm fine."

"You've got to be careful in these basements, all that dampness. It's not good for you."

Cora nodded.

"My son had to pull out all the carpet in his basement," Mrs. Williams said. "It was growing things. I always got sick when I went over. I told them, but they didn't listen. They didn't believe me."

"Really?"

"Marjorie always thinks she knows better—my daughter-in-law. That's why they don't come to church anymore. They always know better."

"That's unfortunate," Cora said.

"But I pray for them like the Reverend says. That's the best thing."

"Yes, he's very smart."

"We're blessed to have him here," Mrs. Williams said.

A pair of women's voices came from the front of the basement. Cora hoped they weren't coming to the kitchenette.

Behind Mrs. Williams, a shadow with a head stretched out like a platter flitted across the wall, heading toward the voices. Cora's stomach lurched, and she leaned against the doorframe of the bathroom.

"Oh, dear," Mrs. Williams said, reaching for one of Cora's arms. "Are you sure you're all right?"

"Yes. Just a little tired."

"Sit down. I'll get Brenda."

"No, please. I'm fine. I just need some fresh air."

Mrs. Williams peered in the kitchenette. "Where did all those silly chairs go?"

"No, really, it's okay," Cora said. "I just ate something funny.

Some seafood."

"Don't worry, dear. I'll get you one," Mrs. Williams said. "They must be here somewhere."

"I should have been more careful," Cora said. "You never know where it comes from."

"It happens to me all the time," Mrs. Williams said. "Everything disagrees with me now."

"I'm fine though," Cora said. "I just need to talk to the Reverend—before I go."

"That's a good idea," Mrs. Williams said. "But there's no rush. The Hendersons are probably talking his ear off."

Cora smiled and took a step toward the old classroom.

"Don't get me wrong, Dolores is a saint. I love her to pieces." Mrs. William shook her head. "I just can't believe she's leaving. I mean, I'm sure it's lovely over there in Vancouver, but—"

"I'll wait for him on one of the pews," Cora said. "You're right. I should sit down. I really appreciate your help."

Mrs. Williams blinked a couple of times. "Oh. Well, all right, then."

"I'll see you next week."

"Yes, dear."

Cora hurried through the old classroom and turned into the stairwell she had used earlier. Once on the landing, though, she stopped and leaned against the yellow plaster of the walls. Her legs felt like sponge cake. Her stomach gurgled. God, what was wrong with her?

In the basement, Mrs. Williams chattered with another woman, and Cora peered around the balustrade but didn't see anyone. Just a long, skinny shadow.

She shivered and hurried up to the landing at the top of the stairs and peeked into the nave. Half-a-dozen people still sat on the pews, and a few more stood by the main doors, talking. She moved under a lamp and pulled out her compact and checked her face. She did look a little pale; but maybe it was the lights?

A pair of voices drifted near the door, and she took a step back, not thinking. Her heel missing the edge of the landing, and she squawked and grabbed at the railing. Her compact hit the floor.

Still clutching the railing, Cora sucked in a breath and straightened up, her heart racing. The voices faded. She took a few more breaths to calm herself and crouched to pick up her compact.

The mirror had cracked down the middle. The wand was missing. She glanced down the stairway. Yes, there on the second step.

Cora eased down the steps and picked up the wand and popped it into her compact. She could throw it out later. She just needed to calm down. Breathe. Get a grip.

Back at the top of the stairs, she turned on her cellphone and saw she had missed calls from Melissa and Nathan. Both of them had left messages too.

"Hey, call you back later," Melissa said.

"There's shit in the fan," Nathan said. After a long silence, he added, "She went straight in. Red, yellow, green light go."

Cora closed her eyes and rubbed her forehead. There was no winning sometimes.

She deleted Nathan's message and called him, but he didn't answer his phone. She said she would be at his place in a couple of hours. She was just leaving church. Then she called a cab, and the dispatcher, his accent thick and goatish, said it would take five minutes.

Cora slid her phone back in her purse and peered into the nave. The people by the main doors had moved elsewhere. The rest were far enough away.

She slipped out of the stairwell and stayed close to the back wall. If only she had worn flats. Her sandals sounded like gunshots.

When she stepped into the narthex, a man said, "Ah, Cora. Hello."

She turned left, startled, but managed a smile. Reverend McLachlan clasped one of her hands with his meaty palms. He was a thick man with white hair and a tanned face that made him look like a Floridian version of Santa Claus.

"I hope you've been well," he said.

"Yes, thank you," she said.

"I know a couple of the lads missed you at the potluck."

"I wanted to come," she said, "but it's complicated—with my brother. But I really enjoyed your sermon."

129

The Reverend nodded. "That happens to all of us. Family's important."

"Yes," Cora said and glanced at the woman standing behind the Reverend. She had a beak nose and a hairy upper lip and looked at Cora with distaste, like she had a zit on her forehead.

"If you ever need to talk about it, about anything, my door's always open," the Reverend said. He leaned forward to quietly add, "You can talk to Brenda too, if you need a woman's perspective. She was a nurse, you know."

"I appreciate that," Cora said. "Very much. Thank you."

"You're never alone in this world. Nor in the next."

Cora smiled and nodded.

The Reverend reached out to shake her hand again.

"Your sermons always help so much," Cora said.

"That's good to hear. Sometimes I wonder," he said and laughed.

Behind the Reverend, the woman with the hairy lip said, "It's our boys in the war who need the help. We don't have nothing to complain about here."

"Yes, they're in our prayers," the Reverend said. "Along with all the people there, the children most of all."

"Yes, the children," the woman said, nodding fervently.

Cora took a step closer to the exit. The woman wagged a finger at no one in particular and continued talking about Afghanistan. Every time she turned on the news, somebody died. Yes, most of it was in Iraq, but they were all the same. It was one big mess.

The Reverend nodded goodbye to Cora. She slipped outside and saw a minibus for people in wheelchairs leaving the parking lot, while people waved to each other, and cars honked.

Cora turned in the opposite direction and walked to the far side of the message board that dominated the small patch of grass in front of the church, hoping to stay out of sight, but a man darted from the parking lot and headed towards her. He was in his early twenties and wore gray slacks, a white button shirt, and a bluish-gray tie. His dark brown hair looked like his mother had dangled a bowl on his head and cut around it.

"Do you need a ride?" he asked. "I think we're going in the

same direction."

Cora smiled, trying to remember his name. "Oh?"

"Yeah, I have to go to Scarborough," he said. "Do some stuff for my uncle. So, you know, I can drop you off."

"That's kind of you to offer, but I have some stuff to do too."

"I'm not in a rush," he said. "As long as I get there by three."

"Well, it's girl stuff."

"Oh." The young man scratched his head. "Uh . . ."

"Sorry," Cora said. "But thank you."

An awkward silence followed while the boy studied the grass. Cora wished her cab would hurry up and glanced at the traffic lights to the west, an intersection overwhelmed by a concrete monolith meant to be an apartment building. Thankfully an orange cab had already turned the corner and stopped behind a red Buick parked on the street.

"I have to go," she said to the boy and turned to leave.

"Maybe next time?"

"We'll see," Cora said.

Once in the back of the cab, she rubbed her for her head and dug through her purse for an aspirin. Why couldn't she have one day without somebody wanting a blow job? Just once? All she wanted to do was go home.

"Yes, ma'am. Exactly where?" the driver asked.

Surprised, Cora straightened up. Had she said that aloud?

"They tell me Skydome," the driver said and pulled his cab into a driveway to turn around.

"Yes, that's close by," Cora said and gave him the address for the grocery store next to her apartment building.

Chapter 15

Around quarter after two, Cora woke up, her head thick with the residue of dreams. The most disturbing had been Nathan sitting cross-legged in a cupboard, playing with himself, surrounded by bottles of cleaner, rubber gloves, and sponges. Eventually he noticed her spying on him and yelled at her, calling her a pervert and a bitch, which became even more horrible when she realized he had no voice. Someone had taped off his mouth. It was actually his penis yelling at her.

She walked into the master bathroom, took an aspirin and rinsed her face. Feeling somewhat better, she sifted through her closet and tried on several shorts and jeans and decided on a pair of white shorts and the blue camisole she had bought a few weeks earlier. It was Sunday. She was not going to clean.

Half an hour later, at the grocery store next her building, Cora picked up green beans, baby carrots, red potatoes, the leanest cubed beef, and two butterfly pork loins. She still had breadcrumbs and eggs at Nathan's place. Bananas and orange juice she had picked up the day before. But the green grapes were on sale, so she walked back to the fruit section and searched for a bundle without any bruises.

At the opposite end of the stand, a middle-aged man with a sunburned scalp and a red, bulbous nose snuck glances at her, the mangoes in his hands forgotten, and she moved to the stand of cantaloupes and the honeydews, more tired than annoyed, and caught his reflection in the window staring after her, next to a man wearing a black shirt and a big, black hat.

Cora fumbled with her grocery basket and turned to look past the sunburned man clutching his mangoes. No one stood next to him. None of the other half-dozen customers roaming through the front of the store wore a black shirt. None of them wore a hat of any sort.

She turned back to the window and leaned her grocery basket against the stand holding the cantaloupes and honeydews and took a deep breath. She saw the reflections of tomatoes and oranges and apples. She saw the sunburned man scurry toward the cereal aisle. Outside, two streetcars clanged as they passed each other, and people sped by on the sidewalk, some pulling out their umbrellas as a light rain began to fall.

Cora gripped her basket and walked past the deli counter to the dairy section. She picked out two small containers of low-fat yogurt—blueberry and strawberry—and hurried to the line for the cashiers. The rest would have to wait until tomorrow. She was late enough already.

~

While climbing the stairs of Nathan's building, Cora caught the smell of burnt coffee and ran up the last flight. She knocked on his door and fumbled with her keys.

"Nathan? Are you home?" she said, opening the door, and found knives, forks, spoons, drinking glasses, and marbles strewn on the floor.

God, not again.

She maneuvered through the mayhem of tableware, watching for the marbles in particular, and dropped her umbrella and the grocery bags in front of the refrigerator and unplugged the coffee machine. She also checked the stove was off and glanced in the microwave.

From the bedroom, she heard movement. "Nathan? It's me."

She stepped around the groceries and knocked on the door-frame of the bedroom. Her brother sat beside the window, wrapped in a sheet, his hands trembling on his knees, his feet tapping on the floor.

"I'm just going to put the groceries away," she said. "Or do you want something? Maybe some fruit? I brought some more grapes. They're really good."

He shook his head and stomped on the floor.

"Okay," she said and stepped back into the kitchen and put the meat and yogurt and vegetables in the fridge. She washed a handful of grapes in a small bowl before adding the rest of them to the crisper.

In the bedroom, Nathan swore. Cora circled the apartment and checked the bathroom and the coat closet. Other than the mess by the door, everything looked fine. Though where had he gotten the marbles? She hoped he hadn't taken them from any of the kids in the building. She didn't know any stores in the neighborhood that sold them.

She washed the bowl of grapes again and poked her head in Nathan's bedroom. "Is it okay if I come in?"

Nathan pulled the sheet over his face. She waited, giving him a chance to get used to her being there, and glanced at the Playboys lying on top of the chest of drawers. One of the covers was torn and dangled over the side of the chest like a sad flag.

When the jittering of his hands and feet slowed down, she sat down across from the foot of the bed and waited again, munching on the grapes. Nathan shifted away from her. He was still in a bad place.

Cora waited in silence. She remembered how he used to boast in high school about his big plans for the future. He must have told her a hundred times how was going to move to California and meet movie stars and learn to surf. Then he could say all his scars came from a shark bite. Cool, huh? Work was no problem. Everyone there was rich and wanted new patios and fences and wooden floors. And if that didn't work out, so what? He was ready for anything.

Except for what happened, of course.

The treason from within.

Nathan shook his head and muttered to himself. Cora nibbled on her grapes. He shook his head again and eased the sheet away from his face.

"I'm going to make your favorite soup," she said. "Just the way you like it."

"It's too late," he said.

"I'm also going to make breaded pork chops with green beans and potatoes."

"They're next door," Nathan said. "I can hear them."

"The neighbors?"

"They couldn't catch me, so they came inside."

"It was raining pretty hard," Cora said.

"She's got a secret, the way she does it," Nathan said. "Like a thief. The forks don't work with her."

Cora leaned her head against the dresser and waited a few minutes before asking, "I need some of the forks for dinner. Is that okay? Some spoons and knives, too. But the rest I can leave on the floor."

"They won't stop her," he said. "They're all in the shadows."

"Is there anything I can do to help, Nathan? Or do you want anything? A banana? Or a glass of water?" She held up the bowl of the grapes. "You can have these, if you want. There's more in the fridge."

Nathan frowned. "What day is it?"

"Sunday."

"No, not that," he said. "I'm not an idiot."

"Sorry, I didn't know what you meant."

"Just shut up, okay?"

Cora looked down at the translucent apricot polish on her toenails and nodded. Outside, the sky rumbled. Rain pelted the window and the cardboard she had wedged in the bottom since the stupid thing wouldn't close anymore.

After a few more minutes, Nathan pulled the rest of the bedsheet off his head and looked at her, actually meeting her gaze.

"Soup?" he said.

"Yes, I'm going to make a fresh pot," she said.

"No, that shit gives me a headache."

"What about dessert?" she asked. "Do you want anything special? There's still some ice cream in the freezer, French vanilla, I think, or I could make pudding. Chocolate mousse?"

"I don't remember," Nathan said.

"That's okay. Just think about it and let me know what you want. Ice cream or pudding."

"Pop goes the weasel."

Cora eased to her feet and paused in the doorway. What else could she say? What else could she do? Explanations were never as powerful as the random permutations of his brain.

"I'll be in the kitchen," she said.

"May the force be with you."

Cora pulled on the apron with the picture of a cow and scrutinized the soup pot she had cleaned the day before. Though the pot looked spotless, she rinsed it twice before filling it half full of water and turned on the stove. While waiting for the water to boil, she dumped the burnt coffee in the sink, threw out the grinds, and scrubbed the coffee pot with an old toothbrush.

By the time she finished, the water on the stove bubbled vigorously, and she added bay leaves, sea salt, peppercorns, an onion cut into wedges, two chopped carrots, a stalk of celery, and the cubed beef. When the water returned to a boil, she skimmed off the scum coming from the meat and turned the heat to low.

Her cellphone chimed, and she set aside the skimming spoon. The caller was Katrina.

Cora peeked around the fridge, making certain Nathan was still in his bedroom, before answering the phone.

"It's about tomorrow," Katrina said. "Mr. Big had his credit cards stolen, so he wants to pay the rest in cash."

"So you want me to text you?"

"Yes, but you can keep the whole amount. We'll work out the rest on Wednesday."

"Okay."

"Are you sure?" Katrina asked. "I don't want any more surprises. No more mysterious stomachaches."

"I know, I'm sorry. I'm feeling a lot better. Definitely no more seafood."

"Good. I don't like surprises. That's why we do things a certain way. It's better for everyone."

"Yes, I'll be more careful. I promise."

"I know you try really hard, helping out your brother and all. That's why I know I can rely on you."

Cora murmured, "Yes," and glanced at the door to the bedroom.

"Good, I'm glad we understand each other," Katrina said. "I'll call you tomorrow and let you know what Mr. Big wants. He wasn't sure yet. My bet is the Catholic schoolgirl."

"At eight?"

"Yes, but I'll text all the details later, so you'll have them when you get home."

"Okay."

"And tuck in early, have a long bath. Be good to yourself."

"I'll definitely try."

"Yes, do," Katrina said and ended the call.

Cora sighed and slid her phone back in her purse. Yes, it was always tomorrow. Tomorrow this, tomorrow that. She felt like she never had a day to herself anymore.

"Are you stealing my stuff again?" Nathan demanded, stepping around the fridge.

She jumped, startled.

He grabbed her purse. "This is bullshit."

"Nathan!"

He spun away from her and pulled out her compact—a new one from her stash at home—and threw it on the floor. The lid snapped off, the mirror cracked, and eyeshadow spattered on the floor.

"Nathan! Stop! That's mine."

"You're fucking calling them all the time, making deals, stealing my shit."

He threw her lipstick and mascara and tissues on the floor and then dumped the rest of her purse on the floor and stormed into the living room.

"I'm just making supper. See? The soup." Cora took the lid of the pot. "It'll be ready in a couple of hours."

"That's too long. Hesus is hungry." Nathan yanked open the door to the hallway. "Hesus be back. The gods are angry."

"Wait," she said. "It's raining outside."

"Fuck you," he said and stumbled on the marbles by the door. He swore again and kicked at them, smashing two drinking glasses. Shards skittered across the floor.

Still swearing, Nathan disappeared into the hallway and stomped down the stairs. Cora steadied herself against the fridge and pressed a hand to her face. Why couldn't they have a normal Sunday? Just once? Was that too much to ask?

~

After taking an aspirin, Cora changed into a pair of old jeans and the red T-shirt she had brought Friday and got the yellow rubber gloves from under the bathroom sink and the broom and dustpan from the coat closet. She swept up the pieces of her compact and threw them in the garbage and piled the utensils, drinking glasses, and marbles in the sink. With great care, she swept up all the broken glass, checking under the couch and the coffee table and in the corners. Glass had a way of getting everywhere.

She dumped the broken pieces in a thick plastic bag and pulled out the Dustbuster, which was tucked in the bottom of the microwave stand, and found several slivers of glass hiding against the walls and the cabinets. She swept and dusted a second time and threw the plastic bag with the broken glass in the garbage and tied it shut.

Cora returned the yellow gloves to the bathroom and pulled on the green pair for the kitchen. She rinsed the utensils piled in the sink and put the marbles in an empty yogurt container and tucked them in the cupboard with the cleaners. If Nathan didn't notice them missing, she would leave the marbles in the laundry room for one of the neighbors—maybe the Muslim woman with the two little girls—or drop them off at the Salvation Army. Somebody would find a use for them.

Cora rubbed her forehead. With Nathan it was always a gamble. He might never notice; or get really upset.

~

With the rain drizzling around him like a fairy tale, Nathan heard a snap on the other side of the garbage bin and clapped his hands over his ears.

"Why do you think you can hide?" the devil said. "You are a stinking fire."

"Go fuck yourself," Nathan yelled.

"I do not know why Teresa's men are so stupid. They should have found you a long time ago."

"That means get lost. Kiss my ass. Take a hike."

"Yes, very brave. Did you beat your little sister to have such confidence?"

"I'll use them all," he said. "Right up your wazoo."

"Time's running out," she said. "I know where to find them. I don't have to wait anymore."

"Yeah, and you can fuck your dog sideways."

The devil slammed into the garbage bin, and it lurched toward him. He flattened himself against the wall and scrambled to get his feet under him. The devil smashed into the bin again, and one of the corners smacked into the concrete retaining wall of the apartment building towering over him.

Nathan scrambled out of the gap on the other side of the garbage bin. The devil stood a dozen feet away, holding a black umbrella, and kicked the garbage bin a third time. He gave her the finger and scrambled up the slope of the driveway.

"Go ahead, run," she said. "It won't do you any good. They'll find you. I'll make sure of it."

~

Cora lay on the couch, dozing, when the door of the apartment burst open. She lurched upright, knocking her cellphone on the floor. Her brother slammed the door shut and glanced around like a bomb might fall any second, his clothes soaked, water dripping on the floor.

"Nathan?" she said, pressing a hand to her aching forehead.

He jumped and stumbled against the wall behind him.

"Are you okay?" she asked. "What happened?"

"Fuck you," he said and ran into his bedroom and slammed the door.

For a second or two, the words stung more than her headache, but then she fetched a clean bath towel from the cabinet beside the TV and put the towel by the bedroom door and hoped he would at least pull off his wet clothes. Knocking didn't seem like a good idea yet. Maybe in half an hour.

In the kitchen, she washed her hands and fished the meat out of the stock and strained it. After adding the meat back, she chopped a fresh stalk of celery, two leeks, and three red potatoes and added them to the pot. She also added a small bag of baby carrots and the last of the cauliflower.

While the soup simmered, she turned on the oven and breaded the pork loin and spread them on a skillet. Ten minutes later, the oven beeped, and she slid the skillet inside and turned on the burner for the pot of peeled potatoes. She waited another ten minutes before adding the pot of green beans to the stovetop and added noodles to the soup. Ten more minutes passed. She drained the potatoes and beans, took the meat out of the oven, and filled a plate for Nathan, sprinkling a bit of nutmeg on the beans. On the side, she added a bowl of soup.

She knocked on the bedroom door. "I just wanted to let you know I made supper. I'll clean up and put the rest of the soup in the fridge, if you want any more. You can heat it in the micro-wave."

Cora waited. The bedroom remained silent.

"I'll go in a few minutes," she said. "You can do whatever you want. But call me if you need anything. I'll be home."

Again Nathan said nothing. She stepped into the bathroom, swallowed an aspirin, and rinsed her face. Once she felt calm enough to return to the kitchen, she divided the extra food into two Tupperware containers, the smaller one for herself, and washed the pots and pans. She wrote a note reminding Nathan of the settings for the microwave.

With the rain still rattling on the windows, she retrieved her umbrella and stowed her supper in a plastic bag. She wasn't the least bit hungry, but she might manage a few bites later. She just hoped she could get a hold of Nathan's doctor tomorrow and find out what was wrong. Things couldn't keep going on like this. For either of them.

Chapter 16

Teresa stood in the kitchen on the first floor of her mansion, looking at the pots, pans, ladles, knives, onions, garlic, basil, oregano, and various other herbs hanging over the granite-topped center island, while a pair of old women in black dresses cowered in the doorway leading to the pantry and the wine cellar. In her right hand, she held a glass of red wine. From her left hand dangled the rosary she had taken from a dead Cardinal during the French Revolution. In those days, she had rediscovered the transient pleasure of decapitation and the taste of duck, pheasant, goose, and pigeon, even though she rarely ate more than a bite or two. Now, she didn't bother. They all tasted like dung. They all died too quickly.

She opened one of the ovens, still warm from the Monsignor's supper, and shook her head at the stench of charred meat. He called it well done, making excuses for his weak stomach, but she found the whole notion repugnant. Bloody was the only way to eat lamb.

One of the old women lurched into the kitchen, bowing her head, but Teresa glared at the woman, and she scampered back into the passage. Teresa traced a finger over one of the metal racks in the oven and thought of the kitchens her mother oversaw seven centuries ago: the baking bread; the spit-fired capon; the sizzling pig fat; the fruity pastries His Eminence had loved so much, next to little boys. Sometimes Teresa still heard the knives at work, scissoring flesh and bones, the ladles banging on the cauldrons, the thump of platters thick with meat. Sometimes she still felt the heat of the fires and the weight of the stone walls and the dampness of the cellars. Father had tried to destroy those memories many times, but she had never let him win. She would never let him break her.

In the midst of closing the oven door, her ears began to burn. The glass in the oven door quivered. She hopped away from it and slid her wine glass on the granite counter. The tingling shot down her neck and across her back. She dropped into a crouch, clapping her hands over her ears, and a screech like a wild animal ripped through the kitchen. The tempered glass in the oven cracked. Pots and pans crashed on the granite island and the tiles of the floor. On the far counter, the wine bottles exploded. She kept her hands over her ears, pushing out the noise with her own thoughts.

You'll get nothing from me. You have no dominion here.

One last iron pan rolled off the center island and hit the floor. Wine streamed off the counter in a row of dark red waterfalls. The servants wept and prayed to God, though neither would do them any good. They were only alive because of her.

Another minute or two passed. Teresa stood up, brushed her hands over her dress, and stepped away from the counter to avoid the wine spattering on the floor. One of the servants hovered at the edge of the kitchen, terrified to enter, but equally terrified to displease her mistress.

Teresa ordered the woman to fetch the phone. After a quick bow, the servant scurried into the dining room and returned with one of the portables. Teresa grabbed the phone and ordered the woman out of the kitchen. She bowed again and scurried back to the passage leading to the wine cellar.

Teresa pressed one for Mobius's Blackberry, and his voicemail greeted her.

Though furious—at his failure to answer—she simply said, "Check on Father. He must have killed the prisoners again."

She would deal with his impudence later.

~

Alex sat in his car, drinking a bottle of Hoegaarden, and watched the rear entrance of the Four Seasons hotel. Despite the wankers clogging the street with their expensive cars, he had managed to park on the same block. The girl wouldn't come back—the pattern was all wrong—but he hated driving around for hours on end, waiting for some mystical sign to smite him over the head. Now he had a picture—a solid lead—like all those clever dicks in the movies.

A foursome ambled out of the hotel. Two of the women wore

bright dresses and high heels, and the man primped himself in a gray sport jacket. The third woman, wearing a white dress that showed more legs than a giraffe, had blonde hair, but she was too old and too tall to be the right one.

Alex guzzled the rest of his beer and fished out a Stella Artois from the case in front of the passenger seat. After a couple of gulps, he tugged a large manila envelope out of the glove compartment. The computer technician had printed off thirteen pictures of the girl, and Alex stuck one of the smaller ones in his jacket, reminding him of the war when he had mimicked his buddies with their pictures of their sweethearts, real or imagined. He had never felt the same way about those girls, but he had tried his damnedest and carried around a shot of Betty Grable in a swimsuit for three years. At least she had reminded him of a world that was sane, the world before Hitler—before Teresa and Father came along and blew the whole concept of sanity to shit.

Alex gulped down the Stella and stuck the manila envelope behind his duffel bag. Christ, why did he have to think of that? He didn't need another fucking trip to the war. He didn't want to see his buddies getting their arms and legs blown off, the rats fattening themselves on the flesh of idiots and boys.

He shook himself and stepped out of his car. A gray Jaguar honked at him. He slammed his door shut and waited for the Jaguar to pass. Once across the street, he paused by the revolving door of the hotel. Sebastian had said the girl had run out the main entrance, which had to be where the monkeys waited for cars.

Alex walked through an underpass, past a pair of loading docks and a green dumpster filled with cardboard, and found the main doors of the hotel around the next corner. Three men stood by the doors, wearing three different uniforms: a white doorman in a gray jacket and cap; a Latin bellboy in dark blue; an Indian in a black suit, standing behind a podium.

"I need some information." Alex said. He took out the picture of Sebastian's mystery girl and showed it to the men.

"I'm sorry, sir. We can't help you with that," said the Indian man behind the podium.

Alex looked at the other two men. The doorman recognized

her, judging by his face. The bellboy, too. The man behind the podium was hard to read.

"I know how things are," Alex said. "I'm not here to cause trouble. I'm just trying to help an old woman find her granddaughter. She got into drugs, you know, got herself into trouble. You know kids these days. They're always getting into trouble. Maybe they have too much time on their hands."

"We still can't help you," the Indian man said.

The white doorman fiddled with his cap and pretended to eye the red Lamborghini parked beside him.

"I know you've seen her," Alex said. "On Friday."

"Then why you asking us?" the bellboy said.

The man behind the podium glanced sharply at the bellboy, who shrugged and looked down at his shoes.

"All right, I see how things are," Alex said. "I think it's a dirty trick to pull an old woman, but I guess you don't know what it means to respect your elders."

A flicker of anger passed over the Indian man's face. "We respect the privacy of everyone who stays here. Sorry we cannot help you."

"Well, if you see her, let me know," Alex said and snapped up a pen from the podium. "I'll make it worth it."

"Please, sir, I think it's best if you go."

"Of course, here you are." Alex took out his wallet and wrote down his phone number on a twenty dollar bill and threw it on the ground, along with a few more. "There's lots more where that came from."

"Sir!"

Alex nodded to the bellboy and walked past a black limousine pulling up to the doors and turned the corner back to his car.

When he reached the sidewalk, he stopped abruptly. Someone was watching him. A split second later, a blow hit him in the back and knocked him to the sidewalk. He rolled left, avoiding the stomp of a foot, and kicked his attacker in the shin. The attacker caught Alex by the leg and flung him a dozen feet, in front of the patio belonging to a small cigar shop. He rolled and sprang upright and darted to the next patio, where people scrambled out of their seats and backed up against the glass wall of the Starbucks.

From the sidewalk, Mobius ripped out a metal pole about three feet long. "This is my watch now. You do not belong here."

"You always were a cheap shot," Alex said. "A real yellow-belly."

Mobius scowled and pointed the metal post at Alex's head.

"Do you want to bring the cops?" Alex said and glanced at the people standing around like popsicles. Dozens more gawked from the patios of the restaurants further down the street.

Mobius twitched. Alex ducked and sprinted into a walkway paved with bricks. The metal post smashed through the window of a restaurant with a gray canopy.

On the next street, Alex darted around a cab dropping off a pair of women dressed in skirts that barely covered their butts. The cab blared its horn. He ran into another passageway, next to a movie theater, and stopped at the end: it was narrow, and there were no bystanders in the way. Easy to control.

Mobius stopped next to a glowing poster of Denzel Washington and glanced at his Blackberry.

"You're wasting time," Alex said. "We have a job to do. We all serve the mistress."

"Your words mean nothing. You are the viper, the eater of snakes."

"How long do you want to argue that? Another fifty years?"

"You won't be here," Mobius said and charged forward.

Alex sprinted onto Bloor Street, which had two lanes blocked off for construction, and hurtled the back end of a green Subaru, moments before it slammed on its brakes. He ran past stores selling clothing, shoes, and jewelry and turned into a side street empty of traffic.

After running another block, he no longer heard footsteps behind him and stopped beside the front doors of a chalky white condominium. Mobius lingered in the shadows of a clothing store displaying suits, holding his Blackberry.

"You are too late," he shouted. "Your boy was not strong enough."

"What the hell does that mean?"

"Find out yourself. Father is calling."

Without waiting for a reply, Mobius trotted back to Bloor Street and disappeared around the corner, heading west. Alex ran to the end of the white apartment building and turned eastwards. When he reached the next intersection, he stopped to dial Sebastian's number, but he didn't answer.

Alex sprinted past the Manulife Centre and a mix of other stores and restaurants, and then zigzagged through side streets where high-rises had not yet replaced the brick houses. Sebastian's apartment was on the third floor of a Victorian house with a green roof, above a store selling condoms and sex toys. The apartment was dark, though, and Alex kicked a fire hydrant. Sebastian turned on every damn light when he was home. Father had a way of crawling out of the dark when you weren't watching.

On the walk back to Yorkville Avenue, Alex stopped in five different bars and guzzled at least a dozen bottles of beer. Once he reached the corner across from the Four Seasons Hotel, he stepped into the shadows of a hair salon closed for the night and watched a police officer talking to an ice cream vendor stationed outside the restaurant with the shattered window. Alex waited until the officer walked into the cobbled walkway beside the restaurant before striding through the shadows of the stores on the north side of the street and pressed the button to unlock his car.

In the walkway, the police officer stopped to scribble in her notepad. A second officer stood next to the patio of a bistro, talking to a waitress. Alex circled his car and climbed in. Everything looked fine. No one had bashed a hole in his hood, which surprised him. The windows didn't have any cracks in them. The car even started.

What luck.

Fifteen minutes later, he spotted Sebastian's blue Cadillac parked in front of Father's building and swore. Alex pulled into the mouth of the alley and grabbed a beer from his duffel bag. On the other side of the street, a guard stepped out of a house with red bricks and green siding. He was a beefy man with olive skin and curly, black hair and wore a black flak jacket over his black uniform, a pistol holstered on his right side.

Alex hopped out of his car and rubbed his nose. The stench of rotting meat was thick enough to spread on toast.

"How long has he been in there?" he yelled at the guard.

The guard looked confused. "Uh . . ."

"Where's Sebastian?"

"He's still in the building, sir."

Two more guards appeared at the door, one tall, the other muscular, both wearing flak jackets.

"How long?" Alex demanded.

"Close to three hours," said the olive-skinned man.

"Just over," said the tall guard. "Three hours, ten minutes."

Alex swore, ran up the alley, and ripped open the door beside the loading bay. The stench of death made him stop, though. He put the beer bottle by the door and shoved it shut. Father was no game. He ate stupidity and fear for breakfast.

Two wooden boxes sat in the center of the loading bay: the first held two bodies, the second had one.

Alex eased open the door to the inner room, but the hinges squawked regardless, warped from when he had hit the door two days earlier. From a spot near the steps leading down to the dance floor, a beam of light cut across the darkness, shining on the cage in the right corner.

Was it the flashlight he had dropped, Alex wondered. Leroy might have left it as a joke. He was such a fucking clown.

Alex inhaled and slipped into the room. A sob came from the direction of the cage highlighted by the flashlight. The prisoner was still alive.

But where was Sebastian? Had he run off?

In the stillness left by the sob, Alex walked to the cage bolted into the floor beside the deejay's booth. The stink of urine and feces made his nose twitch, but he felt the woman's heart beating and the vague in and out of her breath. The prisoner in the far left corner was alive too, but her breathing came in tiny gasps and her heart beat too fast. She would not last the night.

On his way to the front of the building, Alex spotted a long shadow lying on the old dance floor. The shadow was large enough to be a person, large enough to be a man.

Alex ducked under the railing and stepped on the dance floor. Something scraped against the glass of Father's cage. Alex shook his head. Not now.

The air thickened. A faint hiss tickled his ears. Another step turned the air into a smoky grit that burned his nose. Alex resisted the urge to cough and circled the edge of the grittiness, his eyes watering, his brain screaming at him to run. He focused on the body ahead of him, hoping it was only a prisoner despite the black pants and the black shoes that clearly belonged to a man.

A nail of hot pain punched into Alex's skull. He lurched sideways, away from the glass coffin, and pressed a hand to his head.

"Go ahead. Do it," he said.

Another fiery burst cut into his brain. He fell to his knees.

"Do it! I'm tired of your bullshit."

Glass exploded overhead and rained on him. A spotlight the size of a paint can crashed on the floor, barely missing his head. Shadows whipped around the flashlight. He grabbed one of Sebastian's hands, but the rat-tat-tat of a machine gun came from behind, and Alex dove to the floor. Bombs exploded. Mortars whistled. Tanks roared.

"No!" he yelled and scrambled to his hands and knees and grabbed at the body on the floor. He was not going to lose another one.

The shadows screeched and smothered the light. He pulled with all his strength, his lungs burning, his arms screaming. He yelled and continued to heave. A loud pop filled the air. The ground shook. He stumbled and smacked his right elbow against something hard. A metal post. A railing.

Alex swore and grabbed the railing. There was no mud. No machine guns. No bombs. They were just a trick. Father and his fucking tricks.

A raspy hiss erupted from the center of the room. Alex hoisted Sebastian off the floor and staggered up the steps. A gray halo appeared in front of them. For a second, Alex thought it was another trick, but he plodded forward, and the halo grew brighter. It was the door to the loading bay. The way out.

Alex kicked the door hard enough to rip the bottom hinge free and staggered through the opening. He didn't stop until he collapsed beside the gray metal door leading to the alley, somehow protecting Sebastian's head from hitting the concrete, even though it didn't matter anymore. In the mercurial light from the alley, the terror frozen on his pasty face was unmistakable. His eyes glistened like hard-boiled eggs peeled of their shells. His jaw hung open in a scream that seemed infinite in its silence, his mouth impossibly wide, the jawbone broken.

Alex squeezed his eyes shut, trying to keep that face out—or he would always see that face, like all the others who had died.

"You fucker," he shouted. "You never have enough." He slid a hand over Sebastian's face and nudged his jaw shut. "You always have to take them, always the good ones."

Something thudded against the wall to Father's room. Sebastian's jaw popped open again.

"Go fuck yourself," Alex yelled.

Again he tried to close Sebastian's mouth, but his head rolled sideways and his tongue slithered out like a purple snake.

Alex slammed a fist on the floor and stumbled to his feet. He kicked open the security door and hoisted Sebastian onto a shoulder. This time Mobius would pay. He would pay for Sebastian and all the others. Alex would make sure of it, even if he had to beat that fucking bastard for the rest of his unnatural life.

Chapter 17

Cora woke with a start. Her phone was ringing. Where had she left it?

She slid out of her bed, sleep vaporizing, and realized it was already morning. Five after nine. She had actually managed to sleep through the whole night without any bad dreams.

In the living room, she fumbled with her phone, but she was too late. The caller had hung up. The ID said Dr. Goldman, Nathan's psychiatrist. She had also missed a call from Nathan and a text message from Melissa.

The text message said, *Men=shit-brains*.

Cora sent back a smiley face and listened to her voicemail.

"The Devil's fucking trying," Nathan said. "But I know her game. Don't let her follow you." After a pause, he added, "The soup's cold."

During the second message, Dr. Goldman's secretary said he had time to see Cora that morning at twelve, but she needed to confirm within the hour.

Cora opened the balcony door, letting in a refreshing breeze, and called the doctor's office to confirm the appointment. Today? Really? The doctor's secretary sounded annoyed, but Cora pretended not to notice. The woman might have had a rotten weekend too.

~

Nathan sat on a rock inside a large evergreen shaped like a puffball, watching a shaggy white terrier sniff around his secret entrance. The dog's owner was nearby too, a little Chinese lady who kept saying, "Come, come. No, no. Leave those," in such a mincing way the dog completely ignored her.

The dog finally stuck his nose into the Nathan's entrance and yapped at him. He gave the dog the finger. The old woman cooed and moved closer to the evergreen.

"Would you fuck off," Nathan said. "This is my bush."

The old woman gasped and stumbled backwards. The dog barked louder.

"You want a pissing contest?" Nathan said. "I'll fucking drown you."

"Beshu! Beshu!" the old woman called, but the dog continued to yap at Nathan.

"Yeah, shoo you little shit. Shoo!" Nathan said and looked around for something to throw at the dogbut only saw dirt and dead needles.

The dog yelped and bolted toward the west side of the Alexander Muir Memorial Gardens. The old woman cried out and hobbled after the dog.

"I hate their wet smell," a woman said, her voice coming from one of the bushes on Nathan's right. The woman from his dreams. Blondie in the hot pants.

"Go fuck yourself," Nathan said. "I don't believe in you."

"Yes, that is why you are afraid."

"Look who's talking."

"You are the coward who runs," she said. "There is much dog in you."

"You're a bunch of bullshit."

"The bull is fierce animal. He kills the stupid and the slow. You are both."

Nathan swore at her again. She moved toward a bush with pinky-white flowers, trying to block him in. He bolted out of his secret entrance and jumped over a flower bed and ran past a flagpole, through an archway made of sticks, and up a slope covered with wood chips. At the top, he darted across St. Edmunds Drive, giving the finger to a pickup truck barreling at him. It screeched to a stop, and he ran down a grassy slope and passed some bushes and trees where a homeless man slept on an old mattress. The next park had kids playing on slides and teeter-totters while tired mothers and a Filipino nanny rested in the shade, but he avoided them, staying close to the trees in the east side of the park. At the next street, thick with traffic, he had to stop and give them the double finger before they let him cross.

About five blocks later, he scrambled over a fence, gasping for breath, and landed beside the dumpster of a coffee shop. He didn't want to take any chances, though, and ran around to the front and ducked inside. The people stared at him, their drinks forgotten. He told them to fuck off and ran to the men's room. Inside, he found one urinal and one stall, the latter bright orange with graffiti written on the wall above the toilet paper: *Irwin loves pole.*

Nathan locked himself in the stall and crouched on the toilet. The minutes ticked by. Music burbled from the other side of the bathroom door, fighting with the drip of the tap and the gurgle of the pipes.

The door of the washroom creaked open. Nathan swore. He had forgotten to lock the door.

A young man spoke. "Sir? We're not supposed to—"

The blonde woman from his dreams interrupted. "I know this one. I will deal with him."

"Sorry?" the young man said.

"You can go to your counter. He will be gone soon."

"Uh, okay," he said, still sounding confused.

"Chicken shit!" Nathan shouted.

Sneakers squeaked and moved away, but the door stayed open.

"You are a fool always," Blondie said. "You see nothing. You help nothing."

"Yeah, and you're fucking ugly," Nathan said.

"There is no time left," she said. "The old one calls. The bringer of night."

"Shove it up your ass."

"You are full of many fears. That is his power. Like the stories of the Bible. The old ways. But you—"

A phone rang, interrupting her.

"Da?" she said.

A pause followed. The washroom door swung shut. Her voice came muffled from the other side.

Nathan slapped a hand against the wall beside the rolls of toilet paper. As soon as she was done, she would come back. There was no other way out. He was a worm on a hook.

"Then be a worm," he said and lay on the wet floor and wriggled under the stall door.

When he got to his feet, he stood by the washroom door and listened to Blondie.

"I try," she said. "These days are much harder. There is the shadow everywhere, always looking and poking."

Nathan glanced around the washroom. He had nowhere else to hide. The mirror only pretended to go somewhere, like a joke that wasn't funny.

The door to the hallway eased open an inch or two. He pressed himself against the wall beside the sink, one arm jammed against the hand dryer.

"Yes, I will call," Blondie said.

He heard the click of her phone. The door squeaked and swung open, hitting one of Nathan's shoes.

Without thinking, he shoved back. The woman made a sound like a startled squirrel. Her phone clattered on the floor. He hit the door harder, and she cried out, and the door slapped shut.

He stared at the door. Was it really that easy? Had he actually stopped her?

Then he remembered he still had to get out of the washroom and yanked on the door. Blondie sat on the floor, wearing black pants and a red blouse, leaning sideways to pick up her phone. In the sitting area stood a young Chinese man wearing a green apron, his face peppered with acne scars.

Nathan hopped over the blonde woman's legs, but she grabbed his right ankle, and he tumbled to the floor. Gold light flared up her arm. Fiery pain shot up his leg. She yelped and let go while the young man wearing the apron yelled too and fell against a table, knocking a napkin holder to the floor.

Nathan scrambled past the young man and barreled out of the coffee shop. Another man yelled from inside, but Nathan only ran faster, barely registering the words.

~

Forty-five minutes before her appointment at Mount Sinai Hospital, Cora finally settled on an outfit: a beige sleeveless blouse with a matching skirt, a dark brown belt, and dark brown sandals. She also slipped a pink T-shirt into a shopping bag, in case Nathan had any surprises for her, and moved her essentials to her brown Louis Vuitton purse.

On the elevator, heading down to the lobby, she received a text message from Melissa: *Lunch?*

Cora waited until she climbed in her cab to call back.

"I don't really have time anymore," she said. "I have an appointment right now."

"Don't you already have one of your specials tonight?" Melissa asked.

"I don't mean that kind of appointment. I have to go and talk to Nathan's doctor about his medication."

"That's fine. Today is kind of screwy anyway," Melissa said. "Let's do it tomorrow."

"I'd like to, but I'm not sure."

"Yeah, you have to see how your brother's doing."

"It's just been really difficult the last few days."

"You still need some time for you."

"I know," Cora said and peered past the driver as he stopped for a red light. On the sidewalk, a pair of Asian girls walked past, one carrying a camera, the other pointing at the harbor, and a tiny Indian woman with a beautiful face pushed a stroller over an uneven sidewalk.

"Who do you have tonight?" Melissa asked.

"Mr. Big."

"Oh, I remember him. He used to be one of Angie's." Melissa laughed. "She was really pissed about that."

"She can have him back," Cora said. "If she wants."

"Don't ever say that to her. Like never."

"I wasn't trying to take him. Katrina didn't tell me—"

Cora's cellphone crackled, and the call terminated.

"Shoot," she said and glanced at the screen. She hated when her phone cut out like that. She had meant to look into switching carriers, but the others didn't seem much better.

The cab turned right onto Lakeshore Boulevard, the Gardiner Expressway looming over them like an enormous concrete snake, and Cora called Melissa back. After three rings, her voicemail clicked on.

"Sorry about lunch," Cora said. "I'll make it up to you. Promise. Will call you back later."

~

Twenty minutes later, at Mount Sinai Hospital, Cora stepped off the elevator and walked to the reception desk next door to Dr. Goldman's office. His secretary was a small Vietnamese woman with a pixie haircut and a large blemish on her forehead, who always seemed irritated when Cora came to the office, giving her a tight smile that never looked quite right.

"I'll tell him you're here." The secretary picked up her phone, spoke a few quick words, and gave Cora another tight smile. "You can go right in."

Cora thanked the woman and walked next door to Dr. Goldman's office. He stood by the coat rack, pulling on a navy blazer over his pale blue button shirt, perhaps to hide the stains under his armpits or his bright orange tie, which pointed down to his bulbous belly like a glow-in-the-dark arrow.

He flashed Cora a toothy smile and shook her hand. "Ah, Miss Walters. How are you doing?"

"Well, thank you."

"Please, sit down." Dr. Goldman waved her to one of the chairs in front of his desk and closed the office door. Books and papers cluttered the shelves, file cabinets, both ends of his desk, the small conference table tucked away in one corner, and the ground along the entirety of one wall.

"I appreciate you seeing me so quickly," Cora said. "I know you're busy."

"That's what we're here for." He sank into his black leather chair and flashed his toothy smile.

"I just don't know what to think," Cora said. "Nathan's been more erratic than usual. I was worried it might be the medication." She went on to describe how he had scattered utensils and dishes on the floor and the phone calls about the dream woman, but she avoided mentioning the visit from the police. She wanted the doctor to help Nathan, not lock him up.

She finished by saying, "I know I worry too much."

"He's fortunate to have you, someone who truly cares about

him," Dr. Goldman said. "That's incredibly important."

Cora nodded and turned to look at a stack of books leaning against the wall.

"Does anything else stand out?" Dr. Goldman asked. "With regards to his behavior? Or perhaps something you feel triggered this recent change?"

"I don't know if it's because of the summer," she said. "It's almost July."

"Because of the accident with your parents?"

"He talks like he doesn't remember, but I know he does. You never forget something like that."

"Yes, I see," the doctor said and opened a folder on his desk. He flipped through some of the pages. "You've mentioned that before."

For a moment, Cora felt like she was fourteen again, sitting in the office of Mr. Dietrich. He had been the second counselor she had talked about the car accident and kept asking her about the giant serpent that glowed like the sun.

I know it wasn't real. Okay? I told you a hundred times.

Did it have a big head?

Can't I just go home?

Draw it for me.

"It's possible," Dr. Goldman said.

"What?" Cora said, turning back to him.

"Holidays can be difficult because of the emotions and memories tied to them. But ultimately it comes down to personal significance."

Cora nodded and scratched a birthmark on her left knee. Dr. Goldman coughed.

"It was a long time ago," she said. "Maybe he doesn't remember."

"Have you discussed the accident with him recently?"

"No, he doesn't want to talk about our parents."

Dr. Goldman nodded and scribbled on a notepad. "Yes, he's quite adamant."

"Would you be able to talk to him?" she asked. "This week? I mean, if you can. I know you're busy."

"When is he scheduled for his next assessment?"

"In three months," Cora said. "But he has his next injection on the seventh."

"I'll have JoAnn check my schedule."

"Thank you, I would really appreciate that."

Dr. Goldman gave her a toothy smile and scribbled in his notepad, then picked up a picture of a sailboat from a corner of his desk and traced the frame with his stubby fingers.

"If I remember correctly, you asked about transferring his case to another hospital," he said. "Something closer to his home?"

"I don't want to," Cora said. "I think you're a great doctor. But it's sometimes difficult to bring him downtown. He doesn't like it anymore."

"Oh?"

"He keeps talking about the shadows. How the people are so blind, they don't see what's going on."

"Does he do that where he lives?"

"Not really," Cora said. "Not the same way." She paused. "He did say something about a man's shadow a couple days ago, in the park, but I think it was because of the dog."

Dr. Goldman nodded and asked her a few more questions about Nathan's behavior in the weekend before picking up the picture of the sailboat again.

"Have you ever tried it?" he asked, showing it to her.

"Sorry?"

"Sailing."

"No, not really," Cora said, even though she had sailed with her father at least a dozen times.

"You should. It's very relaxing."

"I get seasick."

"Well, that's a shame."

"Yes," Cora said, feeling somewhat guilty, but she didn't want to talk about sailing, and she didn't want to think about what he was actually asking.

The doctor scribbled on his notepad. A minute or two passed.

"I should go," she said. "I've taken up enough of your time."

"Ah . . . of course."

Dr. Goldman stood up, grinned, and shook her hand. Despite the dampness of his palm, she held on till he let go.

In the hallway, she walked around the corner to the elevators and used a tissue from her purse to wipe her hand. On the elevator, an olive-skinned man wearing a white lab coat snuck glances at her breasts while a Latin woman with wild, curly hair glared. Cora tried to turn away from them, but their faces followed her in the mirror-like doors and the metal corners, so she opened her purse again and turned on her cellphone. No new messages.

On the ground floor, she hurried past the cafeteria and the bookstore and paused at the handwashing station for a squirt of sanitizing lotion. She didn't like how the alcohol dried her skin, but it was better to be safe than sorry. Moments later, her stomach clenched. She pressed a hand to her belly and caught a glimpse of an Asian woman wearing a black silk blouse in the glass of the bookstore. The woman hopped sideways and vanished. Cora bumped into a heavy black woman wearing a dark flower print dress.

"Sorry," Cora said and skirted around the woman and darted into the revolving door.

Once outside, Cora coughed from the stench of the smokers sitting on the concrete planters—a mix of visitors, patients, and nurses in blue and two different shades of green—and glanced over her shoulder. The Asian woman wearing the black silk blouse was in the revolving door. The woman from last night. From Paul's apartment.

Cora darted down the steps and stumbled on the sidewalk. People stared at her. One woman pointed. Another laughed. Cora hurried northwards, waving for a cab, and glanced behind her but didn't see anyone wearing a black blouse. Just a lot of strange looks. The kind usually aimed at Nathan.

Chapter 18

The doorknob to Sebastian's apartment snapped off in Alex's hand. He swore, whipped the metal knob down the stairway, and rammed the door, ripping the lock free of the frame.

Once inside the apartment, he paused and glared at the purple, faux suede couch, the puce-colored wallpaper, and the blank face of the TV. This was stupid. He wasn't going to find Mobius this way. It wasn't going to do Sebastian any good.

Alex yanked down a dark blue blazer hanging from the ceiling and draped the blazer on a chair in the kitchen. It had a beige paisley Arborite counter and white cupboards and a bunch of dead herbs sitting on the window sill, looking out over a tar roof spattered with bird shit. In the fridge sat a carton of table cream and an open box of chicken wings and french fries; ice cubes in the freezer; a lot of useless crap in the cupboards, except to the right of the sink, where he found a six-pack of Budweiser and three cans of diced pineapple.

Without blinking, Alex drank the first beer and threw the bottle in the sink. While drinking the second, he heard the door to the hallway creak and glanced in the living room.

"It's about time you showed up," Leroy said. "You're one stupid fucker."

Alex guzzled the rest of his beer and whipped the bottle at Leroy's head. He ducked and pulled a pistol from under his gray Armani jacket.

"Don't waste my time," Alex said.

"I don't give a shit what you do," Leroy said. "But if you rip this jacket, I'll punch you full of holes and see what Father does with you."

"That'd be a good trick."

Alex opened another beer and tossed a second bottle to Leroy.

He caught it with ease but kept the pistol pointed at Alex.

"I had to clean up your fucking mess again," Leroy said. "Mobius tried to make it my fault, but he had to get somebody to swap those fucking carcasses."

"You don't know what the hell you're talking about," Alex said.

"Oh yeah? Where's Sebastian? What's his car still doing over there?" Leroy tossed the unopened beer on the couch. "The guards said you shoved him in the trunk, real cozy-like. Guessing you still got him in there."

"I'm surprised they said anything."

"I had to knock some heads together," Leroy said, grinning. "Get them in the spirit of giving."

"Mobius won't like that."

"Yeah, like you give a damn."

Alex drained his beer and tossed the empty bottle in the sink. "He shouldn't have been there. He should have known better."

"Sebastian was just another dumb shit," Leroy said. "Get over it. They're fucking everywhere."

Alex grabbed a kitchen chair and whipped it at Leroy. He whacked it aside, and it smashed a table lamp. Both crashed on the floor.

"There's the door," Alex said, pointing to the stairway. "Use it."

"Is that all you got? Use the door?" Leroy shoved his pistol back in its holster. "You're one dumb fuck."

"I'm only telling you once. Stay out of it. That's all you gotta do."

"You've been with the old bastard. You know he's gonna blow."

Alex cracked open another beer and took a long swallow. Leroy shook his head and turned to leave.

"We don't know what's going to happen when Father wakes up," Alex said. "Nobody does. Teresa just pretends so you don't ask a lot of stupid questions."

"She's going to make you pay for that," Leroy said.

"If you're right about Father, it won't matter."

Leroy grunted and scooped up an envelope painted with hearts lying beside the doormat.

"Get the hell out," Alex said. "Leave his stuff alone."

"Yeah, yeah." Leroy ripped open the envelope and pulled out a card. "Ain't that nice. Somebody remembered your birthday."

He waved the card in Alex's direction, revealing a picture of teddy bears and balloons and a white cake with seven candles. Alex slid his beer on the counter and stepped out of the kitchen. Leroy's grin froze on his face.

Alex lunged at the birthday card, but Leroy twisted away and slammed an elbow into Alex's chest. He fell against the couch, tearing off most of the card. Leroy darted to the doorway.

"You're a fucking tool," he said.

"You've got two seconds," Alex said.

Leroy glanced at the chunk of birthday card he still held. "Yeah, see ya, loser."

He darted out of the apartment and down the narrow stairs. Alex grimaced at the picture of the teddy bears and birthday cake. Sebastian must have bought the card for his son. The poor schmo couldn't stop torturing himself. He couldn't forget his family. And now it didn't matter anymore.

Alex retrieved his open beer from the kitchen, drank the rest, and opened the card. At the bottom, underneath the generic well wishes, someone had written, *You threw away your chance at the hotel. Very foolish. One more chance to find her. Monday*—

The rest of the message was torn away.

Alex whipped his empty bottle aside, smashing it against the fridge, and bolted down the stairs. On the street, a skinny Asian woman walked a pair of brown dachshunds, and a man in a black suit talked on his cellphone. The intersection to the east was jammed with traffic. To the west, a blonde jogger wearing a light blue top and green shorts ran across an intersection empty of traffic, heading northwards along a residential street.

Alex ran to the latter intersection and heard the screech of tires. A black Mercedes disappeared around the first corner south, heading westwards. He continued running westwards, but when he reached the next intersection, the Mercedes had already turned southwards and roared straight through a set of traffic lights.

With no time to go back for his car, Alex waved at a gray cab.

The driver ignored him and turned into a side street. He swore and ran three blocks south, until he reached a busier street lined with condominiums and stores and restaurants. More cabs sped by, but he didn't bother waving them down. The Mercedes had disappeared. Leroy was long gone.

~

Back at Sebastian's apartment, Alex drank the last of the beers and called Leroy and Mobius. Neither of them answered their phones. Alex left several messages telling the cowards to show their faces and drove around Yorkville for half an hour, hoping to spot them, even though Leroy had no reason to stay in the neighborhood. He had probably gone to fuck one of his girlfriends or driven to his house by Allan Gardens. The latter would be stupid and lazy, but Leroy was sometimes like that.

Alex stopped at a beer store and bought a two-four of Coors and drank the first while walking back to his car. He drank two more while driving to the park at the corner of Gerrard and Jarvis and passed a greenhouse and a fenced off area for dogs before turning left onto a side street lined with detached houses, most of them built with dark brick and colored siding.

In front of Leroy's house stood two white vans: one on the driveway, one on the street. Beside the latter, Fernandez smoked and talked with a young woman wearing a short jeans skirt and a white blouse, her reddish-brown, frizzy hair draped over her shoulders, a bag of groceries in her right hand.

Alex parked behind the first van, earning him a glare from Fernandez. The woman turned to look too.

Alex stepped out of his car and slammed the door. "Don't you have any work to do?" he said to Fernandez. "Go find a fuck some other time."

Fernandez spat on the sidewalk. The woman backed up a step, her gaze wary.

"Get lost," Alex said to her.

She spoke to Fernandez in Spanish. He scowled and said something short and sharp. She turned to leave, but he grabbed her right shoulder.

She yelled and pulled away from him. Fernandez swore and

grabbed her again.

"Knock it off," Alex said, coming around the front of his car.

Fernandez shoved the woman away and fingered the revolver in his jacket. She started running, her heels clicking on the sidewalk like a wonky piston.

"If the police come, it's your head," Alex said and walked past Fernandez.

"You lucky," Fernandez said. "If only us . . ."

The front door of Leroy's house jerked open. Schwartz stumbled outside.

"Get rid of that idiot," Alex said.

"The boss told us different," Schwartz said.

"Mobius told you different. The boss wants to rip off your head and use it for a football."

Schwartz wiped a hand across his fat lips and glanced at Fernandez.

"What the hell are you doing here?" Alex demanded.

"Go inside," Fernandez said. "They fix you."

"Oh, yeah? How about you call Teresa and tell her what a dumbass you are." Alex pulled out his cellphone. "Here, go ahead. You'll find her under death wish."

"We're just doing our orders," Schwartz said.

"Shut up! We move the van." Fernandez spat on the ground, missing Alex's shoes by a few inches. "Like shitface wants."

Schwartz hesitated, clutching his belly like he had diarrhea. Fernandez swaggered to passenger door of the van and climbed in.

"You have one chance to tell me," Alex said.

"I don't know nothing."

The van's horn blared. Alex scowled at Fernandez, who sat in the passenger seat with one foot on the dashboard.

"Fine, get rid him," Alex said to Schwartz. "But she'll find out, one way or another. She'll make you pay."

Schwartz stumbled down the steps and ran around the front van, his fat belly bouncing like a beach ball. Fernandez gave Alex the finger and swore at him in Spanish.

Alex opened the screen door of Leroy's house. Why did Mobius always have to recruit such idiots?

Inside the house, more of Mobius's men sat on the black couch in the living room, flipping through magazines and books and sifting through Leroy's jackets. A fourth man stood by the front window, peeking through the purple curtains. His name was Tarantino, a husky thirty-something with slick hair and tanned skin who had joined the security force about ten years ago, after working in one of Teresa's casinos in Las Vegas. From upstairs came the rumble of more voices—perhaps two or three men—and the bang of drawers.

"Leroy's gonna be pissed when he finds you here," Alex said. "Especially going through his stuff."

"Orders," Tarantino said.

"He's still going to kill you. Or did Mobius forget to tell you that part?"

"We've got it covered," Tarantino said, his frown deepening. "You shouldn't be here either, sir."

Alex glanced at the men on the couch. Though they tried to keep their eyes on their work, they were watching his every move.

"All right," he said. "What am I not supposed to know?"

"Nothing, sir," Tarantino said. "This is routine."

"I guess that means you're going to my place next," Alex said. "Just make sure you do the laundry while you're there. I never seem to have time."

Tarantino returned a sour smile.

"You can restock the fridge too," Alex said and stepped toward the coffee table, where they had a notepad with numbers scribbled on it. One of the men on the couch grabbed the notepad, flipped it over, and kept his hand on top. He had pale blond hair and bug eyes, and the butt of his pistol stuck out of his jacket. "I'm partial to Hoegaarden. Sometimes Stella. You?"

"Sir, we're going to have to call Mobius," Tarantino said.

"Call Teresa first. She sent me herself, praise to the mistress."

All three men quickly said, "Praise to the mistress." The blond one eyed the front door, as if expecting it to burst into flames.

"Tell me about the numbers," Alex said.

The blond man turned back to Alex, looking startled.

"Have you tried them yet?" Alex asked.

"No, sir. We were told to wait," the blond man said.

Alex jerked the notepad from under the blond man's hand. Tarantino tensed and stepped toward Alex, but Alex ignored him. The writing, though difficult to read, included two phone numbers with Toronto area codes.

"Seems like a lot of trouble for pizza," Alex said.

"Sir," Tarantino said.

Alex crumpled the piece of paper and threw the notebook at Tarantino. "Stop wasting your time. There are more important things to be doing. You're just lucky I won't report this to the mistress."

"Sir, I—"

"If you want, I'll take it up with her," Alex said, "but I guarantee you'll still look like a bunch of idiots. She wants quality intel, not more of this garbage."

Tarantino nodded, his face creased with worry.

"I'm going to move my car and give you five minutes to get your act together. And you'd better pray that idiot Fernandez didn't bring the cops on us." Alex saluted the men. They mimicked him in an awkward way that reminded him of many of the boys who had their legs blown off in the war. "I'll be back."

"Yes, sir," Tarantino said.

"Praise to the mistress," shouted the blond man with the bug eyes.

"Yes, praise to the mistress," Alex said.

Once outside, he paused on the porch to straighten his jacket and wondered how long Tarantino would wait before pulling out his phone. Forever if he was smart. Mobius had even less forgiveness in him than Teresa.

~

The oily shadow slithered inside the mirror above the mahogany sideboard, and Teresa lashed out with her right hand, shattering the glass. A hiss reverberated through the dining room, and the shadow seeped into the window to the left of the sideboard. She flicked her hand again, and the window exploded, spraying glass on the terrace. The hiss deepened into a growl, and the walls trembled. A painting with a thick wooden frame fell from the west wall and knocked over the crystal decanter and candles sitting on the wine server.

"You have no dominion here," she said. "This is mine and will always be mine."

For several seconds, nothing happened. Then the oily shadow surged into the window closest to her, and she struck it with her right hand. The window exploded. Glass sliced through her dress and burrowed like maggots into her skin. She fell against a carved mahogany chair, and a cacophony assaulted her ears—the gnashing of teeth, the rending of flesh, the screams of people burning, the sawing of knives—overpowering the Tchaikovsky violin concerto playing on the other side of the room. Moments later, a dagger of pain slammed between her eyes, the mahogany chair snapped underneath her, and she tumbled on the floor.

Despite her fury, Teresa eased upright, holding the table for balance. The table was real, the rest meant nothing. They were mere tricks, an act of desperation. Nothing more.

The volume on the stereo returned, and the glass burrowing into her flesh fell lifeless to the floor. Her flesh wriggled, closing the cuts. Daylight flooded the dining room. On her right, a chunk of glass from the broken mirror crashed on the sideboard, and Teresa glared at the remaining windows, reining in the urge to destroy them. She needed to save her energy.

A servant wearing a black veil appeared in the doorway leading to the kitchens, trembling so hard she looked like an epileptic.

"Go!" Teresa yelled, and the old woman scurried out of sight.

Teresa sat on an unbroken chair and glanced down at her tattered dress. She grimaced and called the servant back. Two old women without veils came running. They bowed and crossed themselves.

"Get me a new dress," Teresa said. "And a phone."

They bowed again and ran to obey.

A few seconds later, the servant wearing the veil returned with a portable phone. Teresa called Mobius. "You need to check Father."

"You are wise, mistress. I was about to call you with word of him."

"Why? What happened?"

"Father has taken Sebastian back."

"When?" she demanded. "Just now?"

"Has Alex not informed you? They were there together with Father when it happened."

"That's not what I asked," she said, her voice rising in anger.

"Yes, mistress. Of course. But I only learned of it because of the loyalty of your security forces. They knew it was not right."

"If you speak another word without answering me, I will find you right now and make you regret it."

"Yes, mistress."

"When were they with Father?"

"The security men said it was last night, close to midnight."

"Yesterday? You waste me with yesterday?" She hurled the phone against a wall, knocking a hole in the drywall, and struck the end of the dining table. It jerked sideways and groaned.

Several minutes passed before she felt able to speak without killing someone. Then the servant wearing the veil appeared in the doorway, bowing and crossing herself.

"Get me another phone," Teresa said.

The servant ran and returned with another portable phone, followed by two women carrying a new dress made of midnight blue velvet. They bowed and hobbled around the broken glass and the broken chair and squealed in alarm when Teresa ripped open the front of the dress she wore. One of the old women pulled a torn curtain off the floor, cutting her hand, and tried to shield Teresa while the other two women helped her into the new dress.

Once changed, Teresa kicked at the broken glass. "Have someone clean this up. And burn that rag," she said, pointing at the torn dress.

Without looking back, she walked into the central hall, lined with paintings of God's destruction, and turned into the sitting room, which had a fireplace made of speckled gray marble against the west wall, a crystal chandelier hanging from a shallow dome, and three plush white sofas. Over the mantle hung the crucified Christ in bronze. A marble statue of the Virgin Mary stood before the largest of the windows, looking out over an arrow-shaped flower garden that grew along the cobblestone drive.

Teresa sat on the nearest sofa and called Alex. He did not answer his phone. She had a servant bring her a glass of red wine and sipped it before calling Alex again. He still did not answer.

She called Mobius. "Where is he?" she asked.

"The traitor?"

"You are riding thin. Very thin."

"He met with Leroy," Mobius said, "to make plans."

"Where?" she demanded.

"They are both moving quickly, after meeting at Sebastian's apartment."

Teresa hurled her wine glass at the fireplace, sloshing wine and scattering shards of glass on the surrounding tile. She had known Mobius too long to trust him. But was he the serpent of lies this time? Or the serpent of truth?

"May I make a suggestion, mistress?"

"What?"

"I will see to Father," he said, "and replenish the prisoners. Your security force can retrieve Alex. They know what they must do to bring him to you. He must answer your questions. He must be accountable."

"It sounds like you've been planning this."

"We must have answers," Mobius said. "Now, when it is most vital, he tells you you are wrong, that you must do what he wishes. We are to look away, he says, and Father laughs. You have felt him laugh."

Teresa glanced in the direction of the dining room.

"Tell me your wish, mistress. I will see it done."

"He has until dusk," she said and kicked the coffee table before her, splintering one of the legs. "Then you can send your men."

"Yes, mistress."

"And we'll find out if his story is as good as yours."

Chapter 19

When Cora walked in Nathan's apartment, she found the bedroom door wide open, his sheets and pillows tangled together on the floor. On his bed lay a black T-shirt and a pair of blue jeans stuffed with underwear and socks. In the bathroom, more things were tossed on the floor: wet towels, a roll of wet toilet paper, two bars of soap, an empty bottle of shampoo, the jeans he had worn yesterday, a pair of black underwear. The kitchen was tidy by comparison, with only a few cornflakes scattered on the counter and the floor, and a jumble of dishes in the sink.

After checking the stove and coffee machine were off, she knocked on the bedroom door and peeked in her brother's closet to make certain he wasn't home. She had a feeling he had gone to one of the parks. The weather was beautiful: sunny, not too humid.

She returned to the bathroom and changed into a pair of old jeans, a pair of white Pumas, and the pink T-shirt she had brought from home. She hung her beige outfit in the coat closet and swept up the cornflakes in the kitchen. At least the mess today was a normal mess; and he had eaten all the food she had cooked yesterday, including the leftovers in the fridge. So maybe it was better to leave him alone and let him come back on his own? His stomach was one thing she could usually rely on.

Back in the bathroom, Cora pulled on the yellow rubber gloves stored in the vanity and hung the towels and damp clothes on the curtain rod. She picked up the roll of wet toilet paper and dropped it in the garbage. She rinsed the bars of soap, returned them to their respective dishes, and stuck the empty shampoo bottle in the blue bag for recyclables. From the back of the vanity, she pulled out an old towel and used it to dry the floor.

With the bathroom restored to some sense of normalcy, she draped the towel on the rim of the bathtub, pulled off the rubber gloves, and washed her hands. After another quick walk through the apartment, she turned on the TV and searched for the channel that played top 40 but settled for the eighties channel, playing an old Michael Jackson song.

She dug out the green gloves from under the kitchen sink and washed the dishes and utensils, scrubbing off bits of potato and noodles and flecks of meat. Afterwards she stepped into Nathan's bedroom and picked up the pillows off the floor and folded his sheets and tucked them on the bed. She didn't touch the clothes stuffed like a dummy. Maybe she should have left the sheets alone too, but she had just washed them on the weekend. Hopefully it wouldn't matter. Otherwise she would just have to try and explain when he came back.

~

In the south wing of the Locke Library, Nathan sat in a circular chair, staring out a large bay window at the cluster of evergreen trees that blocked out the city. He wished more windows were like that. Trees never yelled at you or shit on your face or stole your stuff, even though they got killed all the time. That was why bums liked to sleep under trees. The animals, too—the raccoon and squirrels and pigeons. They were smarter than people.

Behind Nathan, an old woman coughed and rustled her magazine. A whole pack of them sat around the big coffee table, rooting through the papers and magazines. He wanted to tell them to shut up, but he didn't want Blondie to hear. She was outside somewhere, pissed off, waiting for him to leave. She couldn't come inside. She hated books. They stole her powers, like Superman and kryptonite.

The woman behind Nathan coughed again and pulled out a green checkered handkerchief to rub her pointy nose.

"Get some help," Nathan said. "You sound like a fucking horse." He covered his mouth and turned to her. "You look like one too."

Three of the old women glanced in his direction. One of them clucked. Another dropped her magazine. The woman who wore a small white hat with a bow on the front muttered and fumbled with her cane. Then they shook their heads and buried themselves back in their papers and their magazines.

From the far side of the magazine rack, a man said, "You need to be careful. The police have already come to visit."

The man wore black pants and a long black shirt and a big black hat that made him look like a Jewish Zorro, but underneath the hat he had a face that didn't want to stay together. Nathan scrambled out of his chair and darted down the aisle along the east wall, past a dozen rows of books.

When he reached the emergency exit at the back, he stopped abruptly. What if they were outside already, waiting for him? hiding in the shadows?

The man in black stepped around the opposite end of the last bookshelf, his hands tucked in his long sleeves.

"I know the last few years have been difficult for you," he said. "You are uncertain of what to believe."

"Fuck you!"

"Your sister cannot protect you forever."

Nathan grabbed a book and threw it at the man, but he vanished. Nathan swore and peered through the shelves. A teenager with wild curly hair, sitting at one of the tables, stared back. The man in black was gone. He was running around the building, trying to cut off the exit.

Nathan charged through the emergency door, startling two pigeons pecking at the pavement beside a green Chevrolet, and bolted across the library's skinny parking lot into a stand of trees. He had already figured out the perfect escape route. Those bastards would never find him. It would be way too obvious.

~

Cora took the cauliflower out of the fridge and broke off three handfuls and peeled and cut up two red potatoes and put them in pots of water for later. In the freezer, she didn't have much meat left, beyond a small lump of roast, and put it on a plate beside the sink. She would have to go to the market and pick up chicken breast, more roast sirloin, and sausage, though probably not the Italian one. It was too spicy. Nathan didn't always trust it.

On the kitchen table, Cora's cellphone chimed and identified the local library. She scooped up the phone. Oh God. She hoped it wasn't about Nathan.

The caller was Linda, one of the regular staff.

"I wanted to let you know your brother was here," she said, "but he ran out, uh, a bit excited."

"Just now?"

"Yes, that's why I wanted to call you. But I wasn't sure if you were in the neighborhood."

"Yes, I'm at his place. I'll come right down."

"Well, I don't think he's coming back," Linda said. "He ran into the park somewhere. I caught a glimpse of him through the back window."

"Do you know what happened? What was he doing?"

"I have no idea. He was sitting by the newspapers, minding his own, when he started to yell and ran out the emergency exit. The one in the back."

"I'm really sorry," Cora said. "It's been a difficult weekend. I just saw his doctor about adjusting his medication."

Linda remained quiet for several seconds. "I understand about his illness. Really, I do. But we can't have that happening here. There are other people to consider. I know you understand that."

"Yes," Cora said.

"Anyway, I'm sure you want to find him. I don't think he left with anything, but . . . well, we can talk about that later."

"Yes, thank you. I really appreciate you calling me."

"It's definitely more excitement than we usually get."

Cora thanked Linda again, hung up, and slid the roast in the fridge and washed her hands. She did a quick walk-through of the apartment. Everything was off. Then she locked up, hurried downstairs, and checked the back of the building, where the dumpsters stank worse than usual. For once she would have been happy to find him hiding behind the garbage.

She crossed the dead-end street and walked downhill to the parks. When she reached the wrought iron gate for the Alexander Muir Memorial Gardens, she paused to gaze across Yonge Street into the park behind the gas station but didn't see anyone. She walked through the gate and zigzagged along the paths, looking into the trees and hedges and larger shrubs. In the grassy area where the flagpole stood, a couple around her own age strolled, holding hands, and Cora asked them if they had seen a blond man wearing a black T-shirt and jeans.

"No, sorry," they said and disappeared around a growth of evergreens.

For another fifteen minutes or so, Cora searched the rest of the Memorial Gardens. She then followed a path down to the tennis courts where a group of teens clustered on one side of the courts, whacking balls at their instructors, and two women, both in their forties, walked past with their dogs, one large and black, the other small and white. Neither of the women had seen anyone resembling Nathan.

More people walked past, and Cora sat on a bench shaded by a large elm and fanned herself with her purse. Behind her, scrub obscured a tired-looking stream reinforced with concrete blocks, the water gurgling out of one culvert and disappearing into another a few hundred feet away. If Nathan was upset enough, he would sneak through the trees on the slopes of the ravines and go to the cemetery on the other side of Blythwood or to where the ravines merged into the tree-covered slopes of the Don Valley, another two or three miles to the southeast.

A man with salt and pepper hair, wearing gray shorts and a black Nike T-shirt, jogged from the direction of the ravines and ogled Cora as he neared. She checked her phone for messages. Once past her, he tripped and fell. She closed her purse and hurried away from him, heading toward Blythwood Ravine.

Beyond the tennis courts, the trail widened and passed under a bridge, the underside decorated with bright graffiti. On the other side of the bridge, the stream reemerged from another culvert and curved south, the path narrowing and sloping up to Blythwood Road. A school bus stopped to let Cora cross into the next section of the ravine. A woman wearing black spandex shorts and a purple tank top jogged in the opposite direction, a Golden Labrador trotting beside her.

When Cora reached the next culvert, she stopped by the railing at the top. The stream ahead was more natural looking, the banks mostly exposed dirt, some dead trees stretching from one bank to the other. She wondered if Nathan had ever tried to squeeze between the bars of the culvert and hide within the dark and dank. God, she hoped not. Why did she have to think of that?

On the left side of the stream, kids ran around a playground while women both young and old watched from where they stood or sat. A couple of men, too. The path on the right side of the stream was a flat stretch of gravel and empty of people—the obvious choice for Nathan—but he hadn't gone that way either. Cora felt sure of it.

She returned up the steps to Blythwood Road and eyed the school on her right, sitting at the top of the ravine, and the houses on her left. No. Definitely not.

Back at the tennis courts, she spoke to a woman walking a dog, a black pug, who shrugged and said sorry. Cora then repeated her search through the Memorial Gardens and came across the young couple again, this time sitting on the grass and kissing. She darted into a path covered with wood chips and followed it out to St. Edmunds Drive.

A silver Mercedes drove by and honked at her. She crossed St. Edmunds and walked into a small park shaped like a bowl, wondering why men never grew up.

In a stand of trees, six empty milk crates were clustered around a beat-up mattress. No Nathan, thankfully. She didn't want him hanging out with the homeless again, like he had done in Ottawa. She crossed another small side street and used the stairway at the corner to go down to the playground next to the library. Several children scrambled on the ladders and seesaws and slides while two mothers and a Filipino nanny watched.

Cora took a deep breath and asked the woman standing at the edge of the playground about Nathan. She had brown, frizzy hair pulled back into a ponytail and wore a pink top showing off plump, pale arms.

"Yeah, I think Marg saw him," she said and called to the older, brunette woman standing beside the slide.

The second woman pointed to the Memorial Gardens. "He was running that way, a while ago. When I first got here."

Cora thanked them and walked across the grass to Yonge

Street. At least she didn't have to go in the library yet. She felt foolish enough already.

She glanced at her cellphone and returned to the wrought iron gate at the front of the Memorial Gardens. She felt like she was going in the right direction again, even though that seemed strange. Would he have gone back to his apartment? Or the Tim Hortons further south?

Either way, Cora continued up the hill to Nathan's building. If nothing else, she could use the bathroom and take an aspirin.

In the foyer, she spotted a yellow sticker on Nathan's mailbox and found an envelope inside with his apartment number scrawled on both sides, no doubt from the landlord. He wrote like an eight-year-old.

She sighed and stuck the envelope in her purse and headed upstairs. She hoped he hadn't sent another warning. She already had enough of a headache.

While turning the key for Nathan's door, Cora realized it was already unlocked and knocked twice before stepping inside.

"Hi, Nathan, it's me," she said. "Are you home?"

She heard the creak of his box spring and locked the door behind her. Nathan sat on his bed, staring at a magazine and bobbing his head like he was listening to music, his top sheet wrapped around his torso.

"Have you had lunch yet?" she asked. "I can warm up some soup. I haven't had a chance to make the rest of your supper yet."

Nathan picked up a mug from the chest of drawers and saluted her. "Want some?"

"I'm okay, thanks."

"It comes from the fridge. No slaves."

"I was just going to make something to eat. Do you want anything? I could make some eggs."

"Sunny side up. Don't fuck it up."

About twenty minutes later, after Nathan had eaten and gone back to his bedroom, his bedsheet still wrapped around him, Cora washed the dishes and cleaned the counter and the stove. The window beside the stove looked dirty too and she pulled out the glass cleaner from under the sink. Her cellphone chimed.

"Hey, knock that shit off," Nathan yelled.

Cora saw the caller was Katrina and answered the phone.

"I was going to send a text," Katrina said, "but I wanted to find out how you're doing."

"I'm fine, I promise. No stomachaches."

"Good," Katrina said and confirmed the details for the evening: Sheraton, seven-thirty pickup, fifteen hundred balance. "And he decided on the Catholic schoolgirl, same as in March."

"Okay."

"Call me after."

"I will."

Cora put her phone back in her purse and took out the envelope from Nathan's mailbox.

At first glance, the letter looked like another list of complaints—the noise, repeated warnings, damage to property—but then she realized it was actually a notice of eviction and reread it in disbelief and stared at the scribbles that passed for the landlord's signature.

"That bastard," she said.

"Black or white?" Nathan asked.

Cora glanced up, startled. He opened the fridge, still wrapped in his bedsheet.

"Oh, it's nothing," she said. "I'll talk to him. It must be a mistake."

Nathan began to recite a poem about Jack and Jill, which turned obscene, and Cora blocked it out while she hung her apron beside the microwave.

"I'm going downstairs for a minute," she said. "Or are you still hungry? There's yogurt on the bottom shelf. Strawberry and peach, I think."

"Peach is the best," he said.

"I made sure to get one with natural flavors. It tastes a lot better."

While Nathan rummaged in the fridge, Cora stepped out of the apartment and took the front stairs down to the first floor.

Within seconds of knocking on the landlord's door, she heard the deadbolt turn, as if he had been waiting for her, and he stepped into the hallway. He wore a white undershirt stained with sweat and gave her an unpleasant smile. The stink of boiled cabbage and cigarettes billowed after him, followed by the shouts of his wife in Polish or Ukrainian. Cora wasn't certain what they were.

"You get notice, yes? No more crazy business. End of the month."

"You can't do that. There's rules, you know."

"He is waking everyone with his shouting. The police come. No more. He is done."

"You're exaggerating. He hasn't done anything wrong."

The landlord shook his head and leered at her breasts. Then he grunted and rubbed his belly like a demented genie.

"Better he goes. People come for him," he said.

"What?" Cora said, startled. "Are you threatening him?"

"All crazy. Better go before trouble comes."

Cora turned and hurried back to the stairs.

"End of month," the landlord called after her.

Back in Nathan's apartment, Cora locked the door and went into the bathroom. Her brother still stood in the kitchen, eating his yogurt. She had to sit down. She felt cold and shaky. Even if she could stop the landlord, did she really want Nathan to stay in a building with a man like that? What was she supposed to do?

When she could stand without trembling, Cora flushed the toilet and washed her hands. She checked the clothes and the towels hanging on the shower curtain rod, but they were still damp, and she washed her hands again before stepping out of the bathroom.

In the kitchen, Nathan leaned against the counter, reading the eviction notice.

"Don't worry," she said. "We'll find you another apartment, something you really like. Ten times better."

"It doesn't matter," he said. "The devil's everywhere."

"They're not all like that. There's lots of good people out there too."

"Gandhi my ass."

"I'll bring you some real estate guides tomorrow," Cora said. "You can look at them and decide what you want."

"Yeah, bye."

"No, I don't have to leave yet. I can stay if you want."

Nathan crumpled the eviction notice and lobbed it at her head. She closed her eyes and took a deep breath.

"Tell that dog-fucker to shove it," he said. "He's been letting them in, going through my stuff. They're always trying to get in."

"You won't have to worry about him anymore," she said. "We'll find you a better place."

Nathan shook his head and sat on the couch. After rearranging the bedsheet drooping over his face, he pulled out a deck of cards from the bottom shelf of the coffee table and started to play solitaire.

Cora picked up the crumpled letter and put it on the microwave and turned on the burner for the pot of potatoes. The roast would have to wait until tomorrow. Fortunately she still had a couple of cooked slices in the freezer, left over from last week.

"Fucking cheater." Nathan swept a hand across the coffee table, scattering the cards, and grabbed the remote for the TV. "I'm not playing with you anymore."

He pulled a corner of his bedsheet over his head and skimmed the channels while Cora wiped off the counter and the shelves in the fridge. He complained about the dogs, how Hollywood got them all wrong. The goats, too. They were too fucking nice. They would eat your face off, if they could.

The pot of potatoes began to boil. She turned the burner to its lowest setting and sat beside Nathan. At first, he pulled away from her, but then he shook himself and started flipping through the channels again. She collected the playing cards together and dealt them out for solitaire.

"No, you're doing it all wrong," he said and grabbed the cards from her.

Cora sighed and sat back to watch while he rearranged the piles on the coffee table. At least he was reasonably calm, even if he was wrapped up like a weird monk. She had to take her blessings when she could.

After all, who knew what tomorrow would bring.

Chapter 20

Three hours later, back in her own apartment, Cora pulled on a bra and panties the color of mint ice cream and a white silk blouse and took a black business suit out of the closet. When she arrived at the hotel, Mr. Big wanted her to look like hundreds of other lawyers and accountants in the downtown before changing into something special for him alone. Maybe he even thought he was being original. Katrina said he probably got the idea from television. In that way, he was like everybody else, trying to fill up their lives with somebody else's idea of happiness.

Once dressed, Cora slid a pair of black stilettos into a large, chocolate brown handbag, on top of her outfit for the hotel and started putting on her eye shadow. Nothing too flashy. Some caramel and soft brown. They would look good with both the suit and the school uniform.

While putting on a light rose lipstick, she got a text message from Straw: *Waiting*. She sent back, 5, and studied herself in the mirror of the vanity and adjusted her ponytail.

More or less satisfied, she took an aspirin and zipped up her handbag.

~

Straw said little during the drive to the Sheraton hotel on Queen Street, next to the new opera house. One day, when she had more time, Cora wanted to go to a performance, maybe a ballet. In high school, she had gone to Stratford to see *Romeo and Juliet* and London once for a concert of classical music, but she didn't remember much of either. One of her clients traveled to Europe every month or two just for the operas and classical concerts and theater, so there had to be something to them. He had even invited her to New York for a weekend to see whatever show she wanted, but there was no way she could leave Nathan alone that long.

Straw stopped the car under a concrete walkway that stretched from the third floor of the hotel to the public square on the other side of Queen Street. He drummed his fingers on the steering wheel, staring in the rear-view mirror like she might get naked or sprout a third breast. Cora ignored him and looked through her handbag.

"Are you going or what?" he said.

"I'm just checking my things."

"Whatever. Just let me know when you're done."

Cora stepped out of the car and slammed the door. He honked back and cut in front of a cab. The cab blared its horn, and she shook her head. Why did he have to make everything so difficult? He was such a little kid.

Inside the hotel, she paused in front of a glass wall beyond which a waterfall flowed into a pool and took a deep breath to collect herself for walking to the elevators for the top half of the building and waited with a chubby white man in a blue Hawaiian shirt who fidgeted with the handle of his black suitcase while his gaze darted back and forth.

After he stepped off on the twenty-fourth floor, Cora checked herself over in the mirrored walls of the elevator and turned her cellphone to vibrate mode. A few seconds later, she got a text message from Katrina about the money still owing.

Cora stepped off the elevator and knocked on the door of Mr. Big's suite. He opened it with a nervous smile and waved her inside. He was a squat man with a beak nose and large dark eyes who wore special shoes to look taller and smelled like an ad for Ralph Lauren. She kissed him on the cheek and walked to the beige sofa in the sitting room, where he passed her a fat envelope.

"I'm going to change now," Cora said. "No peeking."

"I'll try," he said. "But it's awful tempting."

She smiled and presented a cheek for him to kiss before heading into the bathroom. After counting the money, she stowed it in a pouch inside the handbag and sent Katrina a text message: *Yes 1500.*

Cora washed her hands twice and stripped out of her business suit and changed into her schoolgirl outfit: a green plaid skirt, a plaid button-up jersey over her blouse, white knee-high socks, and black stilettos. She had no idea if he was actually Catholic, but he beamed as soon as she stepped out of the bathroom.

"If you had cookies for sale, that would be perfect," he said.

"Like the Girl Guide cookies?"

"Yes, the vanilla ones."

She mimed giving him a box, and he laughed.

"You are a clever whip," he said and took one of her hands and led her to the couch.

She sat at one end and hugged a throw cushion against her chest. He poured a glass of red wine for himself and a glass of orange juice for Cora.

After tossing his gray blazer on an armchair, Mr. Big settled beside her. He asked about her weekend, if she had enjoyed the downpour and laughed when she said, "Absolutely!"

When he tried to touch her legs, she nudged his hand away and did her best to look embarrassed. She steered the conversation to his interest in photography and his most recent trip. To France? They sipped their drinks, and he talked about the girls on bicycles with their panties showing and the girls he had seen kissing in Paris and the girls sunning on the benches by the Seine. He had wanted to take pictures, but his wife used the camera too, so he had to be careful. He had enjoyed France more last year when he had gone by himself for a business trip.

"I love pictures," Cora said and fumbled with the top button of her blouse, even though the central air blasted the room with its icicle breath. "Geez, it's so warm in here. Can you help me? Just this one? I can't seem to get it."

Mr. Big fumbled with the button too, his knuckles brushing against her breasts, and she pulled away once he managed to loosen it. He started talking about the girls on the street, wearing skirts short enough to show the curve of their bums and their teeny tight shorts, and groped at Cora's knees. She pulled down her skirt to cover them and shook her head.

"I'm shy," she said.

"It's okay," he said. "That's why you're so warm, with that heavy skirt on your legs. You just need to pull it up a little. You'll feel a lot better."

"Oh, I don't know. I shouldn't."

"It's okay," he said. "Just for a minute. I won't tell anyone."

She pushed her lips into a pout and let Mr. Big's right hand slide her skirt up a few inches. With his other hand, he brushed her hair and wiggled her ponytail.

"I remember you love Japan too," she said. "You have the best trips there."

"I got a lot of good pictures," he said and talked about the girls in their starched uniforms, so respectful and obedient, not like the American girls. He especially liked the Japanese girls in the bubble tea shops in the ice cream shops. They seemed fresher that way, alive, authentic.

Cora let him loosen another button of her blouse but moved his hands back to his own lap when he tried for a third.

With a glow in his eyes, he squeezed her left leg and patted his lap. "Sit here, be a good girl. Daddy has a present for you."

"Oh, I love presents."

"Yes, this is special," he said. "Just for you. So sit on daddy's lap."

"Okay," she said and settled on his legs, and he dandled her up and down like a Wall Street version of Santa Claus. To keep her balance, she *accidentally* fell back against his erection, and he twitched and grabbed her hips.

Cora slipped out of his grasp and darted to the side of the sofa. "Oh, Mr. Mathers. I don't think that's mathematics."

"You're really good this time," he said and wiped at the sweat on his face. "Even better than before."

She wrapped her arms under her breasts, hugging herself, pretending to be embarrassed. Mr. Big clawed at the buttons of the shirt and unhooked his belt, and she glanced at the small green purse carrying her lubes and wipes and condoms. He was in such a rush tonight, already past the point of teasing.

He kicked off one of his shoes, and Cora undid the rest of the buttons on her blouse and draped it on a corner of the sofa. Mr. Big threw his pants aside and yanked down his boxers.

"Right here," she said and pointed to where she wanted him to sit. "Pretty please with sugar on top."

While he sank into the sofa, she retrieved a condom from her purse and kneeled beside the coffee table. She wrapped a wipe around his cock, and he groaned and groped her breasts. After several quick strokes, she dropped the wipe on the floor and slid a condom over his hairy shaft. Moments later, he squirted, and she winced.

Mr. Big swore, stumbled to his feet, and lurched to the bathroom. The door slammed behind him. Cora heard the taps running, more swearing, and the toilet flushed. She wasn't sure what she to do next but would have to figure something out.

The shower turned on. Two minutes later, he came back, a towel wrapped around his waist and grabbed his shirt off the sofa.

"Let's go in the bedroom," she said. "It'll be warmer. More cozy."

"Yeah, wonderful," he said.

Cora picked up her green purse and took one of his hands and led him to the bed. After some more nudging, he slid under the sheets and leaned back against the pillows, but he still looked upset. She sat beside him, her legs crossed, and toyed with her skirt.

"Do you know anything boring?" she asked.

"What?" he said, surprised.

"You know, the stuff you not supposed to talk about. Like economics and politics."

He snorted. "You want to talk about Obama?"

She shrugged.

"That would be different," he said.

He was quiet for a minute or two, and Cora wiggled out of her skirt and draped it over the foot of the bed.

"Have you been to your cottage yet?" she asked. "That must a good place for politics."

"Yeah, if you want to make a fire," he said.

She nodded and nudged him with a few more questions, and he said he probably wouldn't go to the cottage in Vermont this year. Too hard to get away during the weekends, and the kids were too old now. They just wanted to go to the mall and play on their computers. When he had been their age, he had loved fishing, even if it meant getting up at five in the morning and sitting in the rain.

While he continued to talk, Cora took his right hand and stroked his fingers. At first, it seemed like he wanted to her to stop, but he eventually settled back into the pillows and closed his eyes. He remembered his first trip up to Quebec with an uncle who went fishing there every year. Twice he ended up falling out of the boat, the second time with all the bait. It was years before he got invited back.

"How old were you?" Cora asked.

"Nine, I think."

"Did you like girls yet? Or were fish better?"

He snorted and shook his head.

"What about the first girl you really liked?" she asked. "Do you remember her too?"

"Who doesn't," he said.

Cora asked him to describe her. What was her hair like? Did he ever get a peek at her underwear?

"Nice try," he said.

She continued to caress his hand, and he talked about his childhood home in Maine instead: the yard, the bugs, the storms, how he used to hate clams and lobster.

"I haven't thought about that in a long time," he said.

"It's funny how that happens," Cora said. "Out of nowhere."

He rolled onto his side, and she let his hand settle on her legs and rub her in an idle way.

"There's something different about you today," he said.

"Oh? Really?"

"I mean more than usual. More . . ." He paused, looking embarrassed. "Never mind. That was stupid."

"No, it's okay," she said. "I liked that. It was sweet."

He nodded and squeezed her calf. Then he ran his hand up to her knee, and Cora glanced at her green purse, tucked between the pillows. She was glad she had left it within reach. The way things were going, she would probably need it again soon.

~

The next two hours were an uncomfortable rerun of Cora's night with Ling. Mr. Big's penis kept springing up like a jack-in-the-box, and he was always in a rush to shove it in her mouth or between her legs. She didn't want him to ejaculate prematurely, either, but he had to wear a condom, and she needed some lube to make intercourse reasonably comfortable, even if it only lasted for thirty seconds.

When he finally calmed down enough to let her ride him at her leisure, she dreamed about the long shower she would have once she got home, the water peeling away all the aches and unpleasantness, but her stomach lurched as she moaned, and her whole body tensed. Mr. Big yowled and clamped on her left breast. She yelped—what he probably thought was passion—and hunched over, nauseous.

No.

No.

For several seconds, he lay beneath her as limp as a doll. Cora pushed against his chest, trying to straighten up, and he sucked in a breath. She reached down to keep control of the condom and slid off of his wilting penis. Her stomach lurched again. Shadows danced across the walls. Gold light flickered over the headboard.

"No," she said and squeezed her eyes shut. Then she remembered the rules—*Never close your eyes*—and focused on pulling tissues from the box on the nightstand and a wipe from between the pillows and tossed the condom in the garbage.

After taking a shaky breath, she said, "I'm going to hop in the shower."

Mr. Big groaned, his face pale, and wobbled his head. She pretended not to notice and grabbed her green purse and her handbag and locked herself in the bathroom.

Once her breathing calmed down, she stood, flushed the toilet, and washed her hands. She balled up her hair. In the shower, she scrubbed her groin and belly and thighs with a fresh bar of soap. When she stepped out of the shower, a few minutes later, she still felt him on her skin, but she didn't want to take any chances. She would worry about the rest when she got home.

From her handbag, Cora dug out a fresh pair of green panties and a matching bra. The business suit felt cold and clean. Everything was normal. She hadn't been sick. Things had worked out fine.

She smoothed back her hair and pulled it into a ponytail. Since her cellphone had no new messages, she sent Straw a text message: *Leaving 10*.

In the bedroom, Mr. Big lay with his eyes closed and didn't seem to notice as she came out of the bathroom. She eased closer and waited. He didn't move. She tiptoed around the bed and cleaned up several condom wrappers and tissues from the floor and tied up the garbage bag. He groaned and rolled on his side.

Back in the bathroom, Cora washed her hands and fiddled with her ponytail. She checked to make certain she had all her things, including the money in the pocket of her handbag, and slipped into her shoes. Then she washed her hands again, tiptoed through the bedroom, and slipped out of the suite.

~

On the elevator, Cora checked her cellphone again. Straw had not replied to her message yet, but she didn't care. She would take a cab. It was less trouble anyway. Less annoying.

The elevator binged, and a middle-aged couple stepped on. They avoided looking at her but stared out of the corners of their eyes. She fiddled with her phone and glanced at the mirrored wall on her right and patted her hair.

When the elevator reached the main floor, she waited for them to step off and lingered by the elevators until they passed an area sectioned off for a dozen or so computers by dividers that reminded Cora of IKEA. The couple continued straight ahead, cutting through the center of the lobby, toward the bar. She turned left, her stomach fluttering, and started walking faster, hoping Straw was parked by the entrance she had used earlier.

Ahead of her, a man yelled, "Get the fuck out of my face."

She stopped and saw the man shove a woman against the glass wall facing the waterfall. He wore a gray Armani suit and black wing tips and had a bald head, pale and knobby like a peeled potato. The woman was in her thirties, had long frizzy brown hair, and wore a black top with a fat frill that made her breasts look like a pair of saggy balloons.

The man cursed again, and Cora backed into an armchair. He

turned and glared at her, his eyes black holes. Her stomach lurched.

"Leroy!" the brunette yelled and grabbed the man's arm.

He flung her against the glass wall, and she cried out and tumbled to the stone floor. Shadows slithered around him and squealed. Shouts and running feet filled the hotel. Cora wanted to run too, but her legs refused.

And then she was too late. The man in the Armani suit stormed towards her, hate blazing from him like a blowtorch.

A table lamp hurtled from the center of the lobby and smashed against his head. A second lamp shattered against his pelvis. The man roared and grabbed an armchair and hurled it into the center of the lobby, but the chair veered sideways and smashed into the wooden panels covering the bottom half of a pillar.

A dark-skinned man in a black uniform shouted as he ran past Cora. She stumbled backwards. Run, she thought. Run!

The man in the Armani suit boxed the security guard in the head, and he crashed to the floor. A second security guard ran past her. She turned and darted to the opposite end of the lobby. Another lamp smashed against the man in the Armani suit. He swore and charged the second guard and threw him on an end table, snapping the legs.

Cora veered away from a cluster of Japanese people staring at the fight but tripped on a suitcase and tumbled to her knees.

Next to her, a man swore. She struggled to stand, her knees flaring with pain.

"Easy now, darlin'," the man said and reached out to help her. He was in his fifties with a pinched face and shaggy mustache and wore a beige suit that had gone out of style decades ago.

Cora pulled away from him and looked over her shoulder. Where was the man in the Armani suit? Where had he gone?

All around the lobby, people yammered and pointed. Shouts came from the glass wall surrounding the waterfall and the pool. People clustered around the security guards lying on the floor.

"You best sit, darlin'," said the man with the mustache. "You took a fine spill."

"No, I'm okay," she said, still looking around the lobby. "Where is he? The one who started the fight? What happened?"

"He ran off." The man pointed to the exit the Cora had wanted to use. "Bolted out them doors."

Hotel employees carrying towels and an emergency kit ran to help the fallen guards while a couple of the Japanese tourists took pictures with their cameras.

"Don't you worry your pretty little head," said the man with the mustache. "He's good and gone."

Cora nodded vaguely and crouched to pick up her handbag.

"Here, let me help with that," he said.

She pulled it away from him and leaned against the back of an armchair, dizzy.

"Easy, darlin'. Just sit down."

"No, I'm fine, really."

The man frowned and eyed the swirl of people around the injured security guards.

"Don't that beat all," he said.

Cora followed his gaze. The brunette wearing the black frilled blouse sat in a wicker chair, holding a cloth to her face, and swore loudly at the hotel employees hovering around her. Another employee, a young woman with long dark hair and dressed in a blue uniform, hurried to the Japanese pair snapping photographs.

The man with the mustache turned back to Cora. "What's your name, darlin'?"

For a second or two, she stared at him. She glanced around the lobby. Hotel employees ran back and forth, people hovered and gawked, sirens whirred outside the hotel, getting closer every second. They would all want to know her name. They would want to know who she was and what she was doing at the hotel.

"Sorry, I—I need to find a washroom," Cora said. "Do you know where it is?"

"I'm guessing the bar," the man said.

She pressed her lips together, attempting a smile. Dozens of people stood in the bar, gawking into the lobby. Too many people. Too many questions.

"I can give you a hand. Walking, I mean." The man with the mustache smiled, embarrassed.

"Thanks. I'll be okay."

"No trouble, darlin'. Don't want you falling and hurting yourself."

Cora nodded, her gaze drifting to the escalators. One set led up to the mezzanine, the other down to the conference level. She was pretty sure the latter had a washroom. Katrina had mentioned it half a year ago for Cora's first visit to the Sheraton. Convenient and discrete.

The man with the mustache started to talk again. Cora nodded again and walked toward the escalators. He made an annoyed noise and followed her, nudging past two middle-aged women dressed in jeans and dark jackets.

"Where you going?" he asked.

"I'm all right," she said. "Thank you for your help."

A security guard stepped in front of her, blocking her way to the escalators. He was a dark-skinned Indian man with a chubby face and a bulbous nose. His dark hair was combed back with gel and his dark eyes darted around nervously.

"Everything is under control," the guard said. "In a minute, the police will be here."

"The washrooms," Cora said. "Are they . . . ?" She pointed to the escalator behind him.

"Uh, yes," he said. "But come back directly. The police will wish to talk to everyone."

The man with the mustache said, "I'll show her down. She's still shaky."

Cora tried to catch the eye of the security guard and shook her head a little. He didn't seem to notice, though, or didn't understand.

"Yes, go now," he said.

"You should wait here," Cora said to the mustached man. "I know you saw everything. They'll want to talk to you first."

He stared at her, his mouth sagging open.

"Was he with you in the bar?" Cora said. "Did you get his name?"

"You know who did this?" the security guard demanded and stepped towards the man with the mustache.

"No!" he said.

"I'll be right back," Cora said.

The man with a mustache sputtered and shook his head. He had no idea what she was talking about. He didn't know anything. She was crazy.

Cora stepped on the escalator and leaned against the railing. Her legs began to tremble. She didn't look back.

At the bottom of the escalator, the hotel opened into a network of tunnels that cut underneath downtown Toronto, full of shops closed for the night. And a way out. But first she needed to find the washroom. Where was it? She saw the men's behind the escalators, next to a door labeled VIP. Nothing that said LADIES.

Cora clutched the gleaming metal railing on the right side of the escalators as she walked toward the two doors. Further right, next to the elevators, she spotted a second washroom.

Oh, God, thank you.

With her legs feeling like month-old celery, she hurried through the door of the ladies' room and ducked into the last stall. Her head spun. Her stomach churned. She dropped her handbag on the floor, sat on the toilet lid, and closed her eyes and rubbed her arms. Sweat peppered her forehead. Her throat stung.

A few stalls away, a toilet flushed. Cora hugged herself and listened to the clack of a door, the clip-clop of heels, and the gush of water from a tap.

The dryer turned on and off.

The heels clopped out of the washroom.

Cora dug out her pink purse from the handbag and rooted through the lipsticks, lip gloss, compact, and Certs and pulled out a bottle of aspirins. She struggled with the childproof cap. Why didn't they open when you needed them to open? She had to take something. Anything.

The cap popped off, and a score of white pills skittered across the tile floor.

"No!"

She clapped a hand over the bottle and stared at the pills on the floor, tempted for a moment to pick one of them up. Then she shuddered and closed her eyes. What was she thinking?

Cora took a deep breath and glanced in the bottle. She still had three aspirins left. That was enough. Enough to help her calm down.

After swallowing one of the pills, she tucked the pink purse within the folds of her plaid skirt and took out her cellphone. It showed no new messages.

She pressed three, and Katrina answered after three rings.

"Thank God, I thought you wouldn't answer," Cora said.

"Why? What's wrong? Where are you?"

"I thought he was going to come after me. He was crazy. He just started attacking everyone."

"Tell me where you are," Katrina said. "Tell me exactly. Right now."

"In the washroom, the one downstairs. The one you told me about."

"What do you mean? In the suite? Where's Mr. Big?"

"No, under the lobby. I had to get away from them, all those people."

"You mean down the escalators? Next to the PATH?"

"Yes, I remembered what you said. It was a good place to go, if I needed it."

"So you're alone? You're safe?"

"I don't know. I think so."

"Have you called Straw?"

"No, he wouldn't answer," Cora said. "I tried."

"I'll fix that."

"I'm sorry. I didn't mean to—"

"Don't worry," Katrina said. "I'll take care of it. He's just being a stupid prick. I'll call him right now and tell him to meet you."

"But I can't go back upstairs. It's full of people. And the police must be coming. There was a big fight, right in the middle of the lobby. People started taking pictures. I just had to get away."

After a long pause, Katrina said, "Relax. Straw will meet you in the parking lot under Nathan Phillips Square. It should be around the corner from you. There's a short hallway with a bunch of doors. Just go into the PATH and you should see it."

"You mean where the stores are?"

"Yes," Katrina said. "It's easy. I'll call Straw right now and tell him to meet you in five minutes."

Two minutes later, Cora received a pair of text messages—one from Straw, one from Katrina—both confirming Straw's imminent arrival. Cora crept out of the bathroom stall and washed her hands and straightened the jacket and skirt of her business suit. Her stomach still squirmed, but at least she didn't have to go far. No one was around.

"Go," a voice whispered.

Cora pivoted toward the stalls and stumbled against the counter. In the mirror, she caught a flicker of movement, something black and human-like. But there was no one in front of her. The stalls were silent.

Cora grabbed her handbag from the counter and bolted out of the washroom. After passing the escalators, she darted through one of the openings that led into the PATH. At first, she continued straight ahead, but the passage led into a cafeteria full of fast food outlets, and she realized how stupid she was and backtracked to the hotel.

This time, she stopped to take a proper look at the different hallways. The garage was to the right, and she struggled through two sets of doors that were labeled push when she pulled and pull when she pushed.

Thankfully the last set of doors slid open on their own, and a black sedan waited for her on the other side. She felt such a rush of relief she became dizzy and had to lean against the sedan.

The relief vaporized when she grabbed the door handle. It was locked.

Cora rapped on the window and tried to open the back door again. A few seconds later, she heard a click. Straw was such an asshole. She was never going anywhere with him again. She didn't care what Katrina said.

Cora's stomach clenched as she opened the back door. About forty feet away, a pale bald head popped up between two cars parked beside the ramp leading down to the second level. She sprang into the sedan and yanked the door shut. It was the man in the Armani suit.

"What the fuck is wrong with you?" Straw said, scowling over his shoulder.

"Just drive! Hurry!"

"Not until you tell me what's going on."

"Go! He's right there."

"You girls are all fucked up," Straw said. "I don't know why Kat puts up with you."

Cora peered out the tinted window that faced the ramp but didn't see the bald head anymore. Where was he? Was he in one of the cars?

Straw muttered a curse and shifted the sedan into drive. She ducked and waited until they pulled up to one of the pay booths before peering out the tinted rear window.

A silver Cadillac pulled up behind them. Cora's heart jolted. The driver seemed to be tanned with black hair—Spanish, Latin, something like that—but was there someone in the back seat? Was he alone?

"Yeah, you completely lost it," Straw said.

Cora pressed a hand to her stomach. A green car blared its horn. Tires squealed somewhere deeper in the garage.

Straw collected his change from the woman in the pay booth and turned left into the exit for Queen Street. When they reached the surface, a police car with its lights blazing made a U-turn in front of them and pulled in behind a fire engine parked beside the Sheraton hotel. More police cars and an ambulance crowded the main entrance.

Cora sank back in her seat, and Straw shook his head. He turned right onto Queen Street. A block later, he accelerated to make the yellow light at University Avenue and turned left.

Behind them, a horn blared. Cars screeched. Metal and glass smashed together. She jolted upright and looked through the back window.

Straw swore. "That was close."

In the intersection, two cars were mashed together, and a third car nosed the sidewalk on the southwest corner. Cora turned back to the front and shuddered. Her heart thudded in her ears. She couldn't look at car accidents. That was one thing she had never gotten over. They brought back too much.

"What's with you?" Straw said.

"Nothing. I'm okay."

"Bullshit. You're whiter than my ass."

Straw slowed down and stopped beside a stairway leading down to the St. Andrew subway station. Cora dug through her handbag and pulled out her pink purse.

"What are you doing?" Straw asked.

"Nothing."

"Yeah, fuck you. I want a goddamn answer."

She pulled out the bottle of aspirins and shook the last pair of pills into her trembling hand.

"Fuck, you're a basket case," Straw said.

"Do you have any water?"

"Answer my fucking question."

"Please," Cora said. "Whatever you have. I don't care. It's just an aspirin."

Straw swore, grabbed a Coke from under his seat, and tossed the can at her. "That's all I got."

"Thank you."

"Yeah, enjoy."

Cora eased the can open, sucking up the foam that hissed out, and popped one of the pills in her mouth. Straw turned back to the front, shaking his head, and turned his music louder.

When they reached her apartment building, he parked across from the planters. Since she had only sipped the Coke, she offered it back to him. He ignored her. She opened the right door and stuck the can on the sidewalk and hauled out her handbag. It felt like it had gained ten pounds.

Back in her apartment, she vomited twice and sat in the shower, letting the water spill over her, until she felt steady enough to stand. In the kitchen, her cellphone chimed again and again. She washed her hair and scrubbed her body and rinsed her mouth with peppermint soap. She didn't want to talk to Katrina. She would only want to know everything. Every detail.

Finally Cora dried herself off and pulled on a terry cloth robe. She wrapped a towel around her head and brushed her teeth. After gargling, she turned on all the lights in her bedroom and curled on her comforter. Her cellphone chimed for what must have been the hundredth time, but she didn't care. She had done enough already. Why wasn't it ever good enough?

Chapter 21

Gunfire ripped Alex out of his sleep. He rolled left, smacked a wooden edge, and fell on a hard floor. Bottles crashed. Instinct made him flatten out and search for his men, but a coffee table stood in the way. He swore. He was in Sebastian's apartment. The war had happened a long time ago. It was just shit from the past chewing at his brain.

Alex shoved the coffee table away, knocking more bottles to the floor, and crawled to the small windows at the front of the living room. He peered outside, staying close to the wall. His car had a yellow parking ticket on the windshield. Traffic rumbled through the intersection two blocks east. Two teenagers walked by carrying skateboards, tangles of hair sprouting from under their baseball caps.

Alex sat down, keeping his back against the wall, and dug out his cellphone. He had missed a call from someone named Felicia Danon, but the message on his voicemail was from Leroy.

"You think you can set me up? You should've cut me in. You fucking owe me. You want me on your side before Teresa finds out about your friends at the hotel. Smarten up, asshole."

Alex deleted the message. What the hell was that about?

He peered out the windows again, careful to avoid rustling the curtains. The street looked quiet. The kind of quiet could be a trap, like when the Germans popped out of nowhere and shot holes in your friends.

He scanned the street once more before crawling to the apartment door. Opposite the shoe rack, he leaned against the door frame and listened to the building and the street below. Gunfire continued to echo in the back of his mind, jangling his nerves. He eased down the stairs.

Outside, a car drove by, spewing rock music. Dogs barked down the block. He inched open the door to the street and heard another door clap shut. He froze. A couple in their late teens or early twenties appeared on the sidewalk, coming from a building on his left and walked past him, oblivious to the rest of the world, only pausing long enough to kiss beside his car.

Once they had reached the end of the block, he hurried to his car and unlocked the trunk. Inside, Sebastian was wedged around a green canvas bag, his body as stiff as a tire. Alex shook his head and wiggled the bag back and forth until it popped free.

"Sorry, buddy," he said and closed the trunk again.

Back in Sebastian's apartment, Alex dug a roll of duct tape out of the canvas bag. It had taken a lot of work to sneak everything across the border without Mobius and his goons finding out. Now all Alex needed was some gasoline. That would make the surprise even better.

~

Twenty minutes later, the door on the main floor smashed inwards, and boots stormed up the stairs. Alex tossed a grenade at the apartment door and ducked behind the fridge, which he had pulled away from the wall. Someone in the stairway yelled a warning. Alex pulled the pin on his next grenade, and a man wearing black fatigues and a black flak jacket smashed through the apartment door, firing his assault rifle. The grenades Alex had wired at the bottom of the stairway exploded. Screams ricocheted into the apartment. The first man continued to fire into the kitchen, but the grenade at his feet exploded and hurled him against the door of the coat closet.

The rest of the grenades in the stairway exploded. Alex hurled two more grenades through the front windows. More shouts rose up from the street. He dropped behind the fridge again and listened to the explosions and the screams.

Alex glanced at the dead man in the living room, missing chunks of his left arm and his legs, and threw one last grenade through the front windows.

"Nothing personal," Alex said and crawled out the window beside the kitchen sink, onto the small flat roof spattered with bird shit.

While the men continued to scream and shout from the other

side of the building, he grabbed his canvas bag and slung it on his back. He climbed down a rusty ladder and jumped into a poorly lit alley. Now he just needed more beer. It looked like it was going to be a long night.

~

Teresa sat in her chapel, watching one of the servants kneel in front of a statue of the Virgin Mary, the old woman's hands clutched together in prayer. A second old woman stood in front of the neighboring statue of Jesus, counting under her breath while her right hand darted back and forth across his crucified body, making the sign of the cross. At the front of the chapel, the Monsignor lit candles, trying not to listen to the man inside the altar, his voice vacillating between broken moans and pleas for water.

In the past hour, four of the reborn had failed to answer their phones. Sebastian was dead. She still didn't know where to find the Light—the key to destroying Father.

But how could she have been misled? Could it really be a woman? All these years—hunting the wrong person?

Teresa grimaced. Mobius blamed Alex, of course. Everything was always Alex's fault, as if she was too stupid to think for herself.

At the back of the chapel, someone knocked on the oak doors. The Monsignor flinched and glanced up but quickly dropped his gaze back to the candles and murmured a prayer.

"Let them in," Teresa said.

The servant kneeling before the Virgin Mary ran to open the doors. Two men entered the sanctuary and walked single file to the front. The first man, Sydney, had short blond hair and blue eyes and a stubby goatee. He wore a black suit and a black tie, which hid most of the vein-colored tattoo on the side of his neck, a Chinese symbol perhaps denoting luck or prosperity. Sweat beaded on his forehead, but he didn't dare wipe the moisture away. The second man, Mueller, was chubby, wore beige slacks, and carried a leather briefcase several shades lighter than his brown jacket.

Both men dropped to their knees and bowed their heads. She gave them permission to stand, and they thanked her and straightened up. Sydney kept his eyes on the floor in front of her shoes. Mueller's gaze flicked around the chapel.

Teresa said, "Close your eyes, *pater.*"

The Monsignor covered his ears and turned to one of the smaller statues of Jesus. The servants ducked into the confessionals.

"How long have you worked for me?" she asked Mueller.

He glanced at Sydney, startled.

"If you hesitate again," Teresa said, "you will never get the chance to do it again."

Mueller nodded. "Yes, mistress."

"How long?"

"Three years," he said. "Just before we began operations in Ottawa."

"As I understand it, you've worked closely with this man—" she pointed to Sydney "—and understand the full range of his duties."

"Ye—yes, mistress."

"Do you fully understand the error of his ways?"

"I, uh—"

Sydney grunted and scrabbled at his tie. His eyes bulged. Then he fell to his knees, still jerking at his tie, and wheezed. Buttons skittered across the hardwood floor.

"What? Are you stupid?" Teresa demanded. "You've been blindly helping this man hide information from me."

"No! Never!" Mueller said. "I just did what he told me."

"Shut up! I want the truth, not excuses."

"But we reported everything," Mueller said. "Everything! As soon as we knew."

On the floor, Sydney thrashed and let out a horrible gurgle. Mueller stumbled away from the flailing limbs.

"We just called Mobius about Alex," he said. "And the leads we found on Leroy. We know most of his girls, forty-three of them here in Toronto. We've already sent men to find them, track them. We'll find him."

Teresa stood up slowly, her face tight with fury. Mueller collapsed onto his knees and clasped his hands against his chest. Sydney gurgled and convulsed. On the dais, the prayers of the Monsignor grew louder, and the man trapped inside the altar squealed.

At the back of the chapel, the door swung open. Teresa turned to glare at Mobius. He stepped inside the sanctuary and bowed to her.

"You're supposed to be in Yorkville," she said, "finding the Light."

"I came to tell you the news, mistress. It was too important to leave it to these incompetent dogs." He walked up the center aisle and scowled at Sydney and Mueller. "Much has happened in the last hour. The traitors have bared their fangs."

Teresa struck Mobius with her thoughts, hurling him into the pews on her right.

"You are a fool," she said.

Mobius wriggled onto his knees and bowed to her. "I sent a squad to retrieve Alex, as you ordered. The sun had set. But he set a trap for them, and most are dead. Buildings are on fire."

"And Leroy? Have you lost him too."

"They are all one, mistress. You cannot trust them."

Teresa lunged forward and grabbed Mobius by the throat and threw him on the floor.

"We're tracking him," he said. "But Leroy's phone and car are missing. The other transmitter's not working."

She slammed his head on the floor and glared at Mueller.

"No!" he said, still clasping his hands over his head. "Wait! Please!"

"Dog!" Mobius yelled. "Worthless dog!"

Teresa slammed Mobius's head on the floor again. Bone cracked, and his eyes slithered shut.

"Speak," she said to Mueller.

"We found the car, using its last location, at a parking garage downtown. We just sent a unit to check. We're tracing every lead, anywhere he might go."

"But you know where Alex is?"

"Yes, we have his phone, the exact location." He bobbed his head, and sweat ran down his face and dripped on the floor. "More men are moving in to contain him. We'll neutralize him."

"No, I'll deal with him," she said.

"Yes, mistress."

"Tell them to get my car ready. I want to leave as soon as I'm done with the Monsignor."

"Yes, mistress. As you wish."

Mueller stumbled to his feet and glanced at Sydney, whose body gave one final jerk, before fleeing the chapel. Mobius groaned and stirred.

Teresa kicked him in the ribs. "What about the others? What are they doing?"

"Mistress . . ."

"You've already lost three of them, now when it matters most."

"Watching," he said. "Must watch."

"I should have put you in a car, like the rest of them. It's all you're good for."

"I am unworthy."

"More like idiotic," she said. "We finally have the chance to break free of Father, and you let them destroy everything. You!"

"Yes, mistress."

She kicked Mobius again, and he grunted but made no move to protect himself. She shook her head in disgust and stepped over Sydney and sat in the front row of pews. Her glare shifted to the Monsignor. He turned around like a puppet on a string and bobbed his head without ever lifting his gaze from the floor.

"Start your prayers, *pater*," she said. "It must be midnight somewhere."

~

Alex walked into a parking garage next to a construction site, slabs of concrete ushering in the birth of a new condominium. At the back of the first level, he found a chubby teenager getting out of a gray Corolla and slugged him in the head, knocking him out.

In the trunk was a musty sweatshirt, which Alex used to tie the boy's arms behind his back, and oil-stained rags to gag him. Alex then hoisted the boy on top of the spare tire and wedged the boy's backpack behind his legs.

Fifteen minutes later, Alex parked beside a car wash closed for the night. He didn't want to call the other reborn without knowing what was going on, or he might drag them into his trouble. The one exception was Leroy. It sounded like the security forces had already gone after him.

Alex hunted through his jacket for his phone and called the last number Leroy had used. Felicia Danon was probably one of his girls. The name sounded familiar. He always had so many of them, dropping one and finding three more the next day. Last week, he had bragged about a nurse who snuck out of the hospital she worked at to give him blow jobs. He loved the idea of people dying because she was too busy sucking him off.

An answering service clicked on. "Hi, it's me, Felicia. I can't come to the phone right now. But leave a message, and I'll call back as soon as I can. Have a great day."

Alex pulled out the crumpled piece of paper he had taken from the security team in Leroy's house and flattened the paper on the dashboard. Neither of the phone numbers on the paper matched the call from Felicia, but that didn't make Alex feel better. The security forces already had half a day's lead. The only plus was they would have to spread themselves thin to find all the girls Leroy had fucked in the past year.

Alex called the first number.

A woman answered the phone. "Yes?"

"I'm Leroy's connection," he said. "Looking for a party girl."

After a short pause, the woman said, "I don't know anything like that," her accent thickening, probably Russian.

"Well, he sure does, and that's what counts. Or do you want to argue with Leroy?"

"No, no. I don't mean different. I am only wondering your name."

"We got lots of time for that later. I just want to know if you like whiskey. I picked up a big bottle, plus a little extra, something he said you liked a lot."

"What?" she asked.

"Well, shit, it wouldn't be a surprise if I told you. I love surprises."

"Yes, me too. Surprises are exciting."

"Then let's get this figured out. I'm only in town till tomorrow."

"Oh, but I work," the woman said.

"You're damn right you're going to work it, or I'm gonna tell Leroy how lousy his party girls are and take my fucking business elsewhere. I got ten guys who want in on the action. You can tell him you fucked it up."

"No, no!" she said. "I only joke. I bad with jokes."

"Damn right, you are," Alex said. "Wasting my time. I'm gonna hang up right now and tell him what a goddamn—"

"No! Please! I have idea. You love it. Big surprise."

Alex waited.

"You have car?" she asked.

"Jesus Christ. Do I have a fucking car?"

"I leave work one o'clock," she said. "We have party."

"Keep talking."

"You know Rush? Is bar on Yonge Street, close to Bloor?"

"I got it," Alex said. In the past year, he had driven by that bar more times than he cared to remember.

"Good, yes. We go there. Easy to find."

"Forget that shit. I love a fat steak and that's just around the corner. Rango Bull. Meet me there, quarter after twelve."

"Oh, but—"

"Ask for Leroy when you get there," Alex said and hung up.

He dialed the second phone number on the piece of paper.

An Asian guy with a thick accent answered the phone. "Grill 'n Wok."

Alex slapped his cellphone on the passenger seat and swore. He scratched at the stubble on his chin. Maybe there was another way to track down Felicia. The gas station on the other side of the car wash was open.

After straightening his jacket, Alex walked to the booth at the end of the gas pumps and asked the attendant, a skinny black man in his early twenties, for a phone book.

"I believe there is a pay phone at the coffee shop," the attendant said and pointed east. "At the next corner."

"I don't give a bloody hell," Alex said. "I'm right in front of you."

The attendant's eyes popped wide, and his mouth opened, but no words came out. Behind Alex, a fat man wearing a black baseball cap stepped into the booth while fumbling with his wallet.

"Give me the damn phone book," Alex said.

The attendant glanced at the fat man before looking behind the counter and passed Alex the Yellow Pages. He threw it at the window behind the attendant, knocking over an empty coffee pot, and both items crashed to the ground.

"Try again," Alex said.

The fat man wearing the baseball cap bolted out of the booth, and the attendant fumbled with another phone book. Alex grabbed it, glanced inside, and nodded his thanks.

At the last gas pump, the man wearing the baseball cap jumped into his car and gunned his engine. Alex walked past, shaking his head. Tires screeched. The car disappeared northwards. He threw the phone book in the passenger seat of the gray Corolla and drove in the opposite direction, then zigzagged east until he reached an empty schoolyard surrounded by a metal fence.

Parked behind a red hatchback, he flipped through the phone book and found an F. Danon on Christoph Blvd. He yanked open the glove compartment and pulled out half-a-dozen maps, the last one of Toronto, and spread it on the steering wheel. Christoph Blvd. was about twenty minutes away, on the other side of the Don Valley. Close enough for a look. But first he had to meet the Russian girl. He just hoped Mobius hadn't found her yet. Otherwise it would be a fucking mess.

~

Alex parked on the third floor of a four-story garage across from the south entrance to the Bloor subway station and stuffed a pair of grenades in his jacket. He didn't sense any trouble yet, but it was out there, floating in the background. It was just a matter of time.

On Yonge Street, he walked south two blocks, where Rango Bull was wedged between a shop with leather outfits in the front window and a Vietnamese and Thai restaurant. The windows of Rango Bull were small and plastered with pictures of beer and steak while the interior looked bruised and worn out.

Inside, three men sat at the tables—two against the north wall, underneath a shelf of tin cans, drinking and looking bored; and a fat man near the front door, shoving fries and hunks of steak in his mouth.

A middle-aged waitress wearing a pink skirt and a black tank top, her platinum blonde hair pulled back into a ponytail, greeted Alex and pointed to a table near the front. He ignored her and sat at a table near the statue of a bull at the back and dropped his canvas bag on the floor.

"Grab me a Moosehead," he said.

After giving him a sour look, the waitress circled behind the bar, brought the beer, and slapped a menu on the table.

"Are you always this slow?" Alex said. "No wonder nobody's here."

"I guess you need a few minutes," she said and turned away.

"Yeah, grab another beer while you're at it. This one won't last long."

The waitress glared at him but came back with another Moosehead before disappearing through a green door, into the kitchen.

"Yeah, make that two," he called after her.

Three beers later, a dyed blonde woman with fake breasts jammed under a torn blue jean jacket walked into the pub. She had a big black bag hanging from one shoulder and wore enough makeup to paint a truck.

Alex waved her over. She looked like someone Leroy would fuck.

When she reached the table, Alex said, "Sit down," and pointed to the chair adjacent to him.

"Where is Leroy?" she asked, her gaze darting around the bar.

"Later," Alex said. "Sit down."

She sniffed, like she had something better to do, but slid into the chair. Alex shoved a Moosehead toward her.

"You talk different," she said. "Not like phone."

"Yeah, I'm a jack of all trades."

The waitress came out of the kitchen and steered in their direction. Alex told her to fuck off, and the Russian woman continued to glance around. The waitress strode to the main bar and crouched down to move bottles in one of the small refrigerators. The Russian woman started to pick up her bag and stand up. Alex stepped on the strap.

"I go to washroom," she said.

"You won't need that."

"I be right back," she said.

Alex stared at her until she let go of the bag. After a few more seconds, she unzipped a pocket on the side and slipped out a silver purse.

"Hurry up," he said. "I don't have all fucking day."

She nodded and hurried to a blue door at the back of the pub. Alex glanced at his watch. He felt like he was wasting his time. She hadn't seen Leroy in the last few days, the way she was acting. Maybe even weeks.

Alex drained the rest of his beer and frowned at the blue door. Then he swore and jumped to his feet. Both of the doors at the back went to the kitchen. The sign for the washrooms hung from a metal rod at the end of the bar and had a big finger pointing downstairs.

He grabbed his canvas bag and charged through the blue door, ignoring the yell of the waitress from the bar. In the kitchen, one man hunched over a stainless steel sink, scrubbing a pot. The second man stood in front of the grill, tossing cheese on a hamburger and smoking a cigarette.

"What? Do you think this is a fucking zoo?" he said.

"Where'd she go?" Alex demanded.

"Get the fuck out of here."

The other man waved a knife at the back door.

Alex shoved the cook out of the way, knocking him into the grill, and he screamed. Alex smashed through the back door and glanced around an alley stinking of rancid food and burnt grease. To the left, he saw a dark courtyard and dumpsters. To the right, metal fencing from a construction zone narrowed the alley while two cranes hovered overhead like a pair of frozen giants.

From somewhere along the fencing came a squawk of pain. Alex sprinted closer and saw a chasm several stories deep through the mesh of the fencing. The fencing turned left, and he spotted two figures next to a yellow brick building blackened with years of grime.

Alex stopped and swore.

"Looking for this?" Teresa said, clutching the Russian woman by the throat. The woman squawked and flailed her arms at Teresa, but Teresa squeezed harder and shook the Russian until she went limp.

"I guess you got tired of waiting," Alex said.

"Is she yours?" Teresa demanded. "Or one of Leroy's?"

"I was hoping she'd know where Leroy is," Alex said. "I think she's one of his newer girls."

"Why does that matter?"

"I don't know, does it?" Alex said. "Looks like you already decided."

"The only choice I've made is to destroy Father. But you're all too stupid to realize that."

Alex eyed the other branch of the alley and shrugged. Was Mobius hiding in the shadows too, waiting for his turn?

"What about Leroy?" Teresa demanded. "Where is he? What is he planning?"

"The only one who's been planning anything is Mobius," Alex said. "Like he always has."

"Then tell me where Leroy is," Teresa said.

"That's what I'm trying to figure out, why I wanted to talk to her." He gestured toward the Russian girl, wheezing for breath.

"Oh? That's why you didn't tell anyone? That's why you're sneaking around?"

"Mobius made things clear enough tonight. I didn't want to kill those men."

"They're irrelevant," she said.

"What about the girl from the hotel? Mobius sure isn't helping us find her."

Teresa hissed. Shadows bubbled around her. The Russian convulsed and let out a horrible gurgle, like the alveoli in her lungs had started to explode.

"I think Leroy has a lead on her," Alex said. "That's why he's being careful. He doesn't trust Mobius."

"Enough!" Teresa yelled and hurled the Russian over the fence. With barely a whisper, she disappeared into the blackness of the construction pit. "I've heard enough. From both of you."

A fist of air hurled Alex against the grimy yellow brick wall, and he grunted in pain and fell on the ground.

"I'll find the girl," he said, not bothering to get up. "After that, I don't care. Except for Mobius. Leave him to me. Just let me find the girl."

The invisible force slammed Alex into the wall again. Bones and bricks cracked. He tumbled onto a patch of broken asphalt. The hem of Teresa's dress faded in and out, sweeping closer.

"You have until tomorrow," she said. "Twelve hours."

Despite the pain cascading through his body, Alex managed to murmur, "Yes, mistress."

Then the shadows in the alley surged and snapped over his head.

Chapter 22

Alex jerked awake, and the rat crouching by his right foot darted behind a dumpster. He sucked in a breath. His lungs burned. His head throbbed. A light rain sprinkled the alley, and sirens wailed in the distance. He watched the rain bead on his shoes like tiny jewels, each one popping and streaming down the ground, until the sirens faded and the rat scampered into the darkness behind an old, beat-up Ford. Then he let his eyes drift shut and waited for his bones to knit enough for him to stand without falling and breaking them anew.

In the midst of another doze, he heard the rat scampering closer. The little bastards were always looking for toes and fingers to chew off. Rain, mud, guns, bombs—the rats didn't care. They didn't care what side you were on.

Alex slapped a puddle, scaring off the rat, reminding himself he wasn't in the trenches anymore. Asphalt covered the ground. Cars rumbled on the streets. All those boys had died a long time ago. Like he should have died.

He sucked in a breath and tugged at the canvas bag lying by his feet. The pain in his lungs flared. Dark blobs skittered across his vision. He ignored them and struggled to stand and grappled with his bag. More sirens echoed through the alley, this time coming from far away, and he staggered toward the end of the construction zone. Several times he had to stop and grab the fence with his free hand, dizziness threatening to pull him back to the ground.

At the mouth of the alley, he turned north, across from a dozen or so brick rowhouses huddled at the foot of a white condominium. Two blocks later, he turned east and passed a clump of houses converted into restaurants and shops and leaned against the window of a drug store at the corner of Yonge Street. Several teenagers and drunks crossed the intersection. A cab made a U-turn in front of a strip club. Alex wished he had some beer. His head felt like a pot of molasses. He also felt a sharp twinge in his back that had nothing to do with his broken ribs and realized someone was following him. Probably one of Mobius's monkeys. Teresa wouldn't do it herself.

Either way, Alex didn't care. He was tired of their crap.

Half a block later, he turned left into the parking garage where he had left the stolen car and ducked into a stairwell. On the first landing, he sat down for a minute, waiting for the throbbing in his chest to ease.

When he reached the third floor, he dug the car keys out of his pants and gripped one of the grenades in his duffel bag. A white van sat next to the car he had stolen. He also heard banging from inside the trunk. The kid must have gotten his hands loose. Or maybe he was using his feet.

A Schwarzenegger-type wearing a black uniform and black flak jacket stepped out of the van and waited for Alex to approach.

"We can get rid of the car," the man said. "Drop you off wherever you need."

"I'll worry about that," Alex said. "Just duct-tape the kid so he doesn't make so much noise."

The man frowned and glanced at the van.

"That wasn't a request," Alex said. "I know you've been listening. So does the mistress."

Another man wearing a flak jacket hopped out of the van and glared at Alex. He opened the trunk. Inside, the kid struggled to sit up, and the two men sprang forward to stop him. They rolled him over and taped his legs and wrists, and Alex told them to pull out the rag in the kid's mouth before taping it shut. Otherwise the kid would choke to death.

"Now get the hell out of here," Alex said. "Report back to Mobius. I'm sure he'll love that."

~

Several hours later, shortly after seven, Alex sat up and returned the driver's seat to the vertical position. Sunlight gleamed off the windows across the street, and he grimaced and shielded his eyes. His chest still ached but not out of any real pain. He just needed some beer to wash away the sensation. He needed to feel the liquid rolling over his tongue and down his throat.

The rumble of a car jarred Alex back to the garage, and he grabbed the grenade in his lap. A red Honda parked about twenty feet away from him. A young Chinese woman with long, curly hair, wearing a black dress and black pumps, stepped out the car and headed to the nearest stairway, never giving him a look. Everybody was fucking oblivious.

Alex stuck the grenade between his legs and pulled out a second one from his canvas bag. He drove out of the parking garage, watching for the white van, but didn't see it anywhere nor any other vehicles he recognized. No alarm bells went off. Whether that was good or bad, he wasn't sure.

He turned east on Bloor Street and crossed the Don Valley, the bridge rigged with fences to keep people from jumping off. He stopped at three coffee shops to make do with their blackest brew until the beer stores opened. The first coffee tasted like rubber tires. The second burned his tongue. The third he saved until he reached Christoph Boulevard and then gulped the entire cup.

Felicia's house was a sturdy, brick two-story with green shutters and a deep porch, across from a high school where a yellow bus unloaded a score of teenagers. Her driveway was empty. No cars sat on the street. No white vans.

Alex parked around the corner behind a red pickup, and stuffed both grenades in his jacket. On the sidewalk, he passed a pair of teenagers smoking cigarettes and yakking on their cellphones. He spat on a lawn. Kids these days wanted to pretend they were adults but still had Mom wiping their asses. They didn't know a damn thing. They had never seen their buddies explode or found their heads sunk in fields of mud like deformed soccer balls.

At the foot of Felicia's driveway, Alex paused and frowned at her house. A blue bird hung on the front door. Fliers stuck out of the mailbox. On the second floor, the curtains facing the front yard were closed. On the side, a small window made of frosted glass glowed, probably from a bathroom.

He strode to the end of the driveway and unlatched the wooden gate leading to the backyard. A small vegetable garden, mostly tomatoes and lettuce, grew along the wooden fence at the back of the property. Pots of geraniums sat on the patio, which was white and needed a fresh coat of paint. In the yard next door, a straw hat bobbed up and down like a duck on a target range.

Alex stepped on the patio and saw the hat belonged to an old Chinese woman watering her garden. At first, she didn't notice him, but then she straightened up abruptly and stared at him. He waved hello. She ducked back down and continued watering her garden.

Okay, he thought and peered through the patio doors into a kitchen with a beige counter and white cupboards. Everything looked quiet. No one moved around.

Alex tried the back door and smiled. It was unlocked. He eased the door open, the hinges squeaking, and stepped into a tiny coatroom stinking of cigarettes. The kitchen beyond stank too and had a yellow linoleum floor that must have been beige once. Next to the stainless steel fridge, a coffee machine gurgled. From upstairs came the creak of footsteps. One pair? Maybe two?

He turned into the hallway leading to stairs at the front of the house, the wooden floor underneath him crackling. On the second floor, a shower turned on. Except for the coffee machine, the rest of the house remained quiet.

Alex eased up the stairs, pausing each time a step cracked or popped, and muttered a curse. Was he even in the right house? Felicia could have moved or gone to work and left her fat mother behind. He didn't like killing mothers.

He peered through the wooden railing at the top of the stairs and heard a woman swear. The door leading to the shower stood ajar an inch or two. The woman swore again, and something hit the tub. A bar of soap? A bottle of shampoo?

Alex eased up the last steps and crept past the bathroom and turned into a bedroom littered with shirts, underwear, and pantyhose. Mustard yellow sheets lay tangled on a queen-sized bed. A black Sony TV sat on a pine chest of drawers beside the closet. Framed photos were spread out on a dresser with a rectangular mirror: a middle-aged couple wearing plaid and big glasses from the sixties; individual pictures of the couple, but older; a little girl with blonde pigtails smiling for all she was worth; the girl graduating high school, chubbier, sporting a severe haircut.

Half the drawers in the dresser were empty. Others were crammed with crap that didn't tell him anything. In the nightstand, next to a pack of cigarettes, he found an inhaler with a label that said Felicia Dannon.

Alex nodded and set a grenade on the dresser, against one of the pictures. The shower stopped, and the shower curtain rattled. Two or three minutes later, something hit the floor. The woman sputtered a curse. He stepped behind the bedroom door and rubbed his head. He should have checked the fridge before coming upstairs. She sounded like a drinker.

After another ten minutes or so, she walked into the bedroom, a large gray towel wrapped around her torso. Alex kicked the door shut and grabbed her. She screamed. He slammed her against the chest of drawers and slapped a hand over her face. The towel fell to the floor, revealing pale chunky thighs and sagging breasts. She yelped and twisted.

"I'm with Leroy," he said.

The woman froze in his arms.

"We understand each other," he said.

She wiggled her head. Yes.

"I don't believe you," he said and rammed her into the chest of drawers again. She howled and fell to her knees. Alex tightened his grip around her rib cage. "Stop fucking around. I don't have time for your crap."

She managed to nod.

"We're going to chat. Like old friends. And you're going to give me good answers because you like giving me good answers."

Felicia nodded again, and Alex released her mouth.

"He's coming back," she said. "Any minute. He's going to kill you."

"He's welcome to try. Everybody else does."

"He's gonna cut you up. Cut off all your fingers and your—"

Alex rapped her on the head and spun her around. She yelped. The left side of her face was swollen and bruised, and she had more bruises on her left arm.

"Looks like you had fun with Leroy," Alex said.

Felicia backed into the chest of drawers. He pulled the second grenade out of his jacket and waved to her. She froze, one arm wrapped over her breasts, leaving her shaggy, dark crotch exposed.

"Good, you know what it is," he said. "Want to play catch?"

"He's coming back," Felicia said. "He is!"

"That's perfect. We have lots to talk about. The sooner, the better." Alex shoved the TV, and it toppled off the chest of drawers. Felicia flinched and hugged herself. "But I hate liars, as much as Leroy does, and you're a liar."

He grabbed her by the hair and pulled her away from the chest of drawers. She started crying and squawking. He tossed the grenade on the bed and threw her on top. She screamed and tried to wriggle away from the grenade, but Alex sprang on top of her and shoved her face into the mattress until her screams turned into choked sobs.

Alex shifted to her right side and rolled her off the grenade and thrust it between her breasts.

"He's not here," she said, still sobbing. "He's not. He left."

"Obviously," Alex said. "But when did he give you that whack? What time? Where? Was anyone with him?"

"I don't know. I—"

Alex slapped her bruised face. "I've never blown up a woman before, so I'm curious what would happen. Do you have any duct tape? I think that would make it interesting."

Felicia started to scream again. Alex clapped a hand over her mouth and wished she would hurry up and tell him something useful. He hated holding the grenade so long. It brought back too much of the war, all the screaming, mud, and body parts, the fingers that still seemed to wiggle after everything else had been blown to bits.

He swore and shoved the grenade in his jacket. Felicia stopped screaming and started sobbing again. He slapped her across the face, scooped up the gray towel, and tossed it on top of her.

"Put that on," he said. "We're going downstairs."

She shook her head, staring at him through bleary eyes.

"Now!" he yelled. "Move it, move it."

Felicia lurched off the bed and fumbled with the towel. He

picked up the other grenade from the dresser and hauled her after him, down the stairs, and into the kitchen.

"Get me a coffee," he said and sat at the small dining table, made of rubber wood from somewhere in Asia.

She hurried to pour him a cup. Her eyes darted to the phone beside the microwave.

"Go ahead," Alex said. "Call the police. I hear they're good at cleaning up bodies."

She slid the cup on the table and grabbed a carton of table cream from the fridge. As soon as she turned back to him, he tossed the grenade to her. She screamed and dropped the carton, and the table cream spattered on the linoleum floor.

Alex swore and scooped the grenade off the floor. "Christ, you're stupid," he said. "Ever seen anyone with their feet blown off? It isn't pretty. You wouldn't believe how far body parts can fly. You'd never even think they were human. You can't tell anymore."

"Please," she said. "I'll do whatever you want."

"Where can I find Leroy?"

"I don't know," she said, trembling. "I don't."

Alex picked up his cup of coffee and whipped it against the cream-colored wall beside the fridge. The cup shattered, spattering coffee up to the ceiling.

"Please," Felicia said. "I just—I—"

He slammed her into the counter beside the sink, and she cried out in pain. Then he threw her on the floor and opened the fridge. Inside, he found three beers, and he smiled.

Alex turned back to her, the grenade in his left hand, a Labatt in his right. "I hope you're ready to tell the truth now. The truth is always the best. It'll set you free."

He returned to his seat at the kitchen table and opened the beer.

Felicia crawled against the cupboards, blinking back tears, and fumbled with the towel. "I haven't seen him. He hasn't been here."

"Why? Is he too busy with his other girlfriends?"

"No! He doesn't need them," she said.

"Where have you been? He fucks them all the time."

"They're only in it for the money. They don't care."

"Well, the Russian one's dead, so you don't have to worry about her anymore." Alex finished his beer and went to the fridge for a second. "Want to see her? We can go for a ride."

Felicia shook her head.

"Are you sure?" Alex said. "I'm the nice one. My boss threw the other gal in a big hole at one of those construction sites downtown. Can you imagine falling like that? And splat, you're dead."

She kept shaking her head and refused to look at him.

"I'll give you a test," he said. "An easy question first. Did you see him on Saturday? Sunday? Or Monday?"

"No, I didn't. None of them."

Alex knocked her head against a cupboard, and she cried out.

"Remember, I know some of these answers."

"Last night," Felicia said. "I saw him last night. After my shift."

"He wanted you to meet him somewhere specific."

"The parking garage," she said. "He wanted me to drive there. I thought . . ." She stopped and shook her head.

"Which garage?"

"The one by city hall, under Nathan Phillips Square."

Alex finished his beer and got the last one from the fridge. "Keep talking," he said.

"He just wanted my car," she said. "That's all. He didn't—he was too busy."

"Then what?"

Felicia squirmed on the floor. Alex tapped her on the head with the beer bottle.

"I just pretended to leave," she said. "So I could follow him."

"That was pretty stupid."

She wobbled her head, perhaps nodding. "He went into the hotel across the street. The Sheraton. I thought maybe he had a room. But he just walked around the lobby, and I had to hide in the bar."

"How long before he caught you?"

"I don't know, half an hour. He went up to the second floor, and I thought maybe it was better to sneak out, but he saw me and came running back down." Felicia touched her bruised cheek. "But he wouldn't have done anything if it wasn't for those nosy bastards. He would never do that."

"No, of course not."

She glanced up, hate in her eyes.

Alex tapped the beer bottle against her forehead. "Go back to those bastards in the hotel. Did they have flak jackets and assault rifles? Where did they come from?"

Felicia looked startled. "No, it was just some Indian guys. From the hotel. The security guards. And those bitches from the desk."

"He got in a fight with the staff?"

"They should have minded their own business. We weren't doing nothing."

Alex guzzled the rest of his beer and crouched beside Felicia. He pulled out the grenade from his jacket and pulled the pin. She squawked but remained still.

"He must've been there for a reason," he said. "Something really important."

"I don't know. I didn't see nothing. I swear."

Alex studied the grooves on the grenade, their cold, hard reality both beautiful and ugly. Felicia shifted and winced. He remembered the torn birthday card and pulled it from the inner pocket of his jacket, and the photo of the blonde girl from the Four Seasons fell on the floor. Felicia's gaze flicked down to the girl's image.

"What about the rest of this birthday card?" he asked. "The missing corner?"

Felicia shook her head.

He picked up the photo. "And this girl? Have you seen her before?"

"Is that the Russian?"

Alex rapped Felicia on the head with the grenade.

"I want to know if she was at the hotel," he said. "Did you see her? Or anyone else?"

"I don't know. There were lots of people, running all over the place. And the cops came and—"

Felicia stopped, looking alarmed.

"What did you tell them?" he asked.

"Nothing! I just said it happened really fast, I didn't know him."

Alex snorted. "They must have loved that."

"I told them I was meeting a friend for a drink. She was in town for work."

He nodded and toyed with the grenade. Felicia wriggled and clenched her fists, her face tight with fear.

"Let's play a little game." Alex put the pin back in the grenade and returned it to his jacket. From beside the phone, he grabbed a pen and a notepad. "You write down the answers, and I'll tell you if you're right. But for each one you get wrong, you lose a finger."

"Please, I've told you everything, I swear."

"That's what we're going to find out." He tossed the pen and notepad at her and told her to write down her license plate, the color and make of her car, Leroy's phone number, her shoe size, the time of the fight at the hotel, and her work number.

"But I don't know all that, I don't have it memorized."

"You'd better have the answer in one of these drawers, 'cause you've got three minutes, starting now. Then you lose fingers."

"My purse! It's right there."

She pointed to a frilly, brown leather bag beside the blender and fumbled with her towel, trying to keep her crotch hidden. Alex dropped the purse beside her and pulled a long bread knife from the butcher block. He banged the blade against the counter, and she dumped the contents of her purse on the floor, breath mints, lipstick, and loose change skittering in multiple directions.

When she had finished writing, Alex looked over her answers and pulled out his cellphone.

"Let's find out if you got them all right." He smiled and dialed Sebastian's number.

"Wait! I—I forgot something. One thing."

"You're out of time."

"They have my car. They took it last night."

Alex frowned and terminated the call. "Who?"

"The police. They called." She paused, wringing her hands. "Someone smashed it up. Near the hotel."

"You mean Leroy."

She flinched. "He had my keys."

"And?"

"That's it," she said. "I swear. I haven't seen him. He just ran out of the hotel. He didn't even look back."

Alex tossed the bread knife in the sink and picked up the grenade on the kitchen table. Felicia backed into the stove.

"Lie down," he said. "Face down."

"No! I told you everything."

"Down! Now!"

"He has my phone," she said, tears streaming down her face. "And my credit cards. He took my cash."

Alex grabbed a belt from the raincoat hanging by the back door, shoved her down, and tied her arms behind her back. Then he stuffed a dishrag in her mouth and threw her into a tiny bathroom tucked under the stairs.

"It'll take you awhile to get out of those," he said. "But at least you're alive to do it. Don't make me regret it."

~

Half an hour later, Alex found Leroy's black Cadillac sitting in the parking garage underneath Nathan Phillips Square. The ticket in the window had Monday's date with a timestamp of 8:57pm. Alex walked up the nearest stairwell and stepped outside, next to a large rectangular reflecting pool, people scattered about, chatting or eating.

He left the square, and cars honked at him as he cut across Queen Street to the Sheraton Hotel. In the lobby, he talked to several of the employees, all of them eyeing his rumpled suit with distaste or distrust. None of them wanted to tell him anything. The bar wouldn't sell him any beer. Too early. Come back in an hour.

At the front entrance, a bellhop accepted sixty dollars and recited the little he knew: a drunk, who was *not* staying at the hotel, had started a fight in the lobby; two employees had gone to the hospital; the culprit had escaped before the police arrived; and, no, the bellhop did not recognize the photo of the blonde girl.

~

After turning left onto Sherbourne, Alex parked in front of a dollar store across from a park drifting with bums and pigeons and a few seagulls and tossed the keys on the driver's seat. Teresa still didn't answer her phone, so he left a message about Leroy's car.

Alex slung his bag of grenades over his right shoulder and

walked half-a-dozen blocks north and east. In an alleyway behind a restaurant, he sat on a broken chair and wondered if the restaurant had any beer hiding in the back. He could break the lock on the door and look around. One case would be enough to hold him over.

A gray four-door with a dent on the side pulled into the alley and puttered past him, driven by a dark Indian woman wearing a blue and green sari. She parked beside a rust-colored dumpster and glanced at him several times before digging a cardboard box out of the trunk.

The woman ducked into a building with white vinyl siding, the door closing behind her. Alex walked to the red car and spotted a baby seat in the back. He kept walking. Oh well. Next time.

At the end of the alley, he turned right and walked along a street with small houses squashed together, patches of grass spurting here and there from their tiny yards. His phone rang. The screen displayed a number he didn't recognize.

"Army supplies," he said, answering the phone.

"Where are you?" Teresa asked.

"I was looking for Leroy's car. Seems he left it sitting in a parking garage, the middle of downtown. He also caused some trouble in the Sheraton hotel across the street. I think he was looking for the girl, the one Sebastian found."

"Does he have her?"

"Don't think so," Alex said. "Some people decided to be heroes and chased him out of the hotel."

"That sounds idiotic."

"I guess they got lucky."

"Where is he now?"

"That's what I'm working on," Alex said. "He took one of his girlfriend's phones, credit cards, and car, but he smashed the car up already. The cops have it now."

Teresa remained silent for a few seconds. "You have the numbers for these things?"

"Yes."

"Good. One of the computer men will call you to get them."

"You mean Sydney? He's just one of Mobius's cockroaches."

"You'll give him the details," Teresa said, her voice sharp, "regardless of who it is."

She hung up. Alex shoved the phone in his jacket, even though he wanted to throw the damn thing against a wall. What the hell was he supposed to do now?

Chapter 23

Cora swallowed an aspirin and stepped in the shower. She must have woken up a dozen times last night, the dreams always pulling, snarling, groping, swearing, hissing, grabbing. She would have been better off getting up and doing something useful, like laundry or scrubbing the bathroom. Getting to sleep had been hard enough in the first place, thinking about that psycho at the hotel, along with everything else that happened in the past week—the eviction letter, the mess at Paul's, the visit from the police.

Twenty minutes later, she dried herself off and took another aspirin. She skipped the blow dryer, brushed her teeth, flossed, and gargled with mouthwash. In her bedroom, she pulled on a pair of white Lululemon pants and a pink top and checked her cellphone. She had another voicemail message from Katrina, which made five since leaving the hotel last night.

"This is serious, Cora. You need to call me. I'm not upset about what happened at the hotel. But we need to talk."

Cora deleted the message and sorted through her laundry, careful to keep her work clothes and normal clothes separate, and threw a load of colors in the washing machine. She watered the plants on the balcony and on the window ledge. In the kitchen, she washed her hands and cut up the cantaloupe she had bought last week. One end was mushy, and the flesh wasn't particularly sweet, so she only ate half a slice, put some in a Tupperware container in the fridge, and threw the rest in the green bin.

~

The tea kettle clicked off. Cora's cellphone chimed.

She glanced at the screen, expecting another call from Kat, but the ID said Melissa.

Cora hurried to answer the phone. "I'm glad it's you."

"You okay? Kat was telling me some crazy story about last

night."

"You wouldn't believe it," Cora said and described the fight in the hotel lobby and the bald man wearing the Armani suit and the creepy man with the southern accent who wanted to follow her downstairs.

"But you're okay?" Melissa asked. "You got out all right?"

"I thought he was going to come after me, the way he looked. He was completely crazy."

"Some guys just need to be locked up. Or neutered."

"I kept dreaming about him too. I couldn't sleep."

"Yeah, well, forget him," Melissa said. "He's probably on a plane, drinking himself stupid."

"You think so? There must be police at the airport. Lots of people saw him."

"You know what those assholes are like. They think they own the fucking world."

Cora murmured in agreement.

"Are we still doing lunch?" Melissa asked. "I have to go to the mall and pick up a doll for my niece's birthday. You can tell me the rest."

"Oh. I forgot."

"Don't let this guy fuck with you, not for even a second. He's not worth it. He's probably just some cokehead with a lawyer's degree."

"I don't think I can handle a lot of people."

"The third floor's not that busy. Just meet me at the Disney store, like twelve, and we'll go somewhere quieter after."

Cora toyed with the box of chamomile tea, spinning it in small circles. The third floor didn't sound any better, even though she did want to see Melissa. Who else could she talk to? Who else would understand?

"If you're not hungry, we can go to a cafe," Melissa said. "There's some cute places in Little Italy."

"I have to go to Nathan's too," Cora said.

"Yeah, I know. But you need some time for yourself, or you're not going to be good for anybody. And Kat won't let you keep ducking her calls."

"What do you mean? Did she say that?"

"Sort of," Melissa said. "But we can about that later. Now I gotta go. Are you in or not?"

"I wish I could."

"Just meet me at twelve. Your brother's not going to miss you for an hour."

"I know, but I—"

"Seriously, you'll feel a lot better. It'll be good for both of you."

Cora picked up the box of chamomile tea, tilting it left, then tilting it right. She sighed.

"Just say yes. Stop giving me so much grief."

"I can't stay long."

Melissa laughed. "Tell me something I don't know."

"But definitely somewhere quieter. Maybe that cafe?"

"Sure, just meet me at the Disney store. We'll figure it out later."

~

Cora pulled out a plastic bag from under the kitchen sink and took the business suit and white blouse from last night to the dry cleaners at the base of her building. The old Portuguese woman behind the counter avoided meeting Cora's gaze and held her money up to the sunlight as if the bills were counterfeit. She pretended not to notice and draped her three clean dresses over her left arm and hurried back upstairs.

After hanging the dresses in the mahogany wardrobe in the spare bedroom, Cora washed her hands and opened the washing machine. She took out her lingerie and shorts and tops and hung them in the spare bedroom on a pair of drying racks and realized she had completely forgotten about tomorrow night. She was supposed to meet Frank, a sweet guy from Chicago who flew in every few weeks to see her. Katrina had to cancel the appointment before it was too late, if it wasn't already. Maybe the whole week.

That wouldn't go over well, Cora thought and walked into the kitchen. She picked up her cellphone. She stared at the numbers but stopped short of pressing call and carried the phone into her bedroom. After trying on several blouses, she changed into a pair of blue jean with rhinestones on the back pockets and a black halter top. She didn't want to keep making excuses, but she had to think of something.

She changed into jeans with tapered legs and stepped into the bathroom to brush her teeth. Her cellphone chimed a few seconds later, and she hurried back into the bedroom, in case Melissa was calling again. Instead the screen flashed *Kat C.*

Cora rubbed her forehead and answered the phone. She couldn't avoid it forever.

"I was expecting a call," Katrina said.

"I know, I'm sorry. I didn't sleep well."

"Have you talked to Straw?"

"Uh, no," Cora said, surprised. "I mean, he drove me home, but you already know that."

"I mean this morning."

"No," Cora said. Why would she?

"I haven't been able to get a hold of him," Katrina said. "And the car isn't behind the salon."

"Really?"

"You don't know anything about it?"

"No, of course not."

"I'm not blaming you," Katrina said. "I just want to find out what's going on."

"But that's the truth. He dropped me off, like he always does. Around eleven, I think. Maybe eleven-thirty. I don't remember exactly. Everything was a blur."

"Yes, what happened at the hotel? You haven't explained that either."

Cora repeated the story she had told Melissa about the man in the Armani suit starting a fight in the lobby.

"So it was a random guy from the hotel?" Katrina asked. "Nothing to do with you or Mr. Big?"

"No! I've never seen him before."

"You're positive?"

"Yes! You wouldn't forget someone like that. Like, never."

Katrina remained silent, and the phone crackled. Cora switched the phone to her other ear and sat on her bed.

"I guess we'll have to wait and see, then," Katrina said.

"I'm sure Straw's fine."

"He won't be, as soon as I find him." Cora heard another phone ring in the background and the squeak of a chair. "That must be Lindsay."

Cora waited, uncertain of what to say. Lindsay sometimes took care of calls and handed travel arrangements for anything out of the province. She should know more.

"Call me if you hear anything from Straw," Katrina said. "I'll see if I can track him down."

"Okay."

"I'll call you later anyway. We still have things to talk about."

~

The cab stopped across from the north entrance of the Eaton Centre, the sidewalk churning with people on their lunch breaks. Cora took a deep breath. Why in the world had she agreed to come? She didn't want to be around all these people, especially so close to the Sheraton. It was only a few blocks away. The driver had actually wanted to turn onto Queen Street and drive by the hotel, but she had stopped him in time and told him to turn at Dundas Street instead. She would rather take the long way through the mall.

A car honked behind the cab. The driver, a small Turkish man with bushy gray hair and a pockmarked face, coughed and tapped the meter. She hurried to pay him and darted past the people waiting for a streetcar and the teens clustered in front of the H&M store.

A guy wearing a green beer shirt hooted in her direction as she ducked into a revolving door. She hustled through the north atrium and the Sears, passing the discount shoes and the perfumes and the beauty products. The rest of the mall stretched ahead of her, sunshine streaming in from the skylights overhead. Railings surrounded large open sections that overlooked the lower levels. The bottom level was the busiest, perhaps because of the cafeterias, but fortunately she didn't have to go down there.

At the Mendocino store, she paused to look at a blue top in the window, and one of the sales girls standing by the cash register turned, like she had radar, and stared at Cora. She kept walking.

She didn't want to talk to any of them today. She just wanted to meet Melissa and leave.

By the south atrium, the Apple store swarmed with people, some of them spilling in front of her, some of them staring. She was glad she didn't have to go in there either and hurried into the Disney store, weaving through children's clothes decorated with Plutos and Flounders and Dalmations. She didn't see Melissa. Two women rummaged in the back, next to the pile of stuffed toys. On the right, another woman bounced a baby up and down, cooing softly.

In the middle of the store, Cora stopped in front of a stack of dolls from the Princess Collection and glanced at her cellphone. She was a few minutes late. No new messages.

She tucked her phone back in her purse and peered through the plastic cases of the dolls. She used to have all the original ones— Cinderella, Snow White, Sleeping Beauty, the Little Mermaid. The last had been her favorite until the summer she turned ten, when the whole family went camping at Golden Lake, and Nathan told her about the fish that ate people alive. He even had pictures to prove it, ripped out of a National Geographic from the library back home, showing off the fish and their razor sharp teeth.

The next day, he continued to tease her and laughed his head off when she ran screaming out of the water. Their father had not found it amusing, though. Even less so after she woke up at three in the morning, kicking and screaming. For the rest of the vacation, Nathan couldn't sit without a cushion, his bum was so red.

Mom tried to tell Cora the fish were harmless. The minnows nibbled on her toes every year. *Remember, sweetie? They made you giggle, because it tickled.*

But it didn't matter. She didn't swim that whole summer. Maybe not even the summer after.

~

Nathan sat on a rusted paint can, hiding in the bushes on the backside of a chain-link fence, looking down at the people strolling and walking dogs in the ravine. On his left, a pair of gray squirrels chased each other: guys duking it out over territory. This is my tree, you fucking stay away. He felt the dream woman too, hiding down the slope, waiting for her chance. He wished he had worn camouflage. The army gave it away for free, but you had to kill people for oil and virgins and pretend you were God or Jesus or some bullshit like that.

"You cannot hide anymore," the dream woman said.

Nathan spun right, and Blondie stepped out of the air. She wore green pants and a yellow blouse, looking like a parrot with an albino head.

"You must act," she said. "You must know how. The shadows are coming."

He grabbed a rock between his feet and threw it at her, but the rock swerved and bounced off the branches of a beech tree. He swore and scrabbled at the ground, digging up another rock. She backed away and stepped behind the trunk of a crooked maple.

"Yeah, run," he yelled. "I got your number. And it doesn't start with six."

"Then make it so," the woman said. "The time is coming. Too late is too late."

Nathan whipped the rock, and it smacked against the trunk of the maple and fell on the ground. She shook her head and vanished.

"Go back to your fucking country," he yelled. "You don't belong here."

A rock whistled through the air and rattled the branch over Nathan's head. He scrambled to his feet and darted eastwards along the fence, yelling curses. Another rock hurtled past him, and he turned downhill and crashed through the bushes.

From the bottom of the ravine, a dog barked at him. He told it to fuck off and hopped over a fallen branch and skidded down the last of the slope. At least he knew where to get rid of Blondie. She didn't stand a chance.

~

Cora heard her name and put down the baby-sized sweater with a picture of Goofy on the front. Melissa walked around a rack of clothes for toddlers, her heels muffled on the dark carpet. Even without the heels, she was four or five inches taller than Cora, tall considering her Chinese and French Canadian background, and had strong cheekbones and dark eyes and long black hair that sometimes made her look Spanish, depending on what she did with her makeup. Today, though, she looked very Chinese—something about her eyes—and wore a pair of tight, denim Capri pants, a dark green blouse that fit loosely over her small breasts, and gold hoop earrings. She never wore rings but had a fondness for bracelets made of jade or gold. Today they were both gold and on her left wrist, which either meant she was feeling creative, or she wanted to harmonize with the universe.

After exchanging pecks on the cheek, Melissa said, "What happened to your tan?"

Cora glanced down and rotated her arms. The palms of her hands were as pale as cream cheese—from washing them so often—but the rest seemed normal enough, even though she had missed her last two sessions at the tanning salon.

"You really think so?" Cora asked.

"Sorry, never mind. That was a totally shitty thing to say. You already have enough to worry about." Melissa poked the tiny sweater with the picture of Goofy and gave Cora a long look. "Did Kat call?"

"Yeah, she wanted to know what happened last night. And where Straw was. He didn't bring the car back."

"I wouldn't worry. He probably got drunk and hit somebody."

"God, I hope not," Cora said.

"Yeah, well, it's his problem, not yours. Like that guy at the hotel. Screw them."

Cora shivered. She didn't want to think about him. Not now. Not ever.

"The whole weekend was bad," she said.

"No kidding. I had a bunch of assholes too." Melissa leaned closer to Cora. "Sunday night was this fatso from Germany who kept wanting to go bareback. Like, hello, no. But he kept playing stupid, like 'no' was the only word he didn't understand. It was just 'try again later,' or 'better luck next time,' the stupid jerk."

"James is like that too. The one from Vancouver. And that Japanese guy you warned me about."

"Oh, Christ, don't remind me," Melissa said. "That was the guy last night." She laughed. "Honestly, I needed a magnifying glass."

"That bad?"

"Yeah, the condoms wouldn't fit," she said, "so I had to do it the old-fashioned way."

"I haven't had anyone that small," Cora said. "But close."

"Yeah, he wasn't happy. But I think he's used to it."

At the next table, a middle-aged woman frowned at them and hurried to the back of the store. Melissa rolled her eyes and walked to the display of Princess dolls.

"Let's get Annie her doll and get the hell out of here." She tapped two of plastic cases and peered at the different dolls. "Which one would you get? I was never into this stuff."

"Does she have any of them?"

"Just Cinderella, I think." Melissa tapped a plastic case next to one of the Cinderella dolls and went eeny, meeny, miney, mo and stopped at a Jasmine doll. "Space Lego was more my thing. But my parents wouldn't buy it for me, so I had to fight my brothers for it."

"Nathan never liked Lego. Too much work. But he was crazy about Transformers."

"Yeah, they were good too," Melissa said. "But, hey, what do I know. Look how I turned out."

"I'm sure she'll like it. Just like she likes you."

"Yeah, well," Melissa said and took the Jasmine doll to the cash register. "What do kids know."

After paying for the doll, Melissa led Cora past the McDonald's to the La Vie en Rose on the other side of the atrium. "Just quick. Then we'll go."

Cora rubbed her stomach, feeling queasy, but agreed and sifted through the lingerie at the back of the store while Melissa talked about her boyfriend, Derek, how it was getting difficult to hide work from him. He wanted her to come over more often and had mentioned moving in together. She posed in front of a mirror, draping a copper-colored teddy over her green blouse. Her Blackberry rang.

Melissa glanced at the screen and passed the teddy to Cora. "It's Kat."

"I'm not here," Cora said.

Melissa made a face and answered the call and walked to the front of the store, next to the display of mannequins wearing satin chemises and camisoles. Cora poked through the rack of bronze lingerie without really looking at the pieces. Her thoughts turned to Nathan and the eviction letter and what she had to do for supper. She didn't have any spaghetti sauce left in the freezer and needed to make another batch soon. She also wanted to cook the roast she had started to thaw yesterday but needed at least three hours without any surprises.

Melissa came back, frowning.

"What?" Cora said.

"Nothing. She just wants me to meet a guy for a quickie."

"Right now?"

"Yeah, he's sort of a regular. Likes to call last minute."

"Oh."

Melissa spun her Blackberry in her hands. "Sorry, Cora. Normally I wouldn't, but he's actually one I want to keep."

"It's okay, I understand."

"I just have to go downstairs and buy a couple of things."

Cora rubbed her stomach, thinking of all the people on the first floor, but Melissa started walking and Cora followed.

At the drugstore, two young guys with bad haircuts whispered and snuck glances at Melissa while she picked out a box of condoms and a bottle of lubricant.

"See, no microscopic sizes," she said and laughed, but the laugh ended abruptly. She passed the Jasmine doll to Cora. "Can you hold onto this? I won't need it till the weekend."

"Sure."

"We'll have coffee Thursday, maybe Friday."

"That should be okay," Cora said. "If we can do it around lunchtime? By Eglinton again?"

"I guess you're heading to your brother's?"

Cora nodded. They walked to the front of the store and lined up for the cashiers. After paying for the condoms and lubrication, Melissa led the way up the escalators to the atrium at the south end of the Sears and called Katrina back. Cora leaned against the railing overlooking the lower levels and gazed at a shoe store on the second floor.

On her right, a girl about five years old rushed up to the railing and poked her arms through the bars and dropped something small—red, blue, green—resembling candies. Cora glanced around for the girl's mother. A dozen feet away, three women stood around a stroller with a baby, gabbing, but none of them paid any attention to the girl. Another woman, with a tear in her black pantyhose, tromped past with two small children in tow and had no interest in a third.

The girl stuck her arms through the railing again and dropped more candies. Smarties? M&Ms? Cora eyed the group of three women again, but the girl turned abruptly and bumped her head against the railing and started to cry.

"Suzie!"

From the trio around the stroller, a chubby woman with dark, frizzy hair darted forward and yanked the girl away from the railing. The girl squealed. The woman glared at Cora and whisked the girl back to the stroller. Cora pressed a hand against her stomach. It rumbled and clenched. More people stared at her.

"Wow, bitchy or what," Melissa said and stuck her Blackberry in her purse.

Cora nodded, her insides twisting up like sheets in the washing machine. On the escalators coming from the second level, a man yelled. Someone else swore. She turned and saw a man charging up the escalators—a man with a lumpy bald head, wearing a blue jean jacket. She froze. It was the man who had started the fight at the hotel. He flung people out of the way, and several of them fell down the steps. One woman tumbled over the side and screamed.

For a split second, stunned silence gripped the onlookers. Then the mall erupted with a cacophony of shouts and screams, and Cora grabbed at Melissa's arm.

"Yeah, you fucking run," he yelled.

Without thinking, Cora sprinted towards the bright lights of the Sears, and Melissa stumbled. People scattered. Others gawked in confusion. Melissa stumbled again and lost a shoe. Cora continued to pull her friend along, and she swore and kicked off her other shoe.

The two girls ran between rows of cosmetic counters—Shiseido, Anna Sui, Clarins, Guerlain—but Melissa cried out and jerked free of Cora's grip. A split second later, pain exploded in her right shoulder. She tumbled to the floor. A man roared. Her stomach clenched. Her skin burned. The man grabbed one of her legs, but he roared again and shook his hands. Gold light crackled overhead.

Cora scrabbled at the floor, trying to get away from the man wearing the blue jean jacket. He howled and kicked her legs.

"Yeah, your chink ain't so fucking tough this time," he yelled and kicked her in the hips and the ribs. She curled up, trying to protect her belly and head.

"No! She is not yours to take," a woman yelled.

The blue jean man stopped and swore. At the other end of the Lise Watier counter stood a small Asian woman with long black hair, wearing a black silk blouse embroidered with tiny white flowers. He yanked a pistol from under his jacket and fired at her. One of the glass displays for Lise Watier exploded, and a mirror in the next row of cosmetic counters shattered and crashed to the floor.

The woman shook her head. The blue jean man cursed and continued to fire. The front section of the Lise Watier counter exploded. On the other side of the Sears, two more glass booths exploded, and a woman hiding behind one of them screamed.

From the atrium came the sound of running feet. "Stay down!"

The blue jean man fired two shots toward the voice, punching holes through a long purple banner advertising a skin cream. A policeman ducked behind one of the pillars of the entrance to the atrium.

"Yeah, fuck you, pig," the blue jean man yelled and turned the gun on Cora.

The policeman fired. The blue jean man staggered and dropped to his knees. Cora wriggled away from him, fighting against the pain in her side, and he scuttled between the cosmetics counters. The Asian woman wearing the black silk blouse sprang backwards onto the red carpet running down the center aisle of the store.

"Get down!" the policeman yelled.

The blue jean man fired another shot at the Asian woman. A glass display on the far side of the store shattered. He continued to fire at her, more glass exploding behind her, until his gun clicked, empty, and he hurled the gun at her. She caught it with her right hand and vanished.

"Fucking Christ," he yelled and ran toward the escalators in the middle of the Sears. The policeman yelled, "Stop!" and fired several shots at the blue jean man. He ducked between the last of the cosmetic counters, hurtled a railing and fell into the level below. A loud crash followed.

The policeman sprinted along the center aisle of the cosmetics area, yelling into his walkie-talkie. From the level below, someone screamed. The policeman bolted down an escalator.

Cora eased onto her elbows, ignoring the pains in her hips and her ribs. Next to Guerlain counter, Melissa sat up and rubbed her head. She swore and pushed away the stools among which she had fallen. Cora crawled closer.

From downstairs came more gunfire, and she huddled on the floor.

"You okay?" she asked Melissa.

"Yeah, great," she replied and picked up her purse. "Let's get the hell out of here."

"Shouldn't we stay down?"

"We don't know where that fucking guy is."

Cora winced and peered around the counter at the pool of shattered glass in the center aisle. A woman's head popped up from one of the cosmetic counters close to the atrium. Moments later the woman ran into the atrium, her white lab coat flapping behind like an awkward cape.

"Can you get up?" Melissa asked.

Cora nodded and crawled to her purse and the bag with the doll.

"Forget that," Melissa said and darted to the next counter.

Cora dropped her purse in the bag and followed, clutching her right side. At the last counter, two Asian girls about their own age huddled against each other, tears streaking their makeup. One of them stared at Melissa and said something to her in Chinese.

"I'm not waiting to find out," she said and darted into the atrium.

On the other side of the Sears, a woman wearing a red blouse mirrored them, bent over like a centenarian, and sprinted out the exit to Yonge Street, where a police cruiser sat on the sidewalk, its lights blazing. Two police officers charged through the same doors and ran into the Sears. Melissa sprinted to the opposite exit, into a courtyard with a small church huddled against the mall, across from a restaurant with a narrow patio and a long glass façade. She paused once to look at her bare feet before running past a water fountain and a fake stream that led to Bay Street, where the stream disappeared into a grate.

Next to the grate, Cora plunked down on a concrete lip, clutching her right side. Both her thigh and her ribs burned. Black spots floated in front of her.

"You okay?" Melissa asked.

"I think so. Just dizzy."

"He kicked you pretty hard."

"Yeah."

Melissa waved for a cab. "The hospital's not far. Just don't say too much. Play stupid."

Cora nodded. Half a block away, a police cruiser screamed through a red light, heading to the north end of the mall.

"I just hope they don't make you wait ten hours," Melissa said and touched her face. The upper half of her left cheek was red and had already started to swell. Then she scowled at her bare feet and swore. "You know how much those stupid shoes cost?"

"Maybe you can get them back later."

"Right, I'll just go ask for them."

Melissa waved at another cab, and it stopped beside them. She took the bag with the Jasmine doll, passed Cora her purse, and opened the back door for her. She eased into the cab, trying not to flinch. Her entire right side felt like it was on fire.

Melissa closed the door and gazed north and south, chewing on her lips. The cabbie stared at Cora, his face twisting in alarm. Then Melissa swore and grabbed the handle for the front door.

"Don't fall asleep," she said and slid into the cab. "That's supposed to be bad."

"I won't," Cora said.

"Good, we'll be there in a couple of minutes. Just remember, you fell down some stairs. That should be good enough. They don't care anyway."

Chapter 24

Nathan ducked into the trees beside the library, clutching the rock he had scooped from the Memorial Gardens. Blondie was still following him. He could feel her closing in, the shadows around him spitting and hissing.

"I know you're there," he yelled. "Go fuck yourself."

"You must feel him," she said from the direction of the parking lot. "He's calling us, every day stronger."

"I can't hear you," Nathan said.

"Now is the time to throw off your coward's nature and see the truth. You must stop him."

"Yeah? Watch this!"

Nathan whipped the rock at her voice, but the rock veered left and banged off the hood of a green sedan. He swore and ducked back into the trees and kicked at the ground, hunting for another rock. All he found was useless twigs and a crushed water bottle, so he grabbed at a branch overhead and tried to pull it down. The leaves shook and yelled at him. The shadows darted up and down the trees.

"You're a dream," he shouted. "I'm awake. Learn the fucking rules."

The shadows between the trees thickened, rippling over the leaves and needles. Something gurgled like a dying frog. Nathan shook his head and clapped his hands over his ears. A third hand grabbed his right arm, and fiery agony pierced his skin. He screamed and jerked away, and Blondie appeared next to him, hissing in pain. Together they tumbled out of the trees and fell on a patch of hard dirt. Fire cut through his insides. Bubbles of gold light burst around him. Shadows shrieked. He gasped for air. Him, her—it was all the same.

When the pain finally eased, he found himself lying on his back, looking up at the strip of sky between the canopy of the trees and the roof of the library. Next to him, the dream woman coughed. He jerked upright and scrambled away from her. She lay on her side, twitching, and shadows skittered all over her body like cockroaches made of oily smoke.

A dark figure stepped out of the stone wall of the library, wearing a black hat with a wide brim. Nathan stumbled backwards and tripped over his own feet.

"She should not have done that," the Jewish Zorro said. "She is not strong enough to resist Father's pull. I cannot help her anymore."

The dream woman convulsed and gasped. The shadows around her thickened, hissing, growling, grunting.

"You need to run," he said. "The dark one's seed will come after you."

"Fuck you," Nathan said.

The Jewish Zorro reached down to the dream woman and thrust his hand into her chest. Nathan bolted past the bay window for the magazines and newspapers of the library, turned right at the sidewalk, and dodged an old woman wearing a pink hat and pushing a walker. She squawked in alarm. At Lawrence Avenue, he gave the finger to the cars stopped for the red light and ran across and passed an entrance for the subway. To the north, a siren began to scream. He stopped abruptly. The cherries of a police car flashed five or six blocks ahead of him.

Nathan sprinted back to the subway entrance and knocked into a pale teenager wearing iron chains around his neck, a sideways baseball cap, and a black basketball shirt hanging down to his knees. They swore at each other, and Nathan ran down the stairs, turned left, and hurtled the turnstiles. A woman yelled from the collector's booth. He raced down two escalators, shoving past a chunky black woman wearing a purple nurse's uniform and a clump of teenage girls chattering like magpies. He ignored their outbursts and ran along the platform while a train rumbled in the left tunnel, headlights gleaming on the blackened walls.

"Fuck! Hurry up," Nathan yelled and ducked behind a pillar encircled by a red bench.

The train roared into the station, rattling a newspaper lying by his feet. He peered around the pillar for Zorro and the dream woman.

At the south end of the platform, to the right of the escalators, a greasy black slug about the size of a bulldog slithered down the steps. Nathan swore and ran to the back of the train. It made a ding-dong noise, and the doors slid open. He pushed past a skinny thirty-something wearing a suit, trying to step off the train, and darted to the back of the car. People stared. Nathan told them to fuck off. The doors clapped shut, and the greasy darkness splattered against the window behind an old man with bushy gray hair.

"You're all fucking useless," Nathan said. "You don't see anything. Nothing!"

The train began to move, and the darkness wriggled down the glass until only a few blobs remained visible. He jumped on a seat. The young Asian couple sitting in the last row scrambled to their feet and scurried past him to the middle of the train. He took their spots and wedged himself between the last two rows, across from an empty cubicle for conductors.

He stayed down, keeping quiet, until the train stopped at the next station. People rushed off. New people rushed on. Blobs of blackness clung to their sandals and their shoes and slid across the floor toward him.

"I ain't your bitch," he said. "You got that. I don't believe in you. You're not real."

The next stretch of tunnel flashed by in the mirror of the conductor's cubicle: the patches of darkness, the slanted walls, the lights that belonged in an old mine. The train then broke into the daylight, but it didn't stop the black blobs from thickening and bubbling, turning the floor in front of him into an oily pool.

At Davisville Station, people scurried off the train, and Nathan kicked at the blackness. It jerked away from him and hissed. He pulled his feet back and balled up against the wall. The train continued to speed southwards and sucked in more of the oily blackness at St. Clair Station. The morons dragged it in like dog shit. They didn't even know. They were too stupid.

From his hiding spot, Nathan yelled at them. The oily black pool bubbled and wriggled up the door of the cubicle. The train went ding-dong, and the rest of the doors clapped shut. More blobs wriggled across the floor and melted into the thickening pool. He kicked at it again, but the blackness jerked away from his foot.

"You fuckers," Nathan yelled. "Stop helping them."

The pool of gooey blackness rippled and shimmered. He stomped his feet and spat at it. A face pushed out of the oily surface on the cubicle, mocking him, and he gave it the finger. The train sped into another shadowy tunnel, and the gooey face rumbled and hissed. Nathan yelled and kicked at it. The blackness jerked apart like a giant mouth, and the mirror underneath shattered. He kicked again. Shards of glass tumbled on the floor. The blackness roared, and the window behind him exploded. The train jerked and screeched. A second window exploded, and Nathan smacked against the metal back of the seats. People screamed. A light exploded. The train jerked again, and Nathan and bonked his head against the metal backing.

The gooey blackness surged up from the floor and struck him like a wave. He screamed. The train screamed. The blackness ripped into his skin, and his whole body snapped tight. A star exploded. Gold light blazed. The blackness screeched and whipped around his face, trying to push into his lungs. Nathan sputtered and clawed at the goo. Another star exploded. Then everything shattered—the train, light, consciousness. Even time itself.

~

At the Toronto General Hospital, Cora followed Melissa into the emergency room, where everyone seemed to turn and stare at the pair. Melissa pointed to the booth labeled triage nurse. Cora nodded. She had gone to enough hospitals with Nathan to know the routine.

Without another word, Melissa passed Cora the bag with the Jasmine doll and disappeared in the washroom. She sighed, which made her ribs ache, and stepped to the booth. She told the triage nurse she had tripped on the stairs and fallen against a dresser. Her hip and right side hurt, especially her rib cage.

The nurse, a light-skinned Indian woman with an almond-shaped face and thin eyebrows, gazed at Cora for several seconds before handing her a clipboard and told her to fill out the paper-work. They would call her when they were ready to register her.

Cora thanked the nurse and sat down in the cramped waiting room next to another Indian woman, who had a baby snuggled against her red and gold sari. Melissa came out of the washroom five minutes later sporting an extra layer of blush, masking the bruise on her right cheek.

"I guess I won't be working for a couple days," she said.

"Do you want to sit?"

"No, I'm going to head out for a smoke."

Cora nodded, even though she did not want to be left alone, and watched while Melissa walked out the sliding doors, already dialing a number on her Blackberry. Then her gaze shifted to the ladies' washroom, and she realized she should have given the doll back. Her bladder felt ready to explode.

Cora tucked the clipboard on her chair and hurried to the wash-room. The doll would be fine where it was. The waiting room was full of people.

When she returned to her chair, a few minutes later, Melissa was still outside, sitting on a bench, and Cora sat down to finish the paperwork. Even though she had filled out such forms for Nathan more times than she cared to remember, she had not needed to go to a hospital for herself for at least five years. The last time must have been when she and Nathan still lived with Uncle Abner, struggling to come to terms with their unrelenting misfor-tune. Aunt Clara had died of cancer the year before; Nathan had returned home after eight months in the psychiatric hospital in St. Thomas. They still tried to pretend to be a normal family, though, and ate their meals together and sometimes watched TV together, usually a game show or a movie.

One Saturday night, they sat on the porch eating apple pie, barely saying a word, while the sun disappeared behind the trees at the back of the hay fields, creating long shadows across the farm. Bats flitted near the horse barn. Dogs barked from across the road. Nathan wanted more whipped cream, so Cora passed him the can, and something whacked the brick wall next to him. She jerked away from the sound, and her slice of pie slid off her plate and plopped on the porch. A second rock banged off one of the shutters. The third hit her in the head.

Later she vaguely remembered sitting on a kitchen chair, holding a towel to her head, while Uncle Abner tore through his coats, looking for the keys to his pickup. He drove double the speed limit to the hospital in Tillsonburg. Once there, he yelled at the nurses until a doctor came to look.

"It's not so bad. You just need a couple of stitches," the doctor said and patted her leg. "At least they didn't hit that pretty face of yours."

She remembered looking down at her hands, embarrassed, but pleased at the same time. He looked like an older version of Brad Pitt, in a hawkish, angular, sort of way.

The second time he patted her leg, his whole body twitched, and he stepped backwards, looking startled. Moments later he stammered an apology, bumped into the nurse, and rushed out of the cubicle. Cora never saw him again.

By the time the nurse returned to do the stitches, she said Cora didn't need any stitches and scowled at Uncle Abner, who had gotten tired of sitting in the waiting room and stood with his arms crossed on the right side of the hospital bed.

"What you mean?" he demanded. "She's bleeding all over the place. Look at her hair."

"I don't know what's in her hair," the nurse said. "But it's not hers."

Uncle Abner continued to argue with the nurse, who looked ready to throttle him, until a shout from the waiting room interrupted them. Cora slid off the gurney. Another shout came from the waiting room. Something was wrong with Nathan.

Uncle Abner caught Cora by the arm, but she slipped free and hurried past the reception desk. Nathan stood on a chair in a corner of the waiting room, swatting at the air with a magazine, while people scattered to the other end of the room and the entrance.

"Get down," Uncle Abner yelled, tailing Cora.

"Nathan, it's okay," she said. "We can go home. I'm okay."

Her brother swore and kicked at nothing, rocking his chair.

She darted the last few steps and steadied him. "Let's go home. There's still some apple pie. Ice cream, too."

"They're coming," he said. "I saw them. The fuckers flew right through here."

"Get off that chair," Uncle Abner said. "Before you fall and crack your head. It's bad enough already."

"It's okay," Cora said. "I'll help you down."

"They're everywhere," Nathan said and flung his magazine across the room. "Crawling over everything. The fucking floor. The fucking ceiling."

"That's why we're going to go. We'll just go home." Cora took his right hand and led him to the exit. "We'll talk to your doctor tomorrow. I'm sure he can help get rid of them."

"A lot of good that'll do." Uncle Abner paused in the exit and yelled back into the waiting room. "You're not good for nothing."

When they reached the pickup, an old blue Ford with a crooked tailgate, Nathan climbed into the cab without complaining about sitting in the middle.

"You should go back inside," Uncle Abner said to Cora. "We'll get them to look at you proper. All night if it takes."

"I'm okay." She touched the crusty hair above her right ear. "It doesn't hurt anymore."

"This ain't right. None of it."

"Maybe it was just a prank," Cora said. "Some paint left over from Halloween."

Uncle Abner growled and shook his head while Cora climbed in beside Nathan. She buckled her seatbelt and smiled to show him she was fine. He said he would find the boys who had done this, them and their damn pranks, and walked around to the driver's side.

"I'm going to fool them," Nathan said. "They'll never find me."

"Don't worry," Cora said. "He's just upset. He'll be fine tomorrow."

"He's been mad a long time. Longer than God."

"Don't start with that," Uncle Abner said and climbed into the pickup. "We're still a respecting household, whatever they let you get away with in that loony bin."

Fifteen minutes later, after seeing Cora safe in the house, Uncle Abner grabbed his shotgun from a locked cabinet in the basement and checked the barns. She turned the TV on for Nathan and took a shower, which stung her scalp a little but otherwise felt good.

When she came back downstairs, Uncle Abner was still outside, and she didn't see Nathan anywhere. She called his name, but he didn't answer, so she stepped on the porch to collect the plates and forks and clean off the squashed remnants of her pie. She also found two rocks the size of tennis balls, which made her cringe, and dropped them over the railing.

While turning back to the screen door, she noticed Nathan standing beside the pickup.

"Why don't you come inside?" she called out. "I'm sure there's something on TV."

"No, they won't find me. I won't let them."

Cora waited and shivered, the coolness of the night air prickling her bare arms.

"You don't need to worry," she said. "It was just a couple of jerks from town."

"Piggly and Wiggly," Nathan said.

Cora nodded, knowing who he meant. The troublemakers were always the same ones.

"Please, it's been a long night," she said.

Nathan shook his head and walked up the driveway toward the road. She sighed and carried the plates and forks into the kitchen, scrubbed them off, and put them in the dishwasher. Hopefully he would just check the mailbox and come back. She had already taken out the flyers at lunchtime.

It wasn't until midnight, with Nathan still gone, that she realized he had had no intention of ever coming back.

~

At the Toronto General Hospital, an ambulance screamed past the windows of the waiting room, and Cora put down her clipboard and peered outside. Where had Melissa gone? She wasn't sitting on the bench anymore. There was only a pudgy man in Bermuda shorts and a Hawaiian shirt, smoking and talking on his cellphone.

Cora slid the clipboard on her chair and stepped outside and looked around the corner, toward the bay for the ambulances. Past the windows of the waiting room, Melissa leaned against the concrete wall, spinning her Blackberry in her left hand.

"I thought maybe you'd gone," Cora said.

Melissa frowned at her bare feet and wiggled her toes. "I feel like a total hillbilly."

"I'll buy you a new pair, whatever you want."

Melissa took a drag of her cigarette and flicked the rest into a bush in front of her. "You seem a lot better. You're not even holding your ribs anymore."

"Yeah," Cora said and rubbed her right side. "I guess he didn't hit me that hard."

"Bullshit."

Cora gazed at the light brown brick of the hospital across the street—the Hospital for Sick Kids—and realized she was only a block away from Nathan's psychiatrist. For some reason, the hospitals in the downtown were all lumped together like a big concrete sandwich.

"So who was that guy?" Melissa asked.

"What?" Cora said, startled.

"He sure seemed to know you."

Cora winced and rubbed her arms, picturing for a moment the man with the lumpy bald head. "He's the one from the hotel, the one who started the fight in the lobby."

"And he happened to show up at the mall, looking for you?"

"No, I swear. I never saw him before, not before last night."

Melissa pulled out another cigarette and lit it.

After a long drag, she asked, "You think any of your daddies might be looking for you?"

"Why would they?" Cora shook her head. "That doesn't make any sense."

"It depends on how much they want to find you. You've left a few guys behind."

"I don't have time for all of them."

Melissa sucked on her cigarette, looking annoyed.

"Sorry, you know what I mean," Cora said.

"Yeah," Melissa said, still looking annoyed. "That's why none of the girls want to share with you." She took another drag. "They know they won't get those clients back. Or they keel over like that Chinese guy last week."

Cora stared at Melissa. "What?"

"Kat didn't tell you?"

"You mean James?"

"I don't know," Melissa said. "The guy from Friday. She calls him lucky number seven."

Cora leaned against the wall, shaking her head.

"She said it was on the news. Heart attack on the plane."

"Are you sure?" Cora said. "She didn't say anything."

"What about the producer from New York?" Melissa asked. "I think he keeled over a few weeks ago."

Cora shook her head again and pressed a hand to her stomach. It started to roll, as if she had eaten too many sweets, and dark spots floated in front of her eyes.

"Hey, whoa." Melissa flicked her cigarette on the grass and steadied Cora. "Let's get you back inside."

"No, I—" Cora began to say, but a flare of pain cut through her belly, and she dropped to her knees.

"Here, I got you," Melissa said.

"No, wait."

"Christ, what are you doing?"

Cora pulled away from Melissa, the pain gone, and stumbled to the sidewalk and waved at a red and yellow cab coming from University Avenue. Melissa sprang after Cora and grabbed her shoulders.

"No! You don't understand," Cora said.

"Are you crazy? You need a doctor."

"I'm okay. It doesn't hurt anymore."

"You can barely stand," Melissa said.

As the cab passed them, Cora waved again. The driver made a U-turn in the intersection and pulled up beside them.

"What the hell is wrong with you?" Melissa said. "You need to go back inside."

"It's not me. It's Nathan."

Melissa tightened her grip on Cora, but she pulled away and opened the back door of the cab.

"I'll call you later," she said.

"Screw that," Melissa said and yanked on the front door the cab and jumped inside. "You're not going anywhere."

"It's okay, you don't have to come."

"No! Forget it!"

After a few seconds of silence, Cora climbed into the cab and gave the driver the address for Nathan's apartment.

"I hope that's near a hospital," Melissa said. "I'm not dragging your crazy ass back here."

"It's Nathan," Cora said. "He's been hurt. I have to find him. I don't know how to explain it."

"That's the stupidest thing I've ever heard."

"No, I can feel it. I know."

"I still think you're fucking crazy."

Cora nodded. It was crazy. But she knew she had to find him. She had to help him. Before it was too late.

Chapter 25

Under the shadows of a scraggly elm tree, Alex squatted against the painted brick wall of a beer store, drinking a cream ale, and eyed the cars in the small parking lot. Did he want to steal another one? The first car had been easy. And it was better than waiting for Teresa to come get him. Or those butt monkeys Mobius had brainwashed into playing commando.

Alex tossed his empty bottle aside and eyed a purple minivan pulling into a parking space adjacent to him. A blond kid, three or four years old, squashed his face against the window of the passenger seat and wiped his nose back and forth, leaving streaks, though Alex wasn't certain if the kid was actually a boy. They all had long hair these days. The mother, who looked barely out of diapers herself, yanked on the kid and slapped him across the head. The kid bawled. After another slap, she hauled the kid out of the minivan, saying, "You'd better knock it off, or you'll be hurting later."

While she tugged the kid into the beer store, Alex opened another bottle of cream ale. Yeah, the brave new world. That's why he had fought Hitler—saving it for all the decent folk.

He took a long swallow and wiped his mouth. From inside his jacket, his cellphone rang. He grimaced, swigged more beer, and glanced at the call display. It showed the same number Teresa had used earlier.

"Yes, mistress," he said, answering the phone.

"The number you gave for Leroy is located on Queens Quay West, next to the Radisson hotel." Teresa then gave him the address and hung up.

Alex drained the rest of his beer and tossed the bottle aside. After shoving the remaining beers in his duffel bag, he strode through the parking lot and flagged the cab sitting in front of the coffee shop across the street.

About fifteen minutes later, he told the cab driver to stop a quarter-mile before the Radisson hotel. The water of the harbor glinted on his left, partially obscured by a fancy office building with a grocery store at the front. On his right, a wall of condos towered over a broad sidewalk.

Alex paid the driver and crossed the streetcar tracks bifurcating Queens Quay West. He hurried to a long, white building that reminded him of a community center. Inside, he passed a shop selling colorful knickknacks, a bored-looking security guard wedged behind a small desk, and a round counter displaying a variety of pamphlets—fun for the kids, dancing, music, arts.

At the end of the hallway, he pulled another beer out of his duffel bag and ducked outside again. He gulped half the bottle, cut across a patch of grass, and paused underneath an empty white tent. There was a whole row of them next to a slip where a dozen or so boats were docked. On the other side of the slip stood a refurbished warehouse, behind which rose the Radisson hotel. A second warehouse sat closer to the lake, partially obscured by a white bridge for pedestrians that arced over the slip.

On Queens Quay, a streetcar clanged and a car honked at a shirtless guy running across the lanes. Alex swigged his beer and climbed up the steps of the bridge but froze when he reached the landing. What the hell was he doing? He felt like a duck on a shooting range, ready to be picked off by the nearest jackass on a roof.

A chunky white couple carrying backpacks climbed up the steps opposite him and passed him. They laughed at a seagull trying to gobble a french fry before flying out of their way. He muttered a curse and followed them. Right, taking the street was too obvious. That was the whole point of getting out of the cab early. He should have come from the west, though. That would have been smarter.

In the middle of the bridge, the couple stopped to snap a picture of the city, the CN Tower sticking up like a finger behind the wall of condos. Alex crouched beside the railing, patted the grenade in the right pocket of his jacket, and took another swig of his beer. The couple stopped talking and stared at him.

He saluted them with the beer. "Welcome to Canada."

They turned and hustled the west end of the bridge. Alex guzzled the rest of his beer and waited for the next group of people to come on the bridge, some Chinese folks wearing sunhats. They had small children with them, though, so he changed his mind and strode after the chubby couple.

The warehouse next to the lake had a restaurant with a patio where half-a-dozen people ate and drank. Alex plunked his empty beer bottle on one of the tables, ignoring the people who gave him strange looks. At the same time, he noticed the marina on the other side of the restaurant was full of police boats, a dozen steps from the back of the Radisson Hotel.

Yep. Teresa sure picks them. All the best spots in town.

He walked around the south-west corner of the other warehouse, which was decorated with large red pictures of dogs and cats, and paused. Cold rippled across his shoulders and down his back. He slid a hand into the right pocket of his jacket and pulled the pin on the grenade. His gaze flickered over the windows of the hotel. Maybe Teresa had a surprise for him after all. She wasn't one for games, but Mobius always stuck his fingers in everything.

Alex stayed close to the wall of the warehouse and passed two parked cars and a red bakery truck. On the far side of Queens Quay, in front of a Japanese restaurant, sat a white van with party balloons painted on the side. He stopped. He had seen the same van at the Royal York after Peter reported feeling a presence.

Behind Alex, the side door of the bakery truck slid open, trying to be quiet. He turned and saw a flak jacket and Tarantino, his face blue and swollen, his left arm hanging in a sling. Next to him sat a blond man with a pistol aimed at Alex—the man with fish eyes.

"Looking for this?" Tarantino said and held up a cellphone. "We already found it in the garbage. Leroy's long gone."

"Good for him," Alex said and pulled the grenade out of his jacket. Bullets punched into his chest. He staggered backwards, pain rocketing into his head. His hand flicked up. Hot white sparks flashed across his vision.

Bullets continued to punch through his flesh. Others swerved and smashed into cars and brick walls and windows. The grenade flew. Men yelled and jumped, but they were too late.

Alex hit the pavement, his vision obliterated by blood. The van exploded. Men screamed. Then he gasped, and everything went black.

~

Teresa walked out of her mansion, past beds of white and pink and red roses, and climbed into the back of her black SUV. Mueller sat in the front, his hands clutched together, looking frightened enough to vomit.

"Mistress," he said and bowed his head.

She ignored him until the SUV pulled out of the gates and then imagined Mueller's lungs collapsing like a leaky balloon. He squeaked and clutched his chest.

"You've spent too much time with Mobius," she said. "You've forgotten your loyalties."

"No, Mis—mistress. You, only—"

"Then why are you hiding things from me?" she demanded. "You should have found Leroy already. You should have known where he would be."

"Pl—please."

Disgusted, she released him and told the driver to turn on the music. Mueller coughed and slapped his chest.

"Tell me where he is," Teresa said.

"Leroy used us. Our source. The police," Mueller said, between coughs. "Traced license. A car."

"Whose?"

"Katrina Elliott. Owner. Black sedan. Bathurst. The street."

"Why?"

"Yes, looking," Mueller said and coughed. "Just happened. Just now. The call. Team going. On its way."

Teresa grimaced and flipped the music to Stravinsky's *Rite of Spring*. Why did she always have to trade one idiot for another? No matter how many she sacrificed, there were always thousands more waiting to replace them.

A few minutes later, the car stopped for a red light across from a Catholic school with a large green lawn. Mueller's Blackberry rang. He clapped a hand over it and glanced at her, his face screwed up like a frightened child. She scowled and hit the back of his seat.

He hurried to answer the call. Teresa heard the words "Alex" and "explosion."

"Take me there," she yelled. "Now!"

~

The SUV accelerated onto the Gardiner Expressway, and Teresa glared at the high-rises of downtown Toronto, still a mile away. The cities nowadays made it so easy for Father. Thousands of fools huddled in every block, nourishing him with their secret pains, waiting for him to twist and jerk and prod. She felt him too, at the edge of her thoughts, stirring memories of long ago: the mobs in Spain hunting Jews; the bodies of the diseased, filling house after house; the water pulling her down, squeezing the life out of her. Every one of those memories still lurked inside her, hidden in the crevices of her mind.

"Why are you taking so long?" she said to the driver. "We should have been there already."

"We're almost there, mistress," Mueller said.

The driver cut in front of another SUV, a white Cadillac, and pulled into an off-ramp. At the bottom of the ramp, the driver continued westward under the expressway until he reached Bay Street and turned south. Teresa frowned, the wail of sirens coming from multiple directions. Two blocks later, Bay street ended at Queens Quay, at the entrance for the ferry docks, and the driver turned west again, toward the flashing lights of fire trucks and police cars.

"Mistress?" Mueller said.

"Shut up!"

He settled back in his seat and tapped a message on his Blackberry. The driver stopped at the next intersection, a police car blocking the street ahead. A middle-aged officer wearing a yellow fluorescent jacket waved for them to turn right.

"Go around him," Teresa said.

"But, mis—" Mueller said.

With barely a thought, Teresa flung him against the dashboard of the car; then she kicked open her door, sending it scraping across the street, and stormed across the intersection. A blue Civic

Hatchback jerked and squealed as the driver slammed on his brakes. The policeman yelled at her.

Teresa flicked her right hand and hurled the policeman across the intersection. With another flick of her hand, she threw his cruiser aside. She ignored the gawkers standing in front of a coffee shop and an ice cream shop.

At the corner of Lower Simcoe, she passed a second police car blocking westbound traffic and spotted wisps of smoke coming from behind a warehouse. Another fire engine and ambulance roared in from the west. She passed more gawkers, but the majority of them were clustered in front of a grocery store, across from the jigsaw of personnel, gurneys, and emergency vehicles wedged between the Radisson hotel and a warehouse spattered with pictures of dogs and cats.

Teresa stepped on a curb that demarcated the lane for streetcars and frowned at a red van cracked open like a piñata. Amid the wreckage lay two bodies burned like sausages. Another lay on the ground nearby, but too many firemen and paramedics hovered around the body for her to know if it was dead. Probably not considering the fuss.

"Hey! Sweetheart! Get back to the sidewalk," yelled a tanned policeman.

Teresa brushed her hair from her face and scowled at him. He collapsed on the street.

Another officer yelled, "Man down!"

A woman with her chestnut hair pulled back in a bun sprinted from behind one of the fire engines, toward her fallen comrade, while a tall policeman with tattoos on his right arm jogged toward Teresa, one hand on his holster, his eyes scanning the crowd on the north side of the street. She flicked her right hand. He catapulted through the air and crashed on the roof of an ambulance.

A third officer yelled at Teresa to get down. She threw him into a flower bed in front of the animal warehouse.

The officers closest to Teresa drew their guns. She threw the female officer into a streetlight. An officer wearing shorts and a bicycle helmet smashed on the hood of a police car. The Negro rocketed into the air and crashed back to the ground. A fireman, anonymous in his dirty yellow uniform, hurtled through the windshield of a fire engine.

"Enough. Save your strength," a man said, dressed in black from head to toe, a large hat hiding his bald head. "They are not a part of this. Leave them be."

Teresa stared at him.

No. He was dead. He had to be.

Around her, the world snapped back into motion. People yelled from multiple directions. Guns fired. Bullets whizzed past her, and two of the gawkers screamed and tumbled to the ground. Melons and strawberries exploded. Windows shattered.

"Cease fire," someone shouted. "Cease fire!"

Paul waved for Teresa to follow him and strode eastwards while panicked onlookers tumbled over each other on the sidewalk. After a dozen or so steps, he vanished.

Teresa bolted in the opposite direction but tripped on the hem of her skirt. A policeman ran in front of her and grabbed at her. She struck him, shattering his forearm, and he screamed and collapsed.

She hiked up her skirt and ran westwards on the street. Once past the Radisson Hotel, she flung aside a blonde woman wearing a white tank top and pink jogging shorts, her Great Dane barking like mad, and sprinted into a half-empty parking lot. Ahead, a Middle Eastern couple stopped beside a silver Audi, the man fumbling with his keys. His wife yelled at him and whacked him with her purse.

Teresa jolted to a stop. What was she doing? Why was she running? Paul had no power over her anymore. He no longer had Father.

But how could Paul have survived? It was impossible. He had been separated from Father for almost seventy years. No one had ever lasted more than a few weeks. Father always pulled his children back; or destroyed them, taking back the black seed—the dark fragment of his soul—that fed their immortality.

At the southeast corner of the parking lot, a pair of police officers trotted into view and drew their guns. Teresa flicked her right hand to throw a car at them. Nothing happened.

She turned and sprinted diagonally across the parking lot to a concrete abutment for the Gardiner Expressway, which hovered three or four stories above her. Underneath the expressway snaked Lake Shore Boulevard, the eastbound lanes thick with traffic.

She continued running west alongside the boulevard and passed two filthy bums with frizzy beards sitting behind a wooden stockade stinking of garbage. They ducked down and covered their heads. She ripped open a black fence and ran into another parking lot, a narrow one behind a long building with two apartment towers. The sirens of a police car flashed under the expressway, but the car continued speeding eastwards, oblivious to her.

Once she reached the end of the building, Teresa found a streetcar idling on a turnaround loop. Beyond that, traffic clogged the street running north and south. She scowled. Why was she wasting so much energy? Father would notice soon. She was supposed to be more careful.

An old man wearing a blue T-shirt and baggy shorts limped alongside the streetcar and up its steps, his skinny legs as pale as bleached bone, and she remembered her cellphone, forgotten in the SUV. Did old men carry phones? The young ones seemed to grow them from their ears.

Teresa sprinted closer. In the driver's seat of the streetcar, she found a dark-skinned man with a small face, scratching his chin. She darted up the steps, grabbed him by the throat, and jerked him off his seat.

"Your phone!" she demanded.

He squawked and swatted at her. She grabbed his right arm and squeezed. He screamed.

"Your phone," she repeated.

"Here," he said, jabbing at the pocket on the right side of his shorts. "Take!"

"You're a fool," she said. "You deserve to die."

"No!" he said and scrabbled around with his free hand, trying to grab something to support his weight.

Teresa dropped him back in his seat and ripped the pocket of his shorts open and scooped up his cellphone as it tumbled free. He clapped a hand around his throat and coughed.

She turned her glare on the old man, sitting six rows back. He dropped his gaze to his legs and shook his head. She frowned at the cellphone she had taken and realized she only knew two or three numbers in Toronto. Mobius had programmed everything into her phones. Even before phones had such options, he had always offered to make every call or dial the numbers. She should have realized the numbers themselves had power.

The driver jerked towards her. She pivoted and struck his arms, but he still managed to knock her off balance as he shrieked in pain. She fell backwards down the steps and hit the concrete curb.

While the driver continued to scream, she kicked the steps, rocking the streetcar, and rolled onto her knees. Where was the phone? She had dropped the stupid thing.

The doors of the streetcar clapped shut. She scooped the cellphone off the asphalt and kicked the side of the streetcar, putting a large dent in it. The streetcar clanged. With her left hand, she grabbed at the doors. One of them ripped open. Teresa growled and ripped the second door off and sprang inside. The driver cowered in his seat, his face twisted in terror.

"That was stupid," she said.

The driver shuddered and murmured under his breath, praying to whatever god he believed in. She grabbed his head and snapped his neck.

From the back of the streetcar, an all-too familiar voice said, "They are not a part of this. Leave them be."

She glared at Paul, who stood across from the rear doors of the streetcar. "You're dead," she said. "I don't believe in you."

"That would be best, perhaps. But I do not know when His mercy shall come to pass."

Without thinking, she hurled the driver's cellphone at Paul. It passed through him and bounced off the curved window at the back of the streetcar before clattering to the floor.

"See! You're not real. You can't do this to me. Not anymore."

Teresa walked to the old man frozen in his seat, his gaze glued to his pale, flabby legs.

"Enough," Paul said and stepped toward her. "Leave them be."

"No! You're the one who's dead," Teresa shouted and charged

him. Daylight blurred. Sound stopped. Flesh ignited. Shadows surged. Then the shadows roared and exploded and hurled her through a window that no longer had glass. She crashed into the side of a gray Toyota.

"N—no," Teresa said, trying to sit up.

The driver of the Toyota scrambled out of his car, shouting in Chinese. She flung the car on its side, and the driver scrambled behind a red compact.

Teresa shook herself and looked around for Paul but didn't see him anywhere. Instead, only a few hundred feet away, a police car blocked the eastbound lane of Queens Quay, beyond which gleamed the waters of the harbor, and a policeman wearing a fluorescent yellow vest ran towards her.

She darted around the gray Toyota and ran northwards along the empty lane reserved for streetcars. At the intersection under the Gardiner Expressway, a car turning left swerved and slammed on its brakes as she raced in front of it. On the other side of the intersection, she ran up a hill lined with new condominiums, the lanes on either side of her jammed with cars. Sirens screamed from multiple directions.

Once she reached the top of the hill, Teresa saw several clusters of flashing lights coming towards her on the lane reserved for the streetcars. After a quick scan of the surrounding towers, she hopped over the barrier to her right and flung a green Subaru out of her way. It smashed into another pair of cars. She ran into a side street that paralleled the corridor for the railroad coming from Union Station, but the street turned left, blocked by the Rogers baseball stadium, and she ran across a bridge arcing over the tracks. A police car coming from the north appeared on the bridge to the west while a second police car raced up from the south.

Ahead of Teresa, a white van screeched around the nearest corner and raced toward her. She paused. The van slammed to a stop beside her, and the sliding door banged open.

A man wearing a black flak jacket yelled at her to get in. He had a thick, wrinkled face like a bulldog and black hair cropped short enough to reveal a large knob on his crown. A second white van screeched to a stop in the intersection ahead of her.

On the bridge, the first of the police cars appeared, its lights blazing.

The man wearing the flak jacket jumped out of the van and yelled, "Do it! Do it!"

The driver of the first van gunned the engine and charged the police car. The second white van jerked to a stop beside Teresa, and the sliding door snapped open. A second man wearing a black flak jacket waved her inside.

"Get in! Hurry!"

The first van and the police car smashed together. Teresa hopped into the second van, and the man with the bulldog face jumped in after her and slammed the sliding door shut. The van cut across the street, making a wide U-turn. Teresa fell back on a layer of heavy brown blankets covering rifles and heard the driver ask for further instructions. It took her a second to realize he wasn't asking her.

"Where's Mobius?" she demanded.

"He sent us," said the man with the bulldog face.

She flung him into the wall of the van and glared at the other man sitting in the back of the van. He had eyes like black olives and dyed blond hair and a snake tattoo on his neck, reminding her of the man she had killed in her chapel.

"We weren't told," he said.

A third white van sped past them, heading south. Teresa's van turned east. A police car screamed past, heading in the opposite direction. A fourth white van appeared, also speeding south.

"How did you find me?" she demanded.

"Dispatch," the blond man said. "They told us your location."

Teresa glanced at the man with the bulldog face, who sat up slowly, rubbing his jaw. She flicked a finger and threw him head-first against the side of the van again. The driver glanced back, swearing.

"Where are we going?" she asked.

"They haven't confirmed a location yet," the driver said. "They told me to zigzag. The others are running interference."

"Then you'd better find out," Teresa said. "Or you won't have any arms left to drive."

Chapter 26

Nathan's eyes flicked open moments before a thick tentacle latched on his left hand, an alien with a giant glowing eye hanging over him, its other tentacle reaching for his testicles. He squeaked and slapped at it, but the tentacles grabbed him and pushed him down.

"Take it easy," the alien said. "We'll get you out of here."

Nathan jabbed the thick hide of the glowing monstrosity. "Get off! Get off me!"

"Hey, Bernie! Give me a hand with this one," the alien yelled.

A second glowing monstrosity lumbered up behind the first—its evil twin—and Nathan froze. They looked exactly like his father. They even had fluorescent yellow stripes on their hides and oxygen tanks on their backs. Then he noticed the stink of scorched metal and the moans and the crying and pulled away from the firemen and bumped his head against a seat.

"Relax," the first fireman said. "We'll get you out of here."

"I didn't do it," Nathan said. "It wasn't me."

"Yeah, all right," the fireman said and turned to his twin, Bernie. "We need another stretcher over here. All this glass . . ."

"You're not my father," Nathan said.

"Yeah, you're probably right about that," the first fireman said.

The other fireman, Bernie, stomped to the opposite end of the train car where two firemen hoisted someone onto a stretcher. Nathan tried to sit up, clutching his side, but the first fireman stopped him.

"Get off me, you fucking queer," Nathan said.

"Just relax. We'll get you out in a minute."

Nathan slapped at the arm restraining him. When that failed to work, he hit the mask covering the fireman's face. The man lurched back and swore.

Nathan pulled himself up and leaned against the seat behind

him and rubbed his arms. His skin felt itchy, as if something wanted to crawl inside. All around him, shadows wiggled and flickered, but none of them seemed to be alive.

The fireman reached out to Nathan again, but he shook a fist at the fireman.

"All right, if you want it that way," the fireman said.

"Fuck you," Nathan said. "You're not my father."

"Yeah, I think we got that already."

Bernie came back, looking annoyed, and the two firemen talked about how to handle Nathan as if he was deaf and stupid. He looked out the shattered window at the slanted wall of the tunnel, a wonky yellow light glowing off to the right, next to a timber holding up the roof.

"Hey, Lone Ranger. This way," said the first fireman. "Let's get you out of here."

Bernie reached out to support Nathan, but he swore and brought up both fists.

"Don't touch me," he said.

"Yeah, he's a charmer," said the first fireman.

Bernie shook his head and led Nathan past a fireman talking to a Filipino woman with blood spattered on her face and neck. To their left, a pair of sliding doors had been pried open, and Bernie walked down a set of yellow steps hooked on the side of the train car.

Nathan poked his head out and glanced around at the shadows twisting throughout the tunnel. Where was the black goo? Was it still out there? The shadows could hide anything.

"It's not far," Bernie said. "We can help."

"Fuck you," Nathan said. "I know all about your help."

"Good," Bernie said and waved Nathan down the steps. "Easy does it."

"Yeah, we got to get this next one out," the first fireman said.

Nathan glanced over his shoulder at the Filipino woman, wailing something in broken English. Yes, he had to play dumb. That was the way to get out. They were all the same, all playing the same game.

He climbed down to the floor of the tunnel and rubbed his

nose. The air stank of hot metal and stagnant water, the shadows everywhere, growing arms and legs and fangs. Bernie pointed out the tracks and stepped over them to the other half of the tunnel.

About five hundred feet away, a subway station glowed like the sun. Nathan darted toward it and tripped on a metal box between the tracks.

The first fireman swore. Bernie steered Nathan to a narrow concrete walkway on the side of the tunnel.

"I'll go with him," Bernie called to the first fireman. "You can help Ted."

The first fireman ducked back into the train. Bernie hustled to catch up to Nathan and pointed out the steps leading up to the northbound platform. Nathan stopped abruptly and stared at the people in the station, dozens of them standing, kneeling, or lying on the floor, some of them cops, others with needles, the big long needles they used before they tied you down and locked you up.

Bernie called out, "Hey, Mac. Got one for you. Special delivery."

A fireman on the platform glanced in their direction. Nathan tottered back a step. Bernie reached out to catch Nathan. He swore and ran back into the tunnel.

"Hey!" Bernie yelled and chugged after Nathan.

A second fireman lurched out from the shadows of the subway train, a troll with a flashlight strapped to his head, and Nathan clutched his aching side and tried to run faster. He wasn't going to let them get him, not this time. He knew all their tricks.

Two more men yelled from the train. He hopped closer to the wall on his right, which angled up steeply to the eerie yellow lights. About a hundred yards ahead of him, a shaft of sunlight poured through the roof, revealing a ladder. Further on, the tunnel curved left into another station.

When Nathan reached the ladder, he paused and shielded his eyes. It looked like a trap, the ladder leading straight into a little hole, the sunlight a piece of cheese. And snap!

He continued running to the next station, only two people visible on the platforms. As he neared the dirt-stained steps leading up the northbound platform, he slowed down and stayed low. At the top of the steps, he scrambled over a metal barricade.

Opposite him, on the southbound platform, a man wearing a dark blue shirt popped out of an opening and yelled. Nathan sprinted up a cleaner stairway and knocked into a confused-looking Japanese girl holding a glossy pink suitcase.

The guy in the blue shirt spurted out of the stairwell next to a collector's booth. Nathan jumped the turnstiles and ran outside—a parking garage across the street, stores to the right, restaurants, people. He cut around a chain-link fence, the guy in the blue shirt still yelling, and ran past the tunnels for the buses, low-rises made with mud bricks, and houses like clones. Trees appeared at the end of the street—a whole fucking ravine full.

Nathan whipped out his middle finger and sprinted across the last intersection. Car tires screeched. A horn blared. He scrambled over a rusty fence and skidded down the slope of the ravine and didn't stop until he reached the trail at the bottom. Then, his lungs burning, he fell to his knees and vomited.

~

While unlocking the door to Nathan's apartment, Cora asked Melissa to wait in the hall. "Just for a second. I don't think he's here, but—"

"Would you go already? I have to pee."

"Sorry," Cora said and stepped into the apartment.

The sound of dripping of water came from the kitchen, and she rushed to the sink. The cold water tap wasn't quite closed, but the drain was open underneath a bowl, a plate, and some utensils. Cornflakes were scattered on the floor and counter. Next to the microwave, a half-eaten banana dangled from the bowl of fruit.

In the bedroom, she found his sheets tangled on the floor in front of the window. He wasn't hiding in the closet. The bathroom was empty.

"Is he home or what?" Melissa asked, leaning into the apartment.

"No."

"The way you were talking, I thought this place would be a dump."

"It's just the landlord. He's terrible."

"They're all like that. Otherwise they get bored." Melissa pointed to the door of the bathroom.

"Sorry, yeah," Cora said.

"Is it cool if I wash my feet?"

"Uh, okay."

Melissa disappeared into the bathroom. Cora pulled out a blue towel from the cabinet beside the TV, her mind churning over where Nathan might have gone. Her side didn't hurt anymore, so maybe he was okay after all. Except something must have happened—like a fall in one of the ravines? It felt like he was somewhere with a lot of trees.

She checked the landline for messages. Nothing new. She circled through the apartment and looked out the windows and in the hallway. He always picked the worst places to get into trouble.

The bathroom door opened, and Melissa poked her head out. "Hey, do you have a—"

"What?" Cora said, dabbing her eyes.

"Uh, nothing. I just wondered if you had any bandages. I must have stepped on something."

Cora sniffled and dug a tissue out of her purse. "There's a red box in the medicine cabinet. It has lots of loose ones. Or I can cut you one. They're better."

"No, it's just one of my toes."

"It's okay. I'll get the scissors. I think I put them in the kitchen."

"What about your brother? Shouldn't you be calling somebody? Or one of your neighbors? Maybe they know where he went."

"He doesn't talk to them."

"Doesn't matter. Mine are nosier than fuck. I can't sneeze without them calling the police."

"He's probably in one of the parks," Cora said. "Or one of the ravines. I can usually find him."

"You got to be kidding me. You won't go to a hospital, but you want to walk around some fucking ravine?"

"I have to find him."

Melissa shook her head and stepped back into the bathroom. "Great. Give me a call when you do. We'll have a fucking party."

263

She shoved the shower curtain aside and sat down on the side of the bathtub and turned on the spigot. Cora brought the towel she had pulled from the cabinet.

"I have some shoes too," she said. "In the closet."

"Sure, better than nothing," Melissa said.

Cora made another circle through the apartment. After checking the voicemail on her cellphone, she pulled her shoes from the coat closet and lined them up beside the bathroom. Most were probably too small—except for the white flip-flops—but Melissa could take whatever she wanted. Cora didn't care; she just wanted to find Nathan.

She leaned against the door jamb of the bathroom while Melissa turned off the spigot.

"I put the shoes here," Cora said.

"Yeah, yeah, I'll be done in a minute."

"No, I don't mean that. I—I'll wait."

"Go ahead. I'll pull the door closed behind me."

"No, it's okay."

"I might as well go home," Melissa said. "Everything else has gone to shit."

They remained silent while she dried her feet, the truth too obvious to ignore—the gunshots, the exploding glass, the screams. But Cora had to push those thoughts away, or she would crawl into a corner and never want to come out.

In the living room, Melissa slipped on the white flip-flops and glanced at her Blackberry.

"I'm sorry," Cora said. "I didn't know. I never thought I'd see him again. I swear."

"Don't be stupid. I know you're not like that."

"I just don't understand."

"I just hope the cops do something right for once and shoot the bastard."

Cora murmured in agreement and locked the apartment behind them.

Out front of the building, Melissa waved at the northbound traffic and pulled out her cigarettes, then changed her mind and stuck them back in her purse. A gray cab heading south honked and slowed down. As soon as the northbound traffic had passed, the cab made a U-turn and stopped beside the girls.

"Be careful," Melissa said and gave Cora a quick hug. "He still might be out there."

She nodded, even though she didn't want to think about that possibility. She couldn't. Not now. She had to find Nathan. That was the only thing that mattered. The rest would have to wait.

Chapter 27

The white van transporting Teresa turned into a gravel-covered parking lot behind a large warehouse made of red brick, the windows blacked out, pigeons crooning under the eaves. Two more white vans sat in front of a loading dock, next to a black Mercedes and one of her black SUVs.

The man with the snake tattoo, his face now bruised, opened the sliding door for her. She hopped out and glanced at the Mercedes. Mobius was close by. She felt him scuttling around, twitching and muttering.

The driver of the van led her to a large gray door that slid open at their approach. Inside, another man wearing a black flak jacket bowed his head to her and stepped aside. About a dozen wooden crates were scattered in the loading area, their lids pried off. More crates were stacked against the north wall, next to a pair of forklifts covered with tarps. Assault rifles, pistols, grenade launchers, and flak jackets were organized on a row of tables underneath a wall of posters of women in bikinis or skimpy tops and skirts, their breasts bulging out like blobs of pudding. On the far side of the tables, a half-dozen men wearing flak jackets sat on a cluster of couches, holding hamburgers and french fries, their appetites forgotten.

Teresa strode to a small office beyond the couches while the men scrambled to their feet and bowed their heads. Inside the office, Mobius sat at a desk, staring at a laptop. Next to him, Mueller fidgeted like a child who needed to pee.

"Mistress," Mobius said, rising to his feet, and bowed his head. "You are well?"

"Of course. Don't be stupid."

He gestured with his right hand and a man wearing a flak jacket grabbed a chair from one of the corners and put it in front of the desk for her.

Teresa ignored the chair and stepped around the desk to look at the computer screen. It showed a map of the city with dozens of colored dots moving in various directions—blue representing her security force, red the reborn, green their contacts within the police and government.

"Many things are happening," Mobius said.

"What about Leroy and Alex?"

"They try everything to steal the Light."

Teresa flicked her right hand and Mobius toppled backwards, taking his chair down with him. She turned her glare on Mueller.

"Alex was at the Harbourfront," he said. "But Leroy was already gone. We believe he was at the mall downtown. The Eaton Centre."

"He is a traitor," Mobius said, stumbling to his feet. "He destroys everything you have worked to achieve."

Teresa flung him against the wall behind the desk, and the window in the office exploded, showering two of the soldiers with glass. The rest had already moved out of the way and put their food aside.

As she stepped out of the office, one of the bleeding men scowled, and she glared at him. He shrieked and collapsed on the concrete floor and writhed in agony. She hurled a second man across the loading area, his body twisting like a corkscrew, and he smashed into a crate.

Mobius darted after her. "No, mistress. Save yourself. The time is at hand."

"You've done nothing to find the Light. You're too busy blaming others for your failings."

"But Father has spoken. He is calling us."

"What about Paul? Has he spoken to you too?"

Mobius stopped abruptly, his mouth hanging open.

"When was the last time you saw him?" she demanded.

"No, that's not possible. Father would never allow it," Mobius said.

"Paul believed in the Light," Teresa said. "He would do anything to be here."

"But he can't come back. He couldn't have survived. We made certain."

"Apparently you didn't do a very good job."

"But they were destroyed. All of them. None of them survived. Father did not want them anymore, not in the end."

Though Teresa remembered the experiments perfectly well, she flung Mobius across the floor of the loading bay. During the 1950s and 1960s, she had let him use several of the reborn to test the effects of long-term withdrawal from Father. The first had been Duchamp, whom they had sealed underground near Tuscany while Alex loaded Father on a boat bound for New York. Three weeks later, in New York, she had received a message from Duchamp's handlers. He had escaped and killed dozens of people before the police managed to shoot him enough to disable him. After that, he survived for thirteen weeks, escaping twice despite the restraints and the drugs, killing dozens more, before he finally succumbed to his wounds, days of agony Father must have relished like an infant on his mother's teat.

Teresa marched to the sliding door, which a guard jerked open, while Mobius scrambled to his feet. Mueller ran past her to open one of the back doors of the SUV.

"Get in the front," she said.

He bowed and obeyed. The driver backed up the SUV, ignoring Mobius as he ran out of the warehouse.

"Mistress," he shouted. "Wait!"

"What happened to Leroy?" Teresa asked Mueller.

"We have reports he was in a shootout with the police at the Eaton Centre," he replied. "About an hour ago. That's the big mall downtown, on Yonge street. There was also a subway crash, shortly afterwards, a few miles north, but we don't believe he was involved. The train was going the wrong direction." He paused and squinted at his Blackberry. "The police are still trying to figure out how Leroy escaped. They believe by car. But they did find the black sedan we were looking for, the one Leroy traced. It was parked on the street on the north side of the mall and had a dead man in the trunk. No ID yet."

"What about the others?"

"They're still doing their patrols, except for Johan. He went to the mall to look around."

"Take me there."

Mueller opened his mouth to disagree but coughed instead and dropped his gaze to his Blackberry. The SUV sped through an intersection and passed a bus pulling over to let off passengers. A blue car coming from the other direction honked at them, and Mueller fidgeted with his tie and suggested turning on some music.

"It'd be more useful than your jabbering," Teresa said.

"Yes, mistress," he said and fumbled through the digital library. The first piece he selected was by Chopin—one of the longer polonaises—but she wasn't in the mood and told him to play Wagner instead.

Over the next few minutes, he cycled through *Ride of the Valkyries*, *The Flying Dutchman* overture, and the Symphony in C major. She settled on the overture from *Tannhäuser*, the beginning slow and deep, but still felt Father scratching at her thoughts.

In front of her, Mueller returned to his Blackberry. The stink of sweat rising from him reminded her of the priest she had thrown off the cliffs of Dover almost a century ago. During those years, Paul had managed to keep Father fast asleep while searching for the Light in London, always preaching, believing it would rise forth one day and save them, his stupid, ignorant promises belying his hunger, the death he left in his wake.

Teresa grimaced. She would deal with Paul too, when the time came. He was nothing now—nothing but a shadow of the past.

"Turn the music louder," she said.

Mueller hurried to obey and then cleared his throat.

"What?" she demanded.

"Johan suggested we meet on the west side of the mall. Perhaps in the street behind the courthouse? The mall is full of policemen."

Teresa glared at Mueller's head. He cried out in pain and hunched forward, his hands clasping his skull.

"Mistress!"

"You're a serpent of lies," she said. "Every single one of you."

"But it's true. There are! Even more than at the Harbourfront."

"I'll deal with them," Teresa said.

Mueller sat up slowly, gasping for breath. "Whatever you wish, mistress. I only wish to give you options, so you can get what you want, most of all. The police are trivial, not worth your time."

"We'll see."

~

Teresa toyed with her crucifix, the overture trailing off one last time, as a pair of billboards on the northeast corner of the mall came into view, the larger of the two advertising a half-naked girl. The second billboard advertised more half-naked teenagers, hanging upside down like slaughtered animals. She also noticed a line of four or five streetcars clogging the street ahead, which arced around a stage across from the mall. More billboards and flashing signs hung from the neighboring buildings, perhaps meant as a caricature of Times Square, a place she had at first hated. After five centuries in Europe, New York had felt wrong and smelled wrong, even though it served her purposes well.

The driver stamped on the accelerator to keep ahead of the car creeping forward on their right. Mueller looked up from his Blackberry and pointed to a side street running south.

"Johan's in the parking garage, mistress. The one on this side."

The driver slowed down and glanced at Teresa. She nodded. He blared the horn and pulled around the streetcars, into oncoming traffic, and turned left. When they reached the church at the end of the block, he turned right and drove to the entrance indicated by Mueller, a tiny mouth at the base of a massive wall draped with banners advertising perfume and watches.

The ramp wound up like a corkscrew to the first level of the parking garage, where Johan waited at the south end. He was a thin man with a hawk-like nose and wisps of black hair covering his pale scalp and wore a black suit, a light purple shirt, and a burgundy tie. His hands trembled almost constantly.

After a bow he said, "Mistress, you're coming is a surprise to me. Leroy was here, but he escaped through the underground into one of the neighboring buildings. After that, I can't speculate. The police sealed much of it off."

"You were talking with them?"

"No, I will leave that to your soldiers of fortune." He gestured at Mueller, standing on the other side of the SUV. "Mostly I listened to what the reporters were siphoning from those gathered around."

"Idiots," she said and glared at Mueller.

"We're probing our contacts in the police force," he said. "We'll know more soon."

On the SUV, a window cracked. He bowed his head and clutched his Blackberry.

"There were many conflicting stories," Johan said. "But the main confrontation happened in the rather large makeup department of the Sears. It seems that Leroy was targeting women."

"A blonde one?" Teresa demanded.

Johan shrugged. "Unfortunately many of the onlookers saw little but heard much and have many opinions."

"So you have no idea where he went or why he was here."

"I believe it was the Light, mistress. There was a taste in the air, something difficult to explain. It puts me in mind of lightning, the way it burns the air and leaves your ears ringing."

"You can get pictures from this mall?" Teresa asked Mueller.

"Uh, yes. I'm sure we could. As long as their security system was functioning. We have a number of avenues."

"Respectfully, mistress, that would take too long," Johan said. "The best hope is to find Leroy directly. Perhaps Alex can—"

He lurched back from Teresa's glare and clutched his head.

"You've spoken to him?" she demanded.

"No, not today," he said. "Not since Saturday, I believe."

"What are hiding?"

"I'm sorry, mistress. It's clear to me something has happened, but no one has spoken of it. Mobius told me to report any contact immediately. And it is your will, so that is enough. By your grace, we live and serve."

"Yes, my will," Teresa said, scowling.

Behind Johan, a blue four-door honked as it turned toward him, and he stepped aside. Teresa glared at the car, and one of the headlights burst. The driver, a woman with her hair in a bun, stamped on the accelerator, and the car spurted past them, almost clipping a white Subaru parked next to a concrete pillar.

Johan bowed his head. Mueller bobbed his head too, keeping his gaze down, one hand resting on the SUV.

With a hiss of disgust, Teresa turned away from them and strode toward the exit. The windshield of a red Pontiac parked on her right blasted inwards, eviscerating a pink furry doll hanging from the rear-view mirror. The car's alarm began to wail. She threw the car into the concrete wall that separated them from the interior of the mall, and a black Mercedes sped out of the entry ramp and screeched to a stop in front of her.

Mobius jumped out of the back and bowed. "Mistress, we have a lead on Leroy. Your insight would be valuable. I will take you, if you wish."

He waved her to the Mercedes. She flung him into a bronze-colored minivan and glanced behind her. A few feet away, Johan stood waiting, his trembling hands folded in front of him.

"I want to know what Leroy was doing here," Teresa said. "I want to know if she was here."

Johan bowed and sprinted to a stairwell. In the Mercedes, classic music began to play. Vivaldi? Bach?

Teresa grimaced and strode back to the SUV. Mueller scrambled to open a door for her. Inside the SUV, Wagner began to play: *Ride of the Valkyries*. She told Mueller to put on Tchaikovsky instead, and he fumbled with the buttons of the digital player while Mobius ducked into the Mercedes, and it raced to the exit, bashed through a gate arm, and led the way down to Yonge Street.

Chapter 28

Disturbed by the smell of waffles coming from Eglinton Avenue, Nathan sat in the doorway of a vacant building and watched an old woman with a mop for a head lurch out of a grocery store on the other side of the street, carrying so many bags her arms looked ready to snap. His stomach grumbled. They had potato chips near the entrance, but the place was crowded, full of shadows. People were dragging them everywhere, trying to surround him. They wanted to trick him. One wrong move, and he was a goner. Smash, bang, boom, game over.

A chubby white guy wearing khaki shorts came from the direction of the waffle house, carrying a duffel bag and a box of pizza. Nathan clapped a hand over his nose. The chubby guy turned into the neighboring parking lot, and Nathan darted to the corner of the building, keeping his head down.

Game on! Game on!

The chubby guy slid the pizza on the roof of a gray four-door and opened the trunk. After a yawn, he tilted his duffel bag sideways and wiggled it into the trunk.

Nathan sprinted toward the car. "Hey, look out," he yelled. "Look out!"

The chubby guy straightened up, startled, and glanced in the direction Nathan pointed. He snatched the box of pizza off the roof and ran back to the street. The guy yelled and stumbled after his pizza but remembered his trunk and darted back to slam it shut.

Nathan ran northwards past a mix of townhouses and apartment buildings, the box of pizza tucked awkwardly under his right arm. The curses from the chubby guy petered out as he tried to keep up.

At the second intersection, the guy in the khaki shorts stopped and yelled one last time. Nathan kept running, past houses waiting to be torn down for the next wave of condos. When the street ended at a T-junction, he cut across a park between two white apartment buildings and turned eastwards. He knew where he was now. The street ahead was busy, but the other way was even worse—the longest street in the world, straight to hell and back.

Behind the last apartment building, Nathan ducked between a pair of blue dumpsters, gasping for breath, and dropped the box of pizza. A minute or two passed before he could straighten up and open the box. Inside, the pizza was a mash of crust and cheese and pepperoni and ground sausage. He smiled and dug his fingers into the pizza. At least it was warm—that was the important thing. Better than a poke in the eye. Now he only needed something to wash the gooeyness down.

~

The traffic on Yonge Street seemed heavier than usual, full of people honking and blaring their music. Cora wished she had brought a bottle of water. She hated swallowing aspirins dry. Her feet hurt too, her sandals a poor choice for trekking around Nathan's neighborhood. There was no sign of him in the Alexander Muir Memorial Gardens or the park on the other side of Yonge Street.

At the library, she peered through the front doors, reluctant to go inside. A man wearing glasses and a brown cardigan stood behind the counter, a librarian she had seen once or twice before, the type who licked his lips while fantasizing about his secret fetish. She didn't want to deal with that now. And would they really have let Nathan in after what had happened yesterday?

God, only one day. How could everything have gone so wrong?

After a glance at her phone, she walked around the south side of the library. She peered into the bushes and the trees, but the stench of burning rubber made her stomach lurch, and she hurried to the far side of the small parking lot.

With one hand pressed to her belly, Cora weaved through the trees, scaring off a gray squirrel. When she reached St. Edmunds Drive, she followed it southwards, peering into the trees on her right, more or less ignoring the houses on her left, until she came back to the Memorial Gardens, where the St. Edmunds turned right and intersected with Yonge Street.

Her cellphone chimed. She fumbled with her purse. The call was from Katrina, though, and Cora let it go to her voicemail.

She gazed north and south on Yonge Street. A cab slowed and honked. Her cellphone chimed anew. She glanced at the caller ID, but it was Katrina again.

More cars slowed down, and Cora realized the traffic light had changed. She crossed Yonge Street and walked to the park behind the gas station. Much like half an hour ago, the park was empty, and she sat down on her brother's bench. Even though she had moved only a short distance from the street, the noise of the traffic faded, broken only by the occasional guttural rumble. That was probably why Nathan liked sitting there so much. He was part of the world but separate. Safe but aware.

Her cellphone chimed again, this time with a text message. She had a message on her voicemail. From Katrina, of course. Cora shook her head. Her appointment with Frank hardly seemed important now.

Back on Yonge Street, she hurried up the slope to her brother's apartment. She walked through the rooms and looked in the closets, but he wasn't home and nothing had moved.

After using the washroom, she took an aspirin and checked the landline for messages. There was only one from herself, asking him to call her cellphone.

Cora saved the message and pulled out a pair of white, low rise socks from the cabinet by the TV. Her white Pumas still sat on the floor nearby. At least they would be more comfortable. The way things were going, she would see a lot of the ravines before the night came.

~

When Nathan reached the third floor of his building, he saw the door to his apartment hanging open and swore. The landlord was always stealing his stuff, the fucking bastard. He was too fucking cheap to buy his own. Then a squawk of pain came from the apartment, and Nathan charged the door, his box of pizza still jammed under his right arm.

The man standing in front of the TV looked nothing like the landlord, though, with a head like a turnip and dressed in torn blue jeans and a matching jacket. Behind the man, an Asian girl wearing a green blouse staggered to her feet, one hand pressed against the side of her head, the other clutching the TV cabinet.

Nathan glanced around the apartment. It looked like his. He had the same boxy TV and the same green couch. He also had the same poster hanging on the wall beside the kitchen table: a print of a painting of three deer standing near a pond in a forest.

"Where's the other bitch?" the man demanded. "The blonde one."

"Stay right there," Nathan said and shook his pizza box. "Or I'll slap you with one of these."

The man sprang forward and knocked the pizza box away and grabbed Nathan. A jolt of pain shot up his arms and exploded in his chest, knocking the breath out of him. He fell against the wall by the bathroom. The blue jean man jerked his hands away and stumbled backwards into the coffee table. Gold fire rippled across the floor between them.

Nathan staggered back to his feet. The blue jean man grabbed Nathan again and threw him into the couch. Nathan yelped, pain ripping up his arms and shoulders, and the blue jean man yelled and kicked Nathan. His stomach heaved. A second kick hit Nathan in the belly, and he collapsed on the floor, gold light spilling around him. His throat convulsed. A third kick hit him in the side. The gold light sizzled. The blue jean man stumbled away from Nathan, swearing and pawing at his eyes, and Nathan clawed at the floor and vomited.

The blue jean man bellowed and bashed the spare cabinet beside the TV. Nathan lurched behind the couch and coughed and gasped, inhaling bits of the vomit still in his mouth. The blue jean man charged after Nathan and kicked his feet. He gagged and coughed and spit out vomit. A loud crash came from the kitchen counter. The blue jean man kicked Nathan again, and gold fire crackled across the floor.

Nathan kicked back and rolled into one of the chairs around the kitchen table. He heard a thump and saw the Asian girl swinging a frying pan, but the blue jean man knocked her away. Still coughing, Nathan scrambled around the end of the couch by the windows.

The blue jean man yelled and grabbed at Nathan's right leg. The girl regained her balance and hit the blue jean man in the head again. He hurled her to the floor and stomped on her. Then he grabbed the frying pan from the floor and whipped the pan at Nathan. It ricocheted off his right arm, and he howled and fell beside the spare cabinet.

The blue jean man booted the Asian girl once more before springing around the couch and scooping up the frying pan.

"You're like the girl," he said. "The same fire."

Nathan kicked at the blue jean man. He slammed the frying pan on Nathan's right shoulder, and he crumpled and curled up, shielding his head.

The blue jean man laughed and whacked Nathan's legs. "This is more like it."

The blue jean man continued to whack Nathan's legs and hips and kicked him in the groin. Nathan yowled and dropped one of his arms. In the midst of another laugh, the blue jean man hit Nathan in the face with a frying pan. Blood spurted from his nose. The blue jean man rapped Nathan's face a second time, and gold fire crackled across the floor. The blue jean man hooted and whacked Nathan a third time. More blood spurted from his nose.

A split second later, the blue jean man shrieked and stumbled backwards and flailed at the air. Gold fire licked up his arms and shoulders. The frying pan clanged on the floor. He spun toward the kitchen, the gold fire clawing at his face, and he tripped over the legs of the Asian girl and fell on top of her. The door of the apartment swung open. Another Asian woman stepped inside, wearing a black blouse embroidered with white flowers.

Nathan scrambled to his knees, keeping his right arm tucked against his torso. What the hell? This wasn't fucking China.

The newcomer scowled at him and pulled a pistol out of her purse. He scrambled to his bedroom but slipped and fell against the fridge.

"You forgot one bullet," the woman said and pointed the gun at the blue jean man, writhing atop the girl wearing the green blouse. "It must have gotten stuck."

The gun flashed and roared. Nathan lurched into the bedroom.

Blood and shadows bubbled from the back of the blue jean man, the shadows howling and screaming.

"Interesting," she said. "I think he's actually dying."

Nathan slammed the bedroom door shut, urine running warm and wet down his left leg. A few seconds later, the door snapped off its hinges and crashed on his bed, and he ducked behind the chest of drawers.

"Are you planning to hide?" the woman said. "Is that the best you can do? Do you think that's going to work for all of them?"

Shadows the size of bats whirled into the bedroom. One of them struck Nathan in the face, and he screamed. Gold light flared around him and burned his skin. The shadow exploded.

The woman tossed the gun on the end of his bed and vanished. Nathan grabbed the gun, but it burned his fingers, and he dropped it on the floor.

Another shadow screeched and struck him in the face. Gold light crackled, and the shadow exploded. He ran into the living room and ducked past the shadows swarming around the frying pan and the ones fluttering over the blue jean man. One of the shadows chased after Nathan and struck him in the face. Gold fire snapped around him. He fell screaming against the apartment door. Someone gasped. He yanked on the door and lurched into the hallway. The shadows continued to scream and howl. One of the lights in the hallway exploded.

Nathan ducked and ran to the back of the building and raced down the stairs. On the second floor, a clump of shadows whirled past him and smashed into the doors of an apartment. Someone screamed. He sprang down to the next landing. More shadows whipped past him, and he crashed on the tiles of the first floor. A head of bushy, gray hair popped out of one of the apartments: the landlord's wife. She spotted him and screamed. Shadows swerved towards her. Nathan scrambled to his feet, hurtled down the last set of steps, and bolted out the back door.

Chapter 29

During her stop at Tim Hortons, Cora used the washroom and bought a bottle of water. The girls behind the counter didn't remember anyone like Nathan sitting in the corner by the window, where he had spent a lot of hours during the winter. He liked that location because the staff, most of them Filipino, left him alone and didn't try to sneak up on him. Sometimes they even gave him a donut to get him out the door at closing time. He hated the one with sprinkles and loved the one with the maple topping. Chocolate was okay.

Two blocks north of the coffee shop, Cora sat down on a bench in a tiny park and sipped her water. Something lingered in the air, making her nose itch. Maybe the smog. Her ribs had started to hurt again too, but she didn't want to take another aspirin. She had already taken too many. Three or four?

A sharp pain knifed Cora in the belly. She yelped and dropped the bottle, sloshing water on her feet. The pain raced up into her chest and down her thighs. She hunched over.

Half a minute passed. The pain faded. She sat up slowly, still clutching her belly. An old man wearing a hideous brown cardigan stood on the sidewalk, staring at her. At the opposite corner a woman pushing a stroller stopped too, wondering what was going on.

Cora coughed and felt a bubble in her nose. She dabbed at it with her right hand. Her fingers came away tipped with blood.

She fumbled with her purse, pulled out a tissue, and held it to her nose. Nathan? She lurched to her feet and started running to his apartment, but her stomach revolted, and she had to slow down.

When she finally reached the nursery next to Nathan's building, someone wearing black appeared for a moment in Nathan's living room window. She clutched her belly and ran into the foyer and up the stairs.

The door to Nathan's apartment hung wide open. She darted inside, then jerked to a stop. Two bodies lay in a pool of blood beside the couch: a man wearing a blue jean jacket on top; the other legs smooth and feminine, wearing Capri pants and a single white flip-flop. One of Cora's flip-flops.

Her legs turned flaccid, and she tottered against the door. She sucked in a breath and fumbled with her purse. Lipstick, eyeshadow, tissues, and keys tumbled on the floor. Her cellphone hit the floor with a crack.

Cora scooped up the phone, praying it still worked. The screen blinked on. She dialed 911. The phone rang and rang. She swore and dialed again. Still no one answered.

God, please, Cora said and spotted the landline phone beside the coffee table, tumbled on its side. A whimper escaped from one of the bodies. She wobbled back a step and bumped against the door.

"Melissa?"

The pair remained silent. She inched closer and saw Melissa's face trapped under the man's right arm and stared at his lumpy bald head.

No. It couldn't be. He couldn't . . .

Cora took a shaky breath and called Melissa's name again. A faint moan answered, then twisted into a whimper.

Cora turned towards the coffee table. She had to keep moving. She had to get help.

Once past the feet of the blue jean man, she scooped up the landline phone and dialed 911. It kept ringing and ringing.

"God, oh God," she said and dialed 911 again. It continued to ring endlessly.

She bumped against the TV, dizzy from the stink of blood, and shook the phone. Her gaze jumped back to Melissa, the life pulsing out of her. Cora could feel it. She could see it. Why wouldn't they answer?

She slid the phone back in its receiver, and Melissa let out another whimper. Cora crept around the feet of the blue jean man, terrified he would jump up and grab her, but he remained limp, even as she kneeled on the floor and stretched out an arm to touch Melissa's left hand.

One of her eyelids fluttered.

"Melissa?"

The eyelid fluttered again.

"God, please," Cora said and swallowed hard, her throat like gnarled pantyhose. She took a shaky breath.

A hiss of air escaped Melissa's lips, both flecked with blood.

Cora tapped the man's right arm but jerked her hand away.

Nothing happened. She shook her head and realized she was shaking all over.

She touched the blue jean man a second time, and Melissa let out a whimper.

As if stuck in a horrible dream, Cora saw her fingers curl around his wrist. Her stomach clenched. She lurched to her feet and pulled the arm away from Melissa's head. Melissa groaned.

Oh please, please, Cora thought and circled the pool of blood, trying not to think about how his flesh like half-frozen hamburger meat as she forced herself to keep pulling until his torso rolled off of Melissa.

Then Cora stumbled and lost her grip on his arm. It banged on the floor. His waxy face glared at her.

She flinched and darted away from him. She had to take several shaky breaths to stop from running. She had to help Melissa. There was no time.

Cora stepped closer and, with both hands, gripped his right foot. She pulled the leg off Melissa. A gasp escaped her lips.

"It'll be okay," Cora said and kneeled, bumping against a kitchen chair. "I'll get help."

Her gaze froze on the upper half of Melissa's blouse, soaked with enough blood to turn the fabric black. Oh God. Was that a hole?

With trembling fingers, Cora nudged the collar of the blouse, but the blood had glued the fabric to Melissa's chest.

"Time is short," a man said.

Cora lurched backwards and banged an elbow on the chair. She barely noticed the pain, though, with her throat clenched tight, and her heart thudding against her ribs. She knew the man who stood in the doorway to the hall, his hands tucked in the sleeves of his black shirt, his black hat obscuring his eyes.

"W—what? How—" she said.

"You need to focus on your friend," Paul said, "or she will die."

Cora glanced down at Melissa, her mouth hanging open in a lifeless way that made Cora's heart lurch.

"You need to act," he said.

"Wait! Do you have a phone? We need an ambulance. Mine wouldn't work. It just keeps ringing."

"Help will come," Paul said. "But you are the only one who can save her."

"What do you mean? You called already? How long will it be? I don't hear anything."

"Pull her out of the blood. You must do it now. Her life will not wait."

"But we need to get help," she said, her voice turning shrill. "We need an ambulance."

"Be gentle and slow," Paul said. "It will make saving her easier, like you would for your family. I will tell you what you must do. There is no more time."

Cora shook her head but slipped her hands under Melissa's shoulders and eased her beside the kitchen table. Only her feet remained in the blood, trailing along like a pair of dark red snakes.

"Far enough," Paul said.

"Shouldn't you do this? I don't know what to do."

"Press your hand on the wound," he said. "Keep it there, re- gardless of what happens."

While Cora's mind darted to CPR, about which she knew prac- tically nothing, she shifted her hands to the top of Melissa's right breast and tried not to think about the stickiness of the blood.

"Am I supposed to push? I don't want to hurt her."

"Focus," Paul said. "She is very strong. You can feel her life force, the breath moving through her."

"What do you mean? Is this enough? Am I supposed to push?"

"Stay as you are. Remain steady. In that there is strength."

Cora shook her head again, disbelief and confusion churning

her thoughts into porridge, and glanced at the man wearing the blue jean jacket. Whose blood was who? Was he still alive?

"Stay focused," Paul said. "Look at your friend and remember her well. Remember how she walked and how she smiled. Remember her words. She is strong. You can feel her breath."

"What are you talking about? We need an ambulance," Cora said. "And how did you get here? Did you follow me?"

"That is complicated, better saved for later. Your friend needs you now."

Cora blinked back tears, on the verge of screaming.

"Stay with her," Paul said. "You value her life. You wish it to continue."

"Just get a phone. Get an ambulance."

"Stay with her a little longer," he said. "Her color is improving."

"Get out!"

A moment later, Cora felt a twitch under her hands, and her palms began to itch. She glanced down, startled. The shallowest of breaths pressed against her hands.

"Oh God."

Melissa's lips trembled, and her chest became warm. Cora's hands tingled even more, and she started to pull them away.

"No! Keep your hands there," Paul said. "She needs you to live. Save her. You must learn. There is no more time."

Though bewildered, Cora eased her hands back to Melissa's chest. The warmth and the itching returned. Cora resisted the urge to pull her hands away and prayed. Maybe it was normal. Bodies were supposed to be warm.

A faint hiss escaped Melissa's lips.

"It's okay, help's coming," Cora said. "They'll be here soon. You just need to hold on."

The hiss turned into a soft cough, and the warmth intensified. Cora's arms tingled, quickly spreading to her shoulders, and she kept telling herself it was normal. She had to stop the bleeding.

"Stay with her," Paul said. "She needs you. Be the giver of life."

Melissa coughed harder, and blood flecked her lips. Purple spots danced through the living room. Cora swooned and closed her eyes, trying to catch her breath. Paul spoke again, but the words sounded far away and no longer made sense.

Melissa sucked in another breath and twitched. Cora's arms began to burn, and her stomach grumbled. The heat spread into her shoulders and her chest, and she tried to straighten up, but Melissa let out a horrible croak, and Cora pressed her hands back down.

"Please, I'm sorry," she said. "It's my fault. He must have been looking for me."

A halo of golden light spilled across the floor. She froze. Melissa sucked in a raspy breath and coughed more blood.

Cora shook her head, blinking away tears. No. No. No.

Melissa's chest rose with another breath. The room spun. She let out a weak cough. Cora continued to blink back tears, the gold light fading, and Melissa lay with her head to one side, spitting and coughing blood.

Then, without any warning, Melissa cried out and jerked away from Cora.

"No!" she said and grabbed onto Melissa. Melissa tried to pull away again, but she was too weak, and Cora tightened her grip. "Don't move. You've been hurt."

"Wha—wha—"

"Just stay still," Cora said. "We're just waiting for an ambulance. They'll be here soon."

She glanced at the hallway, but Paul had disappeared. Had he gone downstairs? What was taking so long? Why didn't she hear any sirens?

"C—Cora?"

"Yes, it's me."

Melissa shifted her head, her eyes darting around the apartment.

"Try to keep still," Cora said. "You've been hurt. You need to keep still."

Melissa wobbled her head and coughed several times. "Wh—where? Him."

"It's okay," Cora said. "You're safe."

"No. Ca—came. Him. S—searching."

"You don't have to worry about him. He won't be able to hurt anyone. Not anymore."

"Where?" Melissa asked, clutching at Cora's arm. "Where?"

Cora glanced at the blue jean man and wished she had a towel to cover his face. It looked even worse now, like the bones under his skin were melting.

Melissa swiveled her head, trying to follow Cora's gaze. "Dead?"

"Yes."

"Good. F—fucker."

Melissa closed her eyes and coughed up a gob of red phlegm. Cora rubbed her bloodied hands together, looking around for something to wipe off Melissa's mouth, and grabbed the tea towel hanging on the side of the fridge.

Another minute or two passed. With the tea towel now bloodied and clutched in her hands, Cora stepped to the apartment door and glanced in the hallway. What in the world was taking the ambulance so long? Why wasn't there anyone? The firemen? The police?

From the bathroom, she grabbed a larger towel. Melissa coughed and wiggled her arms closer to her hips and struggled to sit up, her blouse peeling off the floor like sticky toffee.

"No! Don't get up," Cora said, darting back to Melissa.

She muttered a curse and rolled onto her side. Cora continued to protest but helped as best she could until Melissa sat against the couch.

"God," Melissa said. "Wanna puke."

Cora glanced at the chunks of yellow and orange and dark lumps spattered on the floor beside the coffee table. Though the vomit stank worse than the blood, she had barely noticed the chunks before.

Melissa looked down at her blouse and lifted a shaky hand to dab at the congealed blood.

"Maybe you should lie down?" Cora said. "Isn't that better? Help must be coming."

Melissa shook her head and tugged at the right side of the blouse, exposing a pink puckered scar above her breast.

"What about your phone?" Cora asked. "Your purse? Maybe they're having trouble finding us, they don't know the address."

Melissa continued to shake her head. Cora looked around the

living room, but she didn't see Melissa's purse anywhere.

"Didn't want to," Melissa said and coughed. "Tried. But kept hitting. Hitting. Wouldn't stop."

"It's okay. You're safe now."

"Waiting," Melissa said. "My place. Waiting. Had Kat. Kept hitting. Hitting her."

Cora shook her head. Melissa shuddered and tugged at her blouse.

"Wait! Be careful," Cora said.

Melissa swore and kept pulling. A button popped off.

"Okay, wait, I'll help," Cora said and glanced at the hallway, but it remained silent and empty.

Melissa continued to tug at her blouse, and Cora fumbled with the buttons and slowly peeled the fabric off of Melissa's skin, frightened that blood would start spurting out somewhere. Melissa winced, rotating her right arm to pull it free of the blouse, but wouldn't stop until Cora managed to pull both arms free and dropped the blouse on the floor.

"I'll get something to cover you," she said and darted to the cabinet holding the extra towels. The other two were already spattered with blood.

Melissa stared at the blue jean man, her right hand scratching at her chest.

"Maybe you should lie down," Cora said, nudging a blue bath towel into Melissa's fingers.

She swore and pushed at the floor, struggling to stand.

"No, wait," Cora said. "Please."

Melissa swore again and started crawling around the pool of blood,fs toward the bathroom.

"At least let me help," Cora said and hunched over to support Melissa. "We'll walk together."

Once inside the bathroom, Melissa grabbed at the shower curtains, snapping one of the plastic rings. Cora pulled the curtain out of the way and helped Melissa into the tub. She fumbled with her blood-soaked bra and popped it open and struggled with the buttons of her pants. Cora helped take both of them off and shoved them into the back corner of the bathroom, by the plunger for the toilet. Melissa sank against the back of the tub and began to shake.

Cora shut the bathroom door, turned on the faucet, rinsed her hands and forearms until the water felt warm, and then switched on the shower head. Melissa continued to tremble while the water began to peel away the blood crusting her torso.

"Does anything hurt?" Cora asked, watching for any cuts or other wounds beyond the pink scar over Melissa's right breast.

Melissa shook her head and started rubbing her shoulders. Cora slipped a bar of white soap into her friend's right hand. After a few minutes, Melissa began to scrub more vigorously, and Cora moved to the sink to wash her own hands and dig out the blood under her fingernails. Only then did it occur to her she had blood all over her clothes and big red splotches on her white shoes, smearing bloody footsteps all over the floor.

From under the sink, Cora pulled out an old towel, a bottle of Windex, and a roll of paper towels. She used the Windex to clean the blood off her shoes and sprayed the bathroom floor and wiped it off with the old towel. After cleaning the floor a second time, she wiped off the side of the bathtub and the doors of the vanity and dropped the towel in the corner with Melissa's bloody clothes.

Cora pulled out another roll of paper towels from the vanity and wiped her shoes again. She would throw them out later. Melissa stopped shaking enough to ask for a comb, and Cora passed over one of Nathan's from the medicine cabinet before hunching down to clean the floor a third time. The rest she didn't want to think about—couldn't think about. Otherwise she would start screaming.

Chapter 30

Teresa's SUV turned into an alley behind an apartment building made of orangey-brown brick. Her security force had several vans stationed around the perimeter of the property, monitoring everyone who tried to leave.

While she watched on a monitor in her SUV, a team of four men wearing flak jackets charged into the building to secure the apartment of the target, Katrina Elliott. They found the door into her apartment already broken. One cat darted out of the kitchen and died moments later due to an itchy trigger finger. A second gray cat hid in the corner behind the plasma TV.

In a small office beside the balcony, they found a coffee on the desk, still lukewarm; a few drops of blood; one laptop, which they promptly confiscated.

Mueller, sitting in the front of the SUV, shook his head and told them to keep looking.

"Explain this to me again," Teresa said, "before I put your head through a window."

He turned his microphone off and bowed his head. "The target's the owner of the business who owns the car Leroy traced. She might have information about the blonde girl too, considering the apparent nature of the business."

Teresa grimaced, annoyed by his prancing words, and squinted at a gray minivan parked ahead of them. "Where's Mobius? I don't sense him."

"I—I'm not sure. I thought—"

He hit the dashboard with a thud. Teresa flung open her door, hopped out of the SUV, and started walking around the apartment building. Fear flowed from the people inside, some of them confused, hiding, trying to make phone calls, the police and 911 unavailable. She felt nothing from Mobius, though. He should have been running after her, trying to convince her to stay out of sight.

Where had he gone?

She turned the last corner of the apartment building, and Mueller called her from the SUV. As soon as he saw her, he started waving.

Teresa sprinted back to the SUV.

"Mistress, my apologies. I was just informed. Mobius went to another building. The same owner, Katrina Elliott. The team there captured a woman. An employee."

Teresa hissed. A large window from the lobby of the apartment building cracked. Mueller ducked and covered his head.

"It's not far," he said. "Ten minutes. The men here can finish searching the apartment. Whatever you wish."

She threw him aside and sprang into the back of the SUV. With one hand clutching his ribs, Mueller climbed in the front and gave the driver the address.

It turned out to be a red brick house with Victorian-style trim surrounded by other houses converted into businesses: lawyers, accountants, dentists, restaurants, salons, spas. A black Cadillac and a white van sat in front of the house, and a green hatchback was parked in an open garage behind the house.

The driver of the SUV parked behind the green hatchback, and Mobius appeared on the back porch of the house. Mueller scrambled out of the SUV and opened Teresa's door.

"Mistress, I have news," Mobius said and bowed to her. "This one is very cooperative. We have obtained an address for the blonde one. Your men are there, verifying it."

Mueller looked up from his Blackberry, a pained expression on his face. "It's at the Harbourfront. Where Alex was supposed to look for Leroy."

Mobius scowled at Mueller.

"Sorry, sir," Mueller said.

Teresa grabbed Mobius by the neck. "You're telling me I was already there? She was practically in front of me?"

"No, mistress. Not if she was involved with Leroy at the mall. The times are incompatible."

"What about Alex? What happened with him? You still haven't explained that."

"We know his treacher—"

She flung Mobius aside, and he crashed into a blue garbage container resting against a wooden fence.

"Mistress, the men are in the girl's apartment," Mueller said.

"How did they get there so quickly?" she asked.

"We had a team watching the police, in case there were any problems. We still don't know what happened to Alex."

Mobius, on his feet again, brushed off his suit and gestured to Mueller, demanding his Blackberry. Teresa glared at Mobius. He hurtled into the wooden fence, snapping several boards. Two windows in the neighboring house exploded.

"There doesn't seem to be anyone inside." Mueller typed a message and waited. "No, the apartment's empty." He patched into the call and continued to relay messages from the apartment. "A lot of dresses . . . shoes, lingerie . . . a vanity full of makeup . . . definitely a woman's apartment. The mail says Cora Walters.

"Wait, no. There's also a Nathan Walters." Mueller paused. "Oh Jesus, the address is different . . . but still in Toronto. On the main street, Yonge. Uptown, I think."

"Are there any men in that neighborhood?" Teresa asked.

"No, the closest is probably fifteen minutes away. Maybe ten. I'm checking the map," Mueller said, tapping furiously on his Blackberry.

"Who do you wish to send, mistress?" Mobius asked, brushing over a tear in his suit. "The prisoner is inside. She may have answers for you alone."

Teresa walked to her SUV, ignoring him. Mueller scrambled after her to open the back door, and Mobius ran to his Cadillac, parked on the street.

About fifteen minutes later, the Cadillac stopped in front of an apartment building that had green paint peeling from the trim. A white van already sat in front of the neighboring garden center. A second white van sat around the corner of what Mueller identified as a dead-end street.

Mobius stumbled out of the Cadillac and stared up at the apartment building like a retarded child, oblivious to the SUV as it parked behind the second van.

Teresa frowned and stepped onto the curb. Something felt wrong—a stillness that had nothing to do with sound because a dog barked inside the building and music blared from one of the windows on the main floor. The sunlight stung her eyes too, making them water.

"What is this place?" she asked.

Mobius jumped back from Teresa, startled. "Mistress!"

She threw him into the Cadillac. "Expecting someone else?"

"No, I only—"

"Shut up! You've already made enough excuses."

Mobius bowed his head. "There is a strangeness here, a wrong-ness."

Teresa scowled and walked along the length of the building, past the second white van. In the alley behind the building, one of her soldiers stood guard, cradling an assault rifle, and bowed his head. Mobius stopped behind her.

"Something is broken," he said. "The shadows don't speak."

"Watch the front," she said. "No one leaves."

"Yes, mistress."

Teresa yanked on the back door, snapping the lock. The smell of death greeted her, a mix of urine and blood and feces less than an hour old. From downstairs, a baby began to cry. The dog continued to bark.

She climbed the stairs to the first floor and walked through the hallway to the front of the building and heard the swish of cats, a woman mouse-like in her fear, a young child sobbing, and the thump of gangster music. On the second floor, one of the lights in the hallway flickered and exploded. She heard more music, African or Middle Eastern, with drums and chanting; the burble of a TV; a man dying, his gasps thick and rapid. Another man was sprawled in his living room, the door of his apartment hanging wide open.

When she reached the third floor, Teresa stopped and rubbed her eyes. At the other end of the hallway, the shadows thickened. She took two more steps. Paul pulled away from one of the walls and bowed his head, his hands hidden in the sleeves of his heavy black shirt.

"You're dead," she said. "You can't trick me anymore."

"Perhaps it would have been better that way."

Teresa looked around for something to throw at him, but the hallway was empty, except for the cone-shaped lights that hung between the apartments.

Paul nodded to the door on his right. "Father wants you to kill her. He'll try to make you. Are you strong enough to resist him? You have already let his anger infect you."

Teresa clenched her fists and darted toward him. He rushed into the door he had indicated and vanished. A toilet flushed.

She lunged after him and hit the door. It ripped off its hinges and smashed on the floor. To the right of the door, Leroy lay sprawled on his side, his jacket and shirt soaked with blood. More blood spattered the floor beside him, including bloody footsteps leading to a white door, the toilet within still gurgling.

Chapter 31

Cora sat on the lid of Nathan's toilet and watched while Melissa pulled on one of his black T-shirts, which looked baggy and strange on her, and a pair of jean shorts Cora had scrounged from her spare clothes. She had already changed into her cleaning clothes—her red T-shirt and old jeans—but still needed to swap her shoes.

"Do you want a different shirt?" Cora asked. "I might be able to find something smaller."

"Are you kidding me?" Melissa said. "There's a fucking dead guy in the living room. There's blood everywhere."

"I know, but—"

"They're not just going to let us walk out of here. Somebody must have called the cops."

"But we didn't do it."

"Yeah, like they'll believe us." Melissa yanked down the collar of the T-shirt, revealing the pink scar below her right collarbone. "It's like nothing happened. Nothing! But I felt it rip into me. I know I did. I never hurt so bad in my life."

Cora shook her head.

"He hit me with a frying pan and kicked me. But there's nothing." Melissa pointed to her face. "Do you see a single bruise? Even one?"

"No, I—I don't know. It just . . . happened."

"At least I feel like crap," she said. "At least that's normal."

"I have some aspirin."

"Are you fucking listening?"

"It's okay," Cora said. "I need one too."

Melissa rubbed her face and swore. Cora rummaged through her purse, but she couldn't find the aspirins. She must have dropped them. In the hallway? In the living room?

She eased the bathroom door open and peeked in the living

room. The blood, the dead body were still there, all too real. She tried not to look at them while stepping around the bloody foot-prints on the floor, past the fridge, into the kitchen. She pulled out the tin behind the spices. It was the only section of the cupboards Nathan left alone. He hated the smell on his fingers. Spices were for girls.

God, where was he? For once she would be happy if the police had him, if it meant he stayed away from the apartment.

Cora pulled the seal off the aspirin bottle and grabbed a plastic cup from one of the cupboards over the sink. Voices drifted from the hallway. She froze. One sounded angry, speaking in Spanish or Portuguese. Or Italian? The other was a man, familiar but different. He wasn't speaking English.

Cora rubbed her stomach. It had to be Paul. But what was he doing? How was he involved?

On the far side of the living room, the shadows around the TV rippled and hissed. Cora clutched the counter and shook her head. No. They weren't real. The blood was bad enough.

From the bathroom came the rumble of the toilet. The faucet turned on. Moments later, the apartment door smashed inwards, and Cora stumbled against the stove. She glimpsed a thin arm covered in blue, the back of a midnight blue dress, and long black hair as someone charged inside.

A girl?

The intruder kicked the bathroom door, and it ripped off its hinges. A second kick snapped the door into several pieces.

Melissa!

In the bathroom, the shower curtain ripped, and the metal sup-port rod crashed on the tub. Someone squawked in pain.

"Where did he go?" a shrill voice demanded. "Paul? The firstborn?"

Cora peered around the fridge, clutching the door handle. A scrawny teenager stood amid the broken pieces of the door. She couldn't have been more than four and a half feet tall, maybe seventy or eighty pounds, but she only needed one hand to hold Melissa up by her throat and shake her.

"Who are you?" the girl demanded. "Where is the bringer of the

Light? The—"

She stopped abruptly, and her gaze flicked to Cora. Cora stumbled backwards, the girl's anger like a punch in the stomach.

"You," the girl said and dropped Melissa.

With surprising speed, the girl hopped out of the bathroom. Cora clutched her belly.

"You're the one from the picture," the girl said, rubbing her eyes. "But different."

"Yes, it is confusing." Paul appeared in the opening to the hallway. "It took a long time to understand them. Years of study."

"Stay out of this. You already had your chance."

"Even better to listen, then."

"Shut up!"

"T—the police are coming," Cora said. "You'd better leave. Both of you."

"Where is the Light?" the girl demanded. "You must know. You've been touched by it."

"They'll be here any minute," Cora said. "I can hear them."

Paul stepped into the living room and stopped by the feet of the dead man.

"Your brother has gone to the cemetery," he said to Cora. "Through the ravine."

She glanced at him, startled. Nathan? In Mount Hope?

"Yes, it is strange," Paul said. "We have known each other for almost a year, but we meet for the first time."

The girl scowled and stepped toward Cora. To avoid getting cornered, she darted between the couch and the kitchen table.

"You're a fool to trust him," the girl said. "He is the firstborn."

"We are all children of the Cross," Paul said.

"I don't know what you want," Cora said. "I don't care. Just let us go."

"You must find your brother," Paul said. "You must join together. The Light as quick is still divided."

From the bathroom came a squawk, and the broken door shifted as Melissa struggled to sit up. The teenage girl jumped past the couch and grabbed Cora's left arm. An explosion of pain surged up to her shoulder, and she cried out. Gold light exploded around the girl. She sprang away from Cora and tumbled over a kitchen chair. Cora stumbled around the end of the couch and the coffee table, clutching her left arm.

Paul moved closer to the kitchen and stretched out his arms, blocking the girl as she sprang to her feet. She yelled and charged. The living room went dim. A blast of cold air flung Cora against the cabinet beside the TV, and the windows in the living room and the kitchen exploded. Time seemed to hang and flap. She staggered into the hallway. Then Paul blasted apart in a spray of black mist, and the teenage girl hurtled into the microwave. Cora fell against the opposite wall of the hallway, the skin of her left arm burning with pain.

Sunlight streamed back into the apartment as Cora pushed herself upright and shook her arm. The girl sprang to her feet, and the kitchen table hurtled over the couch. Cora scrambled away from the doorway.

The girl stepped into the hallway, radiating enough anger to choke an antelope. Cora sprinted to the stairs at the back of the building. A light exploded.

"Yes, run," the girl said. "Run all you want. I will have the Light. It's mine. Mine!"

Cora bolted down the back stairs. When she reached the second floor, the window on the landing above her exploded. She ducked and raced down the rest of the stairs and heaved on the back door.

Once outside, she lurched to a stop, a hairy man wearing a white undershirt sprawled in the alley. The landlord. A white van blocked the mouth of the alley. A man with the dark hair, wearing a dark suit, stood in front of the van and turned to stare at her.

Cora spun right and sprinted past the stockade for the garbage and ducked into the narrow walkway behind the neighboring garden center. The man wearing the dark suit yelled. From Nathan's building came an explosion of glass and wrenching metal, and she caught a glimpse of a door hurtling through the air.

At the other end of the garden center, Cora darted past a green pickup truck loaded with bags of peat and sand and hickory shavings and turned left onto a street of brick duplexes lined with decades-old trees.

On Yonge Street, tires screeched. Windows exploded in the garden center. Dogs barked from every direction. She sprinted through a T-intersection, her gaze fixed on the trees at the end of the next block—the start of the ravine.

A brunette in her forties, wearing jeans and a yellow tank top, stepped out the front door of a brick duplex with white siding and stared at Cora.

Behind her, an engine roared. She glanced back. A white van accelerated past the girl in the blue dress as she ran along the left side of the street, her anger rolling off of her like waves. The windows of the white van exploded. It swerved in front of her, and she screamed and tripped. The van slammed on its side. More windows exploded in the surrounding cars and houses. Sparks flew as the van screeched across the asphalt and smashed into a parked car.

At the end of the street, Cora ducked between the metal railings meant to block traffic and bolted down the dirt path into the ravine. She didn't glance back. She didn't need to—the girl was still there. She was still coming. The only thing left to do was run.

~

Nathan sat against a spruce tree in the northwest corner of the Mount Hope Cemetery and wondered where the Asians had gone. He hadn't seen them for at least an hour. No freaky bald guys, no freaky shadows. Just some stupid birds. The kind that loved to shit and call it art.

From the west, another boom echoed over the rooftops. Smoke twisted above the trees and houses, lunging for the sun, but the sun was too high and laughed at those stupid morons. They wanted to blow up everything and cover up their mess. Like 9/11. But they needed more Hollywood, more jets and big helicopters. Then they could really rake in the dough, win the big jackpot.

Along the fence on the north side of the cemetery, Nathan spotted movement and rolled onto his belly. A girl with blonde hair, wearing a red shirt, scrambled out of the brush and clambered on the wire fence. Fuck, what did Cora want now? Why couldn't she leave him alone for five fucking minutes?

She tumbled over the fence and fell on the grass of the cemetery. From the ravine came the crack of a tree. He looked around for somewhere to hide, but none of the gravestones were big enough, so he balled up behind the spruce tree. He was too late, though. She had already seen him and called out to him.

Nathan swore and kicked at the grass. Cora called out to him again and stumbled toward him.

"Yeah, yeah," he said.

When she finally reached him, she dropped to her knees, panting like a dog, and grabbed at him.

"Would you fuck off," he said and pushed her away.

"Run," she said, glancing over her shoulder. "Have to run. Not safe."

"You know the rules. You're supposed to mind your own business. This is off limits."

"P—people chasing. Girl. Bad people."

"Yeah, your friends are stupid. I'm going to kick their ass."

Cora shook her head and grabbed one of Nathan's arms again. He swore and pulled away from her.

On the other side of the fence facing the ravine, another girl appeared, this time wearing a dark blue dress. She kicked a wooden post, and it snapped, and she hopped over the sagging fence.

Cora tottered to her feet. "Run!"

"Yeah, bye."

A cold wind snapped around the cemetery. Large shadows rippled the grass in front of the girl, reminding Nathan of submarines and whales when they broke the surface. She shielded her eyes and strode closer: a teenager dressed like the Goth kids but without the face paint.

"Trouble," Cora said, still breathing hard. "Your apartment. A man came."

"It's just bullshit," Nathan said. "None of it's real. You told me to watch out for it—you and that fat prick."

The girl in the midnight blue dress stopped next to a small black tombstone, about a dozen feet away from them.

"This is not the way it should be," she said. "Father never dreamed this. There's only supposed to be one of you."

"Yes, it is confusing," a man replied.

Nathan glanced left. The Jewish Zorro, wearing his big, black hat, stood in the shade of the next spruce.

"Go back to hell," the girl said, glaring at the newcomer. "You don't belong here. You're just a shadow. You're not real."

"Teresa always believes she knows best," the Jewish Zorro said. "She has no patience for the truth."

The girl hissed, and the branches above Nathan cracked. He looked up, but Cora grabbed him and pulled him away from the tree.

"I have dozens of men with me," the girl said. "More are coming. All the reborn are mine. You have nothing."

Another cold wind snapped through the cemetery. Nathan let Cora pull him further away. Shadows swirled across the grass, and the girl grabbed a granite tombstone as wide as her shoulders and ripped it out of the ground. Nathan swore and backpedaled. The girl hurled the granite slab at Zorro, but he stepped aside, and the slab smashed into a second tombstone, breaking them both into big chunks.

"The reborn are nothing," said the Jewish Zorro. "They are simply vessels."

"You haven't changed at all," the girl said. "You still pretend you're not what you are."

"I do not know what I am. I never have. But I can see the creature inside Father, a thing that does not belong in our world. The dark twin of the Light before us."

"You're nothing," the girl said and ripped another tombstone from the ground.

The Jewish Zorro bowed his head and melted into the spruce tree in front of him. The girl cursed and smashed the slab of rock on a pair of smaller tombstones. Then her hate-filled gaze fixed on Nathan, and she yanked a third tombstone out of the ground. He turned to run. After only two or three steps, though, Cora hit him in the back and knocked him down. The tombstone sailed over them and slammed into a spruce tree.

On the west side of the cemetery, a white van roared through the gated entrance. Nathan scrambled to his feet and bolted in the opposite direction. Though the van wasn't an ambulance, it looked just as bad. He knew what happened when the doors opened and the men came pouring out with their rubber hoses and their handcuffs.

A second white van sped through the west entrance, and Nathan hopped over a wreath of flowers. Cora yelled and stumbled. He darted across one of the paved lanes that looped through the cemetery while the first white van screeched around a bend and turned into the same lane.

Another figure appeared by the fence that separated the cemetery from the ravine. His head was bald and yellowish-white like a peeled turnip, and he wore an expensive gray suit writhing with shadows.

Nathan swore and veered to the northeast corner of the cemetery. Behind him, the first van made a loud bang and then another as the back tires jumped the curb. Cora cried out. He tripped and hit the ground.

The first van skidded to a stop, spitting dirt and grass, and whacked a small gravestone. Doors banged open. Nathan scrambled to his feet, and men wearing black flak jackets dove on Cora. A third white van sped into the cemetery, followed by a black SUV.

Something heavy hit Nathan in the back, and he tumbled to the ground. Men yelled and grabbed his arms. He kicked and flailed, but the men pummeled him, knocking the wind out of him.

By the time he managed to recover his breath, they had pinned his arms behind his back and strapped his wrists together. He struggled, but they only tightened their grips, making his shoulders burn, and shoved his face into the grass. He yelped and kicked.

A short distance away, the girl, Teresa, spoke in French or Spanish.

"He does not look like much," a man replied.

"We'll find out soon enough," she said. "Throw him in the van."

Chapter 32

In his entire life, unnatural as it was, Alex had never felt so battered and bruised. Everything inside him burned—every muscle, every tendon, every joint—and something jabbed his throat, something he couldn't spit out. Nothing worked. His arms and legs were hunks of lead. Only his mind teetered back and forth, a toy between two giants, the pain and the darkness, until the pain finally exploded in his chest and threw him back into the darkness.

How long it lasted he had no idea. It didn't matter. Nothing mattered. Not until the light cut through his eyelids, and he tried to jerk his head away, and the pain ripped him apart.

After a time, he regained consciousness and realized his arms had flopped away from his sides. His legs had sagged open. He lay on a hard flat surface, cold air caressing his face. Something hissed. The surface underneath him was cold too, and he dimly remembered throwing a grenade.

His eyes flicked open, and the light cut into his brain. His mouth popped open, but he had no breath to scream. A chicken bone banged around his throat. Again he tried to scream. His arms and legs jerked. Agony splintered his back and his chest. Blackness smashed over him.

When next he awoke, Alex focused on wiggling his fingers, rather than the pain shooting through his chest and the light jabbing through his eyelids. Time scurried along—minutes, hours, it was all the same. His right hand clenched. His left hand refused. He continued to twitch and wriggle his hands and discovered the surface underneath him was smooth and metallic.

He wriggled his right hand away from his hips, and the surface dropped away. The same thing happened when he inched his left hand away from his hips.

Shit, Alex thought and fluttered his eyes, letting in some of the light that cut into him like glass. A gurgle escaped his throat.

He wouldn't let the pain win, though, and fluttered his eyelids, stopping, starting, stopping, starting, until the intensity of the light became bearable. A cough tickled his throat, and the pain in his chest flared. His head flopped to one side. His throat clenched. Something hard hit his teeth. Alex tried to push it out, but his tongue felt like a lump of clay, and his curse came out as a gurgle.

Another cough jiggled his throat, making it burn, and his eyes flicked open. The light scraped his eyeballs. He flinched and groaned.

After another five minutes or so, he eased his eyes open again. Despite the pain, he kept them open, letting his vision wobble in and out of focus. Walls covered with blue tiles and stainless steel cabinets arced around him. A white ceiling. A pair of heavy doors with windows.

Shit. Was he in a hospital?

Alex wiggled his fingers and toes and stretched his arms. He could rest later. First he needed to find out where he was. Everything was happening much faster this time: the knitting of bones, the sealing of flesh.

On the other side of the doors, a man appeared wearing a blue uniform. He stopped, wobbled his head, and pushed on one of the doors. Alex narrowed his eyes.

From beyond the doors, a woman said, "How long you gonna be?"

"I have to process this guy before Dick gets back," replied the man. "Said it's a priority."

"Should I get my watch?"

The man laughed and stepped into the room, letting the door swing shut. Alex heard the snap of latex gloves. The man strode closer but stopped beside Alex's feet.

"What the hell?" the man said.

Alex waited, preparing himself for the pain. The man stepped closer and leaned over Alex. He swung out his right arm and grabbed at the man's blue scrubs. He squawked and stumbled backwards, tripping over his own feet, and fell beside the gurney. A wave of blackness swept over Alex as he tumbled on the man's legs, but Alex ignored the pain and clawed at the man's scrubs.

The man managed to find his voice and cried out. Alex yanked on the scrubs, ripping them, and struck the man's face. The blow seemed to stun him, and Alex whacked the man's head on the floor to make certain.

In the silence that followed, Alex pushed himself into a sitting position, clenching his teeth, and squinted at the gurneys and stainless steel cabinets surrounding him. No one had come to check on the noise yet, but that wouldn't last forever.

He coughed up a chunk of congealed blood and yanked at the camera hanging around the man's neck. The man also wore an ID badge that said Theodore Wilson. He was in his forties and had swarthy skin and dark, cropped hair that thinned into nothingness on his crown. Under his torn scrubs, he wore a cream-colored T-shirt and blue jeans, the crotch of the latter darkening with piss.

Alex coughed again, spattering blood on his pants, and looked down at his own shirt. He had at least five bloody holes around his heart and fingered them. The skin underneath felt smooth, but the blood had hardened into crusty patches that stuck to his skin like oatmeal.

He muttered a curse, closed his eyes, and waited. After a minute or two, Theodore groaned. Alex slapped the man's face and clapped a hand over his mouth. He jerked, and his eyelids flew open.

To prevent any shouts, Alex hit the man in the belly several times. He sputtered and flinched. At the same time, a burning sensation shot up Alex's throat, and he bent over and started to hack. Blood burst from his mouth and spattered Theodore's belly. He twisted sideways, but Alex smacked Theodore's head on the floor, and his arms flopped down like a pair of dead fish.

Something hard pinged on the floor by Alex's right hand. He straightened up, coughing, and wiped blood from his mouth. On the tiles by his hand lay a red-smeared bullet. A second bloody bullet lay beside the front wheels of the gurney.

Alex scanned the rest of the room. On one of the metal coun-ters, he spotted a plastic bag holding a cellphone, a watch, keys, and other trinkets. His things? What about the grenades?

Theodore groaned.

Alex grabbed the man by the throat. "Sh—shut. Shut up."

"Please," Theodore said. "Help, I'll get help."

"Where? This?"

"We just have to go upstairs. The hospital. Just let me go. I'll get help."

"Where? Address?"

Theodore twisted sideways, struggling to free his neck. Alex slapped the man's head and banged it on the floor. He sagged back down, his eyes slipping shut.

After another glance around the room, Alex pushed at the floor, trying to stand, but his legs went rubbery, and he fell on Theodore's midriff.

Several minutes ticked by while Alex rested, focusing on his legs. Then he slapped Theodore's face and pointed to the counter with the plastic bags.

"Help. There," Alex said.

Theodore stared at Alex. He slapped Theodore again and repeated the orders.

"Okay," the man said. "No more. Please, no more."

Alex kept one arm hooked around Theodore's neck while he lurched to his feet. Together they stumbled to the nearest stainless steel counter. Alex ordered Theodore to rip open the plastic bag and sift through the contents, none of which looked familiar. Alex glanced down and felt his pockets and realized he still had his wallet and his keys. His cellphone too, though it was matted with blood.

"Who?" Alex asked, pointing at the items on the counter.

"One of the others," Theodore said. "One that came with you. From the Harbourfront."

Alex picked up the unknown cellphone and checked the call log. He recognized two of the numbers: Mobius's Blackberry and central command.

"My bag?" Alex asked. "Green?"

"I don't know. I didn't see one."

Alex glared.

"No, we don't get it," Theodore said. "We don't handle explosives."

"Where?"

"I—I don't know."

Alex grimaced, but a purplish fog swirled in front of his eyes, and he leaned against the counter to steady himself. He needed to rest soon, for a few minutes at least.

"Please, just let me get help," Theodore said. "I swear I'll get help."

"Car?" Alex said and rubbed his eyes. "You? Car?"

Theodore shook his head and avoided Alex's gaze. Alex poked at bloody holes in his shirt.

"Car," he said. "Now. Or big mess. You big mess."

~

Fifteen minutes later, Alex sat in the passenger seat of a red coupe while Theodore drove west past the University of Toronto. Several times Alex's vision blurred, turning the cars and buildings and people into a gray soup, reminding him of the war—the fog, the mud, the rain. Rubbing his eyes didn't help. It only made Theodore more nervous, his hands fluttering up and down the steering wheel like a pair of horny butterflies.

"Always hated you," Alex said, thinking of the boys who had had their guts splattered in the mud in the rain. "Always got somebody killed. Always blamed somebody else."

"Please, you can have my wallet. I'll give you the pin numbers. Whatever you want. I won't tell anyone."

"Drive," Alex said. "All you need to do."

Theodore stayed quiet for a few more blocks, turning south after passing the busiest part of Chinatown. When they reached Dundas Street, he turned west again and started whining again.

Alex muttered a curse. "Stop. There. Now."

Theodore looked alarmed as he slowed down and parked beside a restaurant with a black awning and dirty windows. Alex grabbed Theodore's head and smacked it against the steering wheel.

"You wouldn't have survived," Alex said. "Not five minutes."

He yanked the keys out of the ignition, opened his door, and hauled the dazed Theodore out of the car. On the opposite side of the street, two girls carrying backpacks stopped to stare. Alex smacked Theodore's head against the side of the car, and he fell on the curb. Thirty feet behind Alex, an old Chinese man with a cane turned around and hobbled down a side street.

"Look," Alex said. "You scared the natives."

Several cars slowed down. None of them stopped. He dragged Theodore to the back of the car, opened the trunk, and shoved him inside.

"Lucky you," Alex said and slammed the lid shut. "So lucky. Busy neighborhood."

Theodore yelled and banged on the lid of the trunk. Alex started walking westwards.

Halfway along the next block, he tossed the car keys over a fence into a patch of purple and white flowers. Then he turned into a lane lined with old garages and rickety fences, and wondered how far he would get before he passed out.

Chapter 33

Cora struggled to sit up, fear turning her insides into mush. She was in the back of a van on a thick musty blanket. Her wrists were pinned together behind her back with a zip tie. In front of her, on a dark green crate, sat a bald man wearing a charcoal gray suit, glaring at her with black bottomless eyes that never seemed to blink. The other two men wore black uniforms and flak jackets and sat in the front, pretending not to look over their shoulders. One held an assault rifle. The second, the driver, spoke on his cellphone and turned a corner.

"Where's Nathan?" Cora asked. "My brother? What did you do with him?"

"You are the girl from the picture," the bald man said. "But you are not."

"I just want to know where he is. Is he okay?"

"Tell me about the Light. Where is it?"

"Please, this is a mistake. We didn't do anything."

"The Light has touched you," he said. "You are known to it, you cannot hide. The mistress sees it and will have answers. Father will have answers."

Cora suppressed a shiver and nodded while the bald man continued to ramble about the Light, like she sometimes had to do with clients, praying she would wake up from this nightmare.

A phone rang, and the bald man stopped mid-sentence. He pulled out a Blackberry and spoke in Spanish or Portuguese.

After ending his call, he said, "We go to a place for answers. You will not like it."

"Is this about Paul?" Cora asked. "Does he—"

The bald man surged forward and grabbed her right arm. She screamed and jerked away from him. It felt like her arm was on fire. He fell back against the green crate, hissing. The driver slammed on the brakes.

"No! Keep driving," the bald man yelled before turning back to Cora, his face twisted in anger. "You speak of Paul? The firstborn?"

Hindered by the zip tie cutting into her wrists, she wriggled on her right side, trying to stop the burning on her arm. The bald man barked an order, and the guard with the rifle passed it to the bald man. He jabbed the muzzle into Cora's ribs, and she yelped.

"Tell me!" the bald man said.

Tears stung her eyes, obscuring her vision, as she gasped out, "W—wait. Please."

"How do you know of him? Has he come to you? What is his form?"

"I've seen him a few times," she said. "But he doesn't like to talk about himself. He's more interested in history. And he has things he likes to show. A lot of religious things, from all around the world."

"He has come to steal the Light," the bald man said.

"Yes, he talks about light. He always has candles. He likes paintings too. Old ones."

"Where is this? When?"

"He was in the cemetery, just before you came. But you must have scared him off."

The bald man glared at Cora.

"It's true," she said. "The girl saw him too."

He rammed the gun into Cora's ribs, and she cried out in pain.

"Do not blaspheme the mistress," he said. "She is the mistress. She is no other."

"Yes! Sorry," Cora said, blinking back tears. "I didn't know. She's the mistress."

"She has seen the Light. Nothing will take her from the path. The first son is treacherous, a deceiver. He has eaten the snake."

"Yes, I understand. He's a deceiver."

The bald man sat silent for a minute, glaring at Cora. She kept her gaze on the blanket by his feet. Moving only made her ribs hurt more. The van turned a corner, and he took out his Blackberry and talked to someone in a guttural tongue reminiscent of German.

During his second call, he switched to another language, possibly Italian, and jabbed Cora with the gun. She flinched but remained on her side and prayed Nathan was all right.

"Sir, we're almost at the warehouse," the driver said.

"Yes," the bald man said. "Father comes."

The van shook, as if struck by a stormy gust, and the shadows along the walls of the van stretched out and melted around the bald man. One of the guards swore.

"There is no escape," the bald man said.

Cora shivered and nodded. The van slowed and turned into a gap between two brick buildings and jounced through several potholes. She wiggled her arms, hoping the zip tie had loosened a little, but it continued to cut into her wrists.

"Why are you doing this?" she asked. "What do you want?"

"You dare to pretend ignorance?" the bald man said and speared her with the gun.

She yelped. The van jerked to a stop.

"Sir?" the driver asked.

"Yes," the bald man said. "Take her to the mistress."

Both men jumped out of the van. A few seconds later, one of the back doors jerked open. The driver grabbed her by the legs and hauled her out of the van. The second man, built like a warhorse, threw her over a shoulder and trudged to a warehouse made of red brick stained with soot. Another white van and a black Cadillac were already parked in the alley, beside a chain-link fence about ten feet high, on the other side of which extended a property overgrown with shrubs and grass.

"Please, let me go," she said. "Please. Just put me down."

The driver, a step behind them, cuffed Cora across the head, while the man carrying her tightened his grip. She blinked several times, trying to clear the spots from her vision, and pivoted her head. Where was Nathan? Was he in the warehouse?

A door reinforced with metal bars squawked open. Another guard wearing a black uniform and a flak jacket waved them inside, an assault rifle hanging from his right shoulder.

"Please," Cora said. "I can walk."

The driver slapped her across the head again, and the warhorse strode into a large room, racks of crates filling two of the walls.

Cardboard covered the windows. The warhorse dropped her butt-first on the seat of a wooden chair, and she winced. At least half-a-dozen other men wearing black uniforms and flak jackets stood nearby, obscuring the girl Paul had called Teresa and someone sitting on a second wooden chair.

"Nathan!" she called out and started to stand.

The driver snapped an arm around her throat. Her brother swore and kicked at Teresa. The two guards holding him tightened their grip, and a third guard punched him in the head.

"I have been hearing a lot of stupidity from this one," Teresa said, glancing in Cora's direction. "But no answers. Only the Light matters now."

"Please, let him go," Cora said. "He hasn't done anything. This is a mistake."

Teresa strode to Cora and prodded her forehead. A burning sensation shot down her face and across her scalp, and she jerked back. Teresa flinched too and frowned at her finger.

"Yes, mistress," the bald man said. "They must be hiding the truth. We only need to break it from them."

"How did you come to touch the Light?" Teresa demanded.

"I don't understand what you mean," Cora said.

Teresa scowled and gestured to the men around Nathan. The shortest of them, a blond man with a face like a hog, punched Nathan in the chest. Nathan sputtered and doubled over, but two other men pulled him upright again.

"No! Stop! Leave him alone," Cora said.

"You're the one keeping secrets," Teresa said. "I only want what's mine. Tell me where it is. Who controls it?"

"Is this about Paul? Did he take something?"

The short guard belted Nathan again.

"Please, I don't know what you mean," Cora said. "I swear, please don't hurt him."

Teresa repeated her question about the Light. Cora shook her head, stumbling through her tangled thoughts. The girl could mean anything—the sun, jewels, lamps.

"What does it look like?" Cora asked. "Maybe I saw it, but I didn't know."

"She is a deceiver," the bald man said. "She has eaten the serpent."

Teresa scowled at him.

"Please, I'm trying," Cora said. "Can't you tell me anything? What sort of light?"

"Take them in there," Teresa said and pointed to a room in one of the corners, a corkboard hanging beside the doorway. "Do what is necessary."

The men standing around Cora and Nathan looked puzzled. Several glanced at the bald man.

"Now!" Teresa shouted.

The two men holding Nathan hauled him off his chair, and he kicked and yelled. A third man slugged Nathan while they dragged him into the room. The guard built like a warhorse slung Cora over a shoulder and carried her after them, the driver following behind, cuffing her across the head until she was too dizzy to kick or yell.

The first pair of guards threw Nathan on the floor, lifting a cloud of dust. He coughed and wriggled toward a stack of chairs and another of metal filing cabinets piled in the back. Both men kicked him, and he collapsed on the floor.

"No," Cora said, blinking, trying to stop the room from spinning. "No."

In a low voice, the guard carrying Cora asked, "What are we supposed to do?"

"Whatever it takes," the driver said.

A man with garlic breath and a thick black mustache pulled Cora off the warhorse and shoved her toward the file cabinets. She stumbled toward Nathan, but the man with the garlic breath grabbed her and laughed. Her brother balled up on the floor, his arms clutched in front of his face and belly. One guard continued to kick Nathan's backside. The other stepped on Nathan's head, pushing it into the floor.

Cora tottered sideways, trying to pull free of the man with garlic breath. He yanked her back and snapped an arm around her neck. She stomped a foot and kicked back at his shins, but he jerked her off balance and tightened his grip. After about ten seconds, the room began to wobble, and the sounds around her dimmed.

He loosened his chokehold and squeezed one of her breasts. "How you like that? Better?"

Cora wiggled her head, disoriented. He squeezed her breast again, and a third guard joined in to kick Nathan.

"No," she murmured. "S—stop."

The man with the garlic breath thrust his hips against her. She struggled to get air. His right hand tightened on her breast again, and his erection jabbed into her pelvis. Then he stumbled, and his arms dropped away.

Cora tumbled on the floor. The rest of the men in the room scattered.

Still dizzy, she rolled onto her knees and bumped against the man with the garlic breath, lying beside her as limp as wet laundry. Teresa stood just inside the doorway while the bald man with the maggot-hued skin hunched beside a coffee machine plastered with dust.

Behind Teresa shuffled a thin man wearing a brown suit and brown loafers, his hair wispy and gray. His jaundiced eyes bulged out of his face, and he had a tick that made his head bob toward his left shoulder.

The bald man barked an order. The men wearing flak jackets scrambled to the back wall and lined up.

Cora crept toward Nathan and reached out to him. No one stopped her. He jerked away and gasped in pain.

"Sorry," she said. "I'm sorry. Just stay still."

"You fucking tripped me," he said. "You always fuckin—"

Teresa interrupted. "This is Peter. He missed you the first time, at the Royal York. Thursday, I believe."

"Yes, mistress," said the man with the tic. "Forgive me."

Cora glanced at him. The hotel? What did that have to do with this?

Peter stared at her, his eyes bulging like tumors, his head bobbing sideways. She shifted in front of Nathan.

"Do you feel her now?" Teresa asked.

The man named Peter shook his head, looking worried. "No, mistress. It's not like before. Not the same."

"What does that mean?"

"There's something around her," he said. "Shiny like a new penny. But I can't feel it. Not really."

"What else?"

"I think it's moving," he said. "Around both of them."

"Yes, mistress," the bald man said. "They are hiding everything."

"I don't understand, mistress," Peter said. "But looking at them makes me dizzy."

Teresa nodded and said something to the bald man. He barked an order at the guards lined up against the back wall. A short, stocky man with a black beard ran forward and passed over a knife, which the bald man handed Peter.

"Start with the boy," Teresa said.

"No!" Cora yelled.

The guard with the black beard grabbed her and hauled her away from Nathan. She tried to bite him and kicked at him, but he wrenched her arms and threw her on the floor. Nathan swore and struggled to sit up, clutching his right side.

"Run," Cora yelled, but the guard clapped a hand over her mouth, and she gagged on the stench of carbine on his fingers.

Two more guards jumped forward from the wall and pulled Nathan flat on his back.

"Get off me, you fuckers," he yelled. "Get off!"

"Start with a small cut," Teresa said to Peter. "Just enough to draw blood."

"Yes, mistress."

"You fuckers ain't sticking me," Nathan yelled. "I know your fucking tricks."

Another pair of guards grabbed Nathan's legs. He thrashed and kicked, and Cora jerked her mouth free.

"No!" she yelled.

The bearded guard slapped a hand over her mouth again and shoved a knee into her back, pushing her into the floor. One of the guards around Nathan yanked his T-shirt up to his shoulders. He swore and managed to pull a leg free and kicked wildly. The same guard jerked the front of the shirt over Nathan's face and punched him in the chest until he sputtered and collapsed.

Peter brushed a hand over his suit and kneeled, his head jerking like a demented bobblehead, and scraped the knife across Nathan's belly. He screamed. The guards shoved him back down and smacked his head on the floor.

All around the room, the shadows rippled. Peter pulled away from Nathan, alarmed.

"Again," Teresa said.

"Yes, mistress."

Despite the hand clamped on Cora's face and the sharp pain from the knee in her back, she screamed at them to stop. Someone grabbed her legs and held them. The knife flicked down. Nathan screamed and jerked. The knife flicked down a third time. Blood squirted. Peter shrieked and stumbled away from Nathan.

A split second later, gold fire roared around Nathan, and lightning exploded around Peter. The guards cried out and sprang away from Nathan, clutching their eyes. Cora kicked and wriggled, but the guard with the black beard tugged her head back and drove his knee into her spine.

Another blast of lightning shook the room. Her guard yowled and tumbled on the floor. Gold fire sizzled and snapped, blinding her. Nathan screamed and screamed.

Cora scrabbled at the floor, surprised to find her hands free, but didn't have time to think about it. Nausea rippled her throat. Purple spots zigzagged in front of her. One man tripped over her legs and fell. Another whimpered. A third swore. Someone else sobbed, loud and deep.

Nathan?

She struggled onto her knees, blinking repeatedly, fighting her dizziness, and crawled towards him. God, please. Please let him be all right.

Chapter 34

Teresa felt the explosion of light moments before it happened and sprang into the main bay of the warehouse with her eyes closed. Men yelled. Peter shrieked.

A second explosion burned through her eyelids, and she dropped into a ball. Yells turned to screams. Mobius called out to Father, and a guard bumped into her, knocking her sideways. She whipped a hand out. Bone snapped. He screamed and tumbled beside her.

She counted to five. The light faded, leaving a smudgy darkness on her eyes, and she stomped on the screaming guard, snapping one of his arms and a dozen ribs. A second kick silenced him.

While easing her eyes open, Teresa darted to the shadows of the nearest wall, the sunlight from the skylights jabbing her pupils like knitting needles. Three guards squatted on the concrete floor, two with pistols drawn, the third holding an assault rifle. Mobius huddled on the floor just outside of the shipping office, his scorched hands clasped over his eyes.

She eased her eyes open a little further and winced. The nearest of the skylights exploded and rained glass.

From the shipping office came a ragged cough, and Mobius scampered inside. She hissed and darted after him. He grabbed a rifle from the floor and swung the butt at the boy's legs. He wailed, and the blonde girl tackled Mobius. Both of them screamed and tumbled away from each other.

"Enough!" Teresa shouted.

Mobius swung the rifle at the blonde girl and kicked her. Teresa sprang forward and yanked Mobius away from the girl. He swung around to hit Teresa, and she hurled him into the wall beside the file cabinets, knocking a large hole in the drywall.

He staggered to his feet and lurched toward another rifle. The blonde girl crawled in front of the boy, and Teresa sprang in front of both of them.

Mobius hopped around Teresa and tried to swing the rifle at the blonde girl. Teresa flung him in the opposite direction, smashing another gaping hole in the drywall.

"Idiot," she said.

For several seconds, Mobius remained unmoving. Then he coughed and wriggled out of the hole in the wall and bowed on the floor.

Teresa scowled and turned to the prisoners. The boy huddled on the floor, crying, while the girl hovered over him.

"Why are you doing this?" she said. "What's wrong with you?"

Teresa opened her mouth to speak, but Mobius interrupted. "Mistress! The time has come. The darkness speaks."

"Shut up!" she said.

"Please, let us go," the girl said. "We won't tell anyone."

"How long has he carried the Light?" Teresa asked. "How did he come by it?"

"He needs help. He's bleeding."

"Answer the question," Teresa said. "Or you can help him pick his fingers off the floor."

The girl pulled at the boy's T-shirt, trying to staunch the blood seeping from his belly. That idiot Peter must have cut an artery. He should have waited before going that deep. They needed answers, not pudding.

One of the guards stirred, his hands clutched over his eyes, and rolled away from Peter, who lay twisted like a child's marionette, all of his exposed flesh blackened. Wisps of shadow drifted from his head. Teresa kissed her crucifix and stepped closer. Was it really that easy? She couldn't sense anything inside him anymore but also had difficulty sensing Mobius, only fifteen feet away. The air had become too crackly, like rice paper, and the stink of ozone overwhelmed the grittier smells of must and urine and sweat.

On the other side of the doorway, two of the guards whispered to each other, wondering what to do, their voices full of fear. She lifted a hand to shut them up, but nothing happened. She growled, and she kicked Peter in the head. His skull burst apart.

She sprang back, startled. His chest and arms collapsed, then his legs and feet.

Teresa grimaced and stepped on a blackened finger, crushing it into a sooty streak. The blonde girl hunched over her brother, oblivious, pressing her hands to his belly. Mobius muttered prayers and brushed at the wisps of shadow flickering over his shoulders.

"Tell those idiots to shut up," Teresa said to him. "Do something useful."

"The others will come, mistress. They will see to it."

"Now!"

Mobius nodded, but he wasn't looking at her. Instead, his face clenched in fear, and he raised a hand to shield his eyes.

Teresa flinched. A golden mist drifted around the blonde girl's fingers, burning Teresa's eyes.

"Mistress?"

"Shut up," she said and backed up to the doorway, one hand shielding her eyes. The golden mist spread over the boy's belly, the edges swirling and dipping into his flesh.

"It's both of them," she said. "That's why we couldn't find it. The Light's hiding in both of them."

"The Light is death," Mobius said. "There is no other."

Teresa hissed and grabbed him by the jacket and hurled him out of the room. Something that felt like hundreds of ants crawled across her exposed skin, and she tried to brush the sensation away, but it only grew stronger. The air rippled and vibrated. She backed out of the doorway. The golden mist continued to spread on the boy's chest and shoulders, and the burning of her eyes intensified.

Inside the room, the shadows hissed and growled and broke apart. Patches of it whipped past her feet, and a guard scrambled out of the room and bumped into her. She grabbed his head and flung him aside, snapping his neck.

The gold mist pulsed. Teresa's vision blurred. She darted sideways, but too late. Gold light surged from the shipping office, scalding her flesh, and she collapsed on the floor, screaming.

~

Alex jarred awake to the rat-tat-tat of machine gun fire and flopped on his belly. With his right hand, he grabbed for his rifle, but the ground was rough and rock hard, and his rifle was missing.

Those bastards had stolen it.

A moment later, Alex realized he was lying on asphalt, not the muddy fields of Holland, and froze. His left hand rested next to a yellow brick wall. A green bin stinking of garbage stood by his feet. A car honked at him—a small gray hatchback—from the mouth of an alley that looked familiar, especially the rickety wooden fence on his right.

He swore and rolled toward the yellow wall, belonging to the Chinese restaurant next to his apartment building. The driver honked again and drove past Alex.

"Yeah, fuck you too," he said and pushed himself up.

After rubbing his face, he limped to the back door of his building and glanced inside. The main floor looked quiet, but that didn't mean a hell of a lot. If those security goons wanted to get him, they wouldn't announce it. He didn't care either, as long as Mobius was there. It was about time the two of them settled things, Father be damned.

On the second floor, Alex dug out his keys and eased open his apartment door. What a surprise. No welcome home party? What were those morons doing?

He locked the door. Shards of brown and green glass and a large yellowish puddle covered the kitchen floor. In the bedroom, he found more smashed glass on his sheets and beer stains on the wall above the headboard. His closet, all his suits, stank of piss.

Alex turned around and listened. He thought he heard the creak of a step or a door, but the shadows in the corners billowed and hissed, masking the sound.

He muttered a curse and stepped into the living room. He had several grenades wedged in the stuffing under the couch, but the shadows hissed even louder, and he heard more creaking in the hallway. He grabbed the hockey stick standing behind the couch, both items remnants of the old tenant, and darted to the wall beside the apartment door. As he swung the hockey stick up, he changed his mind and eased back a step.

Next to the door, bullets punched through the wall. The door smashed inward. A pistol with a long barrel and a pair of chubby white hands appeared, followed by Schwartz's pale face, tense with fear.

Alex slashed the hockey stick downwards and shattered the blade and Schwartz's hands. He screamed. More bullets burst through the wall, one of them punching a hole through his right leg. The TV exploded. Windows shattered. He twisted and rammed the hockey stick through the wall and hit something solid on the other side. A man screamed.

For a moment, the bullets stopped, and Alex charged into the hallway and grabbed a man wearing a black flak jacket and a black mask and slammed him into another soldier. Two bullets tore through Alex's left leg and thigh, and the first soldier screamed. Alex whirled and threw the man at a third soldier standing in the hallway, still firing his rifle, while a fourth man stared stupidly at Fernandez dangling from the end of the hockey stick.

Alex ripped the rifle away from the second soldier, kicked him in the head, and rammed down the door of the apartment on the other side of the hallway. Another pair of bullets hit Alex. A woman shrieked from the bedroom. He ducked left, past the fridge, and crouched beside the sink. One of the soldiers jumped into the apartment and fired into the kitchen, but he aimed too high, shattering the window overlooking the alley, and Alex shot the man in the face. He tumbled to the floor, his screech lasting only a second or two.

Alex sprang over the broken door and fired into the hallway, hitting another soldier in the face and neck, while the last one—the gawker—ran away.

With a single kick, Alex knocked out the soldier wailing underfoot. The other would die in seconds, judging by the blood pumping from his neck. Alex slammed Schwartz's head against a door jamb to stop his shrieking and checked Fernandez was dead.

Back in the neighbor's apartment, Alex opened the fridge and found two beers. He guzzled the first, stuffed the second in his pants, and glanced at his bloody legs. Annoying, but at least he could walk.

He returned to his apartment and eyed the ratty curtains, the worn-out carpet, the sagging couch and opened the second beer. For a year, this had been his own space, his little delusion of freedom. No Teresa. No Mobius.

Alex took a long swallow and shook his head. He was such a damn fool. Then he kicked Schwartz and yanked the shattered hockey stick out of the wall. Chunks of drywall tumbled on the carpet. In the hallway, Fernandez thumped on the floor.

After guzzling the rest of the beer, Alex threw the bottle at a cupboard in the kitchen. The bottle smashed. He flipped the couch upside down on the coffee table and ripped out some of the springs and pulled out three grenades from the stuffing. He tossed them in a paper bag from the liquor store and added two pistols from his welcoming party.

As an afterthought, Alex searched Fernandez and took his cell-phone and a set of keys, which opened a blue van parked in front of a fire hydrant across from his building. No sign of the last soldier. No sirens.

Just as well, Alex thought and climbed into the driver's seat. He didn't want to kill any more fools.

~

Teresa winced and kicked Mobius, who clung to her right foot like a deranged dog.

"Please, mistress," he said. "I am your most faithful."

She kicked him again, clipping the top of his bald head, and hopped to her feet. Though the golden light had disappeared, her skin and eyes still burned, making it difficult to focus. The boy still lay in the office, curled up like a fetus, while the girl sat beside him, talking quietly to him.

"Get up," she said to Mobius. "There's no time to waste. We must take them to Father. Both of them."

"He will never allow it," he replied.

Teresa booted him in the ribs and glanced around at the guards. Most were dead or unconscious. In the room with the prisoners, the big man groaned and lurched upright, rubbing his eyes. A second man stood by the bay door, swearing and struggling with his rifle. Another vomited behind a forklift.

"Get the prisoners," she said to the man holding the rifle. "Put them in a van."

He saluted and scrambled to obey her.

"No," Mobius said, shaking his head. "A trick. Deceivers. All of them."

"The only trickster here is you," Teresa said and kicked him again. "Now open the door. Father's waiting."

Chapter 35

Cora slumped back, the last of the golden light fading, while Nathan muttered and rolled onto his side.

"Are you okay?" she asked. "Does it still hurt?"

"Would you shut up, I'm trying to sleep."

"Please, Nathan. We don't have much time."

One of the guards by the doorway groaned and sat up and rubbed his eyes—the big man who had carried Cora into the warehouse. Nathan lifted his head.

"What's going on?" he asked. "Where the fuck are we?"

"I don't know. But they're bad people."

He swore. "Do I look like I'm five?"

"We have to get out of here," she said.

In the main bay of the warehouse, the girl, Teresa, yelled at someone. Cora glanced around the room, her gaze catching on the guns lying on the floor.

The guard built like a warhorse rumbled and stood up and shook his right leg. Another guard carrying an assault rifle stepped into the room. He had big black eyes with an Asian quirk and a tattoo of barbed wire around his neck.

"Get up. We're leaving," he said.

"Hey, it's Dumb and Dumber," Nathan said.

Cora rested a hand on his right arm, hoping to quiet him, but he swore and shook her off.

"I said, 'Up!' Now!" said the tattooed man.

"Shove it up your ass," said Nathan.

The tattooed man swore and kicked Nathan's legs. Cora glanced at the nearest of the assault rifles again. What if she grabbed it? Could she do it? She had never used a gun before.

Nathan rolled toward the walls, and she shifted closer to the assault rifle. The guard built like a warhorse grabbed her. A third guard limped into the room—the blond with the piggish face—and twisted one of Nathan's arms until he staggered to his feet, cursing and yelling.

The tattooed guard slung his assault rifle over a shoulder and secured Nathan's hands with a zip tie. Cora wriggled and kicked and pulled at the big guard's flak jacket, but one of the other guards—she wasn't sure which—hit her in the head, making the room spin and darken. The big guard hoisted her over a shoulder.

By the time she could focus again, the two guards had hauled Nathan out of the room. The big guard followed, and she lost sight of her brother. A door banged. Nathan continued to swear and cried out in pain.

Cora kicked and flailed her arms, but the big guard only tightened his grip until she couldn't breathe. Once outside the building, he swung her around and plunked her on her feet behind a white van. She grabbed one of the doors to steady herself. In the van, Nathan lay on his back, unmoving, his face flushed.

Despite her dizziness, Cora scrambled in the van and pressed a hand to Nathan's chest. He twitched and shifted his head. His breathing seemed normal. His heartbeat, too.

The big guard climbed in the van and slammed the back doors shut. The girl, Teresa, made a seat for herself on a canvas bag behind the driver's seat, ignoring the protests of the bald man, who then scrambled into the passenger seat.

"Please, just let him go," Cora said. "He hasn't done anything. I'll do whatever you want."

"Your lies are feeble," the bald man said. "Transparent."

"I've waited a long time for this," Teresa said. "More than you could ever understand."

The tattooed man started the van. Another white van honked and pulled up behind them.

While driving around the corner of the warehouse, they bounced through a pair of potholes, and Nathan groaned.

"Are you okay?" Cora asked quietly.

He swore and pushed her away.

For the next few minutes, he remained huddled on the floor, and Cora tried to keep her gaze on something safe—a blob of grease, an oily rag, a dent in the wall—avoiding the eyes that glared at her. She wanted to know where they were going so she wouldn't have to imagine but keeping quiet seemed safer.

Another five minutes passed. The van jerked to a stop for a red light. Nathan swore and kicked at the big guard.

"No, don't," Cora said, reaching for one of Nathan's arms.

He continued to kick, regardless, and the guard belted Nathan in the kidneys. Cora tried to grab the guard, but he shoved her aside and punched Nathan in the kidneys again. He gasped and flopped back to the floor.

"Enough. He won't have any words left soon." Teresa scowled at the driver.

"Yes, mistress," he said and stomped on the gas pedal. The van jolted through the red light. Nathan groaned and wriggled his arms, trussed behind his back.

A streetcar, shellacked in white and plastered with ads for rum, clanged at them. Cora stared at it through the tinted glass of the back windows. Yes, the real world was still out there. It still existed. Insanity hadn't taken over.

Something banged against the right side of the van. She lurched against the big guard, and her stomach clenched. Had they hit something?

The van raced through another intersection, and shadowy faces bulged out of the walls and screamed. The van swerved left. Tires screeched. Horns blared. The big guard slapped his head and groped his ears.

"Mistress?" the bald man called out.

"Ignore them. We'll be there soon," Teresa said.

The van continued to swerve, and Cora slapped her hands over her ears, but the screaming only grew louder. One face was bearded like Uncle Abner. Another had the gaunt cheeks of Aunt Clara after her last round of chemo, two months before she died.

The driver shrieked, and the van whipped left. Something slammed into the right side of the van, and the windshield exploded. A second smash threw Cora and the big guard against the crumpled right wall.

Though dazed, she blinked and struggled to sit up. "Nathan?"

"Get off me, you fucking pig," her brother yelled from under the legs of the big guard.

In front of them, Teresa yelled and flung open the side door and hopped out of the van. The bald man called after her while the big guard groaned.

Cora scrambled over his chest and fumbled with the latch of the back doors.

"Stop!" the bald man yelled.

The left door sprang open, and Cora half-fell, half-stumbled, out of the van. Chunks of glass and metal and rubber littered the street, mostly around a red Corolla with a crumpled front end. Two other cars and a minivan were scattered around the white van like a broken pinwheel.

"Yeah, fucker," Nathan said.

Cora turned and saw him wriggling toward her. She grabbed his ankles and tugged while the big guard struggled to sit up. Nathan's shirt snagged on a metal catch and ripped as he fell out of the van, scraping his back and arms on the fender.

She tried to pull him back to his feet, but the big guard lunged at them and knocked her off balance. She pushed Nathan toward the nearest sidewalk, lined with small shops—a laundromat, a store selling organic food, another selling gelato and ice cream, and several restaurants—people everywhere, all of them gawking.

The big guard stumbled out of the van and caught her right arm. She kicked him in the shins and tried to jerk free, but he threw her against the van, stunning her. Then he threw her inside and slammed the door shut.

"Go get him," the bald man shouted from somewhere on the right side of the van.

"Yes, sir," the big guard said.

In the van, the driver still clutched the steering wheel, blood dripping from his head. Cora scrambled to her knees, scraping her hands on the glass on the floor, and peered out the two holes that had been windows in the back doors. Nathan darted between parked cars and gawkers and ran into an Italian restaurant advertising a wood burning oven. A few seconds later, he reappeared on the patio on the side of the building and tripped over chairs while various customers scattered like pigeons.

"No," Cora shouted and fumbled with the latch of the door. "Run!"

The big guard plowed through the tables and chairs and grabbed Nathan. He swore and kicked, and a man with a black beard jumped to help, but the guard punched the bearded man in the face. He crumpled like a broken toy.

Cora lurched out of the van and ran after her brother. Behind her, something smashed against the van. She ducked and glanced back. The bald man, his eyes goggling out of his head, charged after her. A shaft of metal with a jagged end swished over her head. The bald man lunged again, but Teresa appeared behind him and jerked him off his feet and threw him on the street.

Cora darted around the trunk of a black Toyota with a crumpled fender. Dozens of people stood on the sidewalks, staring, perhaps wondering if the crash was real. Where were the movie cameras? Others peered out of cars and buildings. A few yakked on their cellphones and PDAs, but she didn't hear any sirens. Where were the police? Now when she actually needed them?

With Nathan still kicking and swearing, the big guard stopped in front of Teresa and waited for her command. The bald man kneeled beside her.

"Mistress, forgive me," he said. "I am your most faithful. Striking her was not my intention. It was not my will."

"Bring the boy," Teresa said to the big guard. "She'll follow. Unless she wants to stay with Mobius."

She flung the bald man aside and kicked the black Toyota, knocking a large dent in the passenger door. Cora stumbled backwards, away from the car. The blond driver of the other van ran towards her.

God, what now? Why wouldn't anyone help?

"Mistress?" the big guard said. "I think the other van got rear-ended. Maybe we can grab one of those cars?" He tightened his grip on Nathan and pointed west, the way they had been driving.

Teresa glared but nodded.

Out of sheer desperation, Cora darted around the trunk of the black Toyota and tackled Teresa. It felt like hitting a bag of sand, and the scrapes on Cora's hands burst into agony. She screamed, even as Teresa screamed and flung Cora away.

The burning intensified. Streams of shadow and gold fire writhed around Cora's hands, and she slapped them against her shirt and her jeans. Gold light flared. Nathan hollered. The shadows ripped apart.

Teresa's scream turned to one of fury, and a green car with a busted taillight hurtled into the air and smashed into a gray PT Cruiser parked on the side of the street. The people standing on the sidewalk yelled and scattered.

"Get a car," she yelled. "We're leaving."

"Yes, mistress," the big guard said and dropped Nathan on the street in front of the blond driver with the piggish face.

He hauled Nathan to his feet while the big guard sprinted to a Monte Carlo sitting in the eastbound lane. The car jerked into motion and tried to make a U-turn. The big guard smashed a fist through the driver's window, hauled out a skinny teenage boy rife with pimples, and threw him on the street.

The blond with the piggish face dragged Nathan to the Monte Carlo, and Teresa toed the debris by Cora's face.

"Get up," Teresa said. "Father's waiting."

With tears streaming down her face, Cora lurched to her feet, keeping her hands tucked into her armpits. The big guard dropped Nathan into the trunk of the Monte Carlo.

"No!" she cried and stumbled toward them. The big guard slammed the trunk shut.

"Let him out," Cora said, grabbing at the big guard. "I'll go. You can take me."

He trapped her in his arms and waited for Teresa to join them.

She glared at Cora and slapped a hand on the trunk, denting it. "If you touch me again, I'll cut off his hands."

Cora nodded, tears still spilling down her cheeks.

"Good," Teresa said. "Then get in the back. Father seems to be expecting you."

Chapter 36

Alex drove to a beer store and walked inside, freaking out the staff and customers. He told them to relax, the blood was fake, and poked one of the holes in his pants. It hurt, but not much. He was healing a lot faster this time, even faster than at the morgue, something he took as a bad sign. A gift from Father was a curse for everybody else.

With a great deal of hand-waving, the people in the store let Alex go to the front of the line, and he bought six-packs of Heineken and Hoegaarden. He put them in the front of the blue van and glanced down at his bloody legs. How did people get to be so stupid? Didn't anybody think for themselves anymore?

On his way out of the parking lot, he opened a Heineken. Two blocks later his head began to buzz like a hornet's nest, and he drank half the bottle. He thought about turning on the radio, borrowing Teresa's trick, but then he noticed the crosswalk ahead flashing, and a woman with a stocky golden retriever jerked to a stop in the middle of the street. He slammed on the brakes. She ran back to the sidewalk on the north side of the street, shouting and gesturing like an Italian.

Alex honked and continued driving. If he didn't know better, he'd swear he was drunk—the bad kind that made you vomit, not the dopey, fun kind.

At the next corner, he turned right and parked in front of a pizzeria. He started scrolling through the calls on the cellphone he taken from Fernandez. Alex noticed one labeled M and dialed it. Why not? Mobius would find out sooner or later.

He didn't answer, though, and Alex scrolled through another week of calls. Nothing useful.

He dropped the phone in the case of Heinekens and used his own phone to call Peter's number. The generic message for his voicemail clicked on.

Alex hung up and dialed Dmitri's number.

The Ukrainian answered his phone with a heavily accented, "Yes?"

"This is Satan, looking to trade souls for vodka."

"Alex?"

"No, he's irrelevant. It's official."

"Is good you call," Dmitri said. "They tell us to go to sanctuary. All the men to go."

"I wouldn't go anywhere near there."

"This is true, but the ones who run the soldiers say the mistress is waiting. But she is not. She does not answer. Peter the same."

"Yeah, I just tried to call him."

"Something has happened, I know. Peter was to meet her. She was much excited."

Alex grunted and gulped his beer.

"They have found the Light, yes?" Dmitri asked. "They tell us nothing. Only where to go."

"That's the army for you."

"You go to sanctuary, yes? We meet you there?"

Alex paused, the beer at his lips. "So everyone's supposed to be there? Mobius, too?"

"You are not doing nothing foolish?"

"Of course not. I just need to talk to him about something important." Alex glanced down at the bag of grenades tucked behind the cases of beer. "Something I'm sure he'll love."

~

The Monte Carlo swerved around another corner, and Cora bumped the door, afraid to use her hands for balance, even though the throbbing of her palms had faded to an intense itch that reminded her of poison ivy. The gold fire hadn't been real. It was only her imagination.

In the trunk, Nathan yelled and kicked. Cora winced and hoped he didn't hurt himself.

"Turn on the radio," Teresa said.

The driver hurried to obey and twirled through the stations until he found one playing classical music.

"Louder," Teresa said. "I don't want to hear them. None of

them."

"Yes, mistress."

Cora took a shaky breath and eased her hands down to her lap and turned them face up. She had to look at them. She needed them. No one else was going to help.

Her gaze drifted down. Her hands had no marks, no burns. The cuts had closed.

"Everything he promises is empty," Teresa said. "I'm the one who makes them real. Not the firstborn, not Father."

Cora nodded. The driver stopped for a red light, and the shadows on the floor of the car rippled and whispered. Beside her, the big guard didn't seem to notice, so she lifted her feet and tucked her legs underneath her.

"Keep driving," Teresa said. "Don't stop for anything."

"Yes, mistress," the driver said.

The car shuddered, as if hit by a gust of wind, and he hit the gas pedal. They spurted through the red light. A gray hatchback coming from the north screeched and swerved around their trunk. The shadows on the floor hissed. A fine rain pattered against the windshield despite the sun shining overhead.

Something thumped Cora's seat, and she lurched forward, startled. The big guard grabbed her. In the trunk, Nathan's swearing grew louder, and he continued to kick the back seat. Cora prayed he would stop. Teresa looked angry enough to explode.

Three blocks later, they turned onto a street blockaded by white vans. More white vans and several black cars and SUVS were scattered in front of an old four-story factory made of reddish-brown brick, which partially obscured a smaller brick building painted dark blue. Cora shuddered and pressed a hand to her stomach, fighting the urge to gag.

The Monte Carlo slowed down, and a plump man wearing a light gray suit ran in front of them and fell to his knees. A dozen men wearing black uniforms and flak jackets climbed out of the vans and the cars, several of them carrying assault rifles. More men hovered in doorways and windows.

"Tell that idiot to get out of the way," Teresa said.

The driver honked, and the plump man bowed, his hands

clasped in prayer.

Teresa muttered and threw open her door, snapping the hinges. The big guard fumbled with his handle and pulled Cora out of the car.

Behind them, a gray sedan screeched around the corner and slammed into one the white vans. The bald man stumbled out of the sedan and ran towards them.

"Mistress," he shouted. "I am your most faithful."

Teresa scowled. "Idiot."

Two other men, both wearing expensive black suits, ran forward and bowed to Teresa. The taller of the two also wore a purple shirt and a burgundy tie and stared at Cora. The second, tieless, had a long drooping nose atop a scraggly mustache and pinched, pale lips.

"Get Dmitri off the street," Teresa said.

"Yes, mistress," the two men said and ran to pick up the plump man wearing the gray suit.

The bald man jolted to a stop beside Teresa and bowed to her, wisps of shadow wriggling across his yellowed scalp. Cora rubbed her hands together and glanced around at the dozen or so men carrying guns and wearing black uniforms. They looked so much like the police. But none of them would help. They were all part of this madness.

The big guard let go of her arm and told the driver to open the trunk. As the lid popped open, Nathan burst into a fresh string of curses and wriggled and kicked and managed to get his feet out. Cora darted forward to help him before someone hit him.

Once on his feet, he pulled away from her and kicked at the big guard. He punched Nathan in the head and put him into a headlock.

"You stupid fuck," the big guard said.

"Kiss my ass, you—"

The guard tightened his grip, and Nathan cried out in pain.

"Please don't hurt him," Cora said. "He didn't mean it."

"It's too late for that," Teresa said.

"It is the end of time," the bald man said, sinking to his knees.

"Shut up!"

"Yes, mistress."

A wind stinking of rot and urine and feces whipped through the street. Cora clapped a hand over her mouth and pinched her nose. Nathan wriggled and kicked, but the big guard simply swung Nathan around until his face turned red.

From the north came the faint whir of sirens, and Cora's heart jumped. Thank God. Finally.

The armed men yelled and raced to secure positions at the ends of the block.

Teresa pointed to the man wearing the burgundy tie. "You three bring Mobius. No mistakes!"

The three men in expensive suits looked startled. None of them moved.

"Now!"

"Yes, mistress," they said and circled the bald man. When he failed to stand, two of them scooped him up by his shoulders and carried him to the front doors of the blue building.

Teresa gestured to the big guard, and he hauled Nathan after them. The blond driver fiddled with something in the trunk while inching away from Cora. Teresa didn't seem to care, though, and glared at Cora.

"Okay," she said. "I—I'm going."

What choice did she have?

Two men holding assault rifles stood in front of the metal doors of the blue building, sweat dripping down their faces. The darker-skinned man kept twitching and blinking. The other looked ready to faint.

"Shoot," the bald man yelled. "Shoot them all."

The blinking man shifted his gun, but it jerked out of his hands and smashed into his face.

"Take them inside," Teresa said. "Mobius first."

The tall man wearing the burgundy tie yanked on the left door, releasing a blast of offal and rotting flesh. Even with her nose pinched shut, Cora stumbled and gagged. The faint-looking guard lurched away from the opening and retched. Shadowy faces hurtled out of the doorway and whipped past her. She ducked and yelled.

"Hurry up," Teresa said. "I've waited long enough."

The three men surrounding the bald man nudged him inside, into a dark room, while he yammered in a guttural tongue. The big guard steered Nathan through the doorway, using his bound arms like a lever. Shadows clicked and hissed and sank into the walls.

Cora shook her head. It couldn't be real. It couldn't.

On the street, guns fired. Something roared to the north and exploded. The loudest of the police sirens choked and died.

"Get in," Teresa said and toed Cora's right calf.

A burning sensation shot up her leg, and she fell against the door frame. Screams erupted from the walls. She lurched the other way, and Teresa jabbed Cora in the back.

She stumbled inside the building, biting back a scream. Ahead of her, Nathan and the big guard lumbered to another opening. She hurried after them.

Insane or not, she had to stay with Nathan. Nothing else mattered now.

~

The wail of sirens grew louder as Alex drove west on a one-way street, about three blocks away from the sanctuary. God only knew what sort of mess was waiting for him. Teresa would do anything to destroy Father, even if it meant destroying the whole city.

Ahead, at the next set of traffic lights, a police car speeding from the north jolted to a stop. After a second or two, the police car started forward again and exploded in a fiery ball.

Alex slammed on his brakes, spilling beer on his pants. A second police car screeched to a stop at the traffic lights, and another missile, probably a rocket grenade, streaked northwards through the intersection. The second police car burst exploded, flames and black smoke spurting skywards.

He swore, turned into a side street, and stopped across from a beige brick building with a row of dark green industrial-size garage doors. At least he had another way into the sanctuary. He didn't feel like going back to the morgue yet.

At the end of the street, Alex parked in front of a white office building, in a space reserved for staff. He grabbed the hockey stick, the shattered end still caked with drywall, and tossed a bottle of Hoegaarden into the shopping bag holding his three grenades.

Alex finished his Heineken and peered westwards around the corner of the office building. Two white vans blocked the intersection for Father's street. One or two assault rifles poked out of the windows of the house at the northeast corner. More men were probably hunkered down in the office complex on the other side of Father's street, waiting for Armageddon.

With the hockey stick draped over one shoulder, Alex sprinted across a different one-way street to the warehouse on the south side and ducked into a doorway. Even though the warehouse didn't connect directly with Father's building, they both backed onto the same the alley, and there probably wasn't much security left there if they were busy barbecuing police cars.

From the direction of Father's street came the rattle of gunfire, and Alex ripped open the door of a defunct gym. Once inside, the noise of the gunfire dimmed, and he paused to open the bottle of Hoegaarden.

"Perhaps it would be wise to hurry," a man said.

Alex spun around, swinging his shattered hockey stick in front of him. In the next doorway stood a man wearing a big black hat and a long black shirt over black pants, his hands tucked in his sleeves.

Alex swore. "You're the firstborn."

"We have never met," the man said.

"Yeah, but Teresa's been on my ass for sixty years. She really hates you."

"There have been many years for mistakes. Centuries . . ."

"You didn't do me any favors either," Alex said.

"Perhaps so."

From the floor in front of Alex spurted a shadow with a dog's face and wild hair. The shadow bared its fangs, and he swore and kicked it.

The shadow broke apart and melted back into the floor.

"Yes, Father waits even now," Paul said.

"I don't give a damn," Alex said and stomped on the ground, making certain the shadow beast was gone. "I'm tired of his shit. I don't want it anymore."

"You have seen enough soldiers die."

334

"Stay out of my head," Alex said. "You can't play that bullshit with me either."

"You are the last one."

"What the hell does that mean?"

"Teresa has brought the Light to Father," Paul said. "She will force him to act."

"You mean the girl? She has the Light?"

"It is like the darkness that lives in Father—a creature with its own will, seeking it's dark brother. But neither of them belong here, in our dimension. They must return to their own kind, their own place."

Alex rubbed his face and swigged his beer. "Do you ever speak English? Just tell me what the hell you want."

"You will see soon enough," the man said and melted into the shadows of the doorway.

Chapter 37

Apair of light bulbs snapped on over Cora, helping to cut through the murk that clung to the air like grease. The walls and ceiling of the room were painted black, a yellow poster advertising retro Fridays the only vestige of color. A few feet away, the big guard kept a tight grip on Nathan. The bald man and his escort had already disappeared somewhere: the opening straight ahead was still dark; a second opening to Cora's right led into a room with black stools and cocktail tables.

Teresa snapped an order at the guards outside. One of them shoved the door shut, severing off the sunlight and the clack of gunfire and a third explosion. Screams echoed from deeper in the building.

"You will do what must be done," Teresa said to Cora and pointed to the dark opening.

"Does Nathan have to come?" she asked, her voice trembling. "Maybe he can wait here?"

"What do you think this is?" the big guard said. "The Shopping Network?"

"Keep moving," Teresa said to him. "Do something useful."

The big guard staggered away from her and bobbed his head. "Yes, mistress. Sorry, mistress."

The darkness beyond the opening rumbled and hissed. Nathan kicked and squirmed, and the guard tightened his grip on Nathan's neck. He squawked.

"Please, I'll go," Cora said. "I'll go first. Don't hurt him."

"Life is pain," Teresa said. "The days you live are nothing."

She pointed to the dark opening. The guard shoved Nathan forward, using his bound arms like a rudder, and Cora darted in front of them. The darkness in the next room rippled and growled. In the doorway, she hit a sticky wall of air, and her stomach heaved; then Nathan bumped into her, and the stickiness vanished.

She stumbled through the opening.

From somewhere in the darkness, the bald man yelled. Screams of the dying surged from every direction. Cora clapped her hands over her ears, but the screams only grew louder, and the stench of rot and feces struck her full force. Behind her, Nathan swore and kicked the guard. He clamped on Nathan's arms, eliciting another yelp.

To her right, Cora glimpsed a dark shape with what looked like long hair, hanging from the wall. She flinched and turned away.

No.

No.

Further right, a row of lights flickered on above a glossy black bar, and her gaze froze on a cage in the corner. Another row of lights snapped on, revealing more people sprawled on the floor, strapped together in groups of two with zip ties and handcuffs. A second cage was jammed in the back corner.

The third set of lights flickered, but Cora was too numb to react. The bodies were everywhere, at least a dozen of them, dressed in T-shirts and cheap dresses, most of them women. Asian. Latin. She also saw a pair of boys hanging from a railing in front of a second smaller bar, both boys dark-haired and stripped to their underwear. Beyond the bar stood two of the men from the street, the bald man kneeling between them, facing the middle of the room, where the darkness remained an impenetrable ball.

More lights snapped on. Two more cages appeared in the corners, each with someone slumped inside, and Cora grabbed a handrail beside a pair of steps, her stomach convulsing. A whimper escaped from the nearest body. She lurched in the opposite direction. The body convulsed and gurgled. Red froth spurted out of its mouth and nose.

Cora fell against the wall beside the opening, her stomach and throat clenching. The burning of vomit hit her mouth and spattered on the wall and floor. Her stomach continued to twist and clench well after she had nothing left to bring up.

"M—mistress," the big guard said.

"Take the boy closer," Teresa said.

Cora straightened up, spitting bile, and wiped her mouth. She tried not to look at the bodies, but they were everywhere, in every direction. Even the walls screamed death.

The big guard shook his head and backed up to where Teresa blocked the opening. She hissed and flung him forward. Nathan yelled and fell on the floor. The guard tripped and tumbled down the steps leading to an old dance floor.

Despite the nausea still twisting her stomach, Cora lurched to where Nathan wriggled on the floor.

"I'm not going," he said. "Don't make me go."

"It's okay," she said. "We'll be okay."

"Don't touch me," he said and jerked away from her. "You fuckers!"

In the middle of the room, the dark sphere pulsed with blackish-purple light, and curtains of shadow rippled outwards. One of the men wearing suits screamed. Cora clutched her stomach and shuddered, and several of the lights overhead exploded, raining bits of glass and hot metal on her.

She hunched over Nathan, trying to shield his face. He swore and wriggled away from her. Screams broke out from the middle of the room. Several of the bodies on the floor jerked, and the big guard darted past Cora. Teresa grabbed him and hurled him over a railing, and he crashed on a pair of twitching bodies.

The big guard screamed and rolled off the bodies. Around him, blackish-purple blobs erupted from the floor and bodies, some of them twisting into daemonic faces that shrieked and screeched. Others sprouted wings and hissed and growled.

"God, please," Cora said, squeezing her eyes shut. "Make it stop. Please."

The guard moaned and curled up, burying his head in his hands. One of the blobs flew at him and splattered against the side of his head. He screamed and smacked his hands and his head on the floor.

"They're not real," Nathan said. "It's all bullshit."

"Yes," Cora said, her voice shaking. "Bullshit."

"It gives them an excuse," he said. "They love to fuck with you. Their big fucking needles."

Cora nodded, still feeling numb. How could it be real? How?

A sharp pain exploded in her backside, and she tumbled against a wooden railing that bordered the sunken dance floor.

"Enough talk," Teresa said and punched Cora a second time.

Another burst of fiery pain cut into her back. Nathan flopped on his side and kicked at Teresa, but she sprang back to the opening that led to the front doors.

"No. Won't help," Cora said, gasping for breath. "She—she's too strong."

He swore and rolled onto his knees. At the same time, gold light rippled over her left arm, and the blobs on the dance floor screeched and spattered into the surrounding bodies.

Teresa hissed and shielded her eyes. The roar of an explosion came from the back of the room, and the floor trembled.

"We need to move," Cora said. "Away from her."

"No shit," Nathan said and lurched down the steps to the sunken dance floor.

"No! Not that way."

~

Alex broke through a metal door nailed shut by some moron and stepped into the work yard located at the end of the alley for Father's building. From the front of the alley came a fresh round of gunfire and shouting. The alley itself remained quiet, except for a few shadows skittering across the asphalt.

Alex guzzled the rest of his beer and pitched the bottle aside. He followed the red brick of the warehouse to where it merged with the blue-painted brick of Father's building. A wave of anger and hate slapped against Alex, but he didn't have time for Father's crap and strode to the dumpster wedged in the nook beside the loading dock.

On the other side of the dumpster, he heard someone retch and found one of Mobius's men hunched over, spattering the concrete foundation with blood-laced vomit. A second guard was sprawled against a rain spout, his eyes and ears oozing blood.

"Yeah, the madness gets you every time," Alex said and ripped open the metal door beside the bay door, releasing a gaggle of screams and a stench strong enough to knock him backwards.

Inside the loading bay, a half-dozen coffin-shaped boxes and a pile of body bags were stacked against the wall on the right. More screams reverberated from Father's room, and a voice that sounded like Mobius called out to Father.

Alex stuffed two of his grenades in the pockets of his jacket and pulled the pin on the third grenade. At his feet, a shadowy face burst out of the floor, gibbering like a monkey, and he stomped on the face before it could turn into someone he recognized. The shadow broke apart, still gibbering, and slithered back into the floor.

From the next room came another shout from Mobius. A man bellowed, then screamed.

Alex charged the door leading into Father's room, and the door ripped off its hinges and slammed into someone before falling down. On the dance floor lay several bodies tied up like turkeys. Swaths of shadow whipped around and tangled with the lights, making it hard to see the rest of the room. In the center of the room, the darkness was even thicker, hiding the dais upon which Father rested.

The door shifted, and the man beneath cursed. It was the German, Alex realized and stepped aside. Heimer continued to swear and threw the door toward the cage in the back corner. Before he could get up, though, Mobius sprang out of a pocket of shadows and grabbed at Heimer's head. Alex whipped his broken hockey stick around, and it smashed against Mobius's right arm, sending shards of wood flying. He yowled and yanked on Heimer's head. Alex lashed out with the hockey stick again, and the bottom half shattered. Mobius twisted. Heimer's head cracked and snapped off with a gush of blood.

With a shriek of triumph, Mobius darted to the edge of the darkness surrounding Father and smashed Heimer's head on the floor like a rotten pumpkin. A split second later, a serpentine oiliness spurted out of Heimer's torso and streaked into the darkness.

Alex stumbled and swore, still holding the shattered remnant of the hockey stick. He had never seen the seed do that before, had never seen it so alive. It had always appeared as a shadow—an immortal shadow that merged with the body of its host.

On his left, Johan ran out of the room behind the deejay's booth.

"Alex? What—" He stopped abruptly, staring at Heimer's body.

Shadows boiled out of the floor beneath Mobius and swirled around him. At the edge of the shadows, Alex saw another body wearing a suit, light gray this time, the torso plump and headless. Dmitri.

Johan ducked under a railing and jumped down to the dance floor level.

"No! Watch out," Alex shouted.

Something screamed above him, and lights exploded. He dropped into a crouch, white spots splintering his vision. Mobius charged. A gun fired. More lights exploded. Mobius howled, and Johan screamed.

Alex tossed his grenade, but he was too late. Another oily blob burst out of Johan and hurtled toward Father. The grenade then exploded and threw Mobius sideways. Johan's head toppled on the floor.

Alex grabbed the door he had broken and flung it at Mobius. He bashed it away, losing his balance again, and Alex pulled out one of the grenades from his jacket. Throughout the rest of the room, shadows flapped and shrieked, warping the light.

On the dance floor, Mobius sprang to his feet and ran to the steps leading up to Alex. He darted to the cage in the corner, where a dead woman wearing a pink cotton T-shirt curled atop a smaller woman, possibly a girl, and pulled the pin on the grenade.

"You're nothing," Mobius said and ripped off the railing beside the steps. "You belong to the master."

"At least I'm not a slobbering monkey."

Mobius lunged forward, and Alex ducked. The shaft of black metal swished over his head, but a second swing came back faster than he expected and clipped his right shoulder. He stumbled. The grenade fell between them. Mobius didn't seem to notice, though, and Alex darted toward the cage. The metal shaft slammed into his right arm, snapping a bone, and he yelled and fell against the cage.

Another slash ripped through Alex's jacket and whacked his right leg. He kicked, his pain feeding his anger, and knocked

Mobius back several steps. The grenade exploded. Mobius vaulted through the air and crashed against the bar.

Despite the agony of his arm, Alex scuttled under a railing and dropped into a crouch on the dance floor. He scrabbled his last grenade out of his jacket.

Mobius lurched to his feet, his pale face blazing with hate. Shadows swirled around him and streamed from his eyes and ears and the rips in his suit. Alex pulled the pin.

From the middle of the room came a dull roar, and the floor shook. A cluster of lights exploded. Mobius fell to his knees and clapped his hands to his chest. Alex tossed the grenade at the bastard and backpedalled.

"Yes," Mobius shouted, the shadows thickening and clinging to his flesh.

The grenade exploded and hurled him against the bar. Alex straightened up, keeping his broken arm tucked against his belly, but Mobius shook himself and grabbed at the metal shaft lying by his feet.

"Would you at least pretend to die," Alex shouted and looked around for something else to throw.

Mobius turned and scurried to the front of the building. For a second or two, Alex stared in disbelief. Then he spotted a flash of blonde hair through the murk whirling around the room and limped after Mobius.

~

While Cora stumbled down the steps to the dance floor, Nathan kicked the guard curled up on the floor. The guard wailed and covered his head. Nathan only kicked harder. She grabbed his arms, still trussed behind his back, but he swore and twisted away from her and continued kicking the guard.

Another explosion shook the floor.

"Nathan, please," she said. "We need to get out of here."

"Stop touching me," he said. "I hate it. You're always making me sick."

The murk obscuring the room shifted, and Cora glimpsed two men fighting in the far left corner. On the opposite wall, she spotted another opening, which no one seemed to be guarding.

"There might be another door," she said. "But we need to get away from the girl. We have to pretend to do what she wants."

The darkness at the center of the room rippled, and a wave of screams and shadows knocked Cora off balance. She lost sight of the opening at the back. Nathan swore and ducked down and rubbed his nose against his right shoulder.

"God, that fucking stinks," he said.

From the back of the room came a third explosion. Shadows spurted out of the floor between her and Nathan and hissed at them.

"No!" she shouted and reached for him.

An oily blob the size of a football hurtled out of the dark heart of the room and slammed into her chest, throwing her to the floor. Gold light flared around her. Something wet and thick screeched and wriggled over her breasts and up her throat. She screamed and slapped the blob and flung it away.

"Fucking Christ," Nathan said.

Behind him, a pale, bald head broke through the murk and roared like a demented ape. Nathan turned and stumbled, and a shaft of metal slashed down and clipped his right shoulder. He collapsed, howling in agony.

The bald man squealed and smashed the metal shaft down again, but Teresa darted down the steps and yanked the metal shaft out his hands. For a moment, he stood blinking in surprise as she flung the shaft aside. Then she hurled him back a dozen feet, into the dark heart of the room, and a second man stepped out of the murk, clutching his right arm. He was tall and blond and wore a gray suit torn in dozens of places.

"Why did you throw that away?" he said. "The bastard won't stay down. Father's feeding him, making him stronger."

Teresa lifted a hand, warning him to stop. "No, Alex. You're not with us anymore."

"Fuck that," he said and sprinted to the left side of the room, disappearing into the murk again.

With the grace of a drunk, the bald man lurched to his feet. Swaths of darkness latched on his pale flesh and poured into his gaping mouth. Behind him, the end of a glass case appeared on top of a concrete slab draped with a purple cloth. Inside the glass, Cora saw a pair of desiccated feet, brown with age and pulsing with rage.

She shuddered and crawled to Nathan, his sobs growing louder.

"Stay still," she said. "I'll help. Like before."

She brushed a hand over his hair and eased her other hand to his right arm, trying to remember what she had done at the warehouse. Helping him had seemed so easy there, without the hatred slapping at her, beating from the floor and the walls. The hatred wanted to smash her, pull her apart, crush her into dust, muffling the pain in Nathan's body, the frantic beating of his heart. If she had been alone, she might have succumbed to the pressure of that dark voice, but he needed her, and she felt the warmth inside her release and let it flow into him.

The bald man shrieked and stumbled toward them. Gold mist rippled around Cora's hands. Teresa darted past Nathan's feet, shielding her face, and the bald man charged. The two collided with a loud crack and tumbled on the floor.

Teresa sprang back to her feet first and kicked the bald man. Shadowy limbs sprouted from his body and latched onto her legs like a hungry octopus.

From overhead came a loud ripping noise. A section of lighting swung down. Teresa ducked and stumbled sideways, but the lighting swerved and bashed into her. The bald man scampered after her, the shadowy limbs thickening into tentacles, and grabbed her head and smacked it on the floor.

With a cry of rage, Teresa threw the lighting away from her, knocking the bald man on his back. The shadows streaming around his body tangled her arms and legs. She fell back to the floor.

The bald man ripped off a large light and smashed it against her head. She struggled to kick, and he continued to bash her with the light fixture until her arms stopped flailing. He shrieked like a demented child and pounced on her and bashed her head on the floor repeatedly. Her head made a wet crack.

A split second later, an oily blob burst out of her skull and hurtled to the glass case.

From the murk clinging to the sides of the room charged the

man named Alex, wielding a shaft of metal like a lance. The bald man bobbled upright, and the metal shaft punched through his belly. Both men tumbled to the floor. Alex jerked and twisted the metal shaft, and the bald man screamed louder and slapped and clawed at Alex's head.

A roar thundered through the room, shaking the floor. The two men twisted, rolling on Teresa's body. Alex lost his grip on the metal shaft. The bald man howled and squeezed, and bone cracked. He smacked Alex's head on the floor. After a third whack, his head made a popping noise.

The bald man shrieked and flopped on his side, the blunt end of the metal shaft scraping across the floor. A black blob burst out of Alex's skull and hurtled to the dais and passed through the glass case as if it didn't exist.

Cora sucked in a breath, dizzy, the last of the gold light fading from Nathan's skin. They had to move. They had to get away. There was no one left, no one to stop the bald man.

Her brother muttered a curse and pushed her hands away. "Later. Wanna sleep."

"No, Nathan, please. Not here. Not now."

At the same time, she realized his arms were free. The zip tie had snapped off.

The bald man called out and lifted an arm.

Oh God, Cora thought. He was trying to get up. He was going to get up.

The bald man continued to spew his hate and fumbled with the metal shaft. She lurched to her feet and stumbled toward him. He shrieked and jerked away from her, pulling the shaft with him. It had punched through his belly and stuck out near his spine, which she noticed in an abstract way while grabbing for the blunt end.

As soon as she made contact, a jolt of pain shot up her arm, and the bald man shrieked and clawed at the floor, yanking the shaft away from her.

"No!" Cora shouted and grabbed it with both hands.

The bald man shrieked and convulsed. She struggled to keep hold of the shaft, yelling from the pain, but the bald man roared and twisted, and the metal shaft ripped out of him, pulling out his innards and spewing shadows across the room. Gold fire crackled around her and blasted his gaping wound. His roar turned into a scream. Cora tumbled to the floor. Her stomach and esophagus clenched, but she had nothing left to vomit.

Still shaking, she struggled to sit up and fumbled with the metal shaft. It was heavier than it looked, though, and she dropped it. The bald man spat curses at her and glared with oily black eyes. A chunk of his intestines wriggled back into his body.

Despite the terror clawing at her thoughts, Cora crouched beside the metal shaft and hoisted it off the floor. She stumbled sideways. One of his feet flicked out and clipped her left ankle. She fell. The shaft tumbled next to him. He howled and grabbed it, but she threw herself on his legs to stop him. Fiery pain surged through her arms and chest. She screamed and let go. He screamed too and thrashed his legs.

A part of her realized she had hurt him again—maybe it was the only way to hurt him—and she dug her fingernails into the flesh of his leg, through a rip in his pants. The burning surged up her right arm. The bald man screamed and swatted at her. With one hand, he snagged some of her hair and yanked on it, but she barely noticed. Her entire body burned—her chest, her belly, her face, her legs, her lips, her toes. The only thought left was stopping him. She had to stop him and scrabbled at the gaping hole in his abdomen. Another blast of heat whipped up her arm. He howled and convulsed. Her fingers scraped the bulge of his intestines, and his legs jerked. A knee struck her chin. Flashes of white overwhelmed her vision. Darkness followed.

Cora tightened her grip, fighting to stay conscious, and her fingers punched through the tissue protecting his intestines. A wave of agony blasted her body and bashed her mind. She screamed. The darkness roared. Gold fire exploded.

Then a second darkness, empty of sound, empty of feeling, snapped around her and pulled her down, her fingers still buried in the bald man's intestines.

Chapter 38

Cora jerked back to consciousness. Something yanked on her left arm. Her other arm burned, her hand stuck in a lumpy pudding that wriggled and chewed on her fingers.

She flinched and sucked in a breath. The bald man. His intestines.

Gold fire crackled around her, and the rest of the room snapped into focus—the glass case on the concrete podium, the dead prisoners, Nathan swearing and pulling on her left arm.

The pain in her right arm flared and surged into her chest. The bald man convulsed and screamed. She screamed too and tried to pull her hand free of his intestines. His thrashing intensified, torquing her shoulder until it felt ready to pop.

"Christ, would you knock it off," Nathan said. "Don't be so stupid."

Still holding Cora's left arm, he kicked and stomped on the bald man's legs. The gold fire surged and pierced his flesh. Her hand popped free of his intestines, and the bald man shrieked and thrashed like an earthworm in an alcohol bath.

Despite the agony in her shoulder, Cora rolled away from him. His shriek soared, feverish with terror, and his body snapped upwards like a bow. Nathan tripped over a chunk of metal rigging that had fallen from the ceiling. Then the bald man's body burst in half, and a heaving mass of blackness gushed up toward the ceiling.

For several seconds, Cora sat frozen, staring at the giant black blob hovering overhead. Her mind refused to work. Enough. No more. Too much.

The tip of a large leathery wing burst out of the belly of the blob. Several talons punched from the top, as long as her hands.

"N—Nathan?"

A fiery yellow eye opened above the wing and blinked before rolling in her direction. The floor began to thrum.

"This is bullshit," her brother said. "How do we get our money back?"

From the glass case in the center of the room, a second oily bulge stretched upwards. Rows of teeth glimmered like motor oil, above which opened another yellow eye. The first eye closed, and the surrounding black mass rippled and stretched to the middle of the room and melted into the giant blob writhing above the glass case.

The second eye closed. A guttural rumble shook the room. Lights crashed on the floor, and the churning mass of blackness sank through the glass case and disappeared inside the shriveled corpse lying beneath.

Cora shuddered and pushed at the floor, her arms like rotten bananas, her legs a thousand miles away.

"This place is a shithole," Nathan said. "Why did you want to come here?"

"Please, help me up," she said, reaching for his left arm.

He jerked away from her and shook the arm. "Christ! Would you fuck off."

Then he swore again and darted away from her.

"No! Wait!"

When he reached the big guard, Nathan dropped into a crouch and wiped his left arm on the man's pants. Cora glanced down at the blackened goo slathered on her right hand. Her throat convulsed. She tried to spit, but nothing came up, and she wiped her hand on the floor. That didn't help either.

Still gagging, Cora crawled to Teresa's feet, trying not to look at her crushed head, and fumbled with the hem of her midnight blue dress and wiped at the blackened goo.

Cora shook her head. Her throat convulsed. Nathan limped towards the shriveled corpse in the glass case.

"No!" she yelled.

He took a few steps closer before stopping. Cora tottered to her feet and stumbled after him.

Nathan pointed to the other side of the glass case. "It's that dude in the hat."

She lurched beside Nathan, and Paul stepped out of nowhere

and placed a hand on the glass case.

"You look like a dork in that thing," Nathan said. "You need a horse. Like the Lone Ranger."

"It all comes to you," Paul said to Cora. "I wish it could have been different."

A low rumble filled the room, and she grabbed Nathan. He pushed her away and rubbed his arm against his T-shirt.

An Asian woman stepped out of the air beside Paul, wearing a black blouse embroidered with white flowers—the woman from his apartment and the mall; the one who had tried to stop the blue jean man.

A loud crack came from the glass case. Nathan swore and backed into Cora.

"This isn't what you promised," the woman said. "Where's Tania? She needs to be here too. After everything you put her through."

"The darkness must manifest," Paul said. "We are but shadows."

"You said we'd be free. This would be over."

"Yes, the seeds must be returned," Paul said and thrust his right hand into the woman's belly.

She screamed and convulsed. Black essence spurted out of her and swirled around Paul's right arm, over his chest, and down his left arm. The woman flailed at him, but her arms passed through him. He shook his head.

"My sorrow continues to grow," he said.

A second surge of black oiliness whirled out of her belly, plunged through the glass, and disappeared into the shriveled corpse. The woman let out a final shriek and tumbled to the floor. The glass case imploded.

A split second later, a black serpentine head burst out of the shriveled corpse and smashed into Paul. He shattered into a cloud of black shards, and the serpentine head roared and jerked up toward the ceiling, trailing a long sleek body covered in black scales. The remaining shards of Paul's essence cut into the blazing yellow eyes of the beast, and it roared again, shaking the room.

Nathan stumbled backwards, tripping over his own feet, and

fell. Cora sank beside him.

The serpentine beast twisted in the air and glared at them, its yellow eyes blazing with a hate that hit Cora like a frying pan. She reeled away from the monstrosity, one hand clutching at Nathan, tugging him away. Shadows seeped from the beast's maw, from between its dagger-like teeth, and whipped between Cora and Nathan. Gold light flared around both of them and threw them to the floor.

The black beast screeched and whirled its head away from them. Cora struggled to sit up, her vision blurry. Nathan swore and pushed her.

Another surge of hate struck Cora, flattening her on the floor. The beast hissed and thrust its head higher, its long serpentine neck glimmering like black pearls, its teeth growing longer and sharper as its maw widened, its jaws stretching wider and wider.

"Yeah, fuck you," Nathan shouted. "Go back to the circus, you fucking freak."

The black beast thundered and dove at them, its jaws impossibly wide. Darkness engulfed Cora, cutting her off from Nathan. Hate slashed into her arms and legs and hammered her chest.

"No!" she shouted and reached through the darkness, searching for her brother. Claws and teeth clamped on her arm. She yelled and slapped at them. Gold light flared around her.

Rotting faces boiled out of the floor and screamed at her—her mother, father, Uncle Abner, Aunt Clara, Melissa, Katrina, Straw, James, Nathan's psychiatrist, doctors, countless others. Closing her eyes did nothing. It only made them stronger, clearer, every rip and scab, pus and phlegm and semen oozing out of their eyes and mouths and nostrils.

"Get off me, you fuckers," Nathan yelled. "Get off!"

The rotting faces screamed louder, trying to drown him out. Her mother's face melted like wax on a barbecue. Cora's father blew apart and spattered on the floor. Katrina raged at Cora for every misery, every rape, every beating. Straw shouted, calling her every vile thing imaginable, while the flesh ripped off his face, layer by layer.

She fumbled around for her brother. None of them were real.

They couldn't be real. She had never done those things. She had never meant to hurt them.

Another wave of screams and tortured faces swarmed around her, mixed with men that thrust penises out of their mouths and tried to squirt their black loads on her face. Cora clapped her left hand over her eyes and rolled away from them, straight into a pair of legs. For a moment, she thought it was another dead body, but then Nathan kicked and yelled. The rotting faces screamed. Skulls and ribs and femurs rained on top of him.

"No," she shouted and grabbed one of his hands. "Nathan!"

He thrashed and pulled away from her. Darkness whipped between them, squirming with the faces of the dead.

"What? You want to help him?" Katrina yelled, splotches of bone poking through her torn flesh. "Like you helped me, you bitch, you goddamn whore."

Cora turned away, but Katrina's head darted into view again, yelling obscenities. Bits of flesh fell off and squirmed on the floor like maggots.

More faces joined the chorus, swearing and hurling insults, their flesh dripping, melting, crawling, oozing. Eyes burst. Blood and semen and feces oozed out of their sockets and their nostrils. Bloated tongues lashed out, some of them shaped like penises with thick, black veins and sores dripping pus.

"Nathan! Where are you? Please!"

The faces gibbered and howled.

"It's all tricks," she called out. "You know it is. You know all their tricks. You said so."

"Fucking tricks," Nathan echoed.

Cora crawled left, closer to his voice, and the darkness cracked. A hand appeared. She reached out to grab it, but the hand didn't move, and she jerked back from it. It was too small. Too feminine.

Another hand jabbed her from the right, and she lurched away from it, but this time the owner of the hand yelled and pulled away too.

She scrambled after Nathan's hand and grabbed it. Gold light crackled around her. The darkness roared.

Cora tightened her grip. A blast of gold light shredded the

darkness and jolted her body. The tortured faces screeched and exploded, spraying shadow everywhere. The building shuddered.

A few feet behind Cora, a chunk of ceiling tile smashed on the floor. She coughed and struggled to her knees, keeping a tight grip on Nathan's hand.

He snuffled and blinked back tears. "They said it wasn't real, it was all in my head."

"I know, I'm sorry," she said.

"They tied me up. They hit me."

"It'll never happen again. Never. I promise."

Nathan shook his head and tottered to his feet. Cora glanced at the shattered remains of the glass case. Shadows streamed over the shriveled corpse and the purple cloth that covered the concrete slab, the odd face pushing outwards, their screams and grunts and hisses faint, barely discernible.

"We have to get out," she said. "Before it comes back."

"No, too late," her brother said.

"We just have to find a door, a way out."

"It'll always be there," he said. "Always waiting. That's how they get you. The fucking taxman, axe man."

She squeezed his hand and stepped around a clump of shattered lights and a length of metal rigging. The shadows around the corpse hissed and growled.

On Cora's right, another tile tumbled from the ceiling and crashed on a pair of dead girls. Beyond them, she spotted a dark opening. Was that the one she had come through? She couldn't tell anymore. She couldn't think about the girls. She had to keep going.

Nathan pulled at Cora and pointed to the middle of the room. The shadows continued to thicken around the desiccated corpse, the hisses and growls intensifying, daring her to run.

"It's okay," she said. "We'll be okay. We'll find a way."

"Bullshit."

One of the few remaining lights popped, and Cora shielded her face and shuffled past Teresa's limp feet. The bodies began to tremble. The shadows around the desiccated corpse howled.

"You're always pretending," her brother said. "Everything's always great. But they call me crazy."

"Please, Nathan. We can talk about it later, outside. We need to get out of here."

She pointed to the nearest of the openings and remembered the fighting on the street—the soldiers and the police. But anything was better than staying in that room. Anything.

Her brother pulled away from her.

"No, wait, please," she said. "Let's stay together. We need to stay together. We can try a different door."

"He's moving," Nathan said.

Cora shook her head but couldn't ignore the hatred radiating from the shadows whirling atop the concrete podium. Her brother turned and stumbled back toward it. She followed, pleading with him to stop, a dozen yards that felt even more surreal than the hell she had already suffered.

The shadows whirling around the desiccated corpse growled and hissed. Dead faces bulged out and screamed. One of them hurtled at Nathan and knocked him away from Cora, but she kept a hold of him, and gold light flared around them. The dead face exploded. The shadows on the dais shrieked and collapsed inwards and wriggled into the desiccated corpse.

"Are you okay?" Cora asked, steadying her brother.

"Why do you always ask such stupid questions?"

"Just stay behind me. I'll—"

"Fuck you."

"Wait!"

"You're always nagging," he said. "Like an old fucking woman."

He kicked aside shards of glass scattered around the concrete podium. The arms and legs of the corpse were little more than flaps of dried out skin hanging from bones, the fingers skeletal, the belly hollowed like a bowl, the penis a broken twig between a pair of raisins. Shadows continued to writhe on its head, especially in the hollows of its cheeks and the sunken eyelids and the stubby remnant of a nose.

"I wish I had a lighter," Nathan said.

"I don't think that would help," Cora said.

"Yeah, what are you gonna do? Make pancakes?"

She shook her head and shivered. The screams of the dead echoed from the floor and the walls, and something crashed beside the small bar where the dead boys hung. Next to one of the cages in the back, a light flickered above a doorway surrounded by rows and columns of beer labels.

"No, you're right," she said and took a shaky breath.

Even if they got outside—even if they escaped the soldiers—that oily monstrosity would come after them. Its malevolence was too strong. It didn't care about things like time and money. It wasn't human.

Nathan dug in the pockets of his jeans and pulled out the pink handkerchief he had brought home in the weekend.

Cora said, "Wait, what are—"

He kicked the concrete podium and waved the handkerchief over the corpse's face. "Wakey wakey."

"Nathan!" She grabbed at the handkerchief, but he pushed her away and flicked it across the shriveled face again. "No! Stop!"

"Then this bag of shit should leave me alone."

"We can worry about that later. We just—"

"I didn't sign up for this freak show," he said. "I don't want it anymore."

He picked up several shards of glass from the edge of the concrete pedestal and dropped them on the corpse.

"No!" she said and grabbed her brother.

Even though the corpse's mouth remained closed, a guttural rumble erupted from within its shriveled flesh. He shoved her aside and picked up more glass and dropped it in the cavity made by the corpse's belly.

The darkness rippling on the corpse's head disappeared. Nathan crouched to pick up glass from the floor. Cora wondered if she should help him. How else could she get him out of the room?

Nathan bent down for more glass. She teased a large shard off the lip of the concrete pedestal and held the glass over the corpse's head.

"All right, leave us alone," she said. "Go away, wherever you came from."

"Yeah, douchebag," Nathan said and dropped shards of glass in his bowl-shaped belly. "You're outta here."

Cora lowered her shard to the corpse's face and remembered the fire that had burned her and the bald man. Was that the only way?

Another guttural hiss erupted from the corpse, and one of the last lights exploded. Cora's gaze flicked toward the noise. A glob of darkness surged out of the shriveled head and snapped around her right arm, and a blast of freezing cold raced up to her shoulder and stabbed into her chest, cutting off her cry.

Faces of the dead spurted out of the floor and howled. Nathan kicked at them and threw down the glass he had just picked up. Cora gasped for breath and slapped the corpse, but it felt like hitting a tree. The cold knifed into her lungs and clamped on her throat.

Nathan swore and stomped on the faces of the dead. She fell against the concrete podium, still slapping the corpse, and another viscous blob spurted out of its face and engulfed her free hand. The first blob wriggled up to her shoulder and yanked on her right arm. She yelped. The glass she held cut into her palm. The corpse jerked, and the dead shrieked.

A split second later, a thunderous roar shook the room. Nathan grabbed her from behind, and gold light exploded around her. Fire ripped through her arms. She screamed and fell against the concrete podium.

Another burst of gold light surrounded her, and she couldn't stop screaming. The blackness burrowed into her skin, and the fire burned deeper and deeper until her arms felt ready to explode.

She collapsed, dangling from the black goo like a bug stuck in tree sap. Nathan slapped at the goo, but his hand sank in too, and he hit it with his other hand. It sank in as well, and he cried out.

Cora tumbled on the floor, her arms free. Above her, the gold light around Nathan flickered out. His screams redoubled and turned ragged.

"No," she said and fumbled onto her knees and plunged her left hand into the black goo. Nathan shrieked and buckled. She found one of his arms and squeezed it and felt the fire raging through his flesh.

"Let go," she said, her voice hoarse. "Let go of him."

Her brother continued to scream and convulse. More of the black goo spurted out of the corpse and engulfed his arms.

Back on her feet, Cora slapped at the corpse's head with her right hand while the black goo around her left hand tried to push her away from Nathan. She pushed back, trying to find one of his arms, and clawed at the hardened flesh of the corpse's face. One of the eyelids sank inwards. Her middle finger dug into the spongy socket.

The eyelid clamped on her finger and twisted. She cried out. Black goo gushed out of the mouth and nose and scrabbled at her right arm. Fire ripped through her veins. A thunderous roar shook the room. Something smashed on the floor behind Cora.

She shouted again and plunged her finger into the depths of the eye socket. The corpse screeched. She screamed. Her legs buckled. Its head jerked sideways, and the mushiness inside the socket tried to push her finger out.

Cora struggled back to her feet, her whole body shaking, and thrust her middle finger through the mushiness inside the mutilated socket. Her thumb broke through the eyelid of the other socket. The corpse screeched again, and its head thrashed from side to side, wrenching her fingers. She yelled and pushed with her thumb.

Nathan grabbed her left leg, his arms free. Gold light blazed around them. The corpse roared, and the black goo burst open. She collapsed against the concrete podium. The room tilted and blurred.

Then nothing.

~

When Cora regained consciousness—a few seconds later? a few minutes?—she was on the floor, Nathan poking her arm.

"Have to—can't—" she said.

The corpse convulsed and shrieked. Its flesh cracked. Black goo spurted in various directions.

Gold light flared around Nathan, and coils of it swirled down his left arm. He hopped to his feet and shook his arm.

Only steps away, the chest and belly of the corpse burst open, and a scaly, black head surged upwards and smashed into the rig of dead lights overhead, trailing a long serpentine body with too many feet and claws. Out of reflex, Cora lifted a shaking hand to shield her face from the fragments of glass and metal raining down but froze when she saw the gold coils swirling around her right arm.

The reptilian beast roared, and its head snapped around to glare at Cora with blazing, yellow eyes. She scrambled backwards and knocked into Nathan. He continued to swear and shake his left arm. The gold coils around their arms pulsed and thrummed, the light so bright it stung her eyes.

"Wait," she croaked and grabbed his hand. The reptilian beast roared and dove at them. Their arms blazed.

A shimmering gold head, impossibly huge, erupted from their hands, trailing the same serpentine body, the same glut of claws. The gold beast bellowed and slammed into the black monstrosity. Fire roared across the ceiling, and a boom like thunder knocked Cora and Nathan flat on the floor. Glass and metal rained down as the coils of black and gold lashed around each other and the reptilian pair smashed into the back wall.

Nathan scrambled away from the concrete podium. Cora gasped and kicked at the floor, trying to crawl after him.

The reptilian beasts smashed into the ceiling again, and another section of lighting ripped free and crashed against a cage. Chunks of wood and plaster crashed on the floor. One beast screeched. The other roared. Tails whipped and bashed through walls, and their heads smashed into the ceiling.

More stone, wood, plaster and lighting crashed down. One chunk hit Nathan, and he tumbled beside a dead girl, and Cora stumbled toward him, calling his name. A pair of spotlights crashed in front of her. She lurched around them, past the legs of another dead girl, and grabbed one of his arms.

A thunderous roar erupted behind Cora, and a blast of hot air knocked her to the floor. Nathan yelled. She tightened her grip on his arm, and the reptilian beasts rushed over them, snapping and hissing, and bashed into another wall. Concrete blocks and bricks crashed down. Sunlight poured inside.

The beasts slammed into the wall again, making the hole bigger, and Cora stumbled to her feet. She pulled Nathan. He swore and clutched his head.

"Run!" she yelled.

Flames billowed around the beasts, and they crashed into the ceiling. Cora pulled harder, and Nathan managed to sit up.

"Hurry!" she yelled. "Run!"

The monsters rammed into the ceiling again, bashing another hole. More of the ceiling crashed down. The reptilian heads disappeared out the new hole, and their tails whipped around and smashed through a bar.

One of the beasts roared. Flame belched down around their coiled bodies. Claws scrabbled at the edges of the giant hole, spraying chunks of the ceiling in every direction. Their bodies twisted and surged upwards, the gold and black blurring together into a silvery burst of light. Another chunk of the roof crashed on the floor. Then the tails whipped around one last time, bashing down wood and plaster, and disappeared outside.

Cora coughed and wobbled where she stood, her head spinning. Nathan staggered to his feet and pointed to one of the holes in the walls. Outside, people with guns and dark gray uniforms stared up at the sky, sirens flashing behind them. Gray sirens. Everything silvery gray.

The people yelled and covered their faces. An explosive boom shook the building. Cora tottered sideways. From overhead came a loud crack. She grabbed Nathan and stumbled toward the gray light.

Another crack reverberated through the room, echoed by a groan and several snaps. Nathan stopped to look up.

"No!" Cora yelled and yanked on his arm.

He yanked back and knocked her down. The building roared. She tried to yell again, but he landed on top of her, knocking the breath out of her. She had no chance to move, no chance to scream. Then the rest of the ceiling crashed on top of them, and everything went black.

Chapter 39

On the fifth floor of Sunnybrook Hospital, in one of the back corners of the neurosurgical intensive care unit, Cora sat on a chair next to Nathan's bed, the curtains drawn around them. The police had finally stopped bothering her with questions she couldn't answer anyway and left her to sit with him through the long days, interrupted only by the occasional nurse or doctor. His gown and blanket hid the stitches on his legs and the left side of his abdomen. More stitches marred the right side of Nathan's head and his right arm, and an oxygen mask covered the bottom half of his face while various tubes sprouted from his wrists, his ribs, and his groin, making him look like an alien from another galaxy.

A cast covered two-thirds of Cora's right arm, and she had gauze wrapped around her right hand to protect the stitches across her palm. The cut had been deep enough to nick her metacarpus, but luckily she didn't have any nerve damage. Amazing, the doctors said.

Cora shifted her right arm, hoping to relieve some of the ache and the itch, and picked up her bottle of water from the cart beside her chair. Most of the time, she simply sat next to the bed, listening to the rustle of the other people in the ward and the buzz of their voices, hoping he would blink an eye, wiggle a finger, cough, twitch. Anything, really. The doctors said the operations on his head and abdomen had gone well, but they didn't know when he would wake up. Or even if he would wake up. She tried not to think about that possibility too much, or she started crying. A few times, she had felt the urge to touch him and let the gold light spread over his body, smoothing the scars, knitting the bones, and healing the bruises deep inside him, but her memories of the giant serpents and the dead girls would make her stomach lurch, leaving her nauseous and looking for the nearest garbage can. She didn't dare try again. She didn't even know if she could.

When the police had interrogated her, they had tried to pretend the giant serpents didn't exist, even though a lot people must have seen them. Fuzzy pictures of a silvery comet exploding in the sky had plastered the newspapers for almost two weeks. Those who looked closely enough could see coils in the tail that was pointing the wrong way. Some claimed a weapon had been fired. It must have been a terrorist attack. Or a government conspiracy. Or both. More recently, a nurse had joked about a video on YouTube showing a UFO blasting off from the nightclub district. Cora had simply nodded and asked a question about Nathan's morphine drip. Did it need to be changed? She didn't want to think about those monsters again. Not ever.

During the interrogations, Cora had also remembered another serpent, flying out of the trees before the car accident that had killed her parents. But she had quickly pushed away that memory. For nine years she had convinced herself she had imagined the golden serpent, that something else had caused the accident—a fox, a deer, a stupid truck driver. Anything but the truth.

She slid her bottle of water on the cart and pressed a hand to her stomach. What good would the truth do anyway? The accident had happened a long time ago. She couldn't change the past. No one could. Nathan was the only one who needed her now.

Beyond the curtain, a woman said, "Thanks," and Cora glanced up. The voice sounded familiar, but the nurses weren't supposed to come back for a while.

She wiggled the fingers of her right hand, careful of the stitches, and brushed her other hand over her pink tank top. She hoped it wasn't the police again. She had already told them everything she could, everything that had sounded reasonably sane. And some things that hadn't sounded the least bit sane.

Cora took a deep breath and squeezed Nathan's left hand. The curtains rustled. She froze.

A head with sunglasses perched atop long black hair poked through the curtains.

"Uh, hi," Melissa said. "Is it . . . okay?"

Cora stared, too startled to speak.

"I told them I was your cousin," Melissa said. "Or I don't think they would've let me in."

"Yes! Sorry, yes."

"I wanted to call, but I—I don't know, it felt weird, and I knew you were here. I just—I thought I'd come."

"No, it's okay. I was worried too. Nobody would say anything. The police . . ."

Melissa grimaced. "Don't remind me."

Cora managed a smile, and they exchanged an awkward hug, careful of her hand and cast.

"I'm just glad you're okay," Cora said. "I didn't want to leave. I never would have."

"Forget it," Melissa said and paused. "That crazy bitch wasn't after me."

A curtain rattled on Cora's left, and they both fell silent. She glanced at Nathan and watched while his chest rose with a puff from the ventilator, the monitors beeping like whimsical fairies.

"How is he doing?" Melissa asked.

"The doctors said it went well. All the operations. Now we're just waiting. Wait and see."

Melissa nodded and looked like she wanted to say something more but sighed instead and fiddled with her sunglasses.

"You wouldn't think waiting would be so hard," Cora said. "Not compared to everything else."

"They probably think we're crazy," Melissa said.

"They're not the only ones."

"No kidding."

Again the girls fell silent, and Cora tweaked the hem of her tank top. She hadn't been able to have a proper shower yet, but Melissa looked as fresh as a meadow and wore a purple blouse that showed off enough cleavage to suggest she might actually have some.

"I think there's another chair," Cora said. "The nurses just moved it somewhere."

"No, it's okay. I can't stay long. I—you know . . ."

The awkward silence returned, and a curtain on Cora's left rattled again. This time a shadow stepped out and shuffled away, probably the wife of the construction worker lying in the next bed.

He had fallen off a ladder and cracked his head open on a steel bar and was still in a coma after four weeks. Nathan had just crossed the two-week mark, and Cora didn't want to think about what another two weeks would feel like, sitting beside him, hoping and praying.

Melissa coughed. "I'm going back to Montreal, as soon as the cops let me. They said I couldn't leave the province yet." After a pause, she added, "It's not like I can work here anymore."

"Really?" Cora said cautiously. "Montreal?"

"You know what you're going to do?"

Cora shook her head.

"Yeah, it won't be the same," Melissa said. "But first I need to save some money. That's what I always meant to do."

Cora glanced at Nathan's bruised face. The police would ask him a lot of questions too. She wouldn't be able to hide the truth anymore.

Melissa rested a hand on the metal rail at the foot of the bed, next to the clipboard for the doctors. She said she was already looking for a place in Montreal, she had a friend in real estate. They went way back.

She fiddled with her sunglasses again and said, "It's weird, but this place makes me hungry."

"There's a cafeteria downstairs, on the main floor."

"Yeah, I saw it." Melissa paused. "You want to get something?"

"I'm not really hungry."

"You sure? I don't buy lunch that often."

Cora shook her head, even though her bladder had been pushing her to leave the intensive care unit for the past hour.

"You won't do your brother any good if you pass out on him," Melissa said. "I bet you haven't eaten all day."

"I'm okay. I had a bagel."

"Maybe that works for guys, but you can't fool me."

Cora glanced at Nathan, silent under the ventilator, her eyes misting over, and shook her head again.

"Come on, we'll get something quick," Melissa said.

"I just want him to be okay," Cora said. "That's all. He never did anything, never hurt anybody."

"Yeah, life really stinks sometimes."

Cora blinked rapidly and dabbed at her right cheek, tears trickling down. Melissa passed over a tissue from the box on the cart and fiddled with the doctor's chart until Cora had calmed somewhat.

"We'll be quick," Melissa said. "We'll find a quiet corner. You can come right back. It'll give you a chance to catch your breath."

"Okay," Cora said. "I guess."

"Good. I didn't want to have to drag you out of here. The nurses don't have a sense of humor."

"No, they're really good. It makes it a lot easier."

Melissa shrugged. "Do you want a minute? I can wait by the doors."

"No, it's okay. I don't want to blow my nose in here."

Melissa nodded and slipped out through the curtain. Cora pulled out a fresh tissue, dabbed her eyes a few more times, and then squeezed Nathan's left hand before following Melissa out of the intensive care unit.

~

Half an hour later, after saying goodbye to Melissa, Cora took the elevator up to the seventh floor and headed to the washroom. Even though she had only eaten a turkey salad, her stomach felt tight and kept squelching.

Afterwards, she passed the waiting room for the intensive care unit, which was filled with a dozen or so members of a Sikh family, judging by their turbans and beards and colorful saris and steel bracelets, and pressed the intercom by the double doors. Cora identified herself, and one of the nurses buzzed her in. She hurried past the other patients and their visitors and gave the nurses at the station a quick smile before slipping through the green curtains around Nathan's bed.

Her gaze flickered to the monitors, even though they always looked and sounded the same to her. She didn't even know what two of them did. She must have asked a half-dozen times, but she kept forgetting.

Before sitting down, Cora hung her purse on her chair and gave Nathan's left hand a squeeze. Her stomach still squirmed a little, so she took a sip of water and wondered if the nurses had any antac-ids. Probably a whole pile. But they probably had rules too about giving them to visitors, even if they were the same ones you could buy at the drugstore.

She took another sip of water and screwed the cap back on the bottle. On the bed, something twitched. She pivoted toward the bed, knocking her cast against the arm of the chair, and dropped the water bottle on the floor.

Despite the pain shooting through her right arm, she stared at Nathan's left hand. Did she really see that? Or had she imagined it?

She sat frozen, holding her breath, trying not to blink. What else could it be? What else could move?

Finally her lungs began to scream, and she sucked in a breath. His eyelids flickered.

"Oh, God. Nathan!"

She grabbed his left hand and waited. It seemed to take forever before his eyelids flickered again. Two or three of his fingers twitched.

"Nathan, it's me, Cora. Can you hear me?"

Her brother's lips cracked open, and a gurgle escaped his throat.

"It's okay," she said. "You're safe. You're in a hospital."

His eyes flickered—once, twice. He wobbled his head, ever so slightly, and made another gurgling noise.

"Everything's okay. You're safe, I promise. You don't have to talk. Just rest. I'll be right here."

The fingers of his left hand twitched. She smiled and squeezed them, her eyes filming over with tears. He made another gurgling sound and opened his eyes, wide enough to show the entirety of his irises.

Then his eyes slipped shut, and he didn't open them again for another three weeks.

Epilogue

Cora crouched in front of the gravestone, a rectangular block of pink granite carved with the names of her parents, and laid down a bouquet of red and yellow tulips. Her mother had loved tulips and used to keep a vase of them on the dinner table during the few weeks they bloomed in the garden. Now ten years had passed without her, the tulips blooming all around the city, never giving her a second thought.

"Would you hurry up," Nathan yelled.

Cora closed her eyes. Her brother stood about a hundred feet behind her, leaning against the gnarled bark of a big maple, a cane dangling from his right hand.

"Things are okay," she said. "He complains about the physio a lot, but at least he's doing it. He doesn't need any medication anymore. No needles. No pills. Just the odd Tylenol." She took a deep breath and spread the tulips out a little. "But he still has a lot of bad dreams."

A breeze whistled through the cemetery, rustling the grass and the branches of the trees, some of them already green with buds.

Cora brushed strands of her hair from her face and zipped up her jacket. Sometimes she had the dreams too—the oily blobs, the dead girls, the serpents and their fire—and would get up in the middle of the night and bake or clean or make supper for the next day. Her counselor said it was normal. It was healthy. But Cora had scared herself witless a few times after seeing a teenager with long black hair, wearing a dark dress, or a pale, bald man in an expensive suit. Unfortunately there were a lot of those men in Ottawa, especially in the downtown where she worked.

"The cab's not going to wait forever," Nathan yelled.

Cora brushed a hand over the tulips and sighed.

After a short prayer, she stood and walked up the slope to the maple tree.

"You could have waited," she said. "There are enough cabs around here."

"You can't trust those Indian guys," Nathan said. "They can't tell time."

"Don't start with that. You don't have any excuses anymore."

"You wanted to come here. Not me."

Cora frowned and walked to a red and black cab parked beside a gravestone topped with a small gray statue of an angel. Nathan limped after her, grumbling to himself.

When she reached the cab, she started to open a door for him but changed her mind and walked around to the other side and climbed in.

"You're in a bitchy mood," he said and eased into the cab.

He shifted his right leg several times, until it felt comfortable, and rested his cane against the door.

"I just wish you would've come down with me," she said.

"What does it matter? They're dead. They don't care."

"I'm not."

In the silence that followed, Nathan grimaced and toyed with his cane. The cab pulled out of the cemetery and turned left, heading toward Ottawa's west end. Cora had to work at four, serving food and drinks at Headey's Grill, and needed to change out of her church clothes. The grill wasn't the best place in the world, but the owners were nice and didn't ask too many questions.

A few blocks later, the cab slowed for a red light, and a siren blared from the street to the south. Nathan straightened up and grabbed his cane.

"It's just a fire engine," Cora said and rested a hand on his left arm.

He stared at her for several seconds, his eyes wide with fear. Then he blinked and shook her off.

Her gaze drifted to a pair of brick houses with cherry and crabapple trees crowding their front yards. At least he hadn't freaked when she mentioned visiting the cemetery. That was a start. Another step forward.

The traffic light turned green, and the cab sputtered through the intersection. Nathan muttered a curse and put his cane down. The siren faded out behind them.

That was how life seemed to go—one day at a time, one battle, one sacrifice. Otherwise it would drive you crazy.

And she had already had enough crazy for one lifetime.

About the author:

Lawrence Van Hoof was born in Helmond, the Netherlands, and grew up in southwestern Ontario, Canada. At the University of Guelph, he obtained a B.Sc. in biochemistry. Currently he lives in Toronto.

Children of the Cross is his first novel.

Connect with Me Online:

Website: http://www.lawrencevanhoof.com/
Facebook: https://facebook.com/vanhoof.lawrence